The sorcerer stood and pointed to Gonji with a gloved hand.

"Tell me what you know of the Deathwind, barbarian, he who is called Grejkill." A wave of hushing swept the entire side of the hall.

Gonji was annoyed by the wizard's insult but too intrigued by the abrupt broaching of the object of his own quest to pay it any heed. It was in fact the first time he could recall anyone had mentioned the mystery names to *him*. His heart began to pound.

"It is the name of the thing I have come to seek in the West . . . a thing that is not quite a man — or perhaps it's the other way around. A legend . . . in these mountains the loremongers name the Deathwind as their God's avenging spirit, some protective horror that will lay low their oppressors . . ."

An angry murmur swept the room and the sorcerer, Mord, stared at the samurai. Could he have already divined, by means of some hideous magick, that it was Gonji who had attacked his familiar, the wyvern, with bow and arrows?

The banquet hall fell silent and Gonji's arms stiffened at his sides. He was suddenly sorry that he had removed his swords.

MORE FANTASTIC READING FROM ZEBRA!

GONJI #1: DEATHWIND OF VEDUN (1006, $3.25)
by T. C. Rypel
Cast out from his Japanese homeland, Gonji journeys across barbaric Europe in quest of Vedun, the distant city in the loftiest peaks of the Alps. Brandishing his swords with fury and skill, he is determined to conquer his hardships and fulfill his destiny!

GONJI #2: SAMURAI STEEL (1072, $3.25)
by T. C. Rypel
His journey to Vedun is ended, but Gonji's most treacherous battle ever is about to begin. The invincible King Klann has occupied Vedun with his hordes of murderous soldiers—and plotted the samurai's destruction!

GONJI #3: SAMURAI COMBAT (1191, $3.50)
by T. C. Rypel
King Klann and the malevolent sorcerer Mord have vanquished the city of Vedun and lay in wait to snare the legendary warrior Gonji. But Gonji dares not waiver—for to falter would seal the destruction of Vedun with the crushing fury of SAMURAI COMBAT!

SURVIVORS (1071, $3.25)
by John Nahmlos
It would take more than courage and skill, more than ammo and guns, for Colonel Jack Dawson to survive the advancing nuclear war. It was the ultimate test—protecting his loved ones, defending his country, and rebuilding a civilization out of the ashes of war-ravaged America!

THE SWORD OF HACHIMAN (1104, $3.50)
by Lynn Guest
Destiny returned the powerful sword of Hachiman to mighty Samurai warrior Yoshitsune so he could avenge his father's brutal death. Only he was unaware his most perilous enemy would be his own flesh and blood!

Available wherever paperbacks are sold, or order direct from the Publisher. Send cover price plus 50¢ per copy for mailing and handling to Zebra Books, 475 Park Avenue South, New York, N.Y. 10016 DO NOT SEND CASH.

GONJI #2

SAMURAI STEEL

BY
T.C. RYPEL

ZEBRA BOOKS
KENSINGTON PUBLISHING CORP.

ZEBRA BOOKS

are published by

KENSINGTON PUBLISHING CORP.
475 Park Avenue South
New York, N.Y. 10016

Copyright © 1982 by T.C. Rypel

All rights reserved. No part of this book may be reproduced in any form or by any means without the prior written consent of the Publisher, excepting brief quotes used in reviews.

SECOND PRINTING

Printed in the United States of America

In loving memory of
my most honorable parents,
CHESTER and GENEVIEVE RYPEL

—domo arigato

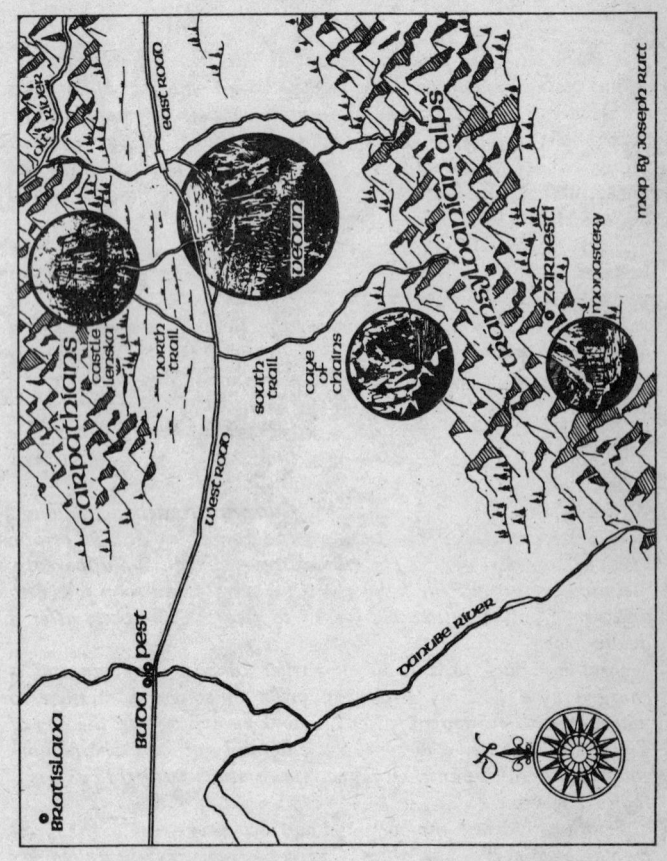

WHAT HAS GONE BEFORE

It is the sixteenth century in Central Europe. A time when sorcerous power, enchanted men, and the haunting things of darkness are receding to the fringes of human concern as men become increasingly urbanized and enlightened. Belief in the eldritch things wanes, but like a dying beast that rears its head for a last plunge at its conqueror, the powers of darkness combine for a final onslaught on a microcosm of humanity.

A half-breed samurai named Gonji Sabataké, son of a powerful Japanese daimyo but cast by circumstances in the role of an itinerant ronin, a landless wanderer, travels through Europe in search of the legendary Deathwind, the Beast with the Soul of a Man. He encounters primal horrors in the dreaded Carpathians, then rescues and joins a company of mercenaries in the employ of a mysterious nomadic king, Klann the Invincible. The king's origin and purpose are cloaked in half-understood tales and legends; few can claim to ever having seen him, though they pledge him their undying loyalty.

Riding with the 3rd Royalist Free Company for a space of days, Gonji learns much of the strange wandering army and its erratic and evil sorcerer, Mord. He grows disgusted with the apparently meaningless outrages he helps them perpetrate and soon falls into disfavor. Gonji is ultimately forced to flee the company after a deadly clash.

Doubling back to a scene of earlier carnage, the samurai is charged by a horribly disfigured priest to convey a message to someone named Simon Sardonis, whom he will find in the city of Vedun. Attacked by a wyvern, a vile flying beast, he is shamed beyond words by his panicked flight. He commits himself to its eventual destruction.

Bringing with him the body of a boy beaten to death in the forest by mercenaries in Klann's hire, Gonji enters the ancient walled city of Vedun, a citadel perched on a Carpathian plateau-aerie. He finds the city already occupied by Klann's army, the magnificent castle of the Lord Protector of the province, Baron Rorka, successfully breached by Klann in a single night's siege.

Gonji learns that the dead boy was the brother of an important *council member, Michael Benedetto, and thus becomes immersed in political intrigue from the outset. Although initially uncommitted to either side, he gradually comes to side with the citizens, who are divided over a course of action. The pacifist faction is led by the Council Elder, Flavio; the militants, by the volatile guildsman Phlegor and a fiery, iron-willed prophetess named Tralayn.*

As enmity between Gonji and Klann's forces, human and inhuman, increases, so dawns his affection for the city and some of its inhabitants, notably, the blacksmith Garth Gundersen and one of his sons, Wilfred. A lovely deaf-mute girl named Helena becomes enamored of him; and he in turn, of Michael Benedetto's wife, Lydia.

Through a series of wild adventures and curious circumstances, the half-breed oriental swiftly rises to a position of influence in the city, though it is, to be sure, a tenuous position, weakened by distrust and bigotry. In a fit of pique, obeying the dictates of his moody disposition and the cry of his empty purse, he hires on as a spy for Klann with Captain Julian Kel'Tekeli, whom he has come to hate. But ever the seeker after noble duty, he also contrives to enter the employ of Flavio, as his personal bodyguard. His love of control, attention, and military game-playing thus satisfied, and characteristically mistaking serendipity for fate, he sees himself committed (in his compromising, half-Western fashion) by the bushido code to following the situation through to the conflict he feels is inevitable. Furthermore, the key to his Deathwind quest—and the now more intriguing mystery of Simon Sardonis—seems to be withheld from him by certain fearful city leaders.

As DEATHWIND OF VEDUN closes, Gonji manipulates himself into the city delegation to the castle banquet being held by the legendary King Klann the Invincible, who has suddenly decided to break with his reclusive tradition.

Breathes there the man with soul so dead,
Who never to himself hath said,
This is my own, my native land!
Whose heart hath ne'er within him burned,
As home his footsteps he hath turned
From wandering on a foreign strand?
—Sir Walter Scott, *The Lay of the Last Minstrel*

In looking on the happy Autumn fields,
And thinking of the days that are no more . . .
. . . O Death in Life, the days that are no more.
Tennyson, *The Princess*

Part I

"Vive le Roi!"

Chapter One

General Gorkin, the castellan, marched through the dank corridors toward the king's chamber. He cradled his helm under a burly arm. His face had an anxious set, jaw muscles rigid.

The general turned into an arch that flanked a shadowed stone stairway, and the huge form jumped him from behind with a fierce battle cry. Gorkin uttered a broken outcry as he was wrestled to the ground. Thick arms squeezed him mightily, stole his wind. He gritted his teeth and strained to break the locked fists at his belly. Then he recognized the labored laughter at his ear.

He tautened and looked back, bewildered, into the face of King Klann.

"You've gone soft on us, Gorkin," the king jested as they sorted themselves out and pushed up onto their feet.

"Sire?" Gorkin said, red-faced.

"We weren't able to take you so readily in the past. But, then, it's been a stretch since we've tilted." The king mopped his brow with a sleeve. "But no more! Things will change around here. Yes, indeed. We're feeling marvelous this morning, Gorkin! And how is our castellan?"

"Fit, sire," the general said, breathing hard, "but troubled. I've just been out in the ward, at the practice ground. I found the—"

"Yes, so you did—you saw the free companions enjoying the run of the place, that's what's bothering you, eh?" Klann smiled. "Yes, it was on my order. The mercenaries have need of training just as the Llorm do. More so, no doubt. And it will keep them out of mischief. They may have the run of the ward, just so there are no firearms."

"All right, my liege, if that is your wish."

"That is our wish, old friend. It's time for some changes. Time for us to shuck our reclusive image. Yo, but I'm feeling grand this morning! Tonight's the banquet, you know." Klann amiably slapped Gorkin on the back.

(don't be so familiar with subordinates—it ill befits our state)

Two scullions, drawn from their tasks by the clatter in the corridor, peered around a corner at them. They goggled to see the king and castellan in such a scruffy, soiled state and hurried back to work.

Klann and Gorkin walked through the maze of corridors toward the outdoors, toward Castle Lenska's expansive wards. They passed chambers jammed with common folk, with the thin, pale dark-haired people who were all that remained of the once proud Akryllonian island race. Hollow-eyed children of Klann's Llorm regulars, worn and wearied by the travails of their nomadic life, wandered about the halls. Listlessly, for the most part. Of late they had seemed to be looking worse. They bowed or knelt at their beloved king's passing. Some were yanked out of his path by scolding mothers, who were in turn admonished by Klann to let them be. He patted young heads affectionately, warmed to see them smile.

"Look at them, Gorkin," Klann said. "They're looking better already, I think, to be relieved of life on the road." He sighed. "These are the important ones. They're us . . . our hope and legacy . . . all that remains of the glory that was Akryllon."

"Akryllon will again be glorious, my liege."

"I wonder," Klann responded gravely. "When was the last birth in the army?"

"Why—just last month, sire, isn't that so?"

"It was *four* months ago. Think back. It was during the severe spring storm in Austria. Remember now?"

The general's shoulders slumped. "Yes, yes, I think you're right, sire. Time does thieve away the days of a man's life." He brightened. "Ananka Kel'Gana is heavy with child. Perhaps within the present moon she'll—"

"And the child will be fatherless."

Gorkin gulped, recalling the dragoon trampled in a recent cavalry engagement. "You're right, sire, I had forgotten."

They walked in silence for a space toward the inner ward behind the central keep. The general respectfully fell a half step behind his king, who walked with hands clasped at his back. Servants scurried past under the heightened attention of stewards as the king ambled by. They were in an area honeycombed with myriad chambers and living quarters, stuffed to overflowing with the families of the hereditary army. Children skittered underfoot and jostled scolding servants. Barking dogs scampered and sniffed. The banquet preparations had set the castle bustling.

Gorkin kicked a yelping hound out of the king's way only to be reprimanded by a chuckling Klann. They broke the fixed gazes of numerous stone-faced sentries, and the general removed two of these from their posts to serve as a personal guard when the king moved out into the ward. Near a sun-drenched exit arch, Klann entered a common garderobe to relieve himself.

Then they were out in the central ward, the sun glaring off flagstones still slick from the recent rains. The ward was alive with activity and noise. At one side soldiers practiced in the training ground before the long, low dormitories that housed them. Steel and wood clashed and clacked as combatants tilted; squeaks and creaks of pulleys and quintains marked the quarter where men trained in strength and agility, attacking spinning wooden man-forms and climbing scaffold ropes.

King Klann watched the activities with informed interest, arms crossed over his chest. General Gorkin's apprehension showed in the tight crinkles around his dark eyes; allowing the free companions so near the king was a new experience. They were encamped between the outer and middle baileys and outside the barbican, but now the king had granted them access to the training ground and castle halls with but few restrictions, and this was a dangerous practice.

As Klann himself should be the first to realize.

The king breathed deeply the arresting cooking and baking aromas issuing from the kitchens and bakehouse across the ward. Tonight they would feast as had the monarchs of old. And this place, this Transylvania, was going to be the beginning of the end of the long, weary quest. Home was in the wind. Yes, soon they would be home.

"Yes, Gorkin," Klann began in a voice edged with resolve, "one final thrust. One more sally after Akryllon, that's all we need. And these poor people will be home at last. Home to the land none of them have ever seen—that's rather silly, isn't it, Gorkin?"

"Milord?"

"To call a place home when you've never seen

it—really seen it, lived in it?"

"No, of course not, sire. Home is home."

"Do you see those mountains?" Klann said, sweeping an arm over the peaks of the Transylvanian Alps. "Such beauty. Such . . . insular comfort. We feel good about this place, Gorkin. Yes . . . this will be a nice, pleasant hiatus for the troops, for the families. We'll winter here, gather strength, and—" He smiled, his eyes narrowing to twinkling slits. "—I think we'll be reliving some past glories, if our intelligence is accurate."

A little boy scooted past behind them. Klann, noticing the motion, halted him in Kunan, the Akryllonian common language.

"Come here, little scalawag. Your king commands you."

The boy was about five, dark-haired and anemic like all the others. Mouth agape, eyes large and liquid and guilt-tinged, he approached the king tentatively, hands behind his back.

"What have you there?" Klann asked. "Come now, let's see."

The boy held forth his hands. There was a large, freshly baked tart in each.

"So you've snitched these from the bakehouse, have you? Come up here, and we'll consider your punishment." Klann scooped him up into his arms with a grunt. "Yes, such fine tarts could wither the integrity of a holy hermit, I should think. But your king is feeling magnanimous today. We'll pardon your crime for the price of a bite from one of them." And he exacted his price, grinning and nodding at the tiny fellow, who could but stare.

Klann set the boy down and sent him off with a pat on the rump, shaking a scolding finger at his popeyed retreat.

"These children will want for nothing anymore, Gorkin, be sure of that," Klann said, tight-lipped. "This land is bounteous and secure—"

There came a sizzling of powder and a *whump!* from the ramparts at their right, followed by a pounding crash in the hills below the outer bailey. The castle troops had begun practicing the use of the mortars mounted in places on the allures. Klann surveyed the castle's defenses: the formidable bombards, the mangonels for hurling stones into any siege party; the enormous cauldrons which could spew boiling oil and molten lead over whole companies. He walked through the middle bailey gatehouse, guards trailing behind him, and appraised the thick ashlar blocks that comprised the high walls, now displaying his coat-of-arms; observed the Llorm bowmen walking their posts behind the battlements' croslets and arrow loops and atop wooden brattices, cut through in spots with holes for firing down onto besiegers; the sturdy casemates built into the base of the walls like bunkers; the nearly completed repair work being done on the drawbridge, torn loose during the castle occupation.

The bombard on the opposite wall blasted its charge in a high arc over the hills. From beyond the outer bailey came the bellowing roar of the cretin giant, Tumo, frightened by the blast. Soldiers on the walls laughed and pointed. Klann looked at the guards, and Gorkin chuckled nervously. Before a word was spoken a deep shadow stretched over the ward: They all looked up, breaths hitching at the sight of the wyvern, unfurling its massive wings in the tower battlement above their heads.

"No enemy shall ever assail us here," Klann said at last. But his voice had quaked ever so slightly.

(don't be so sure of yourself)
(never relax your vigilance never)

Klann shut his eyes and a trembling coursed through him. It passed presently.

"What do you think about our prospects, Gorkin?" he asked without looking at his edgy castellan.

"I believe you're quite right, sire. Next time we'll—"

"Stop agreeing with me because it's what you think I wish to hear. Tell me what *you* think."

Gorkin rolled his eyes groundward. "The astrologers have consulted the stars, and prospects are good for finding Akryllon next spring—"

"A plague on the astrologers!" Klann stormed. "Tell me what you think about our decision to stay here!"

The general's form sagged visibly. "I—I must admit to some apprehension, milord. I don't like this place. It masks something . . . foreboding. Already there's been trouble—the Field Commander's murder—the city seems restive—Have you seen the arrow stub? In the flying monster's hide?" His voice had shrunk to a whisper.

Klann laughed. "Yes—and that's good! Don't look at me like that—I'm making good sense. I understand the guilty have paid the price. But this should be a grand territory for recruiting the kind of men we need, eh? Men who sally forth against monsters? No, you're wrong, Gorkin. This is a fine place to stay, and here will come a turning point for us."

He grew pensive, an ominous shadow darkening his features, moving the soldiers with him to unease.

"One more thrust—and we'll be home—and nothing, *nothing* must stand in our way—"

(don't pay it lip service do it pursue it)
(what else can be done?)
(nothing it is gone forever)

The king shuddered in such a way that Gorkin reached out to catch him lest he fall, but Klann waved him off.

A retainer appeared, seeking the king's attendance on business broached by his counselors. But Klann dismissed them all, wishing to be alone—to the extent the mocking term could apply to him. Against his better judgment, General Gorkin sent the guards back to their duties and himself reluctantly turned to go.

"Gen-kori," Klann called to him.

The castellan turned slowly, eyebrows uplifted. The Kunan term Klann had used was akin to saying "old-timer" or "longtime comrade." It was an affectionate usage.

"My liege?"

"It *was* he at the boxing match?"

"So Captain Sianno said."

Klann nodded and sent him off. A warm nostalgic rush filled the king on whom incident and legend had bestowed the attributive Invincible.

And then, as if out of nothing, the sorcerer Mord appeared at his side.

They stared at each other for a space, neither uttering a word even in greeting. Mord's black marble eyes gleamed impassively from behind the gold filigreed mask.

"Remove that shaft from your beast's hide," Klann said without preamble. "It has an adverse effect on the troops' morale."

He walked off toward the gatehouse and back into the central ward as if the audience were ended, but Mord fell into step with him.

"Not so easily accomplished," the sorcerer's murky voice offered in reply. "But I shall do it when I can spare the time. I carry the reminder here." He patted his abdomen, the same vicinity in which the arrow stub protruded from the wyvern's underbelly.

They walked in silence through the gatehouse, emerging into the ward, out of earshot of any soldiers.

The clamor of weapons practice continued. A small cluster of men gathered around an injured mercenary, whose clavicle had been broken in a fencing bout.

"Why can't you use your power to heal injuries like that one?" Klann asked, pointing. "So much pain might be alleviated."

"Not an easy task, correcting specific ills of the flesh. Spells of destruction are so much more simply wrought, and at far less cost to the worker." Mord's evil grin could be felt from behind his mask, though nothing could be seen through the tiny breathing holes.

Klann scowled, and the sorcerer lifted his hands in a mollifying gesture. "But of course, milord, if a man's faith is strong enough, it may be translated into the mana necessary for healing. However, few men possess such faith."

"Faith," Klann intoned resignedly. He angled away from the scene, affecting regal nonchalance, hands clasped behind him. Mord walked a step to the rear, his gloved hands concealed inside the folds of his sleeves.

"So many men dead in Austria," Klann said, shaking his head sadly. "After all concessions to 'faith' in your god were made, still their god was stronger. You disappoint me at times, Mord."

"Mi-*lord*," Mord minced, "you do me grave injustice. Have I not done all that you've commanded? Any shortcomings being directly attributable to lack of faith among your subjects? We've discussed this matter many times. My Master is implacable in this regard. He demands complete faith and unstinting devotion. Given these, the power he may impart to me is limitless. If you would but permit me the ritual human sacrifice I've suggested—"

"No!" Klann shot, then quickly regained composure

and lowered his voice. "Don't broach that subject again. It's purest animal savagery. It was in allowing such foul dabblings that my father lost the throne of Akryllon. All I ask of you is that you assist me in regaining it. Your time of proof will soon be at hand. Next spring . . . yes, in the spring . . ." Klann waxed reflective, teeth gritted.

"I shall vindicate myself, have no fear," Mord said airily. "But I really cannot understand your attitude toward sacrifice: You've never denied me subjects for my experiments in working at the charm of dividing."

The king looked like a man who had swallowed an emetic. "That is . . . a different matter—how goes it?"

"Very well. Soon I shall be able to show you the result of my most recent progress. But there is another thing that troubles me now. This banquet—I must lodge my protest against it. These people are full of deceit and treachery. They're stubborn and dangerous. They've already murdered your field commander and fired on my familiar. They'll resist you at every turn and will try to undermine your purpose. Why coddle them like this? And releasing the families of Rorka's men, who might well have served as hostages to bend them to your will, that was—"

"Enough!" Klann cried. Several heads turned in the ward, observers self-consciously returning to their tasks almost at once. This day would be well marked, for rare indeed were the king's appearances among them, and rarer still his public displays of anger. "Enough," he said again more calmly, his mood shifting eerily. "We remind you of your duties. We have more than enough effete counselors to question royal mandates. We have our reasons for what we do, and they are sufficient. Leave us now. You have your work."

Klann's face became a blank mask as he began strolling toward the central keep. Mord bowed to his back obsequiously.

"I beg your forgiveness, my liege. I presume too much. But in an effort to appease your anger, may I remind you that it was I who divined the existence of this place, provided the intelligence required for the planning of its invasion, and the power by which the deed was done?" Mord's voice reflected his conviction that an unjust slight had been done him. "All with your sanction at the time," he appended.

Klann's face had a sullen set as he stopped and looked back at him. "True—for the most part. And even this has been tainted by sadness." Mord's head tilted at the cryptic statement.

"Begone now."

Mord bowed in stately fashion and departed.

And in his melancholy Klann heard the voices of the Brethren well up within him. They were stirred to angry, confused counsel. And then he spotted Lady Thorvald, watching him from the veranda of the sweltering bakehouse. He cast her a hateful look. He was abruptly reminded of the mighty man of valor they had all loved and respected but whom only their brother had really known, the brother whose inconstant heart overawed the counsel of his spirit and his kin.

(kill her kill the bitch)

(forget it be done with it move ahead the purpose—that is all that matters anymore)

There came at last the murderous primitive cry of the shameful one, the tainted brother, and Klann could feel the flush of the blood-rage filling his brain. He shut his eyes and swooned as he fought for control of his faculties. And when he had regained control, he suppressed them. Gently. As only one who knows the forlorn feeling of such suppression would do. For they were he.

And he was Klann. And *they* were Klann.

And Klann was five.

Head bowed, hands clung limply behind him, the king who was called Invincible shuffled heavily into the keep, the pungent smells of mildew and damp rot greeting him from the interior.

"Lottie Kovacs—and *Richard*—whatever are you doing in here!"

Genya lowered her voice in mid-sentence to avoid attracting attention to the narrow larder just off the immense castle kitchens wherein she had found the pair huddled together behind the bins. Hunkered down against the wall, Richard sat with arms folded about Lottie, whose head was buried in his shoulder. Genya stood over them, hands on hips, affecting a stern posture.

"Don't the two of you have any sense at all? What if the king's chief steward comes to the kitchens? Lord knows I've had trouble enough with him already. *Hanba na vy!*—shame on you!" She shook a finger at them. "You're just lucky I'm in charge here and not someone else or you'd be—Lottie? What is it, dear?"

She knelt and laid a hand on the sobbing girl's arm.

"Her father's dead, Genya," Richard whispered. "Killed by soldiers. Ferenc heard."

"Oh, dear Lord," Genya gasped. "Lottie—Lottie, I'm so sorry."

Lottie raised her head to reveal a tear-stained face, red and puffy eyes. "Oh, Genya," the girl moaned, "things were so wrong between us. I—I never realized how much I loved him. And now he's gone. It's my fault as much as anyone's."

"Lottie, don't say that."

Genya gazed at her helplessly, momentarily lost for words. Lottie's sad, china-blue eyes stared vapidly.

Her small, perpetually pouty lips were drawn and quivery. Mourning seemed to befit Lottie, who was Genya's best friend and polar opposite. Their alliance was as likely as one between a proud mare and a humble tortoise. Lottie had hired on as a servant at Castle Lenska over her father's protestations, mainly so that she might be near Richard, a baker, whom Papa Kovacs called "bun-brains," which is all that need be said of their strained romantic situation.

Genya rose. "Now listen—Richard, you stay right here and comfort Lottie," she said, shaking her finger officiously. "But only for a while. I'll steer anyone from the larder as long as I can. If anybody comes from the bakehouse, I'll put them off. Just pray the chief steward doesn't poke his birdie beak in here, or I'll have to bounce a salver off his skull! When you leave, leave separately, and *quietly.*" She smiled warmly, patted Lottie's ash-blonde locks. "Be strong, dear. Soon we'll be able to leave and you and Richard can begin a life together."

She nodded curtly to Richard, puffed up her damp hair, and eased out into the steaming, noisy kitchen. At once she began calling out directions in a voice that was both commanding and pleasant.

"*Nahlit sa! Nahlit sa!* Hurry up! Tonight Papa Flavio comes, and if all goes well you'll be home to see your families soon. The king is good and gracious, and I have his assurance from his very own royal lips!"

There was laughter and good cheer all about her, despite the hot and tedious work of preparing a banquet for hundreds. And Genya threw herself into the preparations lustily, lending a hand wherever one was needed. First she helped the Yeoman of the Pantry trundle out and count the silver gilt plates and utensils and lay out the trenchers on which meat would be placed.

The kitchen was huge: sixty feet long by thirty wide with a vaulted roof nearly forty feet high at its apex. On one wall were the cavernous fireplaces—eight feet high and twenty broad—in which cattle and oxen could be roasted whole. And Genya next joined a struggling party attempting to wrestle a side of beef into one of these. Donning a bloody apron, she provided the final push needed to hoist the carcass into position, and by the end of the task her infectious good humor had cheered them all.

She turned her attention to the central hearth slab, where the cooking fires were being lit for the smaller game, which would be roasted on spits turned by dogs in wheelhouses.

"Nahlit sa!" she enjoined, aiding the cooks and drudges in spitting pheasants and geese and capons. "And where are our whimpering turnspits?" Indeed, to see the hearth fires lit the dogs scurried off for cover, for they knew well the work that would soon fall to them. Genya sent scullions to drag the dogs to the wheels. Thick cooking aromas already permeated the withering kitchen heat as Genya brought from storage the great saltcellar that would be placed before the king. She filled it carefully and trundled it by cart through the corridors toward the great hall where the banquet would take place that night.

The saltcellar was of ivory, enameled over with the figures of lions. Standing a foot high on carven legs was the shallow dish that contained the precious salt. Over its top was the golden canopy that protected the ceremonially regarded seasoning. And as Genya pushed the cellar along, she suddenly caught sight of her reflection. She stopped and peered around her: no one in sight.

She raked and molded her dark curls into a semblance of casual charm with practiced fingers. Pinching her cherubic face to instill color, she puckered her red lips—which caused little change inasmuch as nature had set them in a pucker—and practiced a range of expressions, from coyly beguiling to stoically wounded, until they appeared convincingly *un*practiced.

Lord, forgive me, but I'm so clever, she thought, her shoulders hunching to suppress a self-satisfied chuckle. *But praised be for that, since someone has to be . . .*

It had all been trying and frightening at first: the violent overthrow of Baron Rorka on that horrible night and the succession of King Klann; monsters and giants prowling the walls; soldiers parading throughout the castle. The servants had all been too frightened to do anything but cower in their chambers for a night and a day. Those with any backbone at all had been slaughtered with the Baron's men, including the former chief steward. And Klann's newly appointed chief was a nasty, spiteful, vulture-faced old viper. Between him and the proudly strutting Llorm regulars and the pompously demanding ladies of the court and that bastard captain who had grabbed at her, why—

But Genya's anger had finally been stoked, and the lowly scullery maid had dared speak for all the servitors to King Klann himself, presenting their fears to him in a performance that required all her considerable guile. And not surprisingly (to her, at least) Klann had been won over by her charm. He had assured her of the servants' safety and instructed the chief steward to lighten his approach. He had promised that they would be free to visit Vedun once the security quarantine could be lifted, and—best of all—had appointed Genya head of all the local servantry and his personal liaison to them!

His paternal interest in Genya was a great comfort to her, although it had aroused the jealousy of the ladies of court, some of whom from the beginning had found Genya's voluptuous youth and vivaciousness a spur to their cattiness: Before the audience with Klann, for instance, the Lady Gorkin, wife of the castellan, had caught Genya in alleged idleness and sent her to the steamy kitchen for the unpleasant job of shelling eggs. It was all Genya could do to keep from blasting the haughty old wench with a few, just to see how such a fine lady would react to the shocking mess.

And then there was the red-headed virago Lady Thorvald, whom Genya had first supposed the queen, judging by her incessant doting on and flitting about the king. She turned out instead to be a kept-woman in whom Klann had lost interest. Her attentiveness on His Highness seemingly grew in direct proportion to his weariness of her. Genya, in her less charitable moments, thought of Thorvald as a dried-out old shrew who strove to stave off the advance of years with her mock-exotic displays of paint and feathers. She was the epitome of tacky ostentation.

"Such a pampered old puss!" Genya had said that morning to the chambermaid who had overheard that Lady Thorvald would not be in attendance at the banquet, complaining of one of her frequent "head ailments."

Ah, well, Genya thought, steer clear and all's well. All but that scary sorcerer, Mord, him and his hungry looks . . .

She shuddered to think of him and chased the thought. But then there came the reminder of Lottie's murdered father and Genya suddenly wondered about the safety of her own parents in Vedun.

No. No, father would never dream of becoming involved in violence. Safe, sane, and sensible father—he and mother would be there when she came home, of that she was sure. She crossed herself and lipped a curt prayer to fortify her certainty.

Her last warm thought was reserved for Wilf. Darling Wilf. So strong, so stubborn. The only man she knew who had ever kept her thoughts from other men; the only one whose pride couldn't be budged. How I miss you, my love! A whole week apart! But soon we'll be together, and we'll leave this mess, and Papa Garth won't be able to do a thing about it—No, that's wrong. I don't want it to be like that. I do so want Herr Gundersen's approval and love. There *are* those rare men like him, the ones whose expressed distrust of feminine wiles is genuine. They're the hardest to win over. But—

Footsteps echoed along the corridor. She leaned over the saltcellar's canopy and examined her bodice, adjusting its strings minutely to reveal the merest hint of titillating curvature. She experienced a pang of guilt at her shamelessness. She shut her eyes and pursed her lips a second, then crossed herself and pushed the cart forward toward the great hall.

I'm sorry, Lord, but that's me. I need to feel in command. It must all work out—it must. It will. And as usual I'll get what I wish.

Chapter Two

Gonji Sabataké emerged from the tailor shop into the rain-slicked cobblestone lane, suppressing a grin of self-satisfaction. He was freshly scrubbed and shaven. His topknot was tied just so. And he sported the new sleeveless tunic and breeches he had recently commissioned, plus thick woolen socks for under his sandals to replace his worn *tabi*.

He adjusted his swords in his *obi*, the wide sash cinched about his waist, in such a way that they rode nearly horizontally, snug but comfortable as they always must be. He rubbed his stinging face pensively and glanced about in the humid morning air. The day would be hot and thick; murky clouds sagged from horizon to horizon. A good day for an indoor banquet.

He smiled and made off down the street, leading Tora by the reins the short distance to the tanner's. His leather goods—the cuirass, pauldrons and vambraces, and riding boots he had ordered—were not ready; so he mounted and clopped off toward the marketplace at an easy gait. No hurry. Little to do this day until the banquet. But *then*—hah! A first-hand look at storied Castle Lenska! And at long last a meeting with the mystery king and his sorcerer.

This would be a day marked in memory; of that he was certain.

He had risen early to find Garth Gundersen already gone on some business at the foundry. Wilf had been pressed into service at the forge. Sullen and irritable, Gonji's closest friend among the Gundersens was again brooding about the fate of his Genya at the castle; so the samurai had decided it was just as well to be free of his company this day. Strom, the shepherd son, and Lorenz, the Executor of the Exchequer, had been none too gracious in their invitation to breakfast. Gonji had eschewed it in favor of a short practice session in the hills.

Judging by the Gundersens' mixed hospitality, he decided he'd best find lodgings elsewhere soon.

The marketplace was alive and healthy this misty morning, the moist air bearing the sundry sounds and scents of commerce. There was an aura of normality about Vedun, even the soldiers now unwittingly taking their place in the mundane order.

Gonji sated his empty belly with fish and ale, which he consumed languidly on a stone bench near the stalls. The bell tower sounded ten bells, and the shallower timbre of the chapel bell called some to a worship service.

A few of the people Gonji had met at Michael Benedetto's house the night of the memorable boxing matches passed by and greeted him. Among these were Stefan Berenyi and Nikolai Nagy—he couldn't recall which man was which, followed shortly by Monetto, the biller; and Gerhard, the hunter and fletcher, a longbow slung over his back. They carried between them a large sack of small game that evinced the latter's prowess with the bow. Monetto steered them toward Gonji and began to make small talk, but they resumed their course to the stalls at Gerhard's insistence. His concern over the freshness of the game precipitated the usual argument between them that could be heard long after they had departed.

Then Gonji thought he spotted a blonde head that might have belonged to Lydia Benedetto. He craned his neck to peer into the crowd, but from the spot he watched there emerged two Llorm footmen, who suspiciously returned his gaze. He rose then, his thoughts turning to military concerns . . . in a manner of speaking.

Let's see what's on their minds.

He took Tora by the reins and walked down an alley. Turning into the first intersection, he waited. The pack that followed him approached his vantage a minute later, whispering and muting their stealthy steps.

"Eeyah!" Gonji cried, leaping out at them, his scabbarded Sagami's pommel pointing into their midst.

The children screamed as one and stumbled backward. Then they laughed with relief, and Eduardo, their leader, came forward, flashing a hand in greeting.

"All right, you scamps," Gonji said sternly, "what do you want with me?"

A tiny girl clung to the back of Eduardo's breeches, regarding Gonji with big terrified eyes as the boy spoke.

"We just wanted to see what you were getting into. My papa says that where you go trouble will follow. I didn't want to miss anything."

"So?" Gonji replied, affecting petulance. "And he was right, *neh?* Look what's followed me." He waved a hand over them, and they tittered.

"You look *molto buono* with your new clothes," Eduardo said, appending a hand gesture that Gonji took to mean youthful approval.

"Domo," Gonji replied. "Now that I have your seal I can proceed with confidence." He watched with raised eyebrows and folded arms as the boy walked around him appraisingly, the little girl traipsing behind like a shadow.

"Is that your sister?"

"No, that's Tiva. She has no mother, and I get paid for watching her."

"Do you do a good job?" Gonji bent toward the girl and spoke gently. "Does Eduardo watch out for you?"

The boys all laughed. "She doesn't speak Italian," someone said.

She was the most adorable child in Gonji's recent memory and could scarcely have been more than four. When he reached down to lift her up, her large brown eyes seemed to engulf her face. She held a half-eaten roll in one sticky fist.

Eduardo translated what Gonji had asked.

"Nah!" she said in a tiny, piping voice. The boys laughed again.

"He doesn't, eh?" Gonji said. "Well, we'll see about that."

"She says no to everything," Eduardo explained.

Tiva offered Gonji a bite of the roll, and he pantomimed a full belly, but she persisted. He bowed and smiled, taking a small mouthful. *"Domo,* little blossom."

He set her down. "You boys take care of her or—" He raised a threatening fist. "Now be off with you."

"When are you going to teach me the sword? You promised," Eduardo pleaded.

"I did no such thing," Gonji said. "I said we'd have to take it up with your father sometime. What would a ragamuffin like you do with a sword anyway?"

"Kill the soldiers who killed Signor Koski," Eduardo said matter-of-factly, bending to lace a shoe.

The simple poignancy of the statement stung Gonji. "Why would you do that?"

"Because Signora Koski's been crying all the time since he died."

Gonji worked his lower jaw thoughtfully, recalling the dead man, struck down by mercenaries on the day of the city's occupation. "Doesn't your father teach you that killing is evil?"

"Usually. But he's not sure anymore."

Gonji snapped his fingers. "Begone with you now. And watch out for the little one, hear?"

Eduardo bowed, too fast and too deeply, like a bird pecking at seed, and the other boys snickered. Gonji shook his head, corrected him, and sent them packing with a wink to Tiva, who waved her fingers.

He thought about the boy's words as he watched them run down the lane. *He's not sure* . . . Indecision and lack of resolve would be a crippling problem if these people wound up in an armed revolt. Klann wouldn't be shackled by Christian principles. He shook his head. Ah well, the mercenaries have backed off considerably since Ben-Draba was beaten to death by . . . *hai* . . . He smiled thinly. *Our other mystery man* . . .

He leapt astride Tora and rode back into the main street, resolving to check in with Flavio.

Gonji was determined to treat his position as bodyguard to Council Elder Flavio with dignity and seriousness, although he knew that the hiring had been prompted by his own cajoling and Flavio's desire to dispense the city's debt to the samurai for having retrieved the body of Mark Benedetto. Yet bodyguard he was, and he would deport himself as a bodyguard. He had promised not to dog the Elder's steps but had made a point of checking on his well-being from time to time.

He was clattering along easily toward the Ministry building on the Street of Hope when he was halted by the cry of a pedestrian on his left.

"Ho, there! A word with you, *monsieur!*" came the stentorian voice in ringing French.

Gonji pulled up and looked over. It was Alain Paille, the flamboyant and eccentric artist-poet whose revolutionary pronouncements since Klann's arrival had caused the city no end of discomfiture and the occupying troops no little amusement. He was thin, dark, and willowy, with piercing blue eyes, a sketchy shadow of beard, and an unruly mane that no comb had furrowed in recent days. His paint-stained apron evidenced his current commission: an illustration in progress on the ceiling of Vedun's chapel. In his hand he carried a furled paper.

"Behold the Liberator!" he shouted, wide-eyed,

stopping in front of Tora. "He of whom ballades will be sung!"

Gonji glanced about self-consciously. Few had taken special notice of Paille, from whom such outbursts had long been expected. He was, as it happened, Vedun's best-known tippler. Those who watched now watched Gonji for a reaction.

Gonji cleared his throat. "*Ja*, well—what can I do for you?" He had ignored the French, spoke instead in High German.

"I've been seeking you. We must speak. I believe we share a dream. You do speak French, don't you?"

"I speak French . . . of a sort," Gonji replied. "But it gives me trouble. It's a language I—" He groped for an appropriate word, came up with one.

" '*Disdain?*' " Paille repeated with surprise. "But you mustn't! All men of intellect and breeding speak French! I've been inquiring after you, and I believe you *are* such a man. Yours is simply a problem of pronunciation. But be at ease, we shall correct that. Do speak French, *s'il vous plaît.*"

"I don't please," Gonji said with a wry look, "but I'll speak it. What's your business?"

"I think a drink is in order first. Shall we hie us to the *auberge?*" Paille pointed the paper toward the nearest inn, Wojcik's Haven.

"Not now. I've business at the Ministry."

"Wonderful! So have I," Paille said, waving the handbill. "We can talk as we walk, *oui?*"

"*Oui* . . . wonderful," Gonji said softly, glancing at passersby who were listening in on the conversation.

He dismounted and led Tora by the reins. He had been in a mood to ride alone, frankly hoping to encounter the swaggering Captain Julian Kel'Tekeli, to show him that Gonji was just as capable as he of effecting a display of cleanliness, polish, and poise.

But now he stoically accepted the way karma had of laying low the proud . . .

"I am Alain Paille," the artist boomed, "a painter, poet, and balladeer, chronicler of the times and tides of men, and soldier of freedom *par excellence*. And you are—no-no, don't tell me—you are Gonji Sabataké, master of fighting arts from the fabled orient, dispossessed son of Japan's mightiest warlord—"

Gonji winced and rubbed an itching eye, blew a long, impatient breath. Behind him, Tora nickered and bobbed his head.

"—champion of *egalité* and freedom, fated participant in the coming battle that will secure democracy from the strangling grip of monarchy and aristocracy—"

"Whoa, whoa," Gonji groaned. They were tramping through a steep-walled lane, and Paille's words echoed from one end to the other of its tunneling course. "Hold on, *monsieur poete*. Very sorry, but that's a terribly mixed bag of facts and fancies. And listen, don't you ever speak in anything but that blaring herald's voice?"

Paille looked wounded. "Anger, pain, frustration, humiliation—these things are ne'er articulated by the calm and soft voice! But you are right, of course, we must be circumspect. The ears of the enemy are all about us."

He leaned close and laid a finger across his lips with a conspiratorial suspiration, and Gonji caught a full blast of the artist's midday pick-me-up. Wine. And a humble vintage.

"*Oui*, that's best," Gonji agreed, relieved. "Now . . . I'm not sure I understood all this—May we have continued in Spanish?" Gonji stumbled over the words.

"May we continue, not 'May we have continued'," Paille corrected. He sighed. "But, *si*, Spanish then, the cutthroats' language . . . Such a shame. French is so elegant. My brother Guy, he always said that it sings to the ear, and Guy should know—he has only one ear, or still had the last I heard. But no matter—"

"Your brother Guy, who has only one ear . . ." Gonji repeated blankly. But Paille had already launched into a summation of what he had said before.

Gonji shook his head. "Equality? Democracy? Peasants aren't fit to rule themselves. There must always be a ruling class to guide them. And a soldiering class to preserve order."

"Hmm. You're allowing your politics and training to stand in the way of your destiny. But it is a fact, *señor*, that divine right of kings and governing power by virtue of birth to a privileged class are dying concepts. And it is a further truth that men are equals at birth and as such must be free to choose their own political order."

Gonji kicked a stone out of his path. "Is that so? And who has discerned these 'truths'?"

Paille looked surprised. "Why, *I* have, of course!"

Gonji smiled. "Ah, so you are another prophet, like this Tralayn?"

"Nooo! I am a visionary, not a soothsayer," Paille qualified. "My vision is of an ideal, an earthly, temporal one. Not an ideal muddled by vague religious sentiment—oh! thank heaven my brother can't hear me speak like this—"

"Your brother Guy, the one with only one ear—?"

"No-no, my brother David, the one who smiles like a nibbling rabbit—he's a writer, an apologist of Holy Mother Church—"

Gonji looked confused. "Your brother David who—"

"No, I'm not a sleepy Christian like most who live

here," the artist continued. "They choose to cower in wait of a divine Deliverer and wouldn't recognize one unless he came in a blinding light and on wings of a dove. I think they expect that the Christ has reserved His second coming for the plight of Vedun."

"You don't believe in *Iasu,* then—the Christ, the god of the West?" Gonji asked.

"Oh, He is there—somewhere, I suppose," Paille replied. "He seems to play a hide-and-seek game with humanity, and currently it is His turn to hide. That's why it is my duty as a visionary to shake these people out of their apathy and fatalism. But I fear my *esprit* and *panache* are misinterpreted. They believe me to be . . ." He shrugged.

"A madman," Gonji finished.

Paille scowled. "The ugly lot of genius," he snarled. "You understand the Christian doctrines? Those that would proscribe violence even when one's way of life is threatened?"

"That I have trouble understanding," Gonji replied thoughtfully. "But I've traveled in the West a long time, and before that I was a student of Christian priests in *Dai Nihon*—in Japan. I have found that their beliefs are as reasonable as any other in explaining some of the horrors I've encountered . . . the supernatural things . . ."

"Hah! I've yet to encounter anything that can't be explained by reason," Paille asserted. "The natural employed perversely—illusion—the uneducated are easily baffled—these are the ways that—"

Gonji was shaking his head. "So sorry, *señor,* but I only partly agree. There are things in the world that confound moral explanation even as they demand it. I believe that nothing natural can be wrong—although like you I know that the natural can certainly be put to wrongful use. I feel no compulsion to explain the wonders and mysteries of nature, uh—" He rubbed his forehead, trying to remember something. Then he smiled, remembering, and translated the poem into Latin, in which language it best retained the beauty of the Japanese:

> *"Unknown to me what dwelleth here:*
> *Tears flow from my sense of unworthiness*
> *and gratitude*

"That best sums up my attitude toward the unknowable wonders of nature," Gonji said.

"That's quite lovely," Paille observed. "Did you compose it?"

"No, I'm not that profound a poet. It's ancient. My father taught it to me, and his father to him—"

"But—" Paille began.

"But," Gonji interjected, stopping his disagreement short of utterance, "there are those things that demand explanation by their, um, *un*-nature."

"Unnatural quality, you mean."

"Hai, domo—yes, thank you. What do you make of this flying dragon, the wyvern? What possible purpose could it serve in any natural order?"

"It exists," Paille said, "and so we must conclude that it does serve some presently unknown function in the order of the cosmos. Or, quite probably, it is at least part illusion, or the product of natural power as yet harnessed only by the rare few adepts among us. There must be a natural explanation, else all rational order crumbles and there is chaos. Nothing of the sane and mundane in the world could be counted on, even as it has been for untold ages."

Gonji pondered this. Illusion . . . He thought of the fantastic events he had lived through. Of vampires and dragons and beasts of fable that had crossed his path these many years. Can I have imagined that these things were what they were? Have I been self-deluded, misinterpreting every frightful event, recasting every gnome as a giant in flawed memory, even as shadow casts the shapes of things as they are not?

Iyé. No, I have seen truly. Even if it is only I who have seen the truth, whatever that truth might ultimately mean.

The thought vaguely pleased his sense of unfulfilled destiny.

Gonji laughed breathily and changed Tora's reins to his other hand. "Excuse me, *por favor,* but . . . knowing alone what I know of the wyvern, I must say that to call him illusion is fully the most ridiculous thing I've heard all week." Paille looked offended but said nothing. The samurai then recalled Lydia Benedetto's similar reduction of the supernatural to the inexplicably natural. What a difference a change in speakers made.

They were nearing the Llorm garrison, and soldiers passing by sneered to see the familiar artist, some jeering openly at him.

"Now don't be starting any trouble," Gonji found himself advising in a curious reversal of his usual position. He halted Paille halfway through the delivery of an obscene gesture. "So you don't believe in the existence of things that are purely of evil use, yet you ply your craft in churches—I've seen your work, by the way, and it's very good."

Paille brightened. "You think so? *Merci, monsieur le samurai!* But, oh, since these paintings of chapel ceilings became all the rage they've cost artists nothing but stiff necks and aching shoulders and arms. Then one must work under poor light and with inadequate equipment—Ah, but I see that I've slipped back into French again. Eh, may I continue?"

"*Oui,*" said Gonji patiently. "As Guy's ear would have it."

"*Merci beaucoup.* But I was saying that there are more portentous matters to concern myself with now than chapel ceilings. Oh, yes indeed, for here in this place, at this time begins the struggle that will make men forever free of the yoke of monarchy. And *you* shall be the one to lead it."

"Now *wait* a moment, Paille," Gonji said, stopping and facing the Frenchman. Tora nudged his shoulder as he spoke. "Don't be including me in any of your dreams. I've already explained how I feel about your . . . politicals—"

"Politics."

"—whatever, and I make my own decisions about what I become involved in. Besides, this talk is madness, out here in the open like this. You're every bit as crazy as they say."

Paille's eyes shone. "*Oui,* crazy enough to recognize destiny's beckoning call, to see the coming *jacquerie*—the peasant revolution—that will begin in this insignificant place, among these humble mountains, and will echo down the corridors of time. And men will hail these days, for I shall record their moment, and they shall not be forgotten."

Gonji rubbed the back of his neck, and a gurgling sound rumbled in his throat. They began walking again.

"You've taken up your predestined place already, you know," Paille said in a quiet voice.

"How so?"

"Well, the fight at the square, for one. Quite an inspiration to the people. And now you've become Flavio's bodyguard. A stranger, no? Bodyguard to the chief magistrate? And then I've heard other things . . . whispered."

Gonji's skin prickled. "Such as?"

Paille moved closer and said out of the corner of his mouth: "They're saying you killed several bandits single-handedly while trying to rescue Michael's brother. You've become the hero of the masses in a span of days."

Gonji bridled. "Simply not true," he lied. "Nonsense cooked up to produce just the effect it has. Those bandits were dead already when I arrived. And I'll thank you to whisper that back to the whisperers next time, *neh?*"

He deeply regretted the prideful notion that had caused him to reveal how he had slain the boy's killers. Damn that chirruping Strom Gundersen!

"Too late," Paille said, grinning, "you're already included in both my chronicle and in-progress epic! Epic poetry—that's my current aesthetic passion. Ah, the glory of days past!"

"Don't worry. I'll have a look at it before long, and I'll have my blades with me," Gonji advised, tapping the hilt of his killing sword.

"Ah, but those swords of yours will figure prominently in the epic. Of that I'm confident. I wish I had my manuscripts with me—oh! I do have something, the work of a friend—" He fished inside his tunic and produced a crumpled parchment. "—arrived last week—all the way from England. You're a man of intellect. You possess discerning critical faculties. Tell me what you think—"

"Well, I'm no great critic of poetry—"

"Just listen," Paille ordered, holding a hand in front of Gonji's face. "It's a sonnet—tacky, sloppily sentimental form—mercifully dying out, I think, but it goes:

"No longer mourn for me when I am dead

*Than you shall hear the surly sullen bell
Giving warning to the world that I am fled
From this vile world, with vilest worms to—*

"What's the matter?" Paille asked in annoyance, finally seeing Gonji's head shaking.

"I don't understand English," Gonji said.

"Oh—well—let's see—" Paille did a hasty translation of the sonnet into French, which Gonji strove to follow.

After a second reading, Gonji stroked his chin reflectively, then said, "Well . . . I think it's quite good, although I'm sure the language suffers in the translation." Paille made a small squeaking sound. "But is he saying that he should be forgotten when his present life has ended? No life should be forgotten."

"No, of course not. This fellow should forget this sonnet business and apply himself to the stage. My brother tells me he's quite an accomplished actor."

"Your brother—Guy, with the one ear, or David, who smiles like a rabbit?"

"No-no, *Gaston*, the big strong one, who chose the stage against all advice."

"Gaston," Gonji repeated, rolling his eyeballs.

He recalled something he hadn't thought of in years: his twelfth summer—the song of a lark—an indiscretion—the certainty of young death—

He smiled. "Listen to this—

*"The soft white blossom—
  Her eyes, markers of my grave.
My heart yearns for time
  As shadows stretch and move:
The lark remembers my duty."*

"That's very interesting," Paille declared. "What

does it mean?"

"It is *waka* poetry," Gonji replied proudly. "And that was my death poem—composed a bit prematurely, as it happens."

As they neared the Ministry Paille questioned Gonji about his origin and background. The samurai spoke wistfully of Japan, of his father, the *daimyo* Sabataké Todohiro-noh-Sadowara; of *bushido* and its seven basic principles; justice, courage, benevolence, politeness, veracity, honor and loyalty; of the samurai's profound sense of duty; of Gonji's repudiated heritage— but not the details of the duel over star-crossed love fought with his rival half-brother . . .

"This code of *bushido* is marvelously clean and simple," Paille said. "But it can never be espoused here in eclectic Europe. Oh, no indeed. I'm afraid you'll have to exempt yourself from its precepts here if you're to retain your sanity. And as for duty—" He chortled. "—as I've said, you've found it. You're destined to be the great warrior-liberator who will help end monarchic tyranny. Your Western half has caused you to come here seeking fulfillment of that destiny."

"No, *monsieur* wild-eyed poet, I've not come to find death in a radical social . . . upheaval—"

"Oh, good word, *oui*, your French is improving already—"

"—but," Gonji continued, drowning him out, "but to seek a thing of legend called the Deathwind." He explained the quest he had been set by a dying Shinto priest.

"Mmm," Paille mused. "The Deathwind . . ."

"You've heard the legend?"

"Indeed, I know it well. Look about you. The Deathwind is our ever-present companion, the whispering breeze that serenades us when we're alone in the dead of night, reminding us of our helpless, teeth-gnashing mortality." Paille ended with a great theatrical flourish and flutter.

Gonji sighed. "What I need is a concrete explanation, something I can touch. Not more of your airy poetry."

"If you have to ask what the Deathwind is, then perhaps you'll never know—*oww!*" Paille felt his tender jaw, which yet bore the bruise of Gonji's punch on the night of the wyvern battle, when the fleeing samurai had tripped over the drunken artist.

"What happened there?" Gonji asked in amusement.

"Oh, the brigands jumped me the other night. Must have been three or four of them, but I escaped with only this souvenir."

Gonji suppressed a laugh. "So you're a fighting poet, then?"

"My purpose is to inspire others in the fight for freedom, but when the occasion warrants I can take care of myself." He looked about cautiously. Then he produced a dagger from inside his tunic, winking at Gonji.

They stopped before the Ministry of Government and Finance, an imposing stone edifice with huge granite columns guarding its portals, which housed the Chancellery of the Exchequer and sundry bureaucratic offices. Children played on the steps without, waiting for parents on business. The Ministry was the nexus of commerce in Vedun, a short distance from the square and the bell tower and chapel, whose twin peaks fingered the steely sky. A large banner bearing Klann's coat-of-arms now hung limply against the Ministry's facade.

Gonji wondered at the curious appointments: the beast of fable and seven interlocked circles, two of which were blackened out. And as if the thought had spurred him, Paille began to blazon the crest aloud:

"Per bend sinister, Azure and Argent; in dexter, a basilisk (or something still less wholesome, perhaps) rampant-reguardant, Or; in sinister, seven interlocked circles, two of the same Purpure; motto . . . incomprehensible."

"You can blazon such devices, eh?" Gonji said, eyes sparkling with interest. He remembered the other coat-of-arms he had seen several days past. "Listen, Paille, do you know another from these parts, a green-and-red field, with a gold cross at the bottom—"

"Indeed I do," the poet answered with arched eyebrows, "as do all in these environs. Of late it hung here in this very spot. The Rorka crest . . ." He set one foot on a hitching rail and puffed up his chest, then with eyes closed recited rapidly: "Per fess engrailed, Verd and Gules; in chief a lion, Argent, passant-guardant; in base a cross, Or (a hideously garish coloration, that); motto: 'In Vita Sicut in Morte'—'In Life as in Death.' That is, presumably, at the breast of the Lord. 'In Life as in Death' indeed . . ." Paille scowled.

Gonji shook his head sadly, for he had been sure it would be so: It *was* a patrol of Baron Rorka's troops he had helped slay while in the employ of Klann's 3rd Free Company.

"What do you suppose those blacked out, or purpled out, circles mean on the Klann crest?"

"Hard to say," Paille replied. "Purpure is the royal hue, so it doubtless represents Klann. But two of the seven filled, the others not . . . ?" He shrugged and turned his palms up.

A little boy brushed past them as Gonji tethered Tora, another child following quickly in yelping pursuit.

"The *enfants perdus*," Paille muttered, watching them.

"Eh?"

"The children of forlorn hope," the artist explained. "These are the ones who are trampled under the hooves of royal ambitions. They look to you for deliverance, *monsieur le samurai*—will you fail them?"

Gonji frowned, but deep within he was warmed by the pride born of the champion's mantle. His nickname swam on the eddies of his thoughts, that name he had earned farther west.

"Listen, Paille, you're knowledgeable on lore and legend. Ever hear of the Red Blade from the East?"

"Mmm. Let me think . . . *oui*, I do know it. It speaks of a fabled warrior—a cossack, I think—who carries a saber of ruddy metal. Never bested in battle. Some say the blade is colored by the many—what's wrong?"

"Forget it." Gonji's brow furrowed as he mounted the steps to the Ministry, resolving to carefully consider anything the glib Frenchman told him in the future before lending it any credence.

Paille stared after him a moment, wondering what he had said to alter the oriental's mood. They were certainly a touchy lot. He shrugged and loped up the steps after him.

Phlegor, the craft leader, signed the last bill of lading acknowledging receipt of the guild's materials.

"You're sure it's all there?"

"Quite sure, Phlegor," Lorenz Gundersen said with weary indulgence.

"You remember what happened last time the Jew brought the Viennese order."

"*And* you were credited and sent a premium when the shipment was corrected," Lorenz replied without looking up from the sheafs that now occupied his attention. He dearly hoped the discourtesy would send the feisty guildsman packing.

The Ministry was at the peak business hour. Stools and tables were twisted askew in the lobby. Voices chattered incessantly. Stale food and beverage smells clung in the informal air of the heavy late summer caravan trade season. Overworked secretaries argued with traveling chapmen and locals alike in small booths lining the walls. Flavio, the august Council Elder and his snowy-bearded adviser Milorad Vargo could be seen huddled over a desk through the doorway of a rear chamber. Boris Kamarovsky, the ferret-like woodworker, leaned against a foyer window, gazing about him dimly as he waited for his boss to finish signing for the recent trade goods shipment. It was humid after the recent rains, and the atmosphere lent itself well to an epidemic outbreak of irritability and headaches.

Phlegor seemed to thrive on such tense circumstances.

"Listen, Lorenz," Phlegor said, leaning forward over the counter, "is that Jap still staying with you Gundersens?"

"*Ja*, for now," Lorenz responded casually, applying the Seal of the Exchequer to a pile of documents.

"I don't like the way he swaggers around here like he's master of the city."

Lorenz cocked an eyebrow. "Oh? I understand you were quite taken with him the night of that ridiculous brawl on the rostrum."

"That was *then*. Sure, it was amusing to see Klann's bandits take their licks. And he showed he could fight, even if it was only with his feet like some damned fighting cock. But what's he done since then, except strut around town eyeing up the women? You people haven't mentioned the council meeting to him, have you?"

Lorenz stopped in his work. His lips perked and he eyed the craftsman sidelong. "I'll just pretend you never said that."

"Hey, no offense! I just don't trust strangers, that's all. Especially heathens and infidels."

"That's your privilege."

"I understand Flavio's taken him on as a bodyguard," Phlegor said loud enough to turn nearby heads from their business.

"That's *his* privilege," Lorenz said at length.

"Pretty rash, if you ask me."

Lorenz bit his tongue. Then he said, "Weren't you in favor of the hiring?"

Phlegor thought a moment. "*Ja,* I suppose . . . but that was the other night. I've had time to think about it since. Is he really going along to the castle banquet?"

"So I understand."

Phlegor shook his head. He leaned close again. "What about that wildman who killed the big soldier and then jumped over the wall? Anyone know who he was yet? God, that was something!" Phlegor breathed an awe.

The Executor of the Exchequer exhaled deeply and flung down the Seal. Leaning back in his chair, he smoothed the wrinkles out of his doublet and peered up at the insistent craft leader.

"No, Phlegor, no one knows. But I'm sure you'll be the first to find out, and then you can tell us all." Lorenz's voice reeked of the haughty sarcasm that was his trademark.

"Well ten-to-one he's a friend of the monkey-man, and I'd like to know what they're planning. As far as I'm concerned they're just two more invaders trying to make a reputation at Vedun's expense."

Boris snapped to attention at the window. "Phlegor—here he comes now!"

"The Jap?"

"Da." Boris smirked. "Still got his hair tied up on top of his head like a turnip. And guess who's with him?"

"Who?"

"That crazy Paille!"

"Oh, *Jesu Christi!*"

Lorenz's face dropped into a cupped hand, the elbow resting on the chair arm. "Oh no," he grated in a low voice.

When Gonji entered the foyer and bowed to those in the lobby, Boris scrambled over to stand next to Phlegor without a look in the samurai's direction. Several people returned Gonji's bow nervously, the babble of voices diminishing to sporadic whispers.

Gonji spotted Flavio in the rear chamber, and the Elder waved him over. He removed his sashed swords with a slow, elegant motion and carried them, sheathed, in his right hand to Flavio's office.

Then came Paille.

"Gundersen! My paints! Did they arrive with Neriah's caravan?" The artist waved his order form over his head.

Lorenz gathered himself to fend the coming storm. "Not this time, Paille. Can't you just begin on another section with the colors you still have—?"

Then the storm broke in all its aesthetic fury.

Chapter Three

Local musicians had gathered in the square, and drumbeats counterpointed their lilting refrain as the banquet escort party was mounted.

A short column of Llorm dragoons, hefting lances and flying Klann's colors on crisply snapping pennons, awaited the delegation in front of the rostrum. Council Elder Flavio already was there, seated astride a roan of sixteen hands which had been carefully groomed and caparisoned. Flavio himself sat tall and smiling in a long, colorful capote that looked too uncomfortable for the day's heat but would be needed on the return ride that night. Flavio returned the well-wishes of the gathered populace with repeated nods and waves.

Beside the Elder, aboard a gray gelding, sat Milorad, the paunchy ex-statesman, happily affecting a courtly dignity he had little occasion to employ these days.

On Flavio's right sat Gonji, erect and dignified, calm but expectant as he stroked Tora's withers, trying hard to mask his excitement and curiosity over at last visiting Castle Lenska. Clean and polished *cap-a-pie*, he had even oiled his scabbards so that they glistened impressively.

Women and children spread flowers on the roadway to the postern gate. The city's collective hope for peaceful coexistence with the invaders and the redress of grievances would ride with the delegates. The musicians played on, wilting in the midday heat. A muggy breeze lapped the city. More rain seemed in the offing.

A rumble and clink of mounted troops approached from down Alwin Street in the German quarter of the city, and a column of mercenaries wheeled out of the lane and trotted to the square, the richly adorned Captain Julian Kel'Tekeli at their head. It was the 1st Free Company, grinning and chattering in the ranks at the prospect of the castle banquet.

Julian passed close to Gonji and cast him the merest glance. This was the nearest they had been to each other since Gonji hired on with the captain as an operative for Klann. Gonji suppressed a smirk as he observed the captain's proud bearing, the preciseness of his every movement. Julian spoke briefly to the free companions, admonishing them to good behavior, then appointed his second-in-command to lead the column and himself clumped to the head of the leading Llorm squad.

Gonji looked the mercenaries over. They carried the usual array of mismatched weapons—swords, axes, and a few short bows—but it took him a while to notice today's difference: there were no firearms in their ranks. Not a pistol in sight.

Then he spotted Luba, the big ugly trooper with the bald, shining bullet of a head whom he had knocked cold in the boxing match. Luba spat and worked his jaws in a silent insult as their eyes met. The samurai's mouth twisted with wry unconcern, and he languidly turned from the man's view.

They'd have their time of rematch, he knew, and when it happened, it happened. He dispersed all thoughts of Luba, then, relaxing and establishing a sense of inner harmony. He would need control and a keen mind today.

Garth Gundersen, the last of the delegates, arrived and lipped a quiet apology to Flavio for his tardiness. At his side rode Wilf, looking bright-eyed and anxious and, quite frankly, more like a delegate than his blacksmith sire. The young smith was scrubbed and scented and wore clean riding boots, shining breeches, and a new tunic. He eyed the delegates—especially Flavio—breathlessly as if still fostering the hope that he'd be invited along.

Garth, on the other hand, though tolerably presentable aside from the purpling eye and a bruise or two left over from his bout with the ill-fated Ben-Draba, wore a working-class jerkin and faded waistcoat, plus his favorite floppy cap; he seemed sulky and withdrawn, his speech monosyllabic.

Wilf rode up to Gonji and bowed, extending a hand, which the samurai took reluctantly. The young smith pressed into Gonji's hand a blossom of a wildflower.

"Give that to Genya," Wilf said in a strained whisper. "Tell her . . . tell her I'll be coming for her soon."

And with that he yanked his white steed around and lurched off through the parting crowd. Gonji halfsmiled and nodded, pocketing the token. He repositioned his swords more comfortably and waited.

Upon Julian's flashy command, echoed by the subordinate behind them, the delegates joined with the soldiers in the long double column that clattered over the paving stones to the gate. A cheer rose from the crowd as they started off, and Gonji recognized several faces among them: Paolo Sauvini, Aldo Monetto and Karl Gerhard, Lorenz Gundersen on the steps of the Ministry; then he saw Lydia Benedetto, and felt the smile that crinkled the corners of his mouth, and only realized that he had been staring when he saw the smoky eyes of her husband, Michael, over her shoulder. Then he squared his shoulders and set his face in grim dignity, snorting to chase his mild embarrassment and nodding to the waving crowd on both sides of him.

And in an effort at employing the crowd's positive energy, he imagined that it was for him that they were cheering, for their champion.

The farmer Vlad Dobroczy stared hard at Gonji as the delegation party pounded past with clumping hooves and jangling traces and armament.

"I still can't believe Flavio took him along. As if he meant anything to Vedun. That horse's ass Wilf Gundersen probably had something to do with it, through his old man." Dobroczy scowled after the long column as they rode through the gatehouse, where Old Gort waved them through, smiling toothlessly.

Peter Foristek towered at Vlad's side, shifting his scythe from one shoulder to the other. His face was just returning to normal, the lumps shrinking, the bruises fading, from the savage beating he had received at the hands of Ben-Draba.

"You still think he's one of them, Hawk? He's a good fighter, that's for sure."

"He's a *stranger*," the hook-nosed Dobroczy growled. "And no stranger can be trusted, not anymore. Don't forget it. Remember what they tried to do to your sister."

Foristek's face darkened. He shifted the scythe again and nodded solemnly.

"So say it already," Michael whispered to Lydia as he gazed at the departing column over her shoulder.

She half-turned. "Say what, Michael?"

"Whatever's on your mind."

A studied calm crept into her large blue eyes, and she smiled sweetly. "There's nothing on my mind right now—really."

Michael pursed his lips and pushed off through the crowd, Lydia watching him go for a moment and then peering back toward the postern gate, a puzzled frown creasing her soft features.

Tralayn the prophetess stood on the northern rampart, the Llorm sentry casting her a sidewise glance as he passed. Her arms were folded into the ample sleeves of her long jade robes. Her green eyes were sullen slits, heavy-lidded and dreamy, as if she were about to doze off even as she stood. But her thoughts were of dreams that could never be, of the vain and misfit hope of peaceful coexistence with the minions of evil.

Strom Gundersen and Boris Kamarovsky sat with the former's flock on a hilltop northwest of Vedun's encircling walls, gazing down at the delegation and its military escort.

"There goes Papa. He's not too happy about this," Strom observed. "What a grouch this morning."

"Look at that monkey-man," Boris sneered, "riding like he's the cock of the yard."

They shared a laugh, and Strom piped a merry little tune on his reed pipe in accompaniment of the trotting hoofbeats.

"Monkey-man," Strom said then. "Where'd you get that?"

"That's what Phlegor calls him."

"Well, he better not let Gonji hear it."

"Gonji," Boris spat. "What the hell kind of name is that?"

"He's pretty tough."

"Aw, hell, that's just when he fights with his feet like a rooster. Know what the soldiers'll do if he starts anymore trouble?"

Strom looked at him questioningly.

Boris sighted along his hand, which he shaped like a pistol.

"Boom."

The north road out of Vedun was paved only as far as the old Roman road it intersected about half a kilometer from the walls. At this point the plateau melded into the foothills of the Carpathians, and the north road continued as a broad, packed-earth track that meandered through the timbered hills toward Castle Lenska, whose tallest spires and towers could barely be made out from the flatlands.

The banquet delegation rode past the hillock on the left, where Strom's sheep scurried like windblown down. On the right began the checkerboard expanse of cultivation and orchards that fed the province. Beyond, the distant roar of the river that swept past the city to the cataract that emptied into the southern valley.

The road swung left into the hills, and for a time the castle towers were lost to view among the bristling forested woods. The road coursed ever upward, the horses laboring with the increasing strain. The party emerged from a delve in the hills, and suddenly the facade of Castle Lenska lay open to view.

Gonji was momentarily breathless. This was the closest he had ever been to the storied fortress, and its legends seemed indeed warranted. It rose imposingly atop a pine-crowded peak, shimmering in the mist against the jagged gray-white caps in the northern mountain fastness. Men on horseback were dwarfed by even its outer bailey wall, and that one, crowded with soldiers, crouched before a still taller inner curtain, which was also dotted with moving figures.

"Whew," Gonji breathed. "Marvelous." It was not

so sprawling a place as Japan's incredibly complex fortresses, which were composed of acres of mazelike walls. But here in Europe there were none so formidable as this one. The thought struck him again that Lenska *should* have proven impregnable to so small a command as Klann led. And he was stirred with an eagerness to get a look inside.

A lark cried in the treetops nearby, and the bird's call mingled with the memories of Japan to raise up the long-buried details of an occasion he had thought of earlier that day.

The song of the lark, and his death poem. The *waka* he had recited to Paille, which hadn't passed his lips in many a year . . .

He was twelve, charged with tending a garden at the teahouse of a cousin. The cousin's wife, a lusty, voluptuous woman of about seventeen, was alone within for the afternoon. Gonji's awakening sexuality and spirit of mischief had caused him to sneak a look at her through a *shoji* screen while she undressed. But then she had spotted him. And had smiled. He had been seized by fear of discovery and the certainty that his cousin would surely dispatch him upon his return later that day. At the moment of discovery a lark began to sing in a nearby tree. It had remained with him the rest of the afternoon, trilling its song incessantly as he composed his death poem and completed his work in the garden, which he had been sure would be the last duty of his short life. His cousin had returned, but when he had called Gonji inside, it was merely to commend him on the fine work he had done. The matter of his voyeurism was never brought up . . .

A nostalgic smile impishly perked Gonji's lips.

The beating rush of great batwings surged up behind them, shattering Gonji's reverie. All in the party craned their necks and fought their panicked steeds into control as the wyvern soared by. Its shrill cry echoed through the foothills as it flapped toward the castle on its monstrous leathery wings, then orbited the walls in a slow, wide arc.

"Welcome, delegates," Gonji said to the others, grinning nervously. The old fear was rekindled, the hatred for the beast and the fear of the loathsome death it carried in its glands and bowels. Gonji ground his teeth at the fleeting memory of his mad ride from its first strafing attack at the monastery.

Then he noticed that it still carried the broken shaft of his arrow in its belly, and his eyes narrowed. He nodded and patted Tora to calm him. Round one was the wyvern's; round two had been his. He wondered again why it hadn't fried him when it had alighted behind him with devilish stealth that night and only hoped that it wouldn't recognize him today and finish the job.

"All right, the king awaits," Julian called back to them. "Let's go!"

The road steepened and the surrounding terrain grew more rocky as they neared the castle. They swung left and right through hillocks and delves and craggy outcrops of granite or shale, now and again losing sight of all but the tallest towers of the fortress.

Then they emerged onto a flat table of land, the castle yet a kilometer distant, and took in a sight that set their stomachs churning:

"Misericordia!" Milorad cried.

"Great God in heaven!" Flavio gasped, reining in.

The stench was stultifying.

Bodies of Baron Rorka's soldiers, the castle defenders, had been heaped into a shallow common grave to the east of the road. The grave was rimmed by crucified forms hanging on leaning gibbets. A party of mercenaries, their faces covered by bandannas so that only their eyes could be seen squinting out from under chapeaus and helms, were toppling the crucified corpses into the grave. Oil was hauled to the grave in buckets and sloshed over the piled liches, while one man readied a torch for the funeral pyre. Judging by the condition of the bodies—some already bursting with corruption—they were none too soon in getting around to the grisly task.

They pushed on, each man casting a last ambivalent glance at the wretched charnel scene.

Just before the final rise to the outer bailey, the castle road became paved again with cobblestones, and they clattered up a sparsely-treed tor to be greeted by the spectacle of Castle Lenska's dwarfing facade.

Gonji's eyes were alight with anticipation, and he clenched his teeth to suppress his undignified thrill. "An aerie on a wind-lashed precipice," he had heard it called, and it lived up to its reputation. Swirling mountain winds churned about the jagged peak they had surmounted, tugging at their clothes and flapping the column's pennons. Atop the central keep's spires, Klann's banners fluttered wildly. But for the road they traversed, the castle was unapproachable to horses or siege engines. It rose from a depression in the crag on the south and west and backed against a steep incline on the east and north sides. Attack via the latter two directions was out of the question: The slopes were all shale and scrub and bramble, the rushing river rapids at their base, and foot-soldiers scrabbling up their uncertain purchase were target game for the archers on the battlements. On the south and west sides, rocks had been heaped so that besiegers would be forced to mount them, again becoming easy targets, the prize for survival being a plunge into the wide moat that gleamed with oily scum from the southeast corner to the northwest.

They rode past lines of wagons and staring troopers and finally rumbled over the drawbridge and through the raised portcullis of the barbican, the outer gate. A squad of Llorm saluted Julian and the Llorm captain at the head of the column. Gonji began calculating troop strength and committing the castle's defensive deployment to memory when the bellowing roar echoed from around the corner on their left.

Gonji's hand shot to the hilt of the Sagami in reaction to the flaring of his spine. From beyond the southwest drum tower in the outer ward came another awesome bellow of rage, this time mixed with hoofbeats and slapping footfalls—then laughter, both from the approaching clamor and from the escort.

Three mercenaries with polearms, only one on horseback, tore around the base of the tower toward them, peering back over their shoulders with a curious mixture of terror and mirth. The hulking shadow came fast behind them, then the monstrous bulk that tumbled head over heels with a resounding thud that boomed dully in the ward. Soldiers on the ramparts laughed and pointed, but the delegation from Vedun could only stare in shock. For here was their first glimpse of Tumo, Mord's cretin giant.

"*Choléra,*" Gonji whispered hoarsely, still gripping the Sagami's hilt.

The giant pushed himself aright on short stubby legs the thickness of barrels at the thighs. At full height he must have been nearly a rod, but it was difficult to judge because of his stooped, apelike posture. Hairy arms like cannon barrels hung to his knobby knees, which were coarse and callused like the knuckles on his ale-cask fists.

He leaned forward on a fist and peered around him dimly with a face out of a child's nightmare. Then he lurched toward the mounted party on all fours like a gorilla. The horses that were unused to the bestial apparition began at once to curvette and sidestep, neighing and snorting. The three mercenaries who had tormented the giant had split up, one rider and one footman now angling toward Julian soberly and penitently, while the other footsoldier crept backwards along the middle bailey wall. Tumo caught sight of him and made an idiotic caterwauling cry, pushing toward him with a vengeance.

The mercenary screamed as Tumo cornered him, roaring through his yawning, flaccid mouth. The man broke from the wall, but the giant batted him back with a gnarled hand. He hit the wall, breath gushing from his lungs. Tumo tapped him again with a short open-handed blow that knocked him on his side.

"Tumo!" Julian cried out, then said something to the giant in an unknown language. The great beast looked to the captain, bellowed once more at the mercenary, then lumbered over to the delegation party.

A free companion's horse bucked and threw its rider over. It was all the Vedunian party could do to keep their mounts in line. Even Tora, who had seen his share of the unnatural, tossed fretfully under Gonji.

Tumo stopped a short distance from them upon Julian's command. The cretin giant stood erect on his massive bowed legs and regarded them vapidly.

"This is Tumo," Julian said with amusement over the noise of the whinnying steeds. "Tumo is one of our . . . deterrents."

Gonji relaxed his grip on the Sagami as the captain remonstrated with the soldiers who had been prodding the giant into his rage. The samurai could see the disheartening effect Tumo had on the others. The chord it struck in the human heart was difficult to define in all its terrifying complexity, for its appearance had been well designed by whatever dark power had formed it: Slavering lips and grinding splay teeth were continually worked at by an overlong red tongue. The face was broad and squat at the base, the skull so small as to be almost pointed. The giant's brow lay low and heavy over dim, angular eyes. His nose was no more than a tiny stub with pinpoint nostrils. The mouth was the focus of the monster's face. Its body was a great mass of rolling layers of blubber; its weight beggared the imagination. It was naked and hairless, but for knotty tufts on its head and arms and genitals. The overall impression was of some unholy mutation of an idiot child, a perverse mockery of human misery that caused one to flinch in terror and repugnance.

Gonji recalled that Jocko and Jacob Neriah both had spoken of a giant traveling with this army. He had been hoping the tales were exaggerated. Then he remembered the words of the drunken soldier at the inn: *Hey, Cap'n, he reminds me o' Tumo* . . . He felt the anger over the insult working up inside him.

"Tumo will be feasting tonight, too, only he likes his meat raw, don't you, Tumo?" Julian said portentously. The giant ground out a few subhuman syllables that sounded like reproductions of the captain's speech. Milorad shuddered and whispered something to Flavio.

On Julian's command the cretin giant turned and waddled away toward the drum tower, issuing a final warning bark to the prostrate soldier.

"Pathetic creature," Flavio said as they clopped to the middle bailey gatehouse.

"Indeed so," Milorad agreed.

"I hope that's not the king's brother," Gonji jested, leaning toward them. But no one had found it amusing, save Garth, who *tsked* and cast him a sidelong glance. Gonji shrugged and looked once more after the departing giant, wondering what other marvels, strange and sinister, this day might unveil.

The gatehouse was a heavily guarded checkpoint at the entrance to a long tunnel cut completely through the central keep's lower level. Its flanking towers were enormous defensive outworks of the middle bailey wall, which rose like a mighty curtain of stone twice the height of the outer wall and rendering the outer ward a broad killing ground for any besieging party that might breech the outermost obstacles. The towers were cut through with arrow loops and croslets. Archers manning these and walking the ramparts above peered down lazily. At the southeast drum tower far down the wall, Gonji could make out the barrel of a bombard or mortar.

Gatehouse guards saluted the captains and admitted the party. Gonji had just passed through when he was halted by a fierce command at his left hand. He pulled up.

"Remove your weapons and leave them here."

The Llorm guard had spoken in German. His white-knuckled fist gripped the hilt of his sheathed broadsword. Hot eyes glared up at Gonji from under a burgonet helm.

"I'm the Council Elder's bodyguard," Gonji replied evenly. "My weapons go where I go."

"You heard the commander of the guard!"

A polearm probed dangerously close to Gonji's ribs.

Gonji turned slowly to face the soldier on his right. His eyes narrowed menacingly. The Llorm lancer was an ugly man whose bulbous nose looked as if eleven troops had late used it as a training prop.

"Careful with that pike, fig-nose," Gonji said.

Flavio, sensing imminent trouble, began to intercede. Gonji and the pikeman glared at each other. The samurai, remembering his promise to Flavio, felt the dull pang of helpless capitulation rising. But Captain Kel'Tekeli dismounted and strode back to the hold-up.

After a brief explanation, he said to the guard, "I think we can trust the Elder's bodyguard to behave himself, can't we?"

Gonji bridled at the other's patronizing tone but smiled thinly and nodded.

They continued through into the central ward, which was a frenzy of activity, last-minute preparations being attended to by scurrying servants and scullions. The ward was large enough for cavalry practice to be pursued simultaneously with archery and swordsmanship, and Gonji admiringly appraised the training facilities. Only a handful of troops, mostly Llorm, plied their weapons on the grounds now, and the samurai observed their techniques with great interest.

They dismounted, hostlers attending at once to their horses. Garth paused to speak with them awhile. Flavio approached Gonji, an admonishing set to his pursed lips.

"Remember your promise now—no trouble," the Elder said affably, smiling and waving to anxious servants who rushed by in their duties.

"Not unless I'm provoked, of course."

Flavio's concern creased his brow. "Gonji, I would be more at ease if you told me you could extend the limits of your perseverance somewhat . . . at least for this important occasion."

They walked across the ward, Milorad and Garth following.

Gonji sighed. "I *am* sometimes too easily provoked by effrontery, I suppose. And you *are* my master." He smiled at the Elder. "As you would have it."

"Good!" Flavio grinned and picked up his step toward the great hall across the ward. "Now let us meet with our new liege lord and find out precisely where we stand—hello, Frantisek!" He greeted a bubbling servant who nearly tripped over himself as he bobbed his head and walked backward with a heavy ewer.

Gonji was not surprised to find himself a popular attraction. Soldiers and civilians alike scanned him closely as he passed. He wondered what most fascinated them: his fighting reputation? Or had Julian spread the word so quickly that Gonji had become his secret operative?

He took careful note of the Llorm regulars and their people. The Akryllonian nationals were a dark, pale folk who looked drawn, worn by their nomadic life. Lean and hungry. Desperate. Such qualities translated into ferociousness in battle, he well knew. The children, especially, seemed a pathetic lot; scrawny and hollow-eyed, weak and sickly. But the men, the Llorm regulars, were hardy enough, and if their will to live, to preserve their people and ease the burden of their families ran deep enough, they'd not be leaving the province after the winter. Not this winter, nor many winters hence.

It was all absurd. Could this really be the remnant of some lost island kingdom and not simply the camp following of a bandit chieftain? Perhaps they'd have answers soon.

The delegates were led through the portals of the great hall and into a massive groin vault with egresses into three corridors. They turned left, armed guards before and behind them, passed noisy chambers and anterooms, and entered through a broad archway into the hall proper.

It was a cavernous place, richly appointed, alive with the chatter and laughter of soldiers and civilians, servants and animals. Dogs barked and begged, scurried underfoot, awaiting handouts to come. Roistering mercenaries bellowed and clanked their armament, called out ribald jokes; some, already drunk, grabbed at scampering, yelping servant girls.

Gonji sniffed distastefully. He had been expecting a more sedate and august display, something akin to courtly decorum. But this was the epitome of decadence, a scene freshly cut from the Judgment Day perdition paintings he had seen.

Oil lamps and cresset torches blazed in the hall. The only windows were tall, slender affairs set high up on the walls, which admitted a network of murky gray twilight swirling with smoke and dust motes. Halfway up the walls, running its course around them, a canopied gallery bulged out over the hall, supported by ornate ivory columns. Dozens of chamber doors gave egress from the gallery, and at one side sat a group of musicians. Lute and recorder, flute and cymbal valiantly strove against the babble and din.

Stately and heraldic arras hung about the walls, gazing down somberly on the wassail. The long oaken tables already were in disarray, the parquet floor a quagmire of mud and beverage spills. The banquet had yet to be served.

They were led to a solitary table set before the raised dais where several of Klann's advisers had already assumed their places. The four were seated at the end before the dais, Flavio and Gonji facing Milorad and Garth. Several other places at their table were set but untenanted. Servants crisscrossed the room, darting about with pitchers and kegs in a failing effort to keep flagons and goblets full. The air reeked of mead and ale, wine and kvas. Some servants fairly tripped over each other in their effusive efforts to greet the smiling Flavio, Milorad, and Garth. One scullery maid knelt and kissed Flavio's hand, pleading for him to secure her release.

They sat back and observed the orgiastic proceedings as their beverages were served, Gonji and Flavio selecting wine; Garth having an ale; and Milorad, mead. No one spoke for a time, each man content to observe, to ponder the promise of the night's meeting, to seek a comfortable niche for himself in the surroundings.

Gonji saw that the adjacent tables were reserved for the Llorm's women and children and decided that was good. He was beginning to take his ease in this magnificent structure of huge ashlar blocks and sturdy beams which massed beasts of burden might strain at in vain. He worked at a stoic detachment from the nods and chuckles cast in his direction by tactless soldiers. Their childish threat was distant and impotent; it couldn't disturb his harmony. He even met Julian's occasional haughty glances with calm, impassive stares of his own, breaking them off at his leisure. *Dignity will be mine tonight,* he thought with supreme self-satisfaction.

Then the Great Dane sidled up between Gonji and Flavio and began sniffing at the samurai's swords.

"*Damn* you, mangy cur!" Gonji grated in his throat, shooing the animal away in not altogether dignified fashion. "Lift your leg on my swords and someone will be feasting on *your* carcass tonight!"

When his companions' laughter had subsided, he reestablished his lost harmony and rubbed his reddening face. But he couldn't help laughing himself and was pleased to see that he had lifted them from their timid sipping. Removing his *daisho*—his matched set of swords—from his *obi,* Gonji set them at his right side against the bench seat. He ran his hands under the slack left in the sash by their removal.

"Now I've got room," he said, sniffing deeply with eyes closed at the tempting whiffs of meaty aroma seeping from the kitchens. "Looks like no monsters were invited tonight, anyway," he added.

The others' snickers subsided quickly, their memory of the cretin giant still poignant.

"Wonder who's going to be seated at our table," Gonji thought aloud. "Oh, Garth—did the hostlers tell you why you were invited?"

Garth shook his head glumly. "No, I don't know . . . It isn't for smith work," he added haltingly.

Tumo will be feasting tonight, too . . . Gonji shook his head and cleared his throat, was about to say something pleasant when the shriek came from a nearby table of mercenaries.

"How dare you!" a woman shouted. "I'm a personal servant of the king!" She raised a silver serving tray over her head like a bludgeon.

The man who had given her offense raised his eyebrows and leaned back in surprise, his companions roaring their mirth.

"She's a fiery one, eh?"

"Draw on her, Merwyn!"

The woman launched into a tirade, berating the soldier's impropriety, shaking a petite fist in his face all the while. A Llorm regular finally rose from his table and interposed himself between them, dismissing the girl and bending low to admonish the drunken wastrel.

"There's the hoyden," Garth said sullenly.

Gonji looked to him questioningly.

"Wilfred's Genya," Flavio clarified.

"*Ah, so desu*—so that's the lady fair!" Gonji said amusedly.

And then she was heading for their table, adjusting her hair and skirts primly as she pattered over with restored dignity. They all rose to greet her. She looked to be in her late teens, her short stature emphasizing a ripe figure. Her hair was curly, soft and dark, and it frolicked about her shoulders as she moved pertly, calling attention to a cherubic face and sparkling dark eyes. A set of baby-fat dimples framed full red lips that were formed in a tempting pucker. It should not have been surprising that she was much pursued by the young men of Vedun, for nature had fashioned her for allure. But it seemed to Gonji, as the men rose from their table to greet her, that her charm was not without guile and artifice.

"Oh, they're such animals, these soldiers," she said primly. Then she at once melted into wide-eyed innocence. "Oh, Papa Flavio, thank *God* you're here! We've been simply dying inside, all of us, to know what's become of Vedun."

She bent and kissed his hand lightly, her own small white hand fluttering at her bodice modestly. "How are my parents?" She spoke to the Elder in his native Italian.

"They're in good health," Flavio replied, smiling benignly, "and they asked me to convey their love, as have all the servants' families. My heart is heavy, though, for Lottie Kovacs. I'm afraid her father . . ."

"Yes, we've heard—oh, Blessed Mother, what a terrible, terrible thing! Lottie's crushed, absolutely crushed. But at least Richard is here to comfort her. But dear Flavio, you *will* try to gain us our freedom tonight, won't you—?"

And Flavio offered his cautiously optimistic assurances that he would seek the hostages' release. But almost before he had finished Genya shifted her attention to Garth.

"Herr Gundersen, how is Wilfred? I miss him so—oh my!" Quickly dismissing her startled expression at Garth's bruises, she stood on tiptoes to kiss his cheek, and after a moment's hesitation the burly smith self-consciously bent to oblige her.

"He's fine," Garth said. "Stubborn as always." He averted his eyes from hers, rather rudely, it seemed to the others.

"*Bitte*, tell him to have a care. It's so dreadful around here these days. The castle is full of dangers. The soldiers are everywhere. Monsters and giants roam the grounds freely. Have you seen them?" She was whispering with awe now.

The delegates all muttered their agreement. And then, before their voices had ceased to echo, Genya was speaking with Milorad, making a show of interest in his and Anna's well being in the new social circumstances.

All the while Gonji could feel the girl's consuming curiosity about him, though she never once regarded him directly.

She was an operator, of that he was sure. *Good fortune with this one, friend Wilfred* . . . He watched with keen interest how adroitly Genya shifted from dignity to respect to affection to anxiety, coyly affected innocence lubricating the transitions.

Then she was through with Milorad and looking just past Gonji, eyes dropping diffidently floorward. He decided to accept the invitation.

"I'm Gonji Sabataké, a friend of Wilfred." He bowed slightly, and she curtsied, eyelids fluttering closed. "He asked me to give this to you, a token of his undying affection." He handed her the blossom from Wilf.

Her lips parted silently, and for the first time she seemed touched by genuine emotion.

"*Danke*—thank you," she whispered.

And then her breath caught in her throat, and her eyes had suddenly outgrown her face, fear rimming them as she looked over Gonji's shoulder. The others were all staring.

Gonji turned, and a chill shot through his spine. He was gazing into the masked face of Mord. The sorcerer's diamond-hard black eyes appeared to be smiling with private amusement.

Gonji bowed, and a long moment later the magician returned the gesture, bending forward slowly and dreamily, like a reed under water.

"We've . . . met?" Mord asked in his murky basso profundo voice.

Gonji's nape prickled with fine pinpoints of tension. His palms were cold and moist, but his face betrayed nothing of it.

"Not unless you've been to Honshu," he replied evenly.

The sorcerer's gleaming filigreed mask tilted almost imperceptibly, as if the arch reply had thrown him off guard. Then his piercing ophidian eyes appeared to shift, to cloud over with a dull film, to pulsate hideously as if about to burst their sockets.

And an instant later Gonji was gazing with barely disguised shock into the fiery red orbs of the wyvern.

Choléra.

Gonji's face grew hot; his senses reeled with an instant's indecision. He could feel his companions' breathless anticipation. Against his leg—the solid comfort of his sword hilts where they leaned. Then—

"All kneel!"

Gonji slowly joined the jostling, clinking throng in dropping to one knee, striving to control his bewilderment, to plan, to reestablish his *wa*, his harmony of spirit . . .

"Know ye the righteous liege lord of the Isle of Akryllon and all its possessions, Successor to its throne, Preserver of its heritage, Supreme Commander of the Akryllonian Royalist Forces . . . Know ye King Klann, Him Who Is Called the Invincible!"

And in the reverent silence that had fallen during the heraldic pronouncement, it seemed that nothing had moved or stirred the air.

And then the legendary King Klann was among them, and all eyes were on him. All eyes save Gonji's.

Gonji peered furtively over his shoulder.

But Mord was gone.

They sat alone over dinner in the stillness of the house, Michael Benedetto missing his murdered brother's bright chatter more than ever. Two tapers cast their cold glow over the meal. The silence became unbearable, Lydia's smug indulgence insufferable as she served him.

"So say it already, vixen!" Michael growled. "They didn't want me along because of my temper, and I've trodden on the graven image of your lofty ambition." The words were spat more than spoken.

Lydia blinked, but her composure was otherwise unshaken.

"A broken nose and blackened eyes ill befit a statesman."

"Really? I can think of a few statesmen whose noses warrant rearrangement."

"Stop being a child. You're making a shambles of your career—"

"I'm the same child you wanted to keep in Count Faluso's employ in . . . Mi-*lahn*-o," he drawled sarcastically.

"You needn't have stopped there. With a bit of string-pulling by your mother, the de'Medicis might have—"

"The de'Medicis—the *corrupt* de'Medicis—*fie* on the de'Medicis!"

"Hush! You've chosen your position. You'd prefer to administer to peasants. But that's no reason to slander the de'Medicis."

"And then where after Florence, my love?" Michael sneered. "Back to your homeland? To Krakow in triumphant return?"

"Your Polish isn't up to it."

"How very like my courtly mother you are. So thoroughly seduced by the appearances of state and the fripperies of court life."

Lydia spoke softly. "You still don't understand me, Michael. I'm not your mother, I'm your wife. I believe that God has designated leaders and followers. You possess the talent and the education for leadership, but your cardinal humor is choler, and you make no effort to resist it. To fail to live up to your potential is a great sin."

Their meal half-eaten but appetite gone, Michael fell to brooding. Lydia approached him with a wet cloth and touched his shoulder gently.

"Lie back and let me lay this on your battered face."

He shrugged off her hand. "Leave me alone."

She left the room with a soft rustle, the faintest wisp of her perfume trailing behind her. A moment later a servant came and cleared the table, careful not to intrude on her employer's sullen introspection. And then Michael was alone with the hypnotic flicker of the candle flames.

She was right. He was failing miserably in his charge. Even his rightful place in the castle delegation had been usurped by a stranger—and an infidel, yet! And from an angry cell in the dungeons of his mind came the shrill warning that this bold mercenary was going to be real trouble if he went unchecked. In more ways than one . . .

For he had seen how the oriental had looked at his wife.

Michael rose and donned a capote and toque. Lydia stopped him just as he was slipping out through the narrow vaulted foyer.

"Where are you going at this hour?" she asked, eyes flashing with a trace of suspicion or fear.

"Out," he replied without looking back. "To think."

She watched him go through the window grating, then wrapped a shawl about her and stepped out into a crisp breeze that tumbled down from the mountain fastness.

Chapter Four

Two concerns held Flavio captive. There was, of course, the apprehension over the momentous meeting with the warrior-king that was now but seconds away. And then there was the anxiety over Gonji: his temper; his flair for being at the center of contention; and now, most threateningly, the sorcerer's apparent recognition of him.

Could Mord have already divined, by means of some hideous magick, that it was the samurai who had attacked his familiar, the wyvern, with bow and arrows?

Gonji was trouble, and bringing him along—indeed, *hiring* him as bodyguard!—had been a grave mistake.

But then King Klann was speaking.

"Welcome, all of you—my people, my soldiers, free companions who have entered my service, ambassadors from the city of Vedun—welcome, to you all! And now rise." Klann swept his arms upward. "Rise and resume your merrymaking!"

A great cheer swept the hall, and flagons were raised in toast to the king's munificence.

Klann and his retinue marched through the aisles toward the head table on the dais, the king jesting with soldiers and civilians on either hand. It was clear that here was a ruler who cared little for pomp and protocol.

Flavio watched him closely, assessing the province's new Lord Protector as he knew Milorad would be doing. Klann little resembled his swarthy Akryllonian nationals. And, the Elder realized with a disappointment that mildly surprised him, Klann hardly lived up to the aura of mysticism in which he had been enshrouded. He was a big, bluff red-bearded man, rather rotund and quick to laugh, with narrow, close-set eyes that darted and twinkled in a manner which suggested caution or cynicism, a broad melon grin, and high cheekbones which were perhaps his most regal feature. He spoke several languages and drank from the cups of commoners as he swept past.

He avoided looking at the party from Vedun until he had been seated at the opulent table facing them. He sat in the ornate, high-backed chair that had so recently been reserved for Baron Rorka, and his mixed entourage of courtesans, advisers, and military officers joined him. Flavio recognized only Captain Sianno, commander of Vedun's Llorm garrison, and Captain Kel'Tekeli, head of the free companies. The chair at Klann's right was empty, doubtless reserved for his queen or a favorite courtesan. Mord had reappeared and was now seated a few places to the left of Klann, eyeing the delegates somberly. There was neither cup nor place setting before him.

Flavio looked to Gonji, but the samurai sat in dignified silence, expectantly regarding the king. Praised be for that. Milorad sat calmly, shot Flavio a wink of encouragement when their eyes met. Good old Mil. Garth seemed troubled, preoccupied. As well he might be under the shadow of his curious invitation.

Genya directed a stream of servants in attending the royal table under the gaze of an evil-faced chief steward.

Then Klann was nodding and smiling to Flavio, and the Elder prayed for guidance. *Lord God, send me Your Spirit so that I may know the right words . . .*

"Let the feast be served!" Klann called to the chief steward, and immediately there flowed from the sweltering kitchens a procession of foodstuffs held on high in huge serving platters and wheeled into the hall on silver carts. A roar of approval and applause broke from the roistering crowd.

Deer were broken; geese were rered; trout, culponed—all meats and fish and fowl were goodly carved. Beverages sloshed under the botiler's charge. The orgiastic feasting began, strolling minstrels and the gallery musicians serving up festive music for the aid of digestion.

"And now," Klann said in very cultured Italian, indicating the Elder, "you, my friend, can only be the Flavio we've heard of, Council Elder in Vedun. By all accounts a wise and reasonable man—no-no, *sit!* Eat as we speak. Let formality be damned this night. Drink! Eat! Introduce your companions to us."

Klann took a deep draught from his goblet. Flavio drew a breath to relax and sat back down on the bench.

"I am Flavio, sire, even as you say, but I fear your intelligence with respect to me flatters me too much." He bowed deeply. "Here is my close friend and adviser, Milorad Vargo. And our city's chief smith, Garth Gundersen, here with us by your royal edict. And—" He stuttered just a bit when he came to Gonji, whose face betrayed nothing of what he was thinking. "—Gonji Sabataké, a soldier from the Far East, my

". . . bodyguard." The word hitched in his throat, and he dearly wished he could have recalled it. This bodyguard business was absurd.

"Indeed!" Klann replied. "Do you think you'll have need of a bodyguard this night?"

Gonji seemed about to say something, and Flavio waved his hand at his side. He forced out a casual chuckle, and Milorad joined in.

"Hardly, milord king."

"Good. Now let us tell you what you've come to hear and clear the air between us."

And with that Klann launched into his story with a directness and sincerity Flavio had to admire. He ate as he spoke, pausing now and again to lave his hands with the budget and ewer held for his private use by two servants. He tossed scraps to the turnspit dogs that roamed the hall. Flavio listened to him carefully, and it seemed that every so often the conquering king would drift off, become detached, as if searching for words etched in the hall's opposite wall or straining to hear a distant voice. He was addicted to the use of the royal "we," almost to the point of distraction.

"*Signor* Flavio, we Akryllonian nationals are the remnant of a once proud island people, a people gifted in art and artifice and, I think, attuned to powers your mainland folk would find unfathomable. My esteemed parents were rulers of Akryllon. My father was a just and compassionate monarch, but in the end, despite his fairness, he found that the stewards of those powers—a league of wizards and mages—had turned upon him. They wrested the throne and scepter of Akryllon and put our parents to flight. They died in exile, bitter and despondent, and on our heads and the heads of our loyal followers they placed the charge that we should devote ourselves to regaining what is rightfully ours. So our first requisite of you is that you extend us your understanding that we do what we must, and not always as we would have it. But we are driven by an inviolable command to fulfill a destiny and restore a kingdom. For we are the royal bloodline of Akryllon. And we are Klann. *I* . . . am Klann . . . and we are five . . ."

Klann's voice had dwindled to a grating whisper, and his eyes had glazed over with these last words. He seemed to be fighting for control. Flavio felt a wave of disquietude course through him as he listened. Was Klann mad, or—?

"But forgive us," Klann went on, smiling affably, once again rational. "These are things which are no concern of yours. What we would like you to do is look about you—not at the soldiers but at the women and children . . . at the very few aged folk of Akryllon. Can you see in their faces and fragile bodies how they've suffered these many years of nomadic wanderings? If I were to tell you how those years are numbered, I daresay you should call me a lunatic. But we wish you to understand, so we'll say nothing of it. What we will say is that the nations of the world have met us with ill, for the most part. Like wolves pursuing the scent of death, they've hounded us. Met us in our time of need with sword and bow and cannon shot . . .

"And so we've fought back in order to survive. What we've been denied in the name of mercy, we've taken by warfare and sorcery. We came to your Baron Rorka seeking sanctuary, shelter from the coming winter so that we might grow in strength and numbers and, come the spring, once again launch an assault on the usurpers of our father's throne. But the baron denied us what we required. Our situation was desperate, and what happened . . . happened. We were forced to take what we needed for our survival.

"But now we are here, and things are as they are.

Nothing need concern the citizens of Vedun but the continuance of the reciprocal relationship that existed between the city and the baron. Rest assured that your interests will be well protected and that it is of utmost importance to us that our relationship be peaceable. Have I made myself sufficiently clear?"

Flavio collected his scattered thoughts, cleared his throat, and wiped his bearded chin with a linen cloth. A servant boy rushed up with a leather budget of water, but the Elder waved him off.

"Sire . . ." he began slowly, "we appreciate your frankness and candor, and now I hope you'll forgive my impertinence if I, too, speak frankly." He spoke gently, knowing the fragile ground on which he trod. "Was this violent coup truly necessary? So much bloodshed on both sides. We have much room in Vedun, and our grain bins are full to over—"

"Yes, there has been much bloodshed," came the booming voice of Mord, "and it continues. Soldiers on patrol are slaughtered coldbloodedly. King Klann's own *field commander* has been beaten to death in the streets. And insurrectionists have even dared to attack my wyvern, as if their puny shafts could bring down such a thing of power—all by rebel action! Who sanctions these actions, Elder?"

Mord was on his feet, shouting. The closest tables had fallen silent now, watching between sips and bites.

Milorad spoke up before Flavio. "With all due respect, the honored counselor ignores certain facts: First, let it be made clear here that Vedun's council sanctions *no* rebellious activity, certainly not murder. We are a Christian community, and murder is stringently proscribed by the tenets of our faith. Commander Ben-Draba was killed by a stranger. No one in the city ever saw him before—"

"Lies," Mord said flatly.

"—and may I add," Flavio piped in, "that the boxing contests at the square were held at the insistence of the commander himself. The people were threatened for failure to participate."

"And the council had no part in the attack on the wyvern—" Milorad continued, but Mord cut him off.

"Lies—all lies!"

"—why the very sight of the flying monster is enough to send gentlefolk—"

"You lie!" Mord fumed. "It is your intention to resist the king's will and to provoke combat that will see an end to his ordained purpose."

"Enough!"

Klann had been listening impatiently, drumming his fingers on the tabletop. Now he raised a huge red hand, and an uneasy quiet gripped the hall.

"Suffice it to say that enough violence has been done on both sides and that we'll have an end of it, here and now. I have lost a great field commander, true, and he will be missed. But it was not altogether unexpected. Ben-Draba's impetuous nature and bull-headedness were bound to bring him to such an end sooner or later. And as for the wyvern—" Klann chortled. "—I must confess that I, too, might have shot at such a thing flying over my home for the first time!"

A spate of laughter ran through the audience, and Mord's eyes flared hotly. Flavio sensed a certain tension between the king and his court sorcerer, recalling that Baron Rorka had mentioned something of this.

"But let that be the end of it," Klann said as the laughter abated. "I trust that the bold adventurers involved witnessed the wyvern's rather ghastly offensive—and I mean no pun there!—its monstrous offensive capabilities. We'll have no more rebellious incidents."

"I'm quite sure you're right, sire," Flavio agreed.

"But now I've been charged by the city to pursue certain grievances. I beg your indulgence. First, there is the matter of the threats against our worship of the Lord God. Specifically, the cross at the city square has been struck down—"

"I gave no such order. I care nothing for your mode of worship, but it gives me no offense. Sianno—what of this accusation?"

The captain lifted his palms in a gesture of confusion and eyed the other officers at the table.

Then Mord spoke. "Milord, you signed the order. It was merely a routine threat against resistance, part of the standard security procedure in occupied territory."

Klann nodded curtly. "Yes-yes, so I did. Well, their Christian worship offers us no threat—unless it extends to raising another papist army such as the one which gave us such trouble in Austria! You may continue your worship unimpeded."

Flavio and Milorad exchanged a look of relief and triumph. Mord glowered down at them silently.

Then, emboldened by this early victory, the Council Elder tactfully pursued other subjects of concern to the citizens of Vedun: recompense for the families of soldiers and citizens slain by Klann's forces; aggression by the mercenaries; freedom for servants held at the castle against their will . . .

Klann feigned patient indulgence of the bearded Elder as he prattled on. The king knew only too well the necessity for at least hearing the man out. A peaceful respite and recuperation in this province was dreadfully important right now. These people had to be placated. They could be most troublesome if they decided to bare their fangs while the army still licked its wounds.

(don't think such weak thoughts)
(take a firm hand with them you're a king)

But it was exasperating, listening to the council Elder's petty concerns . . .

Recompense and conscripted servants, bullying in the streets—what do we care for these things?! We are king and as such are above the concerns of these small folk! *(be just and merciful wisdom walks hand-in-hand with mercy)* And what of those people Mord has taken for his foul purposes? What shall we tell them of those? Surely they'll demand an answer soon enough. But what is that to us? What can they do about it? We are king; we have our own people to worry after. The problems of these provincials are as nothing to us. *(correct be firm stall them tell them what they want to hear) (no be just and compassionate)*

Be still, my brethren, be still . . .

And then Klann saw the audacious one.

He lurched to his feet and pointed past the Vedunian delegates to a table adjacent to theirs.

"You, there! You in the dirty frock coat! How *dare* you? Guards, seize that man!"

The hall fell silent as a garroted throat.

As the pair of Llorm sentries rushed over, the singled-out mercenary wove to his feet, bleary-eyed from his wine, and held his hands out, palms up, in mute appeal.

"Sire?" he slurred.

"Were you not told that guns were forbidden within these halls?" Klann boomed.

The soldier reached down and slapped the offending pistol at his side, a half-grin twisting his mouth. His eyes came wetly alight with remembrance and guilt.

"I—I forgot, milord king, that's all," he stuttered in Spanish. "But it's not loaded or spannered and—and—"

"Remove him!" Klann ordered. "And if we ever see

you within the middle bailey of this castle again, your head will decorate the towers!"

Then Klann settled himself, self-consciously rubbing his thighs as he sat back, and the buzz of voices and lilting strains of music gradually returned to normal.

Eeyaaiii, but he's a moody one, *neh?* Gonji thought, relief flooding him once the incident had ended. *And that's very bad in a king. Hai, very so.*

For an instant, when Klann had risen and pointed along Gonji's table, the samurai had thought he was the one being singled out.

But what did this obsession about firearms mean? Especially from a king whose army depended on them so. And was he truly a king at all? Gonji's initial suspicion that Klann would turn out to be nothing more than a bandit warlord seemed to be vindicated by Klann's appearance and mien. He had little to commend him as royalty.

Gonji listened as Klann sidestepped Flavio's appeals for redress and release of the conscripted servants. Flavio and Milorad clearly were less than enthusiastic about Klann's declaration that he would take these matters under advisement. All the while Garth idly picked at his food as if it were the last meal of a condemned man.

The samurai himself sampled a portion of most everything that passed his way. The pheasant was especially succulent, and the trout was a rare and marvelous treat. He drank a light white wine, sipping judiciously so as not to wander far from total control of his faculties. For although he had laid his swords at his right side in a gesture of peace and respect, these were still to be considered hostile surroundings.

Klann had steered the conversation away from military and political matters to topics of a more light-hearted, jovial nature, sometimes seeming about to reveal some inner source of mirth. Gonji's curiosity was just turning to the empty place of honor beside the king when a table of mercenaries nearby was cleared, a new troop clumping in shortly thereafter to take their places with many a braying greeting to comrades already present.

A pang of alarm: Would Klann's magnanimity reach out to encompass his entire mercenary force? Would the 3rd Free Company, whom Gonji had quit after the violent incident with the Mongols, be relieved so that they might feast this night as well?

His gaze wandered to his swords, leaning at his side against the bench, then back to the new band of adventurers who were already regarding with puzzlement his topknot and oriental features. There within easy reach was his *katana*, the Sagami, whose noble steel had tasted the blood of many strong opponents. Skewed against it was his *ko-dachi*, the short sword which, if honor demanded, would be used for *seppuku*, for ritual suicide, before he would ever submit to surrender.

If the hours of this night were to be his last, then that was karma. So be it. He dismissed the matter. But not before first offering a short prayer to the *kami* of fortune that he might have an end of his quest before dying.

Then he was suddenly attentive on the king, for Klann had addressed him personally.

"And you, bodyguard," Klann was saying in Italian, "your name is Gonji—?"

"Sabataké Gonji-noh-Sadowara, sire," Gonji clarified, standing proudly and offering Klann a deep bow. "Gonji is my given name."

"I've heard something of your Far Eastern fighting prowess. Were you not one who came forward to fight my ill-fated field commander?"

Gonji was aware of Julian's scornful glare as the captain leaned forward on an elbow at the high table.

"*Hai*, milord—yes," Gonji answered, smiling thinly. "But, so sorry, I was denied the honor of fighting the great boxer. Instead I was placed in a contest with his subordinate, a man of somewhat lesser skills."

He couldn't resist the jibe, and he knew from the oohing and laughter that it had carried to the table of Luba. He could practically feel the heat waves emanating from Luba's table.

Klann chuckled. "They say you use your feet as smoothly as a man might use his fists. I'd like to see that sometime. But what I'd really like to know is, who was your friend?" Klann's eyes narrowed under coyly arched brows.

Gonji swallowed, cocking his head uncertainly. "Sire?"

"The one who so easily killed Ben-Draba."

Nearby conversation dwindled amid shushing whispers. Gonji chose his words carefully.

"So sorry, milord king, but . . . you ascribe to me influence that this simple warrior neither possesses nor deserves." He smiled and bowed again, not so low this time.

"I see," Klann said patronizingly. "Well, then we'll leave it at this: This 'pouncing killer,' or whatever the troops are calling him, had best not turn up in the province again. Unless, that is, he'd like to claim the price on his head for himself. We might make room in our mercenary command for such an astonishingly gifted fighter, eh?"

Klann looked up and down the table at his officers, who grunted or clucked hoarsely.

"I might make room for him at the end of my saber," Julian advanced haughtily. A few nervous laughs came from the table, but they were bled of all their conviction by the still poignant memory of the big commander's helplessness at the ferocious attack by the stranger, the subsequent whirlwind escape, climaxed by the unique warrior's amazing leap over a fifteen-foot wall and disappearance into the forest—with a war arrow embedded in his flesh.

"He's probably dead already of his wounds," one of Klann's captains said from behind clenched hands that supported his chin on bracing elbows. There were mutters of hopeful agreement.

"I'm not so sure."

From his end of the table came the eerie bass voice of Mord. The sorcerer stood and pointed to Gonji with a gloved hand.

"Tell me what you know of the Deathwind, barbarian, he who is called Grejkill." A wave of hushing swept the entire side of the hall.

Gonji was annoyed by the wizard's insult but too intrigued by the abrupt broaching of the object of his own quest to pay it any heed. It was in fact the first time he could recall anyone had mentioned the mystery names to *him*. His heart began to pound.

"It is . . . the name of the thing I have come to seek in the West. I have been told many things about these names. Some conflicting things. There are those who say the names refer to nothing more than a European legend. But others would tell you that they speak of a beast . . . a thing that is not quite a man—or perhaps it's the other way around. My quest after it has led me here, to this province. In these mountains the loremongers name the Deathwind as their God's avenging spirit, some protective horror that will lay low their oppressors . . ."

At this last disclosure there were gasps and whispers all around, for there could be little doubt that Gonji had been referring to the occupying force of Klann.

". . . of course that's all probably peasant talk, the idle chatter of the uneducated. Who can say?" he concluded, smiling slyly.

"I think perhaps you know more than fireside prattle," Mord accused, and Gonji's arms stiffened at his sides. He was suddenly sorry that he had removed his swords.

"What do you know of *this?*" From a concealed pocket Mord produced a large formed metal object. A huge key. The key produced an immediate effect on Gonji's companions; their flaring nerve ends could almost be seen. But Gonji himself could not remember ever having seen it, though it piqued a recent memory.

"Nothing. I've never seen it before." He tinged his voice with gentle menace, weary of the sorcerer's brusque tone.

"I think you're lying."

"Mord, that's enough," said Klann, his tone almost one of boredom.

"I think you're all lying," Mord persisted, "concealing intelligence of interest to the king."

Gonji's mordant tongue, one of the legacies of his Nordic mother, had lost its taste for diplomacy.

"Very sorry, *maho-tsukai-san*—Sir Magician—but I believe your great powers are being wasted on this effort at intimidation. Why don't you try them at divining instead—"

"Gonji!" Flavio warned curtly.

"—I would think it to be a simple matter for one who can call up giants and foul carrion birds."

Mord raised his arms forebodingly.

Chairs and benches scraped at all the surrounding tables, a few screams heard as people scrambled to clear the area. Gonji grabbed up the Sagami, its blade whining from the scabbard as he leaped clear of the table.

"Gonji—no!" the delegates were crying out.

"Mord—stop this!" came Klann's bellow.

The sorcerer worked at forming a shape in the air before him, something long and slithery and fashioned of blue smoke that wriggled and twined its way through the air between him and the samurai.

Gonji stood still as marble with the *katana* in a two-handed clench at middle guard, the hilt before his navel, the point fixed on Mord.

"Disperse it, Mord!"

The shape descended in a sinuous wave. Gonji took a single step back and raised his blade high over his head for a strike. He felt hands at his shoulders, ignored them.

"Send it away!"

Mord brushed one hand across his body in a wave of dispersal, and the shape turned to sparkling blue scintillas that shone an exquisite instant and then fell to the floor as dust.

"Forgive me, sire," Mord said, head hanging low, sullen eyes gleaming out of the golden mask's sockets, "but this barbarian—who knows nothing of what he speaks—kindled my anger. But there was never anything to fear. Merely a warning against disrespectful tongues. I'll take my leave, if it pleases you."

"Yes-yes, go," Klann said.

He moved off but stopped at the end of the table and leered back in Gonji's direction.

"The shape you saw was but an illusion. The creature it suggests, however, is quite real in substance. I should be pleased to introduce you to it one day."

Gonji stood with the Sagami in one hand along his side. He arched an eyebrow. "I'll look forward to it."

And Mord was gone with a rustle of robes.

Gonji took a deep breath, restoring his harmony. He experienced a sudden chill at the cold runlets of sweat that trickled under his tunic. His bristling nape hairs gave him an urge to scratch vigorously. But he forced a placid expression as he smartly returned the Sagami to its scabbard and placed both his swords back in his sash.

Already the hall rumbled with low voices retelling the way the incident had been perceived. By morning it would exist in a hundred versions, each more fantastic than the last.

"All right, everyone—eat, drink; make music, you musicians. We command it!" roared Klann's voice. "This is a time for gaiety. No, not that funeral dirge!" he called to the gallery. "Give us a happy refrain!"

Gonji looked over his shoulder at Garth and nodded. It was the smith who had grasped him by the shoulders in an effort at restraint.

The delegates were sorting themselves out, restoring their dignity after the unsavory incident, when they received a shock that overwhelmed all others on this monumental day.

"And what of *you* all these years, mighty man-of-valor?" Klann was booming. "I see that it will have to be we who shatter your stony silence!"

Klann was addressing Garth.

Chapter Five

Gonji looked to Flavio and Milorad for an explanation, but there seemed to be not a glimmer of understanding between them. Flavio gaped and extended an upturned palm in perplexity as he watched Garth lumber to the king's table.

"Well, Garth," Klann intoned, eyes alight with emotion, "*Gundersen,* is it now? Gundersen indeed! Do you think that beard and a layer of fat can disguise you from us, Garth? Did you really believe we might have forgotten you and all your valiant deeds? Still a battler, I see, if your eye be any indication! We had heard rumors that you might be residing in these territories, and now our good cheer is complete. And yes—things *have* changed, haven't they, *gen-kori?*

"All of you—hear me! Raise your cups in toast to this man you see before me. This is the former General Garth Iorgens, our onetime field commander, a great and noble warrior, if ever there was one, who twice—*twice*—saved us from death at the risk of his own life. All hail!"

A cheer went up from the crowd, and cups were tipped and sloshed in Garth's honor.

Gonji regarded Flavio and Milorad suspiciously.

"Do you swear, both of you," Gonji asked, "that you never knew anything of this?"

"I swear," Flavio replied, as Milorad nodded vigorously. "I have known Garth for twenty-five years. He used to speak of his former military career, but never once did he mention with whom he served. This is all quite incredible."

Gonji scratched his chin pensively as Garth was directed to Klann's side of the table by Llorm officers, one of whom saluted him and clenched his hand warmly in greeting. Klann embraced the smith and bade him sit in the empty chair on his right, and the two began to speak in the Kunan tongue of the Akryllonians. Garth's mood shifted almost at once. He grinned sheepishly as he spoke with Klann, red-faced to be the center of Klann's back-slapping attention and doubtless the object of the mutterings that swept the hall. He avoided meeting eyes with the party from

Vedun, knowing full well the time of accounting that would be his on the return ride from the castle.

Gonji watched the sincere display of nostalgic affection between the two men at the royal table, all thoughts of Mord displaced now. Nor did he miss the cautious looks that passed among some of the officers, especially General Gorkin and Captain Sianno. Something was troubling them.

"It's going to be an interesting ride home."

"Indeed, yes," Flavio agreed.

The festivities bloomed anew. Acrobats performed their gyrations down the central path, followed by a troupe of masked and costumed mummers, performing an ill-chosen somber pantomime that was jeered at by the drunken soldiers. Most of the Llorm families were gone now, and new bands of mercenaries had taken up places at empty tables. The thought again occurred that the 3rd Free Company might turn up in the hall. Gonji saw in memory the snarling captain, Navarez; his toady subordinate Esteban, he of the horse face and scarred eye; and Jocko—that gruff and grizzled old knave who had saved Gonji's hide.

He smiled, tossed off the rest of his wine, and sloshed it around in his mouth. Let them come. It would be one cracking good reunion, *neh?*

Food and drink continued to parade from kitchen and larders. Ribaldry and raucous humor ran rampant. Mercenaries sang and bellowed and belched and chased one another, some tumbling to the floor in impromptu wrestling matches, to be joined by frolicsome dogs.

Gonji, Flavio, and Milorad washed from a ewer and budget brought by a pair of servant children, and the samurai noted with distaste how many of the mercenaries simply wiped greasy hands on the coats of the prancing, barking dogs.

As their cups were being refilled by Genya, Julian Kel'Tekeli strode up to Gonji, adjusting the hasps of his cape and half-armor with foppish élan.

"You seem anxious to use those, bodyguard," Julian said, indicating Gonji's sashed swords. Flavio and Milorad tensed. "I've yet to see them at work. Would you care to join me in an entertainment? An exhibition for this . . . august audience?"

"What do you have in mind?" Gonji's head began clearing at once, the cobwebs of satiety dashed by suspicion.

"A demonstration," Julian replied, smiling insincerely, "for the amusement of the king and his company. King Klann is an avid enthusiast of fighting skills, and it's said that the fencing style of your world differs considerably from conventional saber, rapier, and broadsword fencing. We should all like to judge for ourselves."

Gonji pondered the challenge a moment, drumming his fingers on the oaken planks before him. Two wise *kami* and a screaming demon chased through Gonji's mind: First came the wise counsel that as long as he could avoid an overt display of his swordsmanship skill, he held the arrogant captain at a disadvantage; Julian was obviously consumed with a passion to know how well a man who espoused suicide before dishonor could fight. Then there was the stern voice of *bushido,* admonishing Gonji against showcasing skills that should be humbly held in check until they were needed in true combat. No such insulting request to show off would ever be made to a samurai at court in *Dai Nihon.*

But the demon of hatred was there, too, shouting down all good counsel. Part of him still roared for satisfaction, for a display of *ken-jutsu* technique that would inspire respect and fear in this haughty soldier who had become so large a figure in Gonji's current circumstances. Julian was at once an employer and an iconic object of loathing and vengefulness. Indeed, when the time was right, he must have it out with Julian—had not the captain humiliated him at the inn by breaking the ceremonial short sword given Gonji by his mother? The thought brought an angry fire to his breast. *Damn me for a compromising beggar . . .*

And then he heard Flavio clear his throat tellingly, and remembered his promise.

"So sorry, Captain, but I'm afraid I promised the Elder I'd refrain from contentious displays. It seems I've trodden on my promise already." He bowed to Julian.

Julian sidled over to Flavio, making small circling motions with the pommel of his sheathed saber and displaying his predatory white teeth. Tables were being cleared out of the center of the hall, to their right.

"Oh, come now, Master Flavio. No violence is intended here. Just a matching of pure skills. The king will be presiding. Surely there's nothing to fear. You *do* wish to please the king, to win his favor, don't you?"

Julian leaned close, attempting to intimidate Flavio. The wise old magistrate held his ground admirably and looked Julian in the eyes when he spoke.

"All right," he said with measured calm, "with your assurance that it will only be an exhibition . . ."

"Good! After the lummoxes have their go, then." He grinned toothily at Gonji under a cruelly curled lip.

The last of the mummers and a juggler were bullied out of the hall, and Klann halted the musicians' by now cloying strains. Few women and children were left in the great hall, but all the courtesans remained at the expansive royal table, leaning forward with swollen eyes to leer at the weapons exhibition or snuggling against their escorts.

Klann looked on expectantly, licking beard-smothered lips and clapping the big smith on the back with anticipation.

A target from the practice ground was hastily procured. Soldiers bunched into standing pockets, some seated on others' shoulders. They bellowed and cheered, sloshing their heady beverages as a brief archery contest ended in convincing victory for a squad of Llorm bowmen over their mercenary challengers.

The free companions evened the score in a clumsy staff battle; their giant champion—nearly the size of the dead Ben-Draba—knocked his Llorm counterpart senseless with a blow that sent his dented burgonet clattering halfway across the hall.

The throng heated to bloodlust, fueled by ale and wine. They weren't going to be easy to please.

The samurai scratched at the tension itch under his topknot, breathing deeply and evenly to establish calm at the center of his being, wondering at Julian's purpose in all this. Gonji would lose the advantage of surprise in tipping his fencing technique here. That was something Julian no doubt had thought through more clearly than Gonji himself had. He cursed to himself for having fallen into the trap so easily. Then he shrugged.

Show them what you wish them to see . . .

Flavio eased up close. "I know—it's too late for you to back out honorably now," the Elder said softly out of a corner of his mouth. "But I know that your deft handling of the situation will not disappoint me."

Gonji looked to him admiringly. Smiled graciously and bowed. It was not what he expected to hear, and Flavio's quiet faith at the last both fortified him and instilled respect and affection for the burdened leader of Vedun.

Ignoring a wildly popular wrestling match between two blubbery buffoons who would have given any worthy *sumo* dyspepsia, Gonji began to stretch languidly, to loosen up, wondering what he would be asked to do. The recently injured shoulder still hurt, but it would be all right, certainly no problem during an exhibition. Karma. What was more important was to be alert and cunning; the insufferable commander of free companions had maneuvered him into a tricky position.

Then Julian stepped into the center of the hall amid cheers and braying hoots. Courtesans expressed their admiration of the handsome captain as he ritually doffed his cape and breastplate, then his shirt, revealing a sleeveless tunic, sweat-stained at the armpits.

Four candelabra were placed in a square about eight feet on a side in the cleared space. Julian selected two gleaming sabers and strode to the center of the display. At his order, all but the centermost, tallest candles were removed by servants, and Julian gently stretched out with his slim blades to measure his distance from the remaining four lit tapers.

Raising one sword to direct the audience to silence, he bowed deeply to Klann.

"Milord, a demonstration of speed, blade sharpness, and the economy of movement which are the mainstays of the modern fencer." He bowed again and took a step backward.

A calculated pause. Then—

A sharp, blurring series of saber-passes, right-left, right-left—the four candle wicks were extinguished. . .

A rapid movement of the shimmering right-hand blade—almost all movement confined to the wrist—and like precision machine-work one candle pattered to the floor in sausage-sized chunks. Before the last had hit the floor, the candle to Julian's left was similarly diminished. And as approving cheers rose in pitch from the crowd, the captain performed a brisk quarter-turn and lashed out with both blades at the last two candles, the increased strain showing in broader arm movement as he reduced them to stuttering tallow droplets.

Applause and bellows of delight. Looks of disbelief and deferential chatter.

"Wonderful, Julian!" Klann called out from the royal table, where even Garth clapped his approval.

Genya stood at Gonji's right, lips pursed petulantly. "Show-off," she said. "I can't stand him. I hope you show him up *good!*"

Gonji chortled and tossed his head back, but there was no minimizing the man's brilliance of control.

Julian pointed and nodded at Gonji in invitation. Gonji bowed in return.

The samurai ambled forward with a proud, leopard-like motion. He had already warmed to the competitive atmosphere, feeding off the energy and attention of the crowd. Even the guffaws and insulting catcalls he heard were turned back at the callers in the form of a hard, menacing, self-assured gaze. He was feeling in harmony with the center of his power, and his swords were with him.

He removed his tunic to reveal a tight-muscled, wiry frame and hard, flat stomach, now glistening with a fine film of perspiration. Sarcastic snickers and predictable insults rang in the hall. He could hear the references to his body scars, especially those on the left shoulder—the long white reminder of his once-beloved Reiko's solemn duty and the unhealed dagger-gash, trophy of a Mongol late in King Klann's employ. Luba, the ugly, bald warrior Gonji had dispatched in the boxing match, was saying something to Gonji from across the hall, but it was indecipherable in the din.

As he regirded his *obi* tightly about his waist, he called for uncut melons from the kitchen. These he had skewered atop the candelabra. He crossed his swords in his *obi,* the hilts in opposition, and approached the king.

He bowed deeply to Klann, then to the howling soldiers. Returning to Klann, he said:

"A very effective demonstration, *hai*—if one's enemies are the thickness of tapers, sire—"

A roar of laughter. Julian's ears reddened.

"So sorry. No insult was intended to the captain. But now to repeat the demonstration, with objects of greater substance."

Gonji moved to the center of the square, swords still sashed. He stood motionless a second, stopping the breaths of the onlookers. Then his swords flashed from their scabbards with a sibilant rush from a cross-handed draw. He rapidly whirled the snaking blades with a deadly *whit-wat, whit-wat* sound. . .

Oohs and *aahs* from the women and children; a sporadic chorus of "hey-heys" from the fighting men.

Then with a piercing *kiyai* he lashed out at the melons—

A crossing X-blow with both blades, and the first melon fell in wedge-shaped quarters to splatter on the parquet floor. The return backward double-slash sliced cleanly through the melons at his left and right. The top half of the left slid and dropped off, but the right seemed not to have moved. Gonji leaped into the air in a flying turn that brought him facing the last melon. As his feet touched the floor, both arms arced horizontally across his chest, ripping through the melon, which sat unmoving in neat thirds.

He came to a double-guard position that made him appear as if carved from stone. He held both stance and breath, vaguely aware that he was dissatisfied with the performance but—

A chorus of cheers and applause rang out, and as he moved from the square to bow to Klann and the throng, he swelled with gratitude and pride to realize that his feat had been better received than had that of Julian.

He smiled thinly—and, he knew, insufferably—as he bowed to the captain.

Julian's jaw muscles pulsed with the effort at controlling his anger as he brought up an assistant from the crowd for Round 2. The assistant was a green-clad mercenary of average height with a broad, flat face, humorously oversize scoop-shelled ears, and a big cheshire grin that radiated over the audience in a nervous effort at dealing with the sudden attention. His hands rubbed at his sides apprehensively, and he kept chewing at a large wad of something, switching from one cheek to the other. He wore a warp-brimmed slouch hat; this Julian removed and placed under the soldier's arm.

The mercenary's grin faded and his eyes began to poach as he grasped the captain's intent, placing, as he was, a chunk of oka cheese on each of the man's shoulders and a third atop his head.

The crowd had been sputtering quizzically but now a great burst of uproarious laughter greeted the mercenary's trembling as the cheese quivered off his head and bounced away along the floor. Julian retrieved it and warned the soldier to hold still if he valued his skull. The chewing stopped, and the trembling subsided.

Julian raised a hand to call for silence. Then he snapped his fingers, and by some prearranged signal, a drummer in the gallery began a long, tattering melodramatic roll. Julian postured in the "invitation" *en garde* stance—left arm cocked at his hip, bared saber angled down at the floor before the again quaking mercenary.

Then he sprang, his actions punctuated by emphatic drumbeats.

He slashed right—left—the cheese fell in halved chunks from the man's shoulders—

A retreating step—a blistering lunge like a crossbow shot—the mercenary's mouth gaped—and Julian skewered the third cheese off the top of his head. He withdrew, held up the pierced cheese, then with a flick of his wrist and an audible *thwak!* he split the chunk on the man's skull without marking him.

The mercenary's legs turned to pottage, and he dropped to his knees, his face ashen, a moist *cluck* issuing from his throat as he swallowed the wad he had been chewing.

Howls of laughter and heavy clapping rocked the hall. Some were already pointing to Gonji and chattering speculatively about how the samurai would top this exhibition.

Julian smiled coldly, and Gonji bowed, affecting a look of boredom. Then Gonji bowed again to the king in a more dignified fashion, while the captain saluted his liege lord.

Julian sat with two fawning courtesans as Gonji strode to the forefront. Servants worked swiftly to clean up the melons, candle bits, and cheese.

"I, too, will require a volunteer to assist me," Gonji called out, hands resting casually on his resashed swords.

"How about Smyshlev?" someone yelled, and a chorus of laughter rang out, aimed at the ale-chugging mercenary who had been Julian's accomplice.

"*Nyet,*" the soldier cried, "I'm through performing for the night." More guffaws.

Gonji chuckled. "Someone else, then?" He had spoken first in Italian. He tried again in Spanish and German.

"I'll do it."

Yowls of currish delight and a spate of suggestive comments greeted Genya's bold offer.

Gonji winced and scratched his head, eyeing her sidelong as she stepped up confidently, hands on rounded hips.

"I trust your skill—you did say you were Wilf's friend—?" she added coyly.

Gonji had to admire her pluck. He turned around to see faces reflecting grave reservations about the girl's participation. Flavio's chin rested in one hand. When Gonji's eyes met his, the Elder's eyelids clamped shut with finality. Milorad was rubbing one temple and sipping mead like a half-drowned man gulping at air. Klann looked indecisive under beetling brows, as if about to call a halt to the proceedings rather than risk the safety of his favorite local servant. Even Garth leaned forward, palms gripping the table before him, in an anxious posture, although it was impossible to guess whether his hope was for Genya's health or Gonji's lack of skill.

Oh, well, if I don't go through with it, none of them will be able to sleep, wondering . . .

"Tell me something," Gonji said softly in German, "why are you obsessed with helping show up this captain?"

"He's a *svina*—a pig!" she spat, curling her lip. "He pinched my behind the first day after the castle siege. Made some remarks—you know what I mean."

"You mean you don't find him irresistible," Gonji asked, unable to resist baiting her, "like most of the women who stare when he passes?"

"If I weren't such a lady I'd spit at the suggestion!"

And then the object of their discussion was standing with them.

"Don't you think it's rather ungallant to use a lady as an object in so vulgar a demonstration?" Julian said patronizingly.

Genya spoke up first. "*I'll* be the judge of what's gallant on my behalf." Her small white-knuckled fists were clenched at her sides.

Julian shrugged. "Perhaps I was wrong about the . . . lady." He turned on his heel and marched back to his table.

"*Svina!*" Genya whispered at his back. "*Jesu, Maria*—forgive me!"

"Let's get on with it, then," Gonji said. "Lie down on your back there, and try to ignore these 'gentlemen's' interest."

She nodded and hopped onto the table at his direction, lying back to many a hoot and howl. Gonji commanded a servant to bring over the largest of the melons, this one with a girth larger than Genya's slim waist. He wiped himself down with a scullion's rag, taking special care to dry off his sweating palms.

The melon was placed on Genya's belly, and the throng went wild, drunken soldiers pressing close and jockeying for a better view.

Gonji moved up to the table, leaned near the girl.

"You know," he said with a cocked eyebrow, "this works best with the melon on one's chest."

"Well obviously that's a bad idea . . . here." She stared straight overhead.

"Obviously."

He scratched his neck, dimly aware that he was reluctant to attempt this trick he hadn't tried in longer than he could recall.

"I'm going to have to allow for the curvature of your belly. Why don't you eat more next time?"

"You've got a good thumb's width of corset to play with." She rolled her eyes toward him and fluttered her lashes demurely.

This, Gonji decided, was one hell of a strong-willed woman whose like he had seldom seen in Europe. The thought crossed his mind that should Wilf ever be reunited with her his problems would only just be dawning.

He smiled and turned his back to her, facing the crowd, whose cheering rose to fever pitch. Respectful silence would have been nice, but . . .

Concentrate. Wash them from your mind. Feel the Sagami's familiar hilt. Know the touch that would be required, even as you know the reach of your fingertips in the dark—

He drew the *katana* straight from the sheath high over his head in a mighty two-handed clench. The audience gasped and fell soundless as he shrieked a tremendous *kiyai* and whirled—

Every watcher would have sworn the girl was severed in two by the force of the vicious, whining blow that sheared the air, cleft through the melon, and . . . stopped. As if by an instantaneous mandate of the gods.

Gonji breathed, held his position. Short. He hadn't cloven deep enough. Genya's eyes bulged. She exhaled a choppy, tremulous breath and arched her back.

The melon fell from her belly in perfect halves.

The revelers screamed their approval, cheering madly, sloshing ale and wine over heads and tables and the greasy floor. Gonji bowed to king and crowd and smilingly helped the shaken but composed Genya from the table, then went in search of the cleanest linen or silk he could find with which to cleanse his blade.

"All right, samurai," came Julian's piercing voice at

his back. "The time has come for the true test of fencing skills—a bout! My challenge—your weapons."

Gonji turned ever so slowly, eyes narrowing. *What's this bastard trying to prove?* The crowd noise diminished to expectant murmurs and hopeful jostling. There was nothing more they'd rather see.

"I must protest, sire!" Flavio said. "This is altogether uncalled for—"

"Wait a moment, Elder," the king commanded, eyes flashing with curiosity. "Let's hear him out."

"I propose a fencing bout of the best of three touches, these to be determined by blooding—*nicks* only, Master Flavio, not to fear. Serious wounding would result in the disqualification of the offender. It's a simple contest I'm sure the samurai has played many times before, *n'est-ce pas?*" Julian spoke in French now, the language of the country wherein he had learned the deadly little duelling game. Just one more decadent aspect of the French, for whom Gonji had no great love.

Gonji nodded sullenly. *Choléra. Now* what the hell? What was on Julian's mind? Was he simply trying to pad his reputation at Gonji's expense? He certainly had him in a fine position to do that. *No wonder I have such difficulty finding honorable duty in Europe*—*with employers like Julian . . .*

But he had to accept. And now they'd have some answers as to who was the better fencer. Neither had ever seen the other in a bout, only in exhibitions, but calculating from what he had seen of the swaggering captain's control tonight—and in the lip-slitting incident at the Provender—coupled with the ominous buzzing he heard around him now, Gonji had to assume that his being challenged was quite an honor.

Gonji's thoughts were a maelstrom. He would have to empty his mind, establish a free flow of being emanating from his *wa*. Thoughts were only a burden, and most dangerous among these was the passion for vengeance against this man who had done him grave insult.

Gonji removed his *ko-dachi* and the Sagami's scabbard. They faced each other squarely with naked blades and torsos, each man unflinching, and bowed. Repeated the gesture to the king and the audience. Then they stared at each other for a space.

"Single blade or double?" Julian asked at length.

"Single," Gonji replied without a pause. "Your wish is to test pure fencing styles. Double is best in combat."

"Single is my forte, and my blade is more slender, lighter, more maneuverable. I fear the advantage is mine."

"Advantage," Gonji said evenly, smoothly assuming a two-handed middle guard position with the gleaming Sagami, "is seldom a property of steel. *En garde.*"

Julian sneered and brought his blade into engagement with Gonji's. "A two-handed grip? *Really*, Sir Bodyguard," he drawled.

The captain initiated a series of simple attacks at moderate speed: a disengage, a straight thrust, a cutover. Each time Gonji defeated the attack with brisk flicks of his wrists, the movements scarcely seen, both blades *whanging* sharply, returning to engagement with disciplined economy.

Julian picked up speed. A lunge. A feint-a-disengage. A quick-stepping *pattinando* attack, saber point slicing for Gonji's bare chest. Gonji easily parried each blow, swords clashing and clashing again, the audience heating up, crying out words of encouragement.

Gonji backed up a step, then another, watching, waiting, calculating unconsciously, practiced reflexes responding. He sized up the ever-swifter attacks of the captain, noting tendencies.

Opening up his attack, Julian added complexity to his movements, slashing right—left—feinting a slash and cutting over with a quick straight thrust, redoubling his attacks again and again as Gonji remained content for the most part to fence passively, occasionally offering a token riposte.

Then, when Julian was lulled into false confidence by virtue of his carrying the attack, Gonji made a quick circle with the Sagami, enveloping the captain's blade, confusing him for an instant. The samurai's lightning lunge and sharp *kiyai* drew a gasp from the audience as his sword point whickered past Julian's left ear, bringing in response a wild parry that would have been ineffectual had Gonji aimed at the man's face. Gonji had made his impression. No one watching would have believed his two-handed clench would have allowed so swift and deep a lunge. Julian's eyes were an angry blue line as they returned to engagement. For the first time he had broken good form out of sheer desperation.

The battle was joined for fair.

Slashing, clashing, moving ever faster, the two combatants executed a marvelous series of strokes, parries, ripostes, counter-ripostes . . . Each man's eyes held the other's center with admirable form and courage, ignoring the dancing, all-but-invisible swordpoints. Every witness to the duel knew that something special was transpiring: the classic meeting of Eastern and Western technique, Gonji's exotic *iai-jutsu* style holding the popular favor over the tyrannical captain's, which was nonetheless the apotheosis of European fencing.

Julian backed Gonji near a tableful of shoving, shouting mercenaries, stamping feet vying with clanging steel and blustering voices. Gonji knew his danger even before he heard the outcry:

"Watch the table!"

Julian lunged deeply before the cry was through. Gonji stiffly slapped the thrust aside with the flat of his blade and executed a cunning undercut at Julian's chin from an awkward position. The captain blinked and parried, sword arm bound up close to his chest.

And then Gonji vaulted the table using one arm for a pivot, landing in the midst of a staggering, laughing bunch of brigands, who parted at once before the shimmering *katana*. They poured out from between the tables to give the fencers room.

They eyed each other over the tabletop, stepping balletically like stalking predators toward the end of the table, blades circling tightly.

When they reached the end, Julian attacked at once—low-high—low-high—broad, then tight. Then a demonically fast lunge, parried by Gonji, followed immediately by another to a higher line.

Gonji missed his parry, deceived, slipped his head to the right and saw the saber slide by wickedly.

His teeth ground together as he leaped back, fury broiling in his innards—the thrust had been meant to relieve him of an eye. Julian was playing tough.

What the hell is he doing?

They reengaged, Julian sensing the turn, Gonji's confusion. The samurai's mind reeled with tumultuous thoughts, the enemies of reaction. They clashed, clashed again faster than the eye could follow. Gonji felt the ache in his healing shoulder—

And then the red-hot pain in his wrist. The *phrase d'armes* was ended. Blood ran down Gonji's left arm, plinking to the floor.

"*Touché,*" he said sullenly, jaw tight with the effort at control. His lips had flared once with the pain, his face instantly returning to a composed set as Genya rushed up to bind his wrist with a dark scarf.

All right, so the phrase is done, forget it. Next phrase—choléra! This bastard is good . . .

Murmurs and shouts and scurrying bodies animated the hall, revelers hurrying to refill empty cups before the fencers could engage again.

They approached each other again. Julian saluted; Gonji bowed. Both were breathing heavily, recovering. Sweat ran freely along both their bodies, its pungent smell thick about them. It burned Gonji's wrapped wound, made his thick hair heavy and matted. Julian chest and neck were red with his exertion.

"Your defense is admirable, but your attack leaves something to be desired," Julian appraised, cocky now with his one-touch lead.

"So desu?" Gonji countered. "Very sorry, but attack must not be too impetuous before one knows the enemy."

Julian showed his fine white teeth and confidently angled his blade out for a low engagement. And in the moment before he rejoined his maddening opponent, Gonji realized how wrong all this was for him, what a fool he'd been to accept the challenge out of a bloated sense of pride, his loathing for Julian, and his rigid adherence to the *bushido* code which, given the circumstances, was at best ill-advised. Paille had been right, at least partially: Compromise of principle was inevitable in this land, and the sense of guilt attendant on it was unwarranted. This contest was absurd. It negated the chief function of the *katana,* which was a killing sword, designed for slashing. In Japan such practice bouts were fought with wooden *bokken.* To fight a duel of cuts with so brilliant a swordsman as Julian stretched the demands on Gonji's skillful control to unimaginable levels.

And what did you hope to do, dung-head? Disarm

him, as you have so many other fencers? Shatter his thin, flexible saber as you would a heavier blade? Never have I seen such adroitness as his . . .

And then Julian renewed his attack with a vengeance, sensing his psychological advantage, closing for the finish. The mercenaries howled with excitement, heady drinks mixing with the fury of the bout to arouse the berserker in all of them.

Gonji gritted his teeth and reached deep inside for fresh energy and a heightened spirit of aggressiveness. Their swords sang and flashed, blue and white scintillas sparking as the samurai turned back thrusts and cuts to every quadrant; pressing, pushing, lashing back, until it was Julian who began to give ground.

Taxed muscles forced out grunts and gasps as they dueled, eyes flaring with the passion to win.

Julian leapt back and dropped his point, inviting attack. Gonji feinted, drew a parry, beat Julian's saber to one side, feinted again, then beat the rushed parry across the captain's body, throwing him off balance. *Then* Gonji lunged, the second-intention attack just falling short of an exposed shoulder.

Julian's eyes bulged as he pulled back and lashed across his front with a tight parry that Gonji caught, binding his blade, circling it twice—

A fast *croise*, Gonji's *katana* squealing along the saber's forte, forcing the blade down hard toward the floor. A quick light step forward and an upward flick of Gonji's wrists—

Julian stumbled backward.

Another long, lunging step, an overhand turn of the wrists that sent the Sagami slashing left to right—

Gonji froze. The crowd shrieked and stamped, flinging their cups into the air, applauding wildly. A thin red line trickled across Julian's bare chest, just above the nipples.

Gonji spun briskly in the tumult, nerve ends prickling like porcupine quills as he stepped three paces away. Blood thrummed at his temples; adrenalin rushed through his veins. He turned again and faced Julian, bowing, dimly cognizant of the stinging pain in his left wrist and the aching of the shoulder on the same side. He wrestled back the grin that strove to twist his lips and bowed to the captain, sweat flinging to the floor as he did so.

"*Touché,*" Julian grated in a strangled tone, the word raking his tongue, spilling over his outthrust jaw. He was unaccustomed to its use.

The second *phrase d'armes* had tied them. Bout point to play. Julian mopped the blood oozing from the shallow wound.

They bowed and saluted to the king and audience, to each other. Gonji tested the left hand on the Sagami's hilt, squeezing. A numbness, but less pain now. He'd pay for the workout on the shoulder tomorrow. *Now, Gonji-san, let's see what you're made of . . .*

Both men lunged, blades sliding against each other up to the handguards, bringing them *corps-à-corps*, swordpoints angled at the vaulted ceiling, faces scant inches apart. With a grunt they pushed off, Gonji renewing his attack at once.

Now their roles were completely reversed, the samurai carrying the attack to his backing, deftly parrying opponent. Steel whined and shrieked with increased intensity, sword blades pushed to the limits of pliancy. Julian played a waiting game, probing, lunging now and again with deep, sizzling thrusts. Gonji abandoned caution, seeing at once Julian's new tack. It would be impossible to create an opening with a bind or beat again, for Julian slipped or deceived every such effort with a derobement or passive withdrawal.

The captain's reach was superior. Gonji would have to press to find an opening with sheer ferocity, wearing the captain down, fighting inside his blade when the time was right.

Then—Julian suddenly lashed out with a deceptive lunge that started low and changed direction incredibly in mid-thrust to whiz at Gonji's face. The samurai was caught in mid-step and lurched backward, parrying breathtakingly at the last instant. The crowd sucked in a collective breath—Julian had meant to skewer his head.

Again Gonji wondered at the man's intent and could only reason that Julian was committed to padding his reputation whatever the expense to Gonji. He growled and attacked with irate vigor, rotating his blade with now failing arm strength, the prolonged, constant motion taking its toll. Several forces were at war within him: fatigue and a sense of futility over this pointless touch-duel weakened his resolve, urged him to quit, this, in turn, suffused his soul with fury over his frustrated efforts and the desire to have vengeance against the captain; but through it all whispered the memory of his promise to Flavio that he would cause no trouble, no violence that might redound to Vedun's oppression . . .

Julian taunted him, first with arrogant twists of his swordpoint. Then verbally.

"Come on, samurai. Be done with it. Come after me. Come get it."

Gonji raised the Sagami high overhead along his right side, his right elbow cocked parallel with the floor, ready for a blazing strike. Slowly, gracefully, he stalked. Julian retreated with equal grace, waiting, mocking. A dance of death, their eyes smoldering with mutual hatred, the audience crowding in, bunched on one another's shoulders, eyes and mouths agape with expectation, no cups tipped for fear of missing the fulfillment of blood promise.

Like a scorpion with upraised sting, his whole body seemingly open to attack, Gonji closed. Then Julian lunged.

The saber lanced out, and Gonji's sword arced in a blurring flash that sang off the captain's steel and drove it far to his right, opening him to the death slash . . .

"Nooooo!"

Flavio's cry registered only faintly, and in that instant Gonji knew he might have riven Julian in two. Instead he brought his hilt close and shot out with a two-handed lunge that was not deep enough to catch the quick-stepping captain, too shallow even to force him into a tight parry. The saber's parry came fast and clean, and the slashing wrist-snap followed even faster.

Gonji swung his hips up and out in an evasive move, but the cleaving blade homed in. And Gonji winced at the searing pain at his ribs.

Gasps and screams, then—a general uproar. The bout was over. Julian had won.

Gonji stared in disbelief at the dribbling red line at his side. He eyes narrowed as he clutched at it with his left hand, the fingers coming away slickly wet with the blood that coursed down to his breeches' waistline.

Genya rushed up with a linen cloth to wipe the blood, but he brushed her aside gently and faced Julian. The captain saluted him with a cavalier gesture, his smile smug and carrying an air of finality, as if the business between them was settled. Gonji bowed, forcing an impassive blankness upon his facial muscles. Both men's chests heaved, their skin glistening with cooling sweat that ran into Gonji's wounds, stinging fiercely.

But not so fiercely as his pride. His mother's spirit

cried out for satisfaction, but its cry was muffled, for to do anything now would only add breach of etiquette to loss of face. And now his confidence had been shaken. He needed time to think, to get away from this noisy crowd, who tomorrow would be retelling the details of the duel in a hundred ways.

They bowed to king and crowd and returned to their tables.

"A wonderful duel, both of you!" King Klann called out, though Gonji scarcely heard him.

Flavio was offering his thanks to Gonji for his self-control, and Milorad and Genya, too, were speaking, but Gonji was watching the hated captain, sitting at his table, being ministered to by the courtesans, who were filling a cup for him and bandaging the dark crimson slash on his chest. The mercenary Luba sat near him, grinning Gonji's way.

The samurai sipped his wine glumly as his wounds were dressed, answered questions laconically.

"Now let us return to our revelry," Klann announced. "Eat, drink—musicians, let us have a merry tune! Bring meat and fruits and bread from the kitchens—there are still unsated appetites out there! The jugglers and the clowns—where is that happy troupe? Let us make merry. Tonight Transylvania salutes the god of wastrels!" Klann slammed his goblet on the table to punctuate his jest.

"The king was right, Gonji," Genya said before she hurried off to her duties. "You were wonderful."

Gonji smiled thinly. His wounds burned, and his shoulder ached with the promise of a miserable tomorrow. *Karma*. All karma. His thoughts reeled with kaleidoscopic visions of mocking faces, and pearly teeth, and the broken ceremonial sword. And it suddenly became clear to him why he had hired on as a spy for Julian. At the time his motives had been unclear. Of course he liked the idea of taking the captain's money, but he had believed that his act was partly motivated, too, by his anger at the city for failing to understand him, his code, his actions. But had he ever truly intended to sell out the city's secrets to these invading jackals? *Iyé*. No. Not at all. He had done it to place himself in a position to confound the bastard captain, and to keep himself near him, to keep Julian always at the fringe of his thinking in preparation for the day when they would have their crossing. Now they had done so, and the first tilt had gone to Julian. There would be another. Oh, very so.

Then he began to rationalize his defeat. He could count on one hand the practice duels he had lost in the past. None had ever come in Europe, in all his ten years of journeyings here. Some *kami* had engineered this, perhaps to humble him in his pride. His control had been poor, and the *katana* was not meant for game-playing. His recent illness had cost him more strength and stamina than he realized. The shoulder wound suffered in the fight with the Mongols had weakened his left side. And, he had to admit at last, Julian was without doubt the finest fencer he had ever encountered in all the western lands.

But he should have won. He should have come out the best. Tomorrow he would begin practicing anew. He would strive for perfection of his skill and conditioning. It was his solemn duty to himself, to his masterful warlord father, to his clan and the Land of the Gods. *Hai* . . .

Food platters, held on high, poured out of the kitchens. Fresh wine and ale casks spewed their contents.

Gonji accepted a refill of wine and sat back, sipping and sighing deeply. He nodded repeatedly with resolve. Drink now, for tomorrow begins a renewal of too-long neglected training.

Music wafted overhead, and the drunken revelry rose to fever pitch. Gonji tired of the decadent scene. He washed from a ewer and budget, dressed, and resashed his swords. He relieved his full bladder in a garderobe just off the hall. Returning, he asked Flavio to guide him on a tour of Castle Lenska. Flavio, similarly bored with the decadent festivities, eagerly seized upon the suggestion, Milorad reminding him that there were many conscripted servants they had yet to see.

They obtained Klann's permission, and guards were assigned to each of them. Klann and Garth also took the opportunity to depart with certain other officers to the king's private chambers, late those of the deposed Baron Rorka. Garth looked sheepish, smiled crookedly, now deep in his cups.

The two parties left the hall together in different directions, Gonji resolving to commit to memory the layout of the fabled fortress and its troop disposition. Before he exited the hall, he caught a stealthy movement up on the gallery. A door had been cracked ajar, a shadowed figure peering from the small aperture. But when he strove to look through the smoky haze and the glare of the firelight, the chamber door was abruptly closed.

For a moment he wondered who the skulker might be. And whom the object of surreptitious interest.

Outside the king's heavily guarded private chambers, Klann drew Julian aside, the others having preceded them into the receiving room.

"This Gonji, then—he's the one, eh?" Klann inquired.

"Yes, sire," Julian replied, half-scowling, "that's the barbarian who's selling out his master for gold."

"A shame," the king averred, shaking his head. "All this rotten treachery and intrigue. How we hate it. The days are gone, Julian, when wars were fought nobly. Now the fortunes turn on the squealing of eavesdropping curs and . . . worse. *Sorcerers*. And their filthy magicks and monsters."

"We're fighting no war here, milord," Julian said, anxious to curb the dark leaning of his liege's humor. He thought of the vacant Field Commander position, hungered after it. "But it's wise to maintain a sound intelligence outreach, to stay abreast of the city's thinking."

"I suppose." Klann sighed. "Such a brilliant swordsman, though. Why would he lower himself to . . . slinking about for profit?"

Julian's jealousy was aroused. "Oh, he's not really as good as he looks, milord. He's just a dancer or acrobat, an exhibitionist who's worked the swords into his act."

Klann raised his eyebrows and chortled. "Just an acrobat? It took you a while to dispose of him. We never saw a man stay that long with you in a bout before."

Julian felt his ears redden. "Yes, I'm afraid I overdid it. You see, I felt compelled to carry him for a time—for the benefit of the audience. They would have felt cheated if—"

"Hah!" Klann took him by his shoulders. "Oh, Julian, how like your gallant sire you are! Your father's vain streak finds its mother lode in you! *Carried* him indeed! Since when has a Kel'Tekeli ever disdained the quick, effective kill, eh? Come—there's drinking and reminiscing to be done—oh, and remember to hush us up should we broach any—forbidden subjects, eh?" Klann leaned a hand on Julian's shoulder as they walked toward the chamber door, which was flanked on either side by a Llorm pikeman. "And do they know their duty?"

"Of course, sire. No one enters these chambers while we're here."

"It's the glory days we wish to recount tonight, Julian. No offenses, no . . . guilt—nothing to upset this grand reunion. Do you understand my meaning?"

"Everything will be fine, sire. You'll see. Anyway, as I recall you and my father saying many a time, Iorgens won't be lucid very long once he gets to the serious toasting."

"Oh, what days those were! You must remember something of it from childhood memory, Julian—how you used to beg to sit with us deep into the night, how you were passed along from one officer's knee to the next . . ."

But although Julian nodded agreeably and smiled at his king's words, inside he was fuming. His thoughts were of the samurai. Even in defeat the barbarian had usurped something of the glory that should be his.

Far below the reveling and feasting and reminiscing in the castle's halls and chambers, beneath even the dungeon and subcellar bowels of the fortress, the traitor from Vedun sat in a rock-ribbed cell, facing the masked sorcerer across an ancient blood-crusted torture rack.

"Again," Mord's voice thundered hollowly, "and omit no details."

The traitor repeated the gathered intelligence: Rorka was still alive, he and his soldiers hidden away somewhere by the prophetess Tralayn; it was the barbarian oriental who had brought in the body of the key-bearer boy, Mark, and claimed to have killed several of Klann's men in the process; Gonji was further suggesting rebellion against the occupying army, but not so aggressively as certain militant citizens; the council's official stand was to slowly recruit and train a militia which might join with Rorka and any allies he could muster; and it had in fact been Gonji who had had the sheer audacity to fire upon the deadly wyvern. Still unknown, though, was the identity of the mysterious madman with the superhuman abilities who had slain Field Commander Ben-Draba and then escaped on foot from a whole company of Llorm dragoons and free companions.

"Mmmm. As you've said, Rorka may yet prove troublesome and will have to be dealt with," Mord thought aloud. "Any allies he could marshal against us would only increase the difficulty of my task—and I shall not fail again. Make no mistake, they're lying about the meaning of this key. They know something. *Someone* among them knows something—but *who?* Klann is too soft and sentimental now to pursue the matter with the methods that would pry out answers. But this key is *important*. It has been in contact with someone, some*thing* of terrible potential. Something which must be dealt with, *destroyed*. And yet . . . somehow . . . something with which I feel a strange kinship. I wish I had been there to see this wildman they're all in fear of.

"And this slant-eyed barbarian—how *dare* he attack my familiar as if it were a target in some contest for drunken archers!" Mord felt the spot in his abdomen where the wyvern had been pierced by Gonji's shaft. His obsidian eyes blazed behind the golden mask.

"Now that he's seen its power and portent, I doubt he'll try such foolishness again. And when I've done with him, I'll see his flesh roasted by inches. But in the meantime he shall serve my purpose quite well. Let him foment rebellion among these cross-worshippers. Let his vanity and impudence lead them to destruction."

Mord began to chuckle, a mirthless clucking sound oozing from the breathing holes of the mask like corruption from a festering wound.

"Do you know, I just realized that he cannot escape me—*ever*? I have the means of control over him within my grasp." He blared a deep gravelly laugh that echoed in the vaulted cell.

"But now—the one who awaits you is at hand . . ."

And Mord led the traitor from the cell through an iron-bound door, down a corridor hewn from rock to a similar dungeon chamber, this one appointed not by ancient torturers but rather for the comfort of their administrators.

Then, leaving them alone, the sorcerer hurried back up to the castle's ground level and into the great hall, where drunken mercenaries still sang and jested, half their number already passed out over tables and benches and sprawled on the slippery and discolored parquet floor. No one who remained was sober enough to pay the sorcerer's curious actions any heed.

He kicked a reclining hound out of the way and pushed aside a bench that lay upside down in the center of the hall.

Still there—darkening red spots from droplets of Gonji's blood, spilled during the duel. He carefully scraped all he could find into a small phial, using a sharp, wickedly curved knife. Nodding smugly, he moved toward the arched main doors. A mercenary leaned against one door, barring his way.

"I's the wizard, no?" the man slurred drunkenly. "How's it goin', wiz?"

Mord regarded him balefully. "Have you faith in the Dark One?"

"Sure, why not?" the drunk grated, leering.

"No. You lie. If you had faith in him, you'd also have respect for his servant."

Mord spoke a strange phrase, his gloved hand over his heart, then reached out with a booted toe to press on each of the mercenary's feet in turn. The wastrel's grin faded. He slumped to the floor, peering up at the sorcerer, uncertainty and fear showing in his swollen eyes.

"You can come to me on your knees tomorrow, down in the dungeons, and then we'll . . . talk about restoring what you've lost." And Mord was gone.

And the mercenary lay staring at the smoky ceiling, too drunk now to gag or scream or weep as he would in the morning when he pulled off his boots to see the wriggling things that had supplanted his toes.

Chapter Six

They rode back to Vedun in the pre-dawn gloom under lowering skies, the clink and squeak of saddles and harnesses mingling with the clatter of hooves on the cobblestone road. It was chilly and damp.

Behind them Gonji recognized the ominous "faith chant" of Mord, mistimed and discordant as it rose up from chambers and wards in the castle.

They rode to the edge of the paving and across, where the way began to descend to the plateau. There they waited for their escort to catch up, as they thought they were obliged to do. The mercenary troop slowed and waved them ahead.

They shrugged to one another and were about to move on when Gonji halted them, seeing something on the castle ramparts.

There stood Mord, a black and gold gargoyle,

staring after them. He raised his arms out to his sides, and high above him in the crenelled cradle of a drum tower, the motion was mirrored.

The ghastly wyvern unfurled its batwings and emerged from demon-sleep. Rotating its antlered head languidly, opening its jaws to uncoil a long forked tongue, it screeched once, a cracked morning greeting from hell to the world of the sane and normal. Then it lofted from its perch with a grace that belied its bulk, as if on invisible traces. With a slow, confident flapping it soared down toward the mounted party.

"Choléra-pox!" Gonji breathed through clenched teeth, reaching for the Sagami's hilt. He had no bow along, nothing that could serve as long-range armament.

Not now. Not like this . . .

"Jesu Christi!" Milorad whimpered.

"Stand your ground," Gonji commanded.

The wyvern hovered overhead, and Gonji met its piercing firelick gaze defiantly. It slowed impossibly, looking hollow as a dragon-kite, jackal's head angling down at them. And then Gonji saw: his arrow stub was gone from its belly. For an instant its eyes became Mord's, then it lashed its wings hard and skirred off with a rushing of wind that tore at the chapeaus of Flavio, Milorad, and Garth. Trailing its barbed tail, talons drawn back along its sides, it hurtled over the lowlands in search of morning forage.

Gonji expelled his breath and relaxed. What sort of game was Mord playing? If he was sure Gonji had attacked the beast, why didn't he finish him when he had the chance? Ah—the *king*, that was it. Now that he was Klann's spy . . .

The memory of the mutilated monks at Holy Word Monastery returned to him, and he wondered what this creature ate that turned into searing saliva and filthy corrupting excrement in its innards.

They rode on, the mercenary troop falling ever farther behind, cackling and chattering, still reeling from the night's orgiastic revelry. Soon they stopped following altogether, then doubled back to the castle like bouncers who had expelled *personae non grata*.

"Garth," Gonji called, cantering alongside the big smith, "why in hell didn't you say all you knew about Klann before? What *is* this business about you saving his life?"

"*Ja*, Garth," Milorad added in a voice jouncy from the horses' gait, "you were a *general* in this army once?"

"His Field Commander," Garth replied, raising his eyebrows for emphasis, a small silly grin splitting his face. His eyes were red and puffy. All four were rosy-eyed and irritable from sleeplessness, drinking, and the jading feast, but Garth's eyes seemed especially raw. He had the look of a man spent by maudlin tearfulness.

"Like Ben-Draba?" Gonji pressed, then seeing his nod, added, "But why hide it all this time?"

"What was to be gained? I just didn't think it important enough. And I have reasons for not wishing to call up old memories."

"Your wife's death?" Gonji probed.

Garth shot him a look but didn't inquire as to his source for the information. "*Ja*, for one thing," he answered thickly. "My beautiful wife . . . mother of my sons . . ." His voice now carried a rambling quality, thoughts drifting. "Cut down by the plague in her prime . . . burned . . . cremated with all the other victims . . ."

His lips and eyes began to quiver as if he would begin to cry. Gonji looked away, staring straight ahead along the road.

"And that's what cost you the will to fight, the desire to continue as a soldier?" Flavio asked.

"Ja," Garth said, breath hitching.

He reached down to his saddle for a skin filled with ale and gulped down half its contents. As if it had been a sanctioning signal, Milorad also retrieved a skin from a pouch, this one filled with mead. With a sly grin the snowy-bearded ex-statesman slogged at the thick, sweet liquor.

"Must have my fill before I reach home and Mama finds out how much I've had tonight," Milorad said with an uncharacteristic cackle that made Flavio smile.

Gonji could only grimace to watch the old man's zestful pleasure in the cloying beverage.

Weary and sore, surfeited of feasting and bewildered by the mosaic of castle events he was unable to make sense of, Gonji fell to brooding silence. Sleep. That was what he needed. Refreshing sleep. Then to discuss with the city leaders what they planned to do now that they'd met with the evasive king. Probe this blacksmith who never revealed all he knew of any subject. That's what he'd do later. Then practice. Work at his skills. *Julian.* Forget him. Don't be troubled by the foolish duel. More important things to consider now.

What will be my next move? What is it I want to know about—?

"Well, my friends," Flavio began, shattering Gonji's reverie, "tell me what you all think of our future now. Now that we've met with Klann—eh, those of us who . . . didn't already have his acquaintance." His sheepish smile was aimed at Garth.

"Oh, it's a most optimistic promise for the future," Milorad declared, reeling a bit in the saddle. "He's a very agreeable fellow. I think he's been honest with us."

"He has," Garth agreed curtly.

"Don't be too sure," Gonji cautioned. "So sorry, but too facile trust is a great enemy right now. He's done nothing definite about your request for redress of grievances."

"He will," Garth countered. "He was always . . . fair." There was, Gonji decided, a trace of irony in the smith's statement.

"I believe so, also," Flavio assured. "He has promised recompense, the support of the bereaved families, visiting privileges for those held against their will . . ."

"*Hai*, a lot of hollow promises. Typical political vaguery." Gonji frowned, determined to take the part of the devil's advocate, personally aggrieved as he was by Klann's minions. But deep inside he could find no compelling reason to distrust Klann himself other than the single thing that most bothered him about the legendary king:

"And recall, if you please, his unnerving habit of changing his mind capriciously. To me that's a dangerous sign. You saw how hostile Mord continues to be toward the city. He seems to enjoy much influence with Klann. That, too, bodes ill. Even if Klann is serious about leaving in the spring—and would *you*, if you were in his comfortable circumstances? But even if he does, what happens until then?"

"Until then," Flavio said with growing annoyance, "we shall operate as we always have under Baron Rorka's protection."

"*Hai*, and will you expect the same protection from Klann? What about the mercenary companies? Can you coexist with brigands peacefully for the better part of a year? It looked as though few, if any, are billeted at the castle—even their *king* doesn't trust them! Are you going to live beside them?"

"If necessary," Flavio said brusquely.

"So sorry, but that will be difficult, I think," Gonji persisted. "He'll be recruiting new ones to bolster his army. Your city's going to be overrun with rogues. Every misfit scum for a thousand kilometers in every direction will be heading for Vedun soon. You'll be crawling with them. Where will they all stay when the barracks and inns are filled?"

"We have plenty of room. There's vacant housing—"

"Ah—so then my master will give the city away to them! Certainly, give them everything. And when everything runs out—? What if Klann hires too many and his gold supply dwindles? Suppose they don't like what they're being paid—?"

Milorad choked on his mead. It trickled into his beard. "Hoo-hoo! That's a laugh! They sacked Bratislava, and now they've got the good Baron's treasure vaults, stuffed to overflowing with taxation from the plump years of Transylvanian commerce! Heeeee—!"

They all chuckled, even Garth, for seeing Milorad so out of character wrung much of the tension from them.

"My, aren't we the crew," Gonji said, rubbing his painful rib wound. "Four drunks planning the future of an occupied city!"

They shared a hearty laugh of good fellowship there on the road to Vedun in the dark hour before dawn, bridles jangling merrily in accompaniment.

"You're not drunk enough," Garth said affably, holding out the aleskin. "Here—drink."

Gonji accepted the skin with a bow and pulled at it.

"All right," the samurai began in a less argumentative tone, "then let us suppose Klann's army has both gold and room enough to keep them placid. There are . . . other things."

"Meaning what?" Flavio inquired.

"Mercenaries live at the end of a fragile tether. One that's easily broken. They're meant for the battlefield, not for occupation duty. Most of them are happiest when fighting. When they can't fight, they chafe. They look for fights. You've seen that already in Vedun. Believe me, I've been with enough mercenary armies to know what I speak of. And they're lustful. They're not pleasant when their gold can't satisfy all their lusts. How many pleasure women have you in Vedun?"

Milorad gasped. "Such talk!"

"We would hope there are none," Flavio said uncertainly.

"Come now—I've been to the inns."

"A few, perhaps."

"Quite a few now, I think," Gonji corrected. "And more will be coming to the city even as recruits are added. They're natural camp followers."

"We have an ordinance against them—"

"You have a new social order," Gonji reminded him firmly. "Think about it, please."

Flavio sighed sonorously, his troubles shadowing his face. "You paint a bleak picture, *signor* samurai."

"So sorry, but it is an accurate one, I believe." They guided their steeds around a curve. "The *giant*," Gonji recalled suddenly. "What will you say of him in Vedun?"

The recollection of the creature, his strangely unsettling mixture of the terrible and the pathetic, caused a sweeping discomfort.

"I think . . ." Flavio said slowly at last, "that it would be best to say nothing of him for now."

Gonji's lips twisted, and he shook his head ruefully over the Elder's continued efforts to table matters of military concern.

"That must be the beast that broke into the treasury at Bratislava, the one Jacob Neriah and—" Milorad caught himself before he saw Flavio's warning glance. He had been about to reveal the continued existence of the secreted Baron Rorka.

The conspiratorial silence that followed annoyed Gonji, made him feel once again the onerous lot of the outsider. *To be alone among companions* . . .

"While we're on the subject of threats to Vedun's security, friend Gonji," Flavio said with a hint of humor, "why did you allow yourself to become involved in that duel with Captain Kel'Tekeli? You might have killed him, and who knows what might have resulted?"

"Or, he might have killed me, and you'd be rid of my pessimistic counsel, *neh?*" Gonji replied cynically.

Flavio *tsked*. "Really, my friend, do you think that is my wish? Actually, I'm growing rather fond of your company. Your protective presence makes an old man feel important."

"*Domo arigato*, Elder-*san*, but you *are* important. These people do need your guidance. It's so obvious that they have great respect for you and faith in your administrative abilities."

"Not so much as you'd think anymore," Flavio replied wistfully.

Gonji smiled, deciding the time was right for the revelation. "But you needn't have worried about the duel. My promise to you was never far from my thinking. The duel was a personal matter between myself and the arrogant captain. I could not refuse his challenge. But there was nothing to fear. After all, he, too . . . is my boss . . ."

"Wha-a-a-t?"

They all looked to Gonji for an explanation.

"What are you saying?"

"I hired on with him as a spy to reveal all your

rebellious secrets. So *far* I've had little to tell for his money . . ."

"I don't under—"

"But *why?*"

Gonji pondered his rationale. "To confound him. To relieve him of some of his money—I can't tell you how good that feels! To play him for the fool. He's done me grave personal insult, and until our time of final crossing I wished to keep him in the forefront as an object of revulsion . . ."

"I don't like this one bit," Flavio said, frowning and shaking his head. "Are you using both sides for your own profit?"

"Of course not—"

"You may cause untold damage with such meddling," Milorad added.

"Very sorry, but I must point out the other side of the coin. Think of the potential for control over policy this could give you. I can impart to him whatever information you'd like that might be helpful to your cause. It has already helped. How do you suppose the banquet meeting was arranged? *I* suggested that Julian speak to Klann about it. He's a direct line of communication to Klann."

"But now we have established communication with the king," Gath observed.

"Have we?" Gonji questioned. "We'll see. And if we have, it was—so sorry—owing nothing to you, my friend. I believe you are not telling all you know of Klann and his intentions, and I cannot accept your simple reasoning for not telling your connection to him. Forgive me, and may all due honor attend your wife's spirit."

Garth stared, hollow-eyed, discomfited now to so abruptly have the conversation shift back to his former association with the Invincible.

"That's uncalled-for, Gonji," Flavio said. "I trust Garth implicitly, as do all in the city. His motives are above reproach."

Garth seemed to be struggling with something. "I think . . . perhaps the time has come for an accounting. Gonji is right. Tonight at my home I will read you all a document that will clarify many things about Klann. But come prepared to hear a most curious and frightening tale. Tonight, then."

Riding along with the nagging pain of his wounds and the settling ache the chill brought to his weary thews, Gonji nonetheless felt a surge of triumph. His persistence had broken through the smith's shell of secrecy. Now, perhaps, they'd have some definitive answers to the questions surrounding the wandering king.

But what was it that he had intended to ask Garth about the banquet? Some harping memory buried by the whirlwind events and disclosures of the night . . .

"Iorgens, is it?" Flavio said gaily to Garth. "Just when we begin to think the years have revealed all there is to know of someone!"

"Ja, it is my true surname. Gundersen was my mother's. All will be told tonight—all that I can say I truthfully know. After we sleep—and after I've had the chance to speak with my sons privately first."

"Of course," Flavio agreed readily.

Milorad belched. "To Iorgens!" he toasted, slugging at his mead. The others laughed and joined in, Gonji again sharing Garth's ale, enjoying the warmth that spread through his belly.

"Why dishonor your name by repudiating it?" Gonji asked.

"I wished nothing of my former life to intrude on my new one. That's the simple truth of it."

They clumped over a gently rolling hillock, the

mighty walls of Vedun coming into view in the south.

"Did you really believe Klann wouldn't remember you, Garth?" Milorad asked, still grinning crookedly.

"*Hai*," Gonji added. "After your obvious importance to him in the past? You saved his life *twice?*"

"His, but *not* his," Garth replied cryptically. "You see . . . that's not the Klann I served. I saw him today for the first time, even as all of you did."

His companions casting about in shocked confusion for an explanation, Garth chortled lightly. "Later," he said. "Tonight, I'll tell all, and you can choose to believe what you will when I'm done."

The road sloped down to the plateau's cultivated lowlands on the left. To the right were the gracefully curving foothills of the Carpathians, the verdant meadows on which flocks already grazed, among them the charges of Garth's son Strom. Above and behind, stretching forever into the western horizon, swept the brooding pine forests whose denizens shrugged off the mantle of sleep and began to cry and chirrup a new day's survival concerns. Straight ahead, low on the southern horizon, lay Vedun. Steaming vapors from the flatlands and the valley beyond the city hung thick and dreamlike around its enveloping walls, cutting it off from the precipice that anchored it. It appeared almost to float in the air on a cushion of ethereal mist. A fabulous city out of the realm of dreams.

Out of the swirling mist far down the road, herdsmen approached with their flocks and herds. Behind came rattling drays drawn by draft animals, farmers with their implements. Some were pointing in the direction of the delegates.

"Time to lay up the wineskins, I think, and affect some semblance of decorum, gentlemen," Flavio cautioned. "Mil, I'm going to need your support in a moment."

"Of course, old friend," Milorad assured. He hiccuped and rubbed his red face self-consciously.

Gonji smiled and leaned forward over Tora's withers to peer into the bunched men and animals coming down the road. Strom's reedy piping could be heard wafting down to them on the receptive morning air currents.

They made a sharp right turn along the road, and Gonji snapped a rein. *"Choléra,"* he swore, tossing the broken piece away. "Now I've got to pay a foster's bloated fee."

Garth chuckled. "We have a good one."

"Must you use that awful term?" Milorad asked wincingly.

"Choléra?" Gonji repeated. It was his favorite Slavic epithet, descriptive of a vile intestinal disease whose epidemic outbreaks produced revolting symptoms. It was, in fact, one of the few Slavic terms Gonji understood. "I like it."

"It's such a foul peasant word," Milorad clucked. "And in any case your accent bleeds off all its . . . vigorous vulgarity!" The adviser shrilled a laugh, feeling a tipsy satisfaction with the sound of his words.

"Ahhhh," Gonji growled at him.

Flavio suppressed a smile. "Gonji," the Elder asked, "tell me something—what's in all this manipulation of yours, besides the payment, that keeps you here?"

The samurai thought a moment, a certain warm exuberance filling him that caused him to speak with candor. "I rather like this city of yours, if you must know. I think I've made some friends here, a rare and special occurrence for a lonely half-breed. And these days one must work at keeping friends alive. I do anyway. But, so sorry, that's all silly sentimental talk that probably doesn't answer your question."

"Ah, but it does. Please go on."

"Nothing more to say. Whatever you believe about Klann's intentions, I say you're in deep trouble. I speak from experience. There are other things I—" He drew the line at revealing the savagery he had helped perpetrate in the province while riding with Klann's 3rd Free Company. He shrugged. "And I've told you of my Deathwind quest. I think its secret awaits me here. Maybe you people will help fill in missing information when you decide to—*dozo yurusu*—please forgive—when you loosen your tongues."

He looked sidelong to the Elder with an accusing eye. But Flavio's gaze held the road before him noncommittally.

"What was that key business about last night?" Gonji asked, remembering the object's curious familiarity to him.

"I don't know," Flavio lied. "Something Mord keeps pressing us about that no one can identify."

"It occurs to me that I've seen it around here before," Gonji advanced, seeing the Elder's shoulders stiffen. *Damned stubborn people.*

Sheep and cattle rumbled by all around them now, lowing noisily. The nearest farmers and herdsmen were nearly upon them, quickening their pace and calling out unheard greetings.

Garth looked up the hill to where Strom sat with his flock. "I think I'll go up there and have a word with my son, by your leave."

"Of course, Garth," Flavio said.

And then Gonji remembered.

"Garth!" he shouted at the former commander's departing back.

Garth turned. *"Ja?"*

"That business with the pistol last night . . . What is this obsession Klann has about no firearms in his presence?"

Garth glanced down at his roan's neck and smiled wanly.

"Well, you see," he replied tentatively, picking his words carefully, "you would be too—he was killed by a pistol once. Tonight, eh?" And he wheeled the roan and loped up the hill without bothering to appraise the amazed looks that followed him.

And then they were surrounded by excited townsfolk, led by the farmers Vlad Dobroczy and Peter Foristek. Several voices piped up at once, mostly inquiring after the welfare of loved ones at the castle.

"And how fares the city?" Flavio asked.

"Well, Master Flavio! There was no trouble last night!"

"Most of the soldiers were gone to the castle—"

"We should have knocked out the rest and taken their weapons!"

"Ja!—si!—nyet, that would be crazy!—"

"What is Klann like?"

"Did you see my daughter—please!"

"Si, she was there, she's fine, she sends her love and her assurance that—"

"How about my brother?"

"—Anina?"

"No, I'm afraid I—Mil, did you?"

*"Ja-ja—*in the kitchens, I'm sure of it . . ."

"Did you see the *giant?*"

Gonji understood little of it, for most of the speakers continued to use Slavic tongues which, in his most cynical moods, he was inclined to view as hostility, bigotry, and suspicion directed at him. But he was used to it, and he saw none of the cautious looks or bleak stares that were proffered in his direction. For now his eyes were following Garth.

And what an evening tonight promised to be. He slapped his thigh and gripped the Sagami's hilt, once again flooded by a tantalizing sense of destiny, a conviction of the rightness of his being here in this place, at this point in time.

(Julian)

A pox on Julian. Forget him.

"There will be full discussion and disclosure at a council meeting," Flavio was saying. "You'll all be notified." Spreading encouragement, smiling, he smoothly extricated himself from their pressing attentions.

They pushed ahead toward the city, a rather serious Garth joining them farther down the road. Gonji, feeling a sudden pang of sympathy for his master's administrative problems, loped up alongside Flavio, grinning.

They said nothing more of a coherent nature, all remaining energy spent fighting drowsiness and the spates of chortling and tittering they shared until they clopped up under the shadow of the great walls of Vedun. Before the gatehouse Flavio urged upon them a staid countenance and what decorum they could muster.

Old Gort the gatekeeper greeted them warmly in his cackling tone. His brown, hairless chest was already shirtless, though the sun was still but a glowing ember in the eastern Carpathian peaks, and his shriveled frame and the large growth on his neck lent him the appearance of a baby bird that had fallen from its nest. Not quite dead but with little hope left.

A few mercenary gatehouse guards stood nearby. Gonji appraised them lazily. There was at least one he had not seen before, a sallet-helmed wildman with furry boots who glared balefully at Gonji from astride a black Turk gelding. The mustached brigand was a small arsenal: He wore a broadsword at his waist, a smaller blade angling up from his back. A pistol and dirk hung from his belt; smaller throwing daggers jutted from his boot tops and either side of his helm, the latter pair projecting upward like horns. Lashed to his saddle was an angry looking arquebus; a formidable figure.

One may concentrate on but a single weapon at a time, came a sage voice of experience in Gonji's head.

Gonji ignored the bandit's gaze, long used to such surly assessment. Each new reputation-seeker would feel compelled to regard him like this, especially now, as tales of his battle skills spread.

They rode into the city to see the early risers—and perhaps some who had gone sleepless—clustered around the rostrum and under the infant cupid *amoretti* at the fountain. The square reeked of animal stench and food odors, echoed with the sounds of men and beasts. Upon seeing Flavio, people rushed over for word of the portentous meeting.

Flavio dealt with them briefly, displaying a tact and grace that Gonji found remarkable, given his weary state.

Gonji shivered in the dewy chill and pulled his kimono close at his throat as they rode toward the Via Fideli and Flavio's home. Garth bid them *guten tag* and took his leave of them, saying he'd send for them in the evening.

When they passed the chapel they heard a shouting commotion, and there appeared from around a corner three drunken free companions, scattering an angry farmer's pigs with a staff. They were prodding two rutting swine toward the chapel steps when they saw the delegation party. Milorad *tsked* and crossed himself, lip curling with disgust. Flavio eyed their amusement glumly but said nothing.

Gonji angled Tora toward them at a slow walk. His left hand clutched the pommel of the Sagami suggestively, and his raw, reddening eyes lanced down grimly.

The three mercenaries stopped laughing when they saw him coming. Whether by Julian's censure against provoking him or the threatening sight of the samurai himself, they looked from one to the other and mutely agreed to abandon their sport. Dropping the staff, they staggered off down the lane, their braying laughter resumed only after Gonji was out of sight.

Gonji shot a telling look at Flavio, but the Elder averted his eyes and prodded his mare onward, erect and dignified in the saddle.

Chapter Seven

"That's as much as he would say?" Phlegor fumed above the other dissident voices.

"I think he was quite conciliatory, given the power he holds over us," Flavio countered. The Elder removed his capuchin in the foyer of his manse, which now resembled a meeting hall. Dozens of people crowded in to hear the result of the long-awaited meeting with Klann. The steps and portico without had looked like the entrance to a rescue mission. Some had camped out there overnight, and with the coming of dawn they were joined by curious early-risers.

Gonji stood in a corner of the parlor with Paille, who could barely contain his glee over the general dissatisfaction with Klann's concessions. His eyes flashed wildly, his grin a crooked gash from a night of evident carousing.

The samurai was sleepy, sore, irritable and bored in

equal measures. He watched the jostling, head-shaking grumblers with growing detachment, suppressing a big yawn, all the while wondering where the old statesmen, Flavio and Milorad, found their source of endless diplomacy. Even Milorad now had shaken off the effects of the night's excesses and aided the Elder in dealing with these complaining townsfolk, not one of whom could have begun to construct a plan for the future of Vedun.

Gonji felt himself reeling where he stood. He straightened but let his knees relax. His face felt drawn and squeezed, and his mind was drifting in that peculiar way the mind does when it demands sleep, when even the most pressing concerns dwindle in importance. The burning pain in his wrist and side helped keep him awake in the stuffy parlor.

Tralayn the prophetess leaned against an arch with her hands behind her, her expression sagely sad. The hood of her cloak cowled her sheeny black hair. When she saw Gonji looking, her emerald eyes flashed a tiny smile. The confident lioness. Not long ago she had been a handsome figure of a woman. Hell, still was.

Gonji shook himself and set a scowl on his face. *Choléra,* where did Flavio derive his patience?

"—the craft guilds will not supply goods to these brigands—"

"Phlegor—"

"—positive steps must be taken to—"

"Phlegor, *why* do you remain here in Vedun?" Flavio asked, his patience at last wearing thin. "There is always a demand for militant Churchmen in Austria, you know."

"Afraid of losing the advantages of his status in the great upheaval to come," Paille whispered to Gonji, who displayed no reaction. "So this is how the aristocracy lives," the artist continued, this time in a conversational tone as he rolled a sardonic grin around the manse's rich appointments.

"Shut up, Paille," Gonji said barely above a whisper.

"Mon frere!"

"The man deserves respect, and he *is* my employer."

"Indeed so. And how does one's overseer compare to the chronicler of his glorious achievements? I am deeply hurt, *monsieur*."

But purveyor of histrionic emotion that he was, Paille quickly altered his deep hurt to mere superficial pique when Gonji made no effort to dignify it with an apology. Seconds later it was all forgotten.

"I'm for breaking my fast. Will you join me?"

Gonji grunted an assent.

The angry discussion in the parlor had turned to plans for a council meeting the following night, most of which were hammered out in provincial dialects. Gonji strode up behind Flavio and cleared his throat.

"Will you be in need of your bodyguard this morning, Master Flavio?"

Flavio clapped him on the shoulder amiably, and Gonji passively allowed the gesture. "No, my friend, rest. We'll speak later."

"By your leave, then." Gonji bowed and left the room, irascibly ignoring Tralayn's smiling composure as he moved out onto the portico. No one deserved to look so rested when he felt like a wad of chewed-over cud.

"Decadent," Paille criticized, mashing a feathered cap onto his skull and examining the *amoretto* on either portal and the Madonna and Child *mezzo rilievo* on a stone column. "Decadence. Precious frippery and religious iconography."

Michael Benedetto clumped heavily up the steps, looking tousled and sleepless. He seemed about to say something but merely nodded in answer to Gonji's curt bow as he passed. His twin black eyes had resolved now to ugly green and purple bruises.

"I thought he might have joined you at the feast after all last night," Paille observed. "I saw him out riding. God knows the poor devil's had his troubles lately."

"Well at least he can take solace in his woman," Gonji observed, thinking of the radiant and stately Lydia.

"What—the Polish duchess?" Paille said caustically. "And may we speak French this fine morning, *s'il vous plaît?*"

"Let's stick with German. I'm too tired."

Paille sighed. "German . . . the swaggering Hun language—*all-recht,* as you wish."

"And no talk of your brothers, eh? Your parents must have run a rabbit warren . . ."

They mounted and rode off, Gonji aboard Tora, Alain jouncing whimsically astride a sway-backed mare.

"Ah, what a night it was in Vedun without all those brigands," the artist prattled in desultory fashion, denying Gonji a moment's peace. "All the regulars turned out at the inn for the first time in a week. But I'd venture you had quite a night, as well. What's the warlord Klann like? What did the bastards do to you there?" He pointed to Genya's blood-soaked scarf, still wrapped tightly around the wrist wound.

"Nothing to speak of."

"Couldn't best you, eh?"

Gonji thought of Julian, began to wonder why he was riding with the yammering artist to Wojcik's Haven, half asleep as he was. Ah—the broken rein. The foster. Then sleep.

The harsh morning sun gloated like a conquering

enemy, making Gonji wince. A headache began to pulse over his left eye.

They arrived at the inn. Paille's breakfast consisted of a roll stuffed with salt pork and ale. Gonji had cornmeal cakes and milk, followed by a large goblet of mountain water. He relieved himself in a privy, and they resumed their mounts.

"Listen, Paille," Gonji said, remembering, "what was that death poem, the one from your friend in England?"

Paille thought a moment. "Oh—
*"No longer mourn for me when I am dead
Than you shall hear the surly sullen bell* . . .
"—that one?"

"Hai."

Paille translated the sonnet into French, as Gonji nodded beside him, absorbing it.

"What was the poet's name?" Gonji asked.

"Shakespeare."

"Shake-speare," the samurai repeated, bobbing his head in time to Tora's walking gait and yawning broadly. "Who's this foster Garth spoke so highly of?"

"Probably meant Radetzky, but go to Anton Torok. He's cheaper."

"Is his work as good?"

"Perhaps not, but he has two nubile daughters who work in the shop."

Gonji squinted over at him, saw Paille's puckish grin.

"Harness traces are harness traces. But pretty women are something else."

Gonji shrugged. When they reached Radetzky's Paille's laughter roared to the skies: Gonji passed it by and pulled up in front of Anton Torok's open foster stall. Gonji purchased a new harness for Tora, feeling rather ridiculous for having been talked into this so easily. He could feel Paille's suggestive grin boring into him as one of the Torok girls displayed the available traces and sold him on a harness he might not have bought had he not been in such a hurry to remove the lasciviously leering Paille from the premises. A second daughter eyed the proceedings from a work bench at the rear of the stall. This one Gonji recognized as a friend of Genya who had greeted Wilf once when he and Gonji had ridden together. Both girls were attractive in an earthy, unstudied way, but the father hovered near suspiciously and made Gonji wish to be on his way.

When they were through at the foster's a sudden inspiration drew Gonji to the nearby stall festooned with belts and straps that advertised the lorimer's craft. Gonji found the pungent smells of freshly tanned leather and animal fat pleasant and invigorating. This was the stall formerly owned and operated by Lottie Kovacs' late father. It was not in the hands of his partner and an apprentice, who were suspicious and ill-at-ease when Gonji and Paille ambled in under their canopy.

Gonji was made mindful of a piece of armament, a cross-work harness for carrying his swords on his back comfortably and snugly, which had been stolen long ago. His efforts at improvising the device—such as on the night of his foray against the wyvern—had always proven inadequate. He attempted to order one from the partner, who feigned ignorance and was engaged by Paille in a Slavic argument, the substance of which was not lost to Gonji, who had long since grown used to the hostility and prejudice inspired by his unusual appearance. He was by now growing annoyed with it in Vedun, however, given all he believed the city owed him. But he stood by patiently and watched the irrepressible artist threaten the lorimer with a balled fist.

The apprentice, who had looked on with interest, suddenly moved up to Gonji and, smiling, asked him to describe the device he wished fabricated. The young man was an Austrian, and using a Germanic lingua franca, they established communication. The apprentice at last nodded his understanding, obviously pleased with the challenge of an unusual piece of work.

Paille invited Gonji to sleep the day away in his loft above the millinery shop, and the samurai agreed. But the bath house beckoned when they passed. They tethered their steeds and entered, confronting the horrified boy who tended the baths. Gonji's appearances in the establishment always seemed to catch him off guard, and the sight of his swords would leave the lad speechless. Today, though, he tried to stammer something in Polish, Paille abruptly cutting him short and commanding him to be about his work. He hurried off to see to the coals in the steam chamber.

They undressed and laved, Paille grumblingly removing only his upper clothing, to Gonji's amusement. To the samurai, Vedun's bath house was a wondrous appointment; cleanliness was a matter of personal honor to a Japanese, while many Europeans still regarded bathing annoying or even damaging to the body.

They slumped on benches in the steam chamber, knuckling at sleepy eyes, only the fierce heat of the stone walls preventing them from succumbing to slumber where they sat, there in the moist hot womb of the chamber. Gonji had left his clothing and swords just outside the doorway, near at hand and in plain sight, ever cautious.

Redressing his wounds with clean linen strips obtained from the wide-eyed Polish youth, Gonji grew wistful, his thoughts meandering back to the Land of the Gods. The stinging pain in the shallow saber cuts reminded him of the soothing poltice made of roots and herbs grown in a sacred grove far, far away to the east.

Gonji was almost drifting off to sleep when he saw the attendant boy glance out the chamber door and go goggle-eyed.

He lurched to his feet and scrambled through the archway to his leaning swords. Before he had the Sagami half out of its scabbard, the piercing screams set the hair on his neck standing on end—

Several women in the reception chamber shrilled and gaped to see him naked and on all fours. They pushed and shoved to get back outside, each trying to outdo the others in modesty. Gonji knelt with the drawn *katana*, dimly watching their hasty departure, hearing their muffled laughter, trying to piece together the meaning through a wine-spun haze.

"Dammit!" he cried. "Dammit, Paille, it's the *women's* hours in the bath house now! Stupid barbarian rules—why didn't you remind me?"

"How was *I* to know? How often do I come to this wretched place? *You—mäsohlava!* Meathead! Why didn't you tell us?" Paille scolded the attendant.

The boy stammered something in reply.

"He said he tried to," Paille translated, slapping the boy on top of his head.

"Well, why didn't you listen to him?" Gonji addressed the boy, grinning: "It's all right, *kikusan*—little sir." He fished out a coin and tossed it to the wide-eyed lad, who turned it over in his hand in disbelief. It was more than he'd see for a month of work in the baths.

"Come, Paille, let's get dressed and get out of here. I need sleep."

They dressed and strode out. The women waiting

outside thickened in number as the shocking tale spread swiftly. The younger women tittered and whispered behind their hands. The newest arrivals were merely curious or bewildered, while some of the older ladies *tsked* and shushed them or cast looks of disgust or remonstrance at the offending pair.

"Oh, shit!" Paille breathed. "We'll hear about this. The old hens will lose me my commission at the chapel."

Instead of hurrying away in shame, Gonji walked smartly up to the surprised group of hopeful bathers, whose whispering and cackling was strangled off at once.

"*Ohayo*, ladies—good morning." He continued in German: "So sorry. We were mistaken about the bathing hours—"

And then he saw Helena glide to the forefront, her huge liquid eyes glistening darkly. Confusion and fear shadowed her lovely face in equal measure. No one had yet signed what was happening to the deaf-mute girl who had covered Gonji's escape on that night not long ago.

Gonji bowed to the women as a group and then a second time, deeper, to Helena alone, smiling, allowing the gasping curious among them to make of it what they might. Helena tendered a shaky smile and nodded uncertainly.

Then Gonji and Paille were off for the artist's loft, leaving in their wake the day's most oft-repeated incident.

They reached Alain's small musty room, which was little more than a gable projecting from the highest slope of the millinery's mansard roof. Centuries of gloom seemed to have found a home in the loft; it lay thick with dust and the clutter of the artist's craft; it reeked of paint and linseed oil, of mildew and dry rot from worn shingles fixed to the crowding rafters. Paintings leaned and lay everywhere. The walls were covered with the grim shapes that manifested Paille's dark and gloomy visions, the children of his *angst*.

Paille threw open the shutters to clear the stuffiness, the harsh streamers of blue light clouding with dust motes. Far below, the city stretched and yawned, the scents and clatter of commerce drifting up into the loft. A crier called out his banal news above the babble of men and animals. The bell tower clanged eight bells.

Gonji and Paille maneuvered around each other in the tight quarters, laughing at their absurd ballet. Paille offered the samurai the single cot, but he declined and, undressing down to his linen undergarment, spread Genya's washed scarf before the sill to dry and stretched out on a blanket. The floor was warped beneath him, evidence of the roof leaks that showed up as sharp pinpoints of light.

"They sure love you here, Paille."

The artist cackled from the cot.

"*Hai*, one day someone will discover this loft . . . perhaps make a shrine of it . . ."

"A monument."

"Mmm." As the alcoholic numbness wore off, Gonji counted his aches and pains, each one greeting him in its turn. He breathed deeply, feeling his body sink with the exhale, enjoying the weary satisfaction of another day lived to its fullest, the completeness of having given of one's abilities completely. The slow spinning . . .

Helena's face. Lydia's. The yearning for a woman. The Torok daughters. Reiko . . .

"What part of France are you from, Paille?" His voice wafting up weakly from his reclining form, almost independently of thought.

"Gascony." The reply thick with sleep.

"Gascony. I might have known." Paille's throaty growl, and Gonji's amused smile to think of the legendary boastfulness of that area of France.

Ohayo, Oguni-sama. Good morning—temperance, Gonji-san, temperance and self-denial are their own rewards. Who said that? Oguni. Iyé, not Oguni; the priest, Brother Johannes . . .

The comfort of the *katana* and the *ko-dachi* along his left side . . .

"This town . . . must survive, Paille . . ."

The gentle, sonorous buzzing from the cot.

This town must survive, Paille . . .

"Survival, Gonji-san."

"*Hai*, Master Oguni."

"Come forward, Tatsuya-san. Engage. *Shiai*—fight."

Tatsuya. Bastard. The *bokken* clacking, crossing. Can you see the hate in my eyes, devil-brother? Oh—! The pain! *Iyé!* Show nothing of it. He needn't have done that. My neck burns with pain. No! No tears . . .

No, Mama-san, I didn't cry. That's good, my son. Come close, Gonji-Gunnar, remember that you are *Viking*. You are strong. The red-gold hair, her firm embrace, eyes of blue fire and northern ice. But I'm so alone when I'm with them . . .

Helena and Lydia, laughing together, softly, covering their mouths. What's—what's funny? Helena whispering—*iyé*, not possible—deceiver! *(Why does Mord let you live?)*

Mama-san. Gonji-Gunnar, you are a bear—stern, pointing—showing all teeth and claws. I'm afraid, Mama-san . . .

Show me your best, *samurai*. Don't dispatch yourself until I've seen your *best*. Julian. Julian. . .

Reiko. Crying . . . swinging . . . *iyé*, my love . . .

her *katana* arcing wide long slow . . .

Tonight. All will be revealed tonight. Garth turning, looming, unfurling, becoming—show me your best, your—hee-hee! Everybody's a big boss around here, we got nothin' but chiefs! Rider comes from Klann, rider comes from Mord, from Klann from Mord from *(pounding)* Mord—*Deathwind! What is the Deathwind?* (pounding—*shooting!)* Pounding, beating, sweating—breathe easy! Show nothing! *You have done well, my cousin, the garden is a tribute to your work, my wife wishes to tellyou*—ssss—ssss—Siii—Saaar—*pounding*—whispering sibilance through a honeycomb of dream—Simon—Simon—Simon Sardonis—you have done well—I'll see you dead, barbarian scum—Luba's lips—no sound but—

The booming of timbers.

In days of happy childhood the Gundersen boys were occasioned to think of the musty, forbidding old trunk as a treasure chest whose contents were denied them. Wilfred and Strom would sneak into the storage cellar, wooden swords in their belts, hearts sprinting in fear of the dank moss-and-slime-walled pit. They would circle their prize, finger its iron bands and oak-ribbed lid; pull ineffectually for the thousandth time on the massive lock thrust through the latch. On the boldest sally Wilfred had brought along his father's adz. This he used to pry at the lock while Strom puled and begged him to abandon it, flickering taper trembling in a small fist. The door to the larder above slammed open. Strom screamed. There stood not Papa but a somehow more sinister brother Lorenz, eyes sparkling in the candle glow. Lorenz stormed down the rough stairs, railing at them, something about primogeniture, about the trunk's contents falling into his possession as the firstborn when he would come of age. Then he raised his hand to strike Strom, who cowered against a wall at his oldest brother's uncommon rage. But Wilfred had stepped up, the adz held on high, as if to crash it against Lorenz's skull, and the two locked eyes, their gazes fusing with that irrational sibling hatred that the perspective of adulthood can later recall only with uneasy laughter for fear of thinking on it too long or too deeply. And Lorenz had spat at him and run away up the cold stone steps, and later that evening he had smiled smugly with arms folded while Wilfred had taken his beating, and he had told all Wilfred's friends that he had cried like a baby, but Wilf hadn't cried . . .

Wilf remembered all these things now that the oaken chest had creaked open to reveal its mysterious treasures, and for an instant he wondered why, for the amazing tale they told, the objects within had ultimately proven disappointing.

Garth held up the mildewed banner of Klann's Akryllon. Beneath it lay folded the dark surcoat emblazoned with the crest of Klann and the rest of Garth's former clothing and armament from his days as Field Commander of the Royalist Force of Akryllon. At the bottom nestled a long teakwood box, fastened with a gold clasp. Garth withdrew this last.

"Iorgens," Wilf said hollowly, seeing his father's neck muscles ripple.

"Your grandfather's surname."

"*Der schatz*. The treasure," Strom muttered glumly, the expectation of the treasure chest's wonders now having palled for him also. The mist of youthful memories cleared from his eyes. "Papa, will we have to change our name now?"

Lorenz *tsked*. "Of course not, dunderhead."

"People know us by the Gundersen name, your

grandmother's good name. I can see no purpose in changing it now. You are all men, and may do as you will . . ." Garth's words drifted off into unlit corners of the cellar. His face was still drawn with sleep, his hair matted from the tossing of an unaccustomed daylight slumber.

Lorenz carved a peach into segments, pausing to sniff at each wedge with closed eyes before consuming it.

"What matter a name, when there are those who don't even know their fathers? You should feel fortunate," he advanced.

"This is all madness," Wilf said, crouching sullenly, chin resting on a forearm. "Shouldn't we remember something of this? *You* leading these . . . *bandits?*"

"They're not as they once were," Garth replied sternly. "Nothing is as it once was." He sighed raggedly. "You were barely a year old. Your brother was an infant when your mother died. Lorenz—*you* might recall being hefted by King Klann more than once. He used to turn you upside down—"

"I recall a man with huge hands and a close-cropped black beard. I had nightmares about him."

"*Ja*, that was Klann."

"Did he ask you to rejoin his command?" Wilf asked.

The question disarmed Garth. "Of course not. Don't be silly. Why would I anyway—I—he understood my feelings when I abandoned the soldiering life."

"Did you hope your father would join with Klann again so that you might win an easy commission in this army, Wilfred?" Lorenz teased. "Would your desire to be a soldier even see you enlisting in the band that invaded your city?"

"Shut up, Lorenz. That's not what I meant."

"Or is it your passion to see the fragile flower Genya

that so inflames you with—"

"I said *shut up!*"

"Enough," Garth commanded. *"Bitte."*

"How come the two circles aren't blacked out, Papa, on the shield," Strom asked, pointing to the surcoat.

"Ah," the elder smith answered, thinking a moment. "For that you will have to wait until our guests arrive. This evening all will be known of Klann." He ran a hand along the teakwood box, then appended cryptically: "For those who can believe . . ."

The sons looked at each other quizzically but ventured not another word about the coming revelation. Wilf stood up and stretched.

"You're sure Genya's all right," he said, not a question but an effort at underscoring the assurance he had already been given.

"Ja-ja," Garth said indulgently. "As I said, Gonji can tell you better."

"Ever the exhibitionist—*both* of them!" Lorenz noted, his face brightening as the thought occurred. "They sound like a splendid match."

Wilf's brow darkened, but he held his tongue and simply scowled at the floor.

"I hear Gonji lost a fight at the castle—true, Lorenz?" Strom stroked his soft fringe of tawny beard, grinning vapidly.

"So say the soldiers. Your slant-eyed friend's image has tarnished somewhat, Wilfred. They say he was outdueled by the same captain who backed him down at the Provender on the day of the occupation." Lorenz carefully wiped the knife he had been using, smiling catlike.

But Wilf was unamused. He struggled to deal with the strange conflict inside him. Something troubled him about the business of Genya assisting Gonji at the demonstration. He felt betrayed, angered that he hadn't been there. Yet he wished to be loyal to Gonji, and he was not altogether blind to Genya's displays of brashness.

"Gonji says . . ." he began slowly, picking over his words, "that a wise warrior seldom reveals more than the leading edge of his strength. And he always holds a few tricks in reserve."

Lorenz snorted and shook his head.

Garth was worried by Wilfred's preoccupation with things of the military since the invasion and Gonji's subsequent arrival, but there was, too, a small sense of pride in his middle son's growing wisdom.

"There *were* factors in the duel that weighed against Gonji, I think. But enough of that," Garth said, waving a dismissing hand. "There are other things to think of. First, the evening meal. Then I must get ready for our guests. Wilfred, you may locate Gonji and bring him here. Lorenz—the Benedettos, if you please. And Strom . . ."

Garth's brow furrowed to see Strom shrink back in hope that he might evade the chore he felt coming.

"When were you last at chapel, my young shepherd?"

"*Chapel?* Uh—" Strom rubbed his neck. "What do you mean? When Father Dobret was here last month, maybe. Uh—why?"

"Because the prophetess will be at vespers there now, I think. And Master Flavio is usually with her. You will bring them here when they are done."

Strom winced. "Master Flavio? And *Tralayn?* Why can't Lorenz—?"

"*Gehen Sie!*"

Chapter Eight

Gonji sprang to his knees and slid the Sagami free of the scabbard. His eyes cleared in time to see Paille throw off the door bar to admit Wilf.

"You hid yourself well," Wilf said.

Gonji groaned and lowered the sword, rubbing his tight, numb face. His head ached dully, and his body reminded him of the stress he'd placed on muscles he hadn't thought about in a long time. He bore it all stoically.

Konnichi wa. Good afternoon, Wilfred-san," he said, replacing the Sagami.

"*Guten tag*—good day. Wirfred again—your accent is getting worse instead of better."

"Don't be a smart ass. Paille, do you have a basin here anywhere?"

The artist had flopped back onto the cot. Gonji roused him and repeated the question. Paille grumbled incoherently and shuffled downstairs to the millinery. Wilf sat as Gonji stretched lightly and then leaned out the window to assess the day. Grayish light filled the room from a sky puffed with mounting clouds that had stacked themselves to the zenith.

"Do you know this?" Gonji asked, holding out Genya's scarf. Wilf took it silently. "She's one helluva woman. Good luck, my friend."

The ice was broken, Wilf again feeling at ease with his Japanese friend and mentor. Being in Gonji's presence, once again mindful of the samurai code of honor and loyalty, he experienced a creeping shame for the immaturity of his earlier suspicions and feelings of betrayal. He was soon listening intently as Gonji conveyed every detail of Genya's circumstances and the events at the castle banquet, stopping just short of the blooding duel with Julian.

Gonji continued with his stretching regimen in the tight quarters as he spoke. Paille returned with a sloshing ewer and empty basin, now wide awake, sputtering, and slamming about like a newly escaped bedlamite. Gonji washed, combed out his topknot and retied it. He scrubbed the bloodstains from the sleeveless tunic and hung it to dry. A crimson stain discolored the patch on his left side.

"That looks bad," Wilf observed.

"Not so bad. But perhaps it'll need some help to remain closed." Gonji sighed, frowning. He donned his kimono and wrapped his *obi* tightly around his middle. This done, he placed his swords in the sash and found the shallow wound far more painful than it had been in the morning. It would never heal properly unaided.

"So Genya says she's being treated well?" Wilf persisted.

"Hai."

"The buxom scullion lass, eh?" Paille observed.

"Watch your tongue, Paille."

"Insult his woman, incur his wrath," Gonji gibed.

"Me, monsieur? Really! A Frenchman can have nothing but respect for so special a woman!"

"Oh—Wilf," Gonji said. "Did your father . . . tell you?"

The smith's expression clouded. *"Ja.* What can I tell you? My brothers and I were . . ." He stood shaking his head, lost for words.

"You never knew anything of it? None of you?"

"I swear it," Wilf averred.

"One moment, *monsieurs*—what is this business?"

Gonji explained to Paille the night's revelation.

"Whew!" the artist breathed, eyes bulging. "*Sacre bleu!* So Vedun's *Herr Wunderbar* has an ominous past. But . . . a general with the warlord *Klann?* Why did he say nothing—?"

"There'll be more to tell after tonight, I think," Gonji said.

They departed Paille's loft, the artist exchanging sharp words with his landlady, who greeted Gonji and Wilf pleasantly between snarls at Paille. Once outside, Alain suggested the Provender, Vedun's larger inn and hostel, for supper, but Gonji declined, having no desire to encounter his nemesis Julian again so soon. Paille took his leave of them, anxious to hear the latest scuttlebutt at the Provender.

When he had gone Gonji and Wilf clopped along wordlessly for a time, the samurai aware of his young friend's internal struggle.

"What's on your mind now?" Gonji asked finally.

"Nothing—just—they're saying you lost a duel to this Captain Julian last night," Wilf blurted all at once. "I just—is it—"

"And if I did, what do you make of it?"

Wilf thought about it for a space, watching Gonji's proud carriage aboard Tora. "Well, you're still alive . . . so I suppose there's more to it than they're saying."

"Very wise. Now let's have no more talk of it for now. The conceited captain and I haven't done with each other yet."

"Is he good?" Wilf probed, unable to set it aside.

"He's very good," Gonji responded without a pause. "Let's go see the physician."

They stopped at Dr. Verrico's, found the doctor out on a call. But an assistant, one of his midwives, offered to cleanse and stitch Gonji's rent left side. This painfully done, they supped at Wojcik's Haven, suffering nary an insult from the squad of Llorm dragoons who also ate there, Gonji in fact finding to his surprise that two of the Llorm greeted him of their own accord, if rather curtly.

Riding to the Gundersens', exchanging small talk with the now reassured and ebullient Wilf, Gonji found to his great delight that whatever the lost duel had added to Julian's reputation, it had not been at the expense of Gonji's: Soldiers gave him wide passage, and more townies than ever greeted him with something more than the sullen stares he'd grown so used to.

Garth sat alone at one wide side of the table, the others grouped in a semicircle around it, sipping their drinks reflectively. At his left sat Lorenz, languid and relaxed; then Strom, sitting on his hands, one foot tapping nervously, his discomfiture to be beside the icy Tralayn obvious. Wilfred and Gonji sat opposite Garth, Wilf leaning forward with mild apprehension, Gonji's face a blank mask. Adjacent to the oriental was the settee on which Lydia and Michael were seated, both seeming cool and dignified, their hands entwined in a rare public display of affection. Finally, at Garth's right, were Flavio and Milorad, neither appearing very rested or recovered from the previous night's castle fest.

Garth's hands trembled slightly with anticipation, a tiny thrill of nostalgia rippling through his spine at the prospect of reading from the scroll for the first time in twenty years. He unrolled it a few turns, the faded, musty parchment crackling, yielding up the pungent scent of time. Then he read downward several lines, translating in advance the Kunan script for his own ease of reading. The memory gaps filled themselves in rapidly.

"Chronicle of Tikah Vos. Kanta 16. Scroll 27 . . . Being a continuation of the History of the House of Bel through the bloodline of Durda'Klann . . ."

He skimmed down, rolling the scroll, until he found the passage that caused him to blanch. He licked dry lips and read on.

". . . and so in the days of Sarkanah, when the League of Necromancers had by foul work and insidious treachery vanquished the royalist wizard alliance and savaged their numbers, some inflaming in the night even as they slept such that these goodly spirits were now shunned of men, the wise court mage Zaratakis did counsel flight from Akryllon. All things meet for the lives of men failed on the dwindling isle, once the crowning gemstone of the seas, now a paradise consumed by vermin. Nothing grew, nor did the beasts who were friends to man flourish; men fell as lifeless as stone in the streets, ravaged for mana by evil sorcery.

"King Jari was sore beset, for Queen Sarna was heavy with child, and the astrologers had murmured fearfully of the natal omens for many months. He prevailed upon Zaratakis to contrive some plan by which the throne of Akryllon might be saved, for flight was unthinkable to the scion of the House of Bel. And Zaratakis did fetter himself in the Tower of Primal Knowledge, and he wept and thrashed and suffered the ineffable Prescience for three days and nights, and when he was dragged from his bondage by soldiers who did sear their hands at his touch, the Tower was engulfed in black flames, and crumbled to dust, and was no more seen of men. And the good wizard was rendered aged and sere by his ordeal, and yet there was nothing that could be done for it. His mana was spent, and there was no more to be done, lest he himself resort to the unspeakable effects of the necromancers . . .

"And so, when the defensive gulfs of void and madness had been breached, the king and queen of Akryllon did take flight, with those of the Llorm people yet quick and of sturdy faith . . .

"They took to ship amid furious seas, pursued by the hosts of the Enemy, and when . . . and when the queen's time had come, she cried out in her pain and anguish. And the midwives withered in their charge and . . . threw themselves bodily into the sea . . .

"And Zaratakis and King Jari attended on the birthings with the last staunch midwife, the blind Anka. And they were born alive. And they were seven . . . Seven they were, all dreadfully fragile and in danger of death. And the king and his loyal mage feared the multiple birthing for its portent, but Anka decried their faint hearts and delivered unto them each child in turn, until they at last saw the eerie change that had come over her, the evil of Akryllon reaching to touch them even here, and before Zaratakis could bring her low with his magic, she had brought forth . . . the tainted one. And it struggled in her arms, though she lay dead. And King Jari would have dashed the strange one against the planks until it breathed no more, but Queen Sarna wailed and pleaded with him to do no harm to any of her issue . . .

"And the queen, at the brink of death, begged Zaratakis that he should use his power to save her children, for they would surely die in their frailness. And the wizard pondered, and could find in all the ancient gramarye but one spell that might save them. But it was a terrible spell, and its price would be exacted from all involved. And King Jari rejected the spell, horrified that such a power had ever fallen to the whims of men. But at the last the queen's pitiable pleas touched his heart, and the king agreed to the awful magick that Zaratakis proposed . . .

"And the . . ."

Garth's words caught in his throat. He peered up with darting eyes at his rapt audience.

"And the seven were made *one* . . . and they were a robust, crying man-child, and he was Klann, scion-being of the House of Bel. And *they* were Klann, and they were one out of seven, and seven in one. It had been provided by Zaratakis that each would take up their life upon the death of the last, and the natural lifetime of them all, that is to say of the seven, would be as the life of a man seven times over . . .

"And Queen Sarna, having given up her life force so that her children might live, expired in the arms of King Jari. And the noble Zaratakis, his work in the land of the living complete, followed after into the dark lands.

"And the king looked upon the child left to him, and he wept . . ."

Garth looked up. His listeners were thunderstruck. Flavio's chagrin etched fine lines of worry into his temples. "A—a *phoenix*-king?"

"That is the being you deal with," Garth agreed. No one else spoke, incredulity and confusion shackling their tongues. "I won't read more," he continued, his words tentative and deliberate. "Perhaps I should continue from my own words, about the things I believe to be true of King Klann . . .

"This . . . enchanted child of the scroll grew to manhood, brought up in exile by his father's hereditary army, who propagated only to serve the legacy of Akryllon. They wandered, stayed alive as they could—and here I'll ask that you try to sympathize with Klann, not judge him too harshly for what his agonized life has caused him to do. Any of us might have done the same—but they traveled the world, conquering, stealing when they must to stave off extinction. And when they felt strong enough, they would sally forth by ship with whatever army they could raise in an effort to find Akryllon. And *ja*, that could prove difficult in itself: the sorcerers who wrested it from the House of Bell unfettere it from its moorings in the sea, so it was said. I know only that I sailed once with Klann for Akryllon, and we never found it, though fully a third our number died from the horrors and hardships along the way. Klann is obsessed with finding his homeland and then taking it back from the usurpers . . ."

They kept watching him, waiting to hear more, waiting for some statement by which he could render the tale believable to them.

"I don't know what else I can tell you . . . Maybe you . . . have questions?"

And the spell was abruptly shattered. They began to breathe normally, and move, and, thankfully, to speak.

"Very sorry, my friend, but . . . do you truly believe all this about him?" Gonji queried, gazing at him with suspicion.

Garth thought of the things he had lived through those many years past. "*Ja*, Gonji, I do."

"I myself have reason to believe in the sallies after Akryllon. I've known others who've crossed Klann's path," Gonji ventured, recalling the tale told by old Jocko. "But I think there's more to Klann's legend that—"

"Klann dies and then comes to life again?" Wilf asked. He sat beside Gonji, a carbon copy of the samurai's skeptical posturing.

"Not seven lives—seven *persons*, my son," Garth replied patiently. "Transmogrification, I've heard it called. One person dies and is immediately replaced by another—" His hands fluttered as if to construct an explanation out of thin air. "Like—like the legendary phoenix, as Flavio has said."

"Ridiculous," Milorad blustered under his breath. His eyes were heavy lidded, as if he were courting sleep. He sipped his mead. "In these enlightened times."

"In this day and age," Gonji countered, *"giants* walk the wards of your Castle Lenska."

"What—?" Strom piped in, suddenly alert. *"Giants?"*

"Mord has a friendly giant up at the castle," Gonji said, smiling thinly.

"You never told me that," Wilf said, looking hurt. "Is it—is it—"

"Don't *worry* about it now, Wilfred," Garth urged.

"Your Genya is a match for any giant," Lorenz teased. There were a few chuckles, the tension easing out of them.

Garth was relieved to see the gradual dawning of credulity.

"Have you ever seen one of these . . . changes?" Gonji probed.

"Nein," Garth answered slowly, shifting position, "but I believe in them. Lorenz—you remember earlier I asked you whether you remembered being held by Klann as a babe, and you said you did, you remembered a black-bearded man who frightened you? That was Klann. That was the Klann I rode with. He was the *second*. The first was said to have been killed in battle in Italy not long before I joined the army. The one I knew was shot to death several years ago by a crazed mercenary in his employ. You'll recall, last night, gentlemen—the soldier Klann cast out of

the banquet hall for wearing a forbidden pistol. Klann told me about the shooting when we drank in his chambers. I'm convinced that he *is* Klann. He told me things only Klann could know of our former alliance."

Gonji shook his head gravely. "I'm convinced Mord has something to do with this Klann legend, something more than you know or—"

"Impossible," Garth countered. "Mord is quite new with the army. And I noted a certain ill will between them. It was there, unmistakable, in Klann's every word of the sorcerer."

"Mord is our chief nemesis nonetheless," Tralayn said, at last speaking. "Klann has chosen the power of the Evil One." She seemed strangely smug, some small private triumph perking the corners of her lips.

"Has Klann no sisters?" Lydia asked sarcastically.

Garth looked at her, not liking her tone. For as long as he had known the Benedettos, Lydia had doted on him, held him up as an example to her husband. Now suddenly her entire attitude had changed. Since she had learned the formerly hidden and heretofore unthreatening details of his militaristic background—and now the bewildering history of Klann—she acted as if he had betrayed a trust. She leaned back, her lips pressed together in suppression of a derisive smile and held Michael's hand like an anchor for her shaken reality. If only, he thought, if only you would hold the boy's hand in *support* once in a while . . .

"Ja," Garth replied, smiling affably, "Klann did speak to me of having sisters among the Brethren, as he calls them."

"Oh, Garth," Lydia sighed in exasperation, "this is all so incredible, coming from you."

"We've all seen our share of incredible things lately, Lydia," Lorenz interjected. "If my father believes what he says, then so do I."

"*Himmel,*" Strom whispered, the safety and sanity of his small, predictable world forever dashed.

"It *would* explain certain things . . ." Gonji thought aloud.

"It's all absurd," Michael spoke up, the last person in the room to comment. He had regained something of his former dignity, a calm surety in his mien. He no longer looked disgraced by his bruised eyes and gradually healing broken nose. "All quite absurd—"

"Michael," Tralayn cautioned softly, "*think*. Think of the unnatural things we've been witness to, of the foul sorcery that's touched more than one life—"

"You didn't let me finish, good Tralayn," Michael cut in. "I say it's all madly absurd, yet what choice have we but to take it at face value? *Si,* for the very reason you state. And Garth's word is as good as Flavio's to me."

Tralayn nodded solemnly.

"What was that business of 'mana' being spent, Garth?" Gonji asked.

Garth thought about the things he'd heard many years ago. He cleared his throat. "It's . . . some sort of power magicians draw from the things around them, I think."

"Earth magick imparted to followers of Satan," Tralayn added flatly. They all stared, and one or two shivered a bit at her frankness in discussing cosmic evil. "But unlike the gifts of Providence, mana is drawn from the things the dark agents can smother. Living things, left lifeless . . . soulless . . ."

"You know, you have a lovely city here," Gonji began impassively, narrow dark eyes panning over them paternalistically. "I've come to like it very much. It's amazing that you've survived, given what I've seen of this country, the powers that vie for supremacy in these mountains. And now this invasion by Klann and what he's brought. If a fraction of what Garth says is true—and the councilman's wife will, *dozo*, recall the wyvern and the giant we've seen at Castle Lenska. Then you people must begin thinking of your future security."

Lydia leaned forward, and although she looked across the table to where Strom slouched on his stool, she addressed Gonji. "The councilman's wife's beliefs are of little import to the city's future. But the Elder's bodyguard might remember to uphold the city's social proprieties. I understand you made quite an impression at the baths this morning."

There followed laughter and a few questions, and Gonji's equanimity was disturbed by the slight reddening of his cheeks as the incident was recounted for those who had yet to hear.

"It all fits," Tralayn said, standing suddenly. "Listen to me, all of you, the time of epochal change has come and has centered in Vedun. The Dark Powers join for a final thrust at overt dominion over the world of men. Men of Destiny have gathered here for the playing out of the drama, with all the spiritual world as its audience. I have had a vision that I could not interpret fully until tonight. A vision of a clash between unusual men, men of *strange birthing* . . ." She faced Gonji, the fanatic's torchlight limning her emerald eyes. "Gonji, have you not said that you are a half-breed, your parents' commingling of races being the only such ever known?"

"*Hai*, but—"

"Then it must be true. But can I also have misinterpreted the identity of the Deliverer?" she thought aloud, eyes clouding over, their vision filling with things denied the rest of them. "Can you—to us an infidel—be the promised Deliverer?"

"Whoa, lady!" Gonji said somberly. "Keep me out of your wild visions. If even half this business is true, you people are in more trouble than you know. I'm not sure that it's my karma to become involved any more than I am already. Anyway, I've my *own* visions to interpret, so sorry. And there's nothing strange about my birthing," he concluded, vaguely threatening.

A resolute expression appeared in the hard-set lines of Tralayn's firm jaw. "Garth, I must ask your sons and the good Milorad to leave, please. It's a matter of oath."

Shock pervaded the room. Milorad emitted a querulous grunt and sat bolt upright, now wide awake. Flavio half rose as if he would object but sat back with grim resignation to see Tralayn's determined air of command. He nodded dolefully to his friend and counselor that he must leave. Garth held his breath a few anxious seconds, then in a small voice directed his reluctant sons to remove themselves from the house until called for. Milorad shuffled out behind them, his dignity wounded.

The doors and shutters were closed tight. Tralayn stood at the center of them. Flavio, Garth, Michael and Lydia regarded her with eyes like those of startled forest animals. Gonji looked expectant, hands on knees.

"I fear we've lost the help of Simon Sardonis."

There was not a wisp of breathing in the smith's parlor. Gonji eased backward on his stool, a sly, accusing expression spreading slowly over his angular features. The room lay ablaze with tension and horrified faces.

Chapter Nine

Mord sat before the blood-stained altar, the Book of Philtres open before him to the complex charm of sympathetic-imitative magick he sought. Behind him, shackled head downward from the ceiling, hung the servant, her keening wail filling him with evil heat. His loins flared as he listened to the slow drip of her vital fluids.

The spell called for an adynamic victim, and such subjects were easy to find in his present circumstances. A difficult ritual, but he was becoming better at it all the time as he pressed forward with the Grand Plan. He felt the imputation of dark power, almost stunned by its dizzying thrill. Removing his mask, he performed the chant, drowning out her pain-wracked screaming.

On the altar lay crop samples from the fields and orchards of the lowlands. Mord began to breathe over them rhythmically, and there issued from his mouth a thick, roiling black smoke that caressed the altar, stealing the objects from view, consuming . . .

Sullen gray eyes, eyes blazing with hate, watched from concealment the fuming vapor that descended over the nighted farmland outside the walls of Vedun. Puzzlement furrowed the man's brow as he saw the fog separate, break up, as if with an eerie prescience all its own, rolling over certain fields and furrows, leaving others untouched.

A distant sound. Clumping horse hooves. Two mercenaries, speaking in whispers, rode toward him, watching the fog from the road. Their whispering rasped sharply in the stillness; all wildlife had withdrawn deep into the forest.

He reached back and felt the place where the arrow had pierced his buttock. Already nearly healed. But it had been painful, and they had done it. Just as they'd killed the boy. And then done the unspeakable thing, the outrage at the monastery. He glared upward at the distant castle spires.

Satan's minions had done it. And Hell would be repaid.

The beast within mocked him, and he cursed it back to its curling place, that place he would cut out by his own hand if he knew where inside him it reposed.

He sprinted along the tree line, the death wish burning inside him.

"D'you believe in him? I never believed in him. Not before tonight. Not even with the big birdie, or Tumo." The mercenary shook his head. He removed his sallet and drew an arm across his sweating brow. A chill shook him. "But look at it. He said he'd do it and he done it." He replaced the sallet.

"Shut up," his partner replied. "You talk to much."

"Sure." A cloud covered the moon, and a gloomfast stillness gripped the plateau. "Well, just what we need now. Get lost in the dark and stumble into that . . . mist." His breath came in short gasps, fear clutching at his heart. "If Klann knew anything about this, about what Mord's doin' . . ."

"Why don't you just shout it out?"

"All right, all right, I know. We're sworn. I won't cross him. Not no more. Not after I seen what he done to Lonzo's feet. Uh-uh. You say that chant of his? Say it and really mean it?" His head wagged negatively; in the dark he couldn't see his partner's hand, cautioning him to silence. "I never did. Never really meant it before. I will now, though, I tell you. That's for—"

"Hssst! Shut up. Listen. Did you hear that?"

The horses began to snort and curvette, stamping fretfully.

"What? What? I didn't hear nothin'!"

"Shut up, you damn fool!"

"What *is* it? What do you hear?" he shouted.

And then his steed bolted, whinnying fiercely. His sallet flew off and he lost the stirrups, clung to the reins with one slipping hand and tried desperately to dig into the animal's flanks. The frenzied beast shook him loose, and he fell heavily on his back, stunned, the breath knocked out of him.

His partner howled maniacally, and with a strange nightmarish detachment the soldier stared at the blood-slicked arm, severed at the elbow, that bounced wetly beside him. A mindless moan, cut short by a sharp splintering sound and a jangling crash as horse and rider fell.

He tried to rise, gibbering oaths and half-remembered prayers of protection, and then his shrieking, bolting horse tumbled backward onto him, a twitching carcass.

He shrieked, his leg broken, but in his terror he fought through the nauseating pain and tried frantically to pull free from under the imprisoning bulk.

And then he saw the tall figure, saw the whites of his eyes and the dull glint of clenched teeth. Saw the darkly streaked sword that had been his partner's.

His jaws jacked open unnaturally as he gagged, seeing the wide, blood-freezing arc of steel. And then he saw no more.

Gonji felt a mixture of triumph and indignation, a

heady blend that he wore imperiously as he strutted back and forth, hands clasped at the back of his *obi*.

"So many connivers," Gonji said wryly. "I wouldn't have guessed."

Only Tralayn made eye contact with him. "You take things far too personally. We are under the burden of a solemn oath regarding Simon."

"The awesome mystery man," Gonji guessed aloud, feeling that effusion of thrill in his spine that hinted at fulfillment of his destiny. "The one who killed Ben-Draba and confounded a whole company of Klann's soldiers in his escape."

"The same," Tralayn confirmed.

"He'll be badly injured now."

"It . . . probably won't last." Tralayn drew a deep breath. "Even now I'm not sure how much I dare tell you of him. What is your connection with Father Dobret?"

He started to shake off any knowledge of whom she meant, but then he paused. He'd heard the name spoken before. It was the priest who came monthly to Vedun from the ravaged monastery. But why should he know him? Ahh . . . there could be only one reason—

"The white-haired priest at the monastery? The one who gave me the message?"

"*Si.*"

"I . . . tried to do him a favor once."

Tralayn puzzled over Gonji's evasive words.

"What is happening at the monastery, Gonji?" Flavio asked. "No one is allowed through the Borgo Pass. Soldiers posted there turn everyone away."

"I'll say no more of that until you've told me more of Simon." Gonji's bearing was arrogant, adamant. They looked uneasily from one to the other.

"We swore an oath," Lydia reminded, staring into space.

"Which my brother died keeping," Michael added severely.

Gonji thought about the beating incident, brow darkening. "The key—*that's* where I saw it before. So you do know what that key is for, the one Mord seems so worried about."

Michael and Lydia shifted in their seats. Garth gazed at the floor sullenly. Flavio seemed on the verge of saying something, looking to Tralayn almost imploringly for guidance.

"He has asked of Simon Sardonis, dear Flavio. He has been led unerringly from afar to this place. The timing—his insistence—his actions on behalf of a people who are strange to him—it can only mean that the Lord God has purposed that he shall have a part in our righteous battle. Sabataké Gonji-noh-Sadowara—I have reason to trust you, to believe in your good intentions toward Vedun. We are planning to raise a militia, to bring an underground army into readiness to deal with the invaders and Mord's hellish minions when the time has come. We need your battle skills, your dauntless spirit to help in the training and in the conflict itself. In return we will pay you what you require. And . . . in time I will tell you all you wish to know of Simon Sardonis. Do you accept the charge?"

From the moment she had addressed him by his proper full name he had become intrigued, his heart quickening as she laid out the bold proposal, though his face showed none of it. He inhaled sonorously, his brow overhung with the gravity of his pondering, part of the propriety due so earnest a request. All the while his mind reeled, and his own reply startled him even more:

"*Iyé*—no, so sorry, I think not."

Even as he spoke the words he marveled at the aloofness of their sound, and only after the rejection left his lips did the reasoning become fully framed in his mind. It was the game; ever the psychological warfare, the social game-playing he had learned to pursue with keen interest. Indeed, it was often necessary to survival to maintain this edge, this one-upmanship that kept the other party off balance. In reality he was eager to accept this lofty position he had been offered, which he equated with a generalship.

The *kami* of good fortune smiles on you, Gonji-san. But why do I want it? he wondered. What am I playing for? The money? Blast the money to hell! For friendship, affection? *Hai*, there is that. They have awakened in me feelings I've not felt in a long time. But also . . . for *meaning* to a worthless *ronin* existence. The landless, dutiless wanderer is lower than the lowest grave-digger. So it is for meaningful duty that I will accept. And having accepted, it will be for *acceptance* that I will strive . . .

"I think conflict is inevitable. And if I commit myself to this thing I will probably die here, and my quest will have come to nothing."

He gauged their reactions with relish as he paced solemnly about the room. Tralayn studied him, a confused tilt to her head. "I don't understand you," she said.

Garth and Flavio, seated next to each other, flashed a similar disappointment and mild surprise, which he found gratifying. From the settee on which the Benedettos sat came a flicker of interest. Michael registered a quiet, breathless satisfaction. Lydia's patrician poise and refinement allowed little of the nature of her interest to show. Relief, he decided, was uppermost in her tightly drawn lips, the languid calming of her blue eyes.

"But I'll think on it, ponder the consequences," the samurai concluded, twisting the knife.

"Will you at least tell me now the message you bear Simon?" Tralayn asked earnestly.

Gonji stopped pacing. "Oh no, clever lady, that is my trump. Why don't you instead tell me something I don't already know of him?" A cold recollection welled up. Hadn't Julian asked him the same question not long ago? *Tell me something I don't already know* . . .

Tralayn sighed and looked at the others.

"That's for him to decide, Tralayn," Michael cautioned.

"And it was for me to decide whether to bring in your brother's body," Gonji reminded, rankled a bit at his hostility, "if I may so callously call up the memory."

Michael's bruised eyes dropped in shame.

"It was a solemn oath we swore," Tralayn said resignedly.

"I thought you said he was gone now. So what would be the harm?"

"I'm not really sure. He *said* he was leaving us . . ."

"What is the Deathwind, Tralayn?" Gonji asked imperiously. The room fell silent. "Is Simon Sardonis the Deathwind I've sought all these terrible years in Europe?" He strove to control his sudden trembling, the pace of his heart.

Tralayn stared deeply into his eyes. "I don't know about that. By the cross of Christ I swear that I cannot be sure. He fits certain ramifications of the legends, yet he'll not answer to being the thing of which they speak." Her jaw set with a sudden determination, her eyes becoming green embers. "I will say no more of him now. *You* must proffer your commitment to the city. I will tell you this: Vedun is committed to readiness. The people are prepared to die for their faith and their city. Warriors, tacticians, leaders are needed. You would not be alone—" A coy look crept across her face. "Baron Rorka lives."

She let the statement hang in the air amid the startled gasps of her fellows. Gonji's own surprise shattered his staid countenance. He chuckled softly and shook his head.

"Tralayn, you tell too much!" Michael argued.

"This place is so full of secret intrigues," Gonji observed, "it's like a tale told by a fireside minstrel."

"And there's more to tell," Tralayn assured, "much more. Things that only I know. Will—you—help—us?" She emphasized each word, standing now before him.

Gonji looked at her, admiring her determination. "You have the instincts of a predator. You'd be a deadly enemy, I'd wager—and you can take that as a compliment." By her curt nod he saw that she did. "You say the boy—Mark—*died* to preserve this secret of Simon Sardonis?"

She bowed gravely, the others withdrawing into sullen private thoughts. Gonji's brow creased. He rubbed his chin reflectively.

"Give me the night to think. Tomorrow you'll have your answer. I've training to do. That will help clear my head for a wiser decision than I could render tonight. Garth—something troubles me. Very sorry, but I must be the cynic. You swore fealty to Klann before. What would be your mind now, if—if the worst should happen?"

Garth looked hurt. "My past is behind me. My loyalty is with this city now. You shouldn't have to ask that." Gloom settled over the stocky smith. "But I could never raise a sword against Klann."

Gonji nodded, not altogether pleased with his friend's attitude. "You can do your city a favor, *dozo,* and muzzle Strom about all this. I needn't tell the rest of you, I think, that talk of the castle giant and this tale of Klann's seven lives could only serve to undermine morale. Keep it all to yourselves. A positive attitude, that's what you need. I suppose everyone already knows about the illustrious Rorka's well-being—everybody except the samurai infidel, *neh?*" He smiled wryly and drew an unwonted shy grin from Tralayn.

"I wonder something, though," Gonji said as they began to rise and stretch, preparing to leave. "You all protect this super-warrior Simon, yet I detect a definite fear of him in your manner. Why do you help him? What does he hold over you? And most interesting of all, why does he leave you now in your hour of need?"

They were all looking at him, and he saw the faint tremor that wracked Lydia as Michael helped her with her cape.

"In time, Gonji," Tralayn answered. "All in good time."

Then the door was opened, and Lorenz and Wilf strolled back inside, their offense at having been excluded obvious. Milorad had gone home in a huff, and Strom was saddling a horse to ride off somewhere. Garth called him inside to pass along Gonji's caution. Lorenz poured his indignance into caustic humor, while Wilf took a more boorish tack. An uncommon warmth filled the night breeze that wafted through the door, and the hills seemed quiet.

Flavio sidled up to Gonji and spoke in a low, sheepish voice. "Listen . . . Gonji, will you be talking to Captain Kel'Tekeli soon?"

Julian.

"I don't know—maybe. You don't mind the idea now?"

Flavio shrugged. "You no doubt know what you're doing. But next time would you tell him that we're all still eager for peace? Would you do that for an old man whose influence is waning with the young wolves in council?" He smiled wearily.

Gonji bowed to him. *"Hai,* Master Flavio, it shall be done."

Flavio's shoulders sagged as he left, looking like a man ticketed for the gallows.

Chapter Ten

Feeling the need to be alone to think Gonji eschewed sleeping at the Gundersens' and took a room on the third floor of Wojcik's Haven. He slept lightly and before dawn stirred and laved the sleep from his face. Retrieving Tora from the livery, he rode out through the west gate past wary mercenary sentinels. They didn't detain him, nor did they say a word; Julian was at least keeping his word about restraining his dogs from Gonji's behind.

Clumping into the hills, Gonji found a quiet glade where he ground-tethered Tora. Removing his swords, *obi,* and kimono, he stashed the *daisho* set behind a tree at the far side of the glade. As Gonji began running his laps around the perimeter, the first pink blush of dawn filtered through breaks in the bower to the east.

He finished his run and pushed himself through calisthenics, a regimen of stretches, and several unarmed *kata,* favoring his left side so as not to tear open his stitched wound. The wounds all seemed to be healing nicely, the lips of the rib wound closing without fester. He took up his swords and, sashing them again, practiced speed and precision drills focusing on the draw from the sheath and the immediate strike that followed. He performed each of the amazing variety of sword draws he could remember from the various *ryu*, or schools of thinking, on *katana* technique: one-handed and two-handed draws, sky-to-ground slashes, circular slashes, close-quarter cuts, thrusts at rear attackers. He practiced until he felt the satisfying surfeit that signaled the end of the light workout, the warmup for the rigors he knew were in the offing. Breathing heavily and perspiring freely, he felt lean and hungry, with the heightened sensibilities and predatory confidence of a tiger.

He rode back to Vedun through the sparkling dewy verdure, the moisture of night evaporating rapidly under a hot young sun. Puffy white clouds mounted the western horizon but offered no threat of rain.

Gonji breakfasted from the stalls in the marketplace near the square, where he took note that Flavio had already had the huge crucifix raised again in a display of optimism. There was a nervous buzzing among the soldiers this morning that made him curious.

Then a passing mercenary, nodding and touching his hat brim in greeting, palmed him a note. Winking and bobbing his head again, the man moved on. Gonji discreetly opened the folded brown paper and read the Italian script:

"At the caravanserai behind the Provender at nine bells. The Captain."

Julian. Now what in hell—? A trap? No, that's absurd. To what end? He likely wants to hear more for his money. But what to tell him—?

He tugged at one ear pensively, trying to piece together something that might sound like useful intelligence. Nine bells. Well, he had a little time. And at least now he might learn what had the soldiery so edgy.

He cantered to the tanner's and found that his cuirass was ready, as were the set of pauldrons and vambraces. The cuirass was a fine piece of workmanship, a tough leather shell for protecting the breast and back that was the best he'd ever donned. And the pauldrons and vambraces, constructed of lames, or overlapping scales of hard leather, were designed to protect the shoulders and arms from sword cuts. Gonji found them snug but comfortable and well-oiled for freedom of movement.

It was a fine day for new acquisitions, he found, when he checked in at the cobbler's to discover his new soft leather riding boots awaiting his inspection. They were beautiful and quite comfortable, yet he curiously disdained wearing them, preferring instead to continue with his *tabi* and sandals. He rode off mildly miffed at himself that he had allowed last week's sudden flush of lucre to seduce him to such profligate spending, *and* so tawdry an example of Westernization as a pair of Italian riding boots.

He shrugged and rode to the Gundersens', where he stashed his new belongings in Wilf's bedchamber. After a laconic exchange with the again moody Wilf, he trotted off for the Provender.

At nine bells he sat aboard Tora in the caravanserai, wagons and draft beasts and traveling merchants clamoring around the inn amid odors of food, drink, and animal waste. A mercenary on foot indicated a covered dray in a rear corner. Gonji dismounted and climbed aboard warily, then took a seat facing Julian in the cramped quarters.

"How are they talking since the castle banquet?" Julian probed without preamble. He was dressed like a floppish merchant in dun-colored silks and cowhide breeches. A three-cornered hat sat beside him. His only armament was a dagger fastened to his wide leather belt.

"The leaders, to a man, want peace," Gonji replied. "They're very optimistic since they met with Klann."

"That's all?" Julian's tone denoted disappointment.

"Well . . ." Gonji began, fabricating, not liking being called on the carpet by this contemptible bastard, "there *is* an undercurrent of something. I just haven't gotten the confidence of the right people yet. They still talk of the Deathwind, only now they're calling it a promised Deliverer, some sort of death angel who will free them from oppression. Believe me, no one would like to know more than I what they're talking about . . ." He shook his head and creased his brow, affecting a perplexity that he hoped would be convincing. Julian's face betrayed nothing.

"Where were you last night?" the captain asked flatly.

Gonji's memory raced backward. No, no there was nothing to hide. "At the Gundersens'. All evening. Several others were there . . ." He caught himself, angered that Julian had squeezed a guilty tone from him, and took a more aggressive tack. "Then I took a room at Wojcik's—why? What's on your mind, Captain?"

"Well, that checks out."

"*What* checks out?" Gonji's muscles tautened.

"Two soldiers were killed last night—*butchered*, I should say—along with their horses." Julian smiled sardonically. "A crude effort at concealment was made with the . . . remains."

"And you suspect me?" Gonji's eyes tapered.

"No. No, it wasn't your style," Julian replied, leaning back and relaxing. "But in my position I've learned to extend only so much trust to my hirelings."

Gonji scowled, nodded curtly. "Who found these . . . remains?"

"The same person who verified your whereabouts—Garth Iorgens' son, the shepherd."

Strom. The samurai's thoughts raked over this information, forward and backward, eyes unseeing, though they continued to hold the captain's.

"You know," Julian began leisurely, "I've heard something disquieting about you—"

Gonji returned to the present. *"So desu?* What's that?"

"It's said that you brought back the councilman Benedetto's dead brother from the forest. That you had to kill some men to do it."

They knew.

Gonji tightened, his pulse galloping, a chortle disguising his captive breath. *"Hai,* that's the story I've *told*. Haven't you wondered at how easily I've won their confidence? The truth is that the men I encountered where I found the boy were already as dead as he was. Probably more work of your mysterious 'butcher.' "

"I wonder," Julian said quietly. "Pick up the hat."

"Eh?" Gonji cocked an eyebrow.

"The *hat*."

Gonji reached across and overturned the slouch hat. Beneath lay a shriveled apple, brown and wrinkled.

"What's that?" Gonji queried.

"Pick it up."

He did so. It felt dry and somehow too light.

"The nights have been cold, *neh?*" the samurai observed.

"Not that cold. Squeeze it."

Gonji paused a moment, then crushed the fruit in his hand. It crumbled into powder, soughed through his fingers. It had felt oddly unsavory. He regarded Julian quizzically.

"A third of the farmers' yield looks like that today," the captain said. "What do you know of it? Are the farmers pursuing some sort of . . . passive resistance against Klann?"

"*Iyé*—to what purpose?"

"I don't know. *You* find out. You can tell your Flavio that Klann is learning of all these things right now, and I'd wager there'll be repercussions." He toed the strange powder with his boot. "Like magick, eh?"

Gonji's mind reeled with questions. Caution. *Think*.

"Who told you of this 'death angel' you speak of?" Julian queried.

"Eh . . , the prophetess, Tralayn," Gonji replied absently, then immediately regretted the unguarded, unconsidered admission. *Damn me for a fool!*

"The town witch—I thought as much. Legendary Deliverers and magical crop destruction. I'm going to have her arrested for questioning."

Panic clutched Gonji. He gripped his knees to stave the trembling. *Choléra—not the keeper of the answers to my quest . . . What can I—?*

He laughed abrasively. "So sorry, Captain, but that would be very stupid!"

Julian blustered, losing composure. "What do you mean by that?"

"I mean that she's their holy woman. They're already worried because their priests haven't shown up as they're supposed to, and she's all they've got for leading their devotions. Arresting her would be the surest way of inciting rebellion. Better let me check out what's going on first before you make any rash moves against city leaders."

Gonji rose to go, hunched over in the cramped quarters. "I'll let you know anything that might shed light on these events."

Julian studied him closely. "All right. I'll be waiting. Oh, samurai—no hard feelings about the castle business, eh? It was intended to enhance your cover, and I think it served its purpose. You should have seen the old guy—the Elder's face—when I cut you there." He pointed to Gonji's ribs, and his meaning was clear: It was a brash warning against crossing him and a reminder of the outcome of their duel. Had he learned no respect at all for Gonji's sword in the encounter? From his self-assured posturing it was clear that he hadn't. All that had mattered to Julian was that he had been victorious.

Gonji grinned maliciously around clenched teeth but bowed curtly in assent. *You'll get yours* . . . But the specter of doubt continued to flutter over the memory.

Suddenly squeezing his thick fist, Klann crushed the brittle thing that had been a ripening apricot. He hurled it at the Llorm dragoon, then at once regained his dignity, clamping his fists at his sides, steeling himself. Someone's breath hissed. The dragoon had flinched, turning his face and shutting his eyes, but with goodly discipline he had maintained parade rest. The king espied the people gathered in his chamber, sorely regretting his loss of temper.

General Gorkin stared at him wide-eyed, his wife at his side, nibbling at her lip. The dragoon resumed the professional soldier's mask, while Captain Sianno regarded the floor's gray tiles. Mord stood behind Sianno, the inscrutable golden mask bobbing smugly, arms folded. Leaning against the bedchamber arch: Thorvald, her eyes twitching expectantly. The buxom Genya's nervous clatter of serving ware punctuated the strained silence.

Klann struggled with reason, impulse, and the chaotic council of the Brethren.

(take measures against them—now)
(caution, brother, have a care)
(investigate—move—but trust only in our judgment)

"It is as I have said, is it not?" Mord advanced. "They'll resist you endlessly under that facade of placid religiosity."

"And so what shall we do, Magician Most Sublime?" Klann grated, all joviality of the banquet night dashed by his confused indignance. "Destroy them all?"

Mord met his liege's sarcasm with practiced equanimity. "Oh, I don't think that's necessary, sire. They need a lesson perhaps, that's all."

"A lesson," the king echoed. He pointed at the crumbled fruit. "What is that? How was it done? You're supposed to keep me one step ahead of such treachery. Is it magick?"

"Hardly, sire." Mord walked over and bent to sift the strange substance. He clucked to himself. "No, not magick precisely but a very clever potion nonetheless. An arcane compound known to few but the rare adepts among us. Hmmm . . . there's a witch who resides in the city. Perhaps she—"

Klann waved an arm. "Stop! We don't want to know! Witches and goblins and demons and monsters—we care only about *people! Our* people. We're full up with sorcery, Mord. What sorcery we've encountered has been either antagonistic to us or inept on our behalf."

Mord bowed his head in a gesture of fealty. "Milord, may I remind you, at the risk of being impertinent—"

"No, don't remind me!" Klann roared, cutting short the magician's basso profundo. "Just—just see what you can do about counteracting this—this—blight. And proceed with your other . . . experiments." But the king cared not to think on the foul business, and so he turned to Sianno. "And that is all you have to tell of these ambushed troops?"

"I fear so, sire," the Llorm garrison commander answered.

"Slaughtered," Klann said, his gaze remote, lost in the timeworn stone of the chamber wall. "And what of your Llorm patrols? Haven't they been stationed so that one is never long out of sight of the others?"

Sianno nodded, his palms upturned in penitent bewilderment.

"Can there be a connection between the crop destruction and the ambush?"

"It *was* in the same area, milord. But I fear there's more here than meets the eye. There's disturbing talk among the populace of . . . things you'd care not to hear about, I think . . ." His voice dwindled to a mutter.

"Sorceries and legends," Klann growled. Sianno only shrugged. "Do you suspect rebellious action? Are the people at large to blame?"

"It's certainly possible."

Klann ground out a Kunan curse and pounded his fists on the marble-topped table, startling the servant girl as she laid out his meal.

"We want *peace* with these people—don't they understand? We're tired of conflict. We can ill afford it. One winter's respite from fighting—is that so much to ask? We'll have peace here," he said with grim resolution, "if we have to crush a few skulls to secure it! What do these people want of us? We feast their leaders, and then they claw at our backs like this."

"They're full of deceit, sire," Mord observed.

"Find out what you can," Klann said, sighing, restoring his composure again. "Bring me news. Threaten them. Cajole them. Coddle them—do whatever works! Tell them if they plan to starve us out, *their* children will shrivel before ours. We'll brook no defiance. Tell them that. Shore up the city garrison, and extend the outreach for mercenaries. Send me the paymaster," he said, turning to Gorkin. "We're going to increase the free companions' wage." Then his vision clouded over, a tale from long ago played out before it, a story of lost Akryllon.

"One more thrust," he mumbled. "Just one more thrust . . ."

"Sire," came Mord's booming voice, slashing through his reverie, "I am in need of more . . . assistants in my work. Shall I . . . procure them?"

Klann saw Sianno's downcast look, and he knew they were sharing the same grim thought. What had become of the other conscripted citizens who were taken for Mord's grisly experiments? But of course he knew. He knew, but his conscious mind refused to dwell on the result of the sorcerer's terrible efforts at separating the Brethren. And there would be an accounting. Oh yes. There would come a time when they would come after their hostages, and then what? And *then* what? For this reason Vedun's outrages must be borne stoically; tolerance must be stretched to its limits.

And the voices of the Brethren came to him again from within, crying out against this fatalistic madness, for once in unison in their pleas. *No, no, my Brethren, you must understand. It must be done. If you could know emergence, if you could breathe the air for yourselves, fill your lungs with life, you would yearn for separation as I do . . .*

"Yes, take them," he said in a tremulous voice, "take only as many as you need, and call them hostages. Tell them . . . tell them restoration will be made when we've learned we can trust them." And these last words burst forth in a fast jumble as if muddling through them could make it all true.

And then the vivacious servant girl was speaking soothingly to him in German, and Gorkin's wife and Thorvald were moving forward to hush her.

Genya could understand nothing of the Kunan tongue. She knew only that King Klann was perturbed by the news brought first by Sianno, then by the Llorm rider. She puzzled at the significance of the crumbling substance Klann had hurled at his cavalryman. And she knew that there was something wrong in Vedun.

She had to know what.

"Milord king, your meal grows tepid," she said in the charged air of the receiving chamber, "and the wine will help sooth your ill humor. It's a very fine vintage—"

"Hush, girl!" Thorvald commanded.

"Hold your tongue, scullion!" Lady Gorkin added.

Klann held up a halting hand, and the pair drew back. Genya saw a curious look in his eyes that vaguely alarmed her. There was a sardonic quality in his voice; alien, as if it were the voice of another.

"Do you know what's happening, little minx? Your countrymen are undermining our desires. You know them better than anyone in this room. Tell us why they struggle against us."

"It's not like them to fight, sire," she replied with affected ingenuousness, eager to pacify him now that she had the floor. "But what is it they're supposed to have done?" Klann didn't reply, and she grew uneasy to see the suspicion and cynicism creeping into his stare. "Perhaps if you sent me to the city I might . . . speak with them . . ."

But she knew the words were all wrong. She shrank before his cold gaze. Her abruptness and self-concern had shaken his trust.

"Leave us now," he said curtly.

She scurried out with an awkward curtsy, feeling the angry stares of the women boring into her back, a chill coursing through her when she passed the masked magician, imagining herself a child again, skirting the terrifying black pit of her father's open cellar.

Mord experienced a mixed exhilaration and anxiety.

The unexpected ambush of the mercenary patrol he had sent to scout the deadly fog was a boon he hadn't counted on. The apparent insurgent violence had had predictable effect on Klann, and it should have motivated him to a reprisal that would in turn have escalated the city's desperation. Yet he stubbornly refused to squeeze his grip on these blasted crossworshipers. He was determined to preserve peace at all costs.

I should have destroyed *all* the crops, he thought. No-no, that would too surely indicate earth magick. Patience. All in good time. Don't arouse his suspicions. Just keep placating him with these spells of division. The fool—if I use enough of these people as subjects I'll eventually have my way whatever he does! But that's not enough. Remember the compact with the League: this must be mutually destructive, an internecine clash. Such a fascinating game! And all to the glory of the League and the Dark Master . . .

He smiled beneath his mask, but then he remembered and his mirth was short-lived: The *presence*. That aura that had left its trace with the butchered patrol. The same being the mysterious key suggested but could not declare.

Chapter Eleven

Hell, Gonji thought as he rode, swatting at the flies that buzzed madly in the humidity.

Why didn't I just tell him I killed them in self-defense? Why did I bother perpetrating that stupid lie about finding them dead? Julian knows it's a lie. *Now* what? *Ride out, Gonji-san. Leave this place. You're finished here.* You're going to die here in some stupid, ignoble way, that's what. You're on Julian's death list for certain. An assassin's bullet in the back, or—worse, maybe.

He scanned the lowering sky. Thunderheads now piled up over the Carpathians, smothering the sun. The day waxed threatening. *Ride out while you still—*

Wilf galloped toward him along the Street of Charity, pedestrians parting before his charge. He reined in beside Tora.

"You heard about Strom, what he found?" Wilf asked breathlessly.

"*Hai,* the little rodent," Gonji spat. "So sorry, Wilfred-san, but your brother's chatter has me in big trouble."

"What do you mean?"

Gonji waved the question aside. "Ah, forget it. It may not even have been him. Enough people know. The dead brigands in the valley have returned to haunt me."

"What will you do?"

Gonji blew out an exasperated breath and shook his head gravely. "Where does Tralayn live again?"

Wilf brightened. "Then you're staying!"

"Well, we'll see what the city has in mind anyway, *neh?*" He smiled. "You're in better spirits now than you were earlier."

"Look." Wilf reached inside his tunic and produced the now repaired ceremonial sword which Julian had broken. He grinned broadly.

Gonji accepted it, drew it and examined the work. "Oh, very fine, Wilf! Very good work indeed. I am forever in your good father's debt." He resheathed it and stuffed it into the pouch that housed it.

"Still can't say anything about that secret business at my house last night?" Wilf asked, removing his cap and mopping his beaded brow.

"Eh? Oh—*iyé*, I'm not at liberty, I'm afraid. Anyway, you'd be surprised how little there is to tell, thanks to that devious Tralayn. Your father is full of secrets, though, *neh?*"

"Almost like a stranger to me these days," Wilf agreed.

Gonji patted Tora's withers. "Come on."

"Where to?"

"Your place first. Is Strom there now?"

"He was."

"I want to talk with him. Then out to the fields and orchards to check on this withered crop business."

"Wha-a-at?"

"Never mind now. Let's go." He spurred Tora toward the southwest sector, and Wilf fell in behind. They cantered toward the Gundersens', taking notice of the anxious mutterings passing in relay among the citizenry.

Gonji's expression clouded, and he halted them when he saw the fiercely appointed band approaching them head-on down the Street of Charity.

They yielded right-of-way at their end of the

timbered culvert crossing. The scowling party of ten, weapons bristling from saddles, backs, and belts like whiskered outgrowths, arranged themselves in a double column to negotiate the narrow passage. The timbers creaked and groaned under their clanking, clumping mass: Austrian brigands, by the look of them, and new to Vedun.

They slowed when they passed Gonji and Wilf, eyeing them cautiously and barking gruff greetings. Then, taking them for mercenaries of Klann, their leader inquired after the headquarters. Gonji pointed the way, and they rumbled off, surly laughter and banter left in their wake.

Then Wilf sucked in a breath. One of the last pair cradled on his shoulder what had appeared at first to be a polearm. It was now clearly revealed as an enormous claymore. The Scottish highlander sat stiffly in the saddle, supporting the heft of his great six-foot broadsword, whose point lay deep in a stirrup-like cup that took most of the weight.

"I'd hate to get smashed by that thing," Wilf judged.

"Mmmm." Gonji followed their departure for a moment and then moved off across the culvert.

There seemed a great deal more mercenary activity in the smith shop's sector when they arrived. Gonji observed the bandits' purposeful comings and goings with a calculating eye while Wilf went inside the shop. Garth struggled in the corral with a skittish gray gelding that needed a shoeing. The animals were unaccountably nervous, their temper affecting even Tora when Gonji brought him near.

"Strom's gone," Wilf noted, returning to the corral. "What is it you were saying about the crops?"

"Later. Garth—" Gonji called. "Why all the mercenary activity hereabouts?"

Garth calmed the anxious steed and bridled him. "A new garrison," he shouted. "They've converted the granary back there to a second garrison for free companions."

Gonji looked back toward the southern portion of the bailey wall, where the silo's sloped peak towered.

"Wonderful," he breathed.

He turned back toward the corral just as Wilf grabbed his arm. An electric numbness paralyzed them both. Out of the lead-lined sky swooped the wyvern, long neck undulating as it shrieked its threat, great leathery wings rowing through the air currents.

"Choléra!"

They stared, unmoving as it swept over the quadrant and tilted sharply eastward. The horses kicked and bolted, Garth launching himself for the corral rail, rolling over in an ungainly, muscular leap to avert the lashing hooves.

"Are you all right?"

"*Ja, ja,*" the big smith assured, dusting himself off. He glanced at the sky and then returned to the corral with affected nonchalance. "Funny how quickly one gets accustomed," he added with a shrug as he slowly climbed back into the pen, where the horses still surged and bumped haunches and necks, eyes crazed and nostrils flaring. He collected the gelding and hurried him out the gate.

"You'll forgive me, my friend," Gonji said as he led the animal past, "but I think it's unhealthy to become too comfortable with wyverns in one's skies."

They followed Garth to the forge.

"Where's Strom?" Wilf queried.

"Gone to the pasture. Where else?" Garth replied.

Gonji thanked Garth for the restoration of his mother's gift sword, all the while preoccupied with the wyvern's arcing flight, one eye peeled skyward, his breath coming in short gasps. He felt a frustrated need to lash out, a tightening sensation in his chest and throat.

"What the hell to do?" he said aloud. He could feel Wilf absorbing his tension beside him, clenching his fists.

The flying dragon soared overhead again, and Garth leapt back from the bucking gelding, talking to it soothingly, ignoring the beast above.

"Gonji's staying to fight," Wilf observed, antagonism in his tone.

"Indeed?" came Garth's calm reply. He resumed his work, his file scraping at the gelding's hoof.

Wilf's mention of him snapped Gonji's bonds of indecisiveness.

"What did Strom say about these murdered men he found?"

"Nothing much," Garth said. "He found them and then did the right thing—told someone in authority. They questioned him and let him go."

"What about this crop destruction? Have you heard?"

"Only something about a crop failure—that's all."

Three mercenaries clattered past, heading for the new garrison. Now there were people rushing by on foot and horseback, relaying news in whispers along the street.

"Something's afoot," Gonji said, lips pursed.

"Yuschak," Wilf called out, walking out to engage an excited rider. "What's going on?"

The rider bounded up. "The farmers—they're questioning the farmers. They've hanged Gornick!"

"Hanged—?"

"The Ministry—Flavio!" Gonji whispered. He fixed the wyvern's position; it hovered somewhere over the square now.

"Dammit, I've got to do something, but I hope it doesn't start now—Wilf! Get me those new pieces of armor."

Wilf ran into the house. Garth knelt beside the forge, something on his mind.

"What will you do, smith? The devils *will* force your hand," Gonji probed gravely.

"I don't know. I only know that I cannot raise a sword against Klann."

But his voice lacked conviction, and it contained something else, a wistful sadness that made him seem like a man helplessly imprisoned.

Wilf bounded up to them from the house with Gonji's equipment over a shoulder as he struggled with the couplings of his own sword belt and baldric. Garth's eyes narrowed to see the broadsword that dangled from his son's belt, a short blade with a hand-carved hilt—the sword Garth had presented him on his twelfth birthday.

"Wilfred—?" Garth questioned warily.

"I'm going with Gonji, Papa," Wilf said with a determination that defied challenge.

"Think, Wilf," Gonji urged in a measured tone, donning his armament. "We can't know what might happen this day."

"I'm going, and that's that. I want to be part of this, whatever happens."

"Go then, Wilfred," Garth said icily. "Follow your wayward spirit to your grave, but . . . expect no tears from me."

But he had turned and lumbered off with the last few words, and it seemed to Gonji that his voice had trembled with the very tears he had forsworn, and in that brief instant the samurai recalled similar words spoken by a mighty *daimyo* to his recalcitrant half-breed son.

The wyvern shrilled in the distance and completed its spiraling descent, alighting on a rooftop of sight of their vantage.

Gonji drew a long breath. "You do what I say today. Nothing more, nothing less. *Wakarimasu*—understand?"

"*Ja,*" Wilf agreed in a breathy whisper.

"Let's go, then."

They mounted and spurred off toward the Ministry, toward the area where the fulsome flying monster had appeared to land.

"*Jesu Christi,* Hawk—*look.*"

But Peter Foristek's shout was drowned by the screaming of the crowd before the Ministry, and Vlad Dobroczy didn't need to see his friend's pointing arm. All heads were upturned as the wyvern spiraled down lazily to settle atop the Ministry building's peak. It squalled at the restive throng, its long black tongue protruding from the razor-sharp beak. Its cavernous mouth was slick and moist, blackened by a tarry substance.

Many people now bolted from the square. Some who sat in windows of nearby buildings to witness the questioning of the farmers scrambled inside for cover. A squad of renegade German Landsknechts, now mounted although still bedecked in the Almain rivet armor of light infantry, pressed the farmers into a tight knot lest any break for the alleys.

"*Ja*, our dragon friend is hungry!" shouted Ivar, Julian's lieutenant, from his perch aboard a gray mare. He spanked his horse's haunches with the flat of his blade and lurched away from the cavalry line, at the center of which sat the proud Captain Kel'Tekeli. Two mercenaries with drawn pistols followed in his wake. Ivar looked confidently armored in a waistcoat cuirass and tassets. He yanked in the reins before the huddled farmers, jangling to a halt. The open buffe of his Flemish burgonet helm squeaked as it swung on its hinges. "Who would like to be fodder for the dragon, eh?"

Mutters and grumblings. The crowd across the street pushed in closer, led by the craft guildsmen.

"Why don't you leave those farmers alone!" Phlegor yelled from their center. Several axes, an adz, a staff here and there shifted on twitching shoulders in their midst.

"Now who's looking for trouble?" Ivar growled. "Who wants to take that tough peasant's place?" He indicated the swinging man across the square.

The farmer named Gornick, while not precisely hanged as the hysterical Yuschak had told Wilf Gundersen, had indeed been hoisted on high. He swung from a cucking stool lashed to the gibbet where late had been displayed the corpses of the two bandits shot by Klann's troops. Gornick had flung one of the ruined fruit samples at an interrogating soldier and had been tied to the cucking stool and beaten with staffs by guffawing troops. Bleeding from many superficial wounds, his eye puffed shut, Gornick dangled limply now, as the soldiers had tired of taking whacks at their impromptu practice dummy. Beside Gornick, muzzled and hanged by its neck, twitched a Great Dane, which had bitten a Landsknecht who had cuffed its master. The dog had ceased to emit the *kuh-kuh-kuh* sound from its dead throat now. Its legs kicked reflexively, spastically in death as Gornick's stool glanced off its carcass.

Curses and insults sprang up in the heat and dust. The soldiers glanced about them circumspectly, swords in moist fists. They were greatly outnumbered.

"Farmers! You needn't submit to this unlawful interrogation! Resist them!"

It was Paille, calling from somewhere on high. The bell tower! The madman leaned from the arch where hung the massive bells. Vlad Dobroczy felt a crazy laugh rise up from his chest to see the artist's acrobatic raillery.

"Get that idiot down from there," Julian commanded from the cavalry line, still maintaining his distance from the scuffling throng.

"You — Paille!" a soldier cried. "Get down here!"

"Come for me, knave!" Paille roared, pulling his dagger from his belt. There was laughter in the ranks. Julian pursed his lips and shook his head. And gestured to his archers.

Two shafts twanged forth and hissed toward the snarling poet, only to crash uselessly against the granite facade of the tower. A second later Paille emerged from behind the arch to thumb his nose and stick out his tongue.

Julian sighed petulantly. "Get him. Go up and get him," he said in a low voice. "And try not to make a farce of this. Lunatic's making you look like . . ." His voice trailed off as he watched two soldiers enter the tower at the ground floor doorway. They emerged a moment later.

"He's locked himself into the belfry," a soldier called. Shouts and catcalls wafted over from the gathered citizenry. The Landsknecht squad corraled the farmers against the steps of the Ministry of Government and Finance.

"Ring the bells," Julian said simply.

The two mercenaries looked at each other with bright faces, the thought appealing to them. They dashed into the tower again. A moment later the great alarm tocsin clanged with pendulous fury as if all the legions of Hades had descended on the city.

Seconds later Paille emerged into the arch high

above the Street of Hope, miming, with an eye-popping facial set, the tintinnabulous action of the bells. Then his forefingers came up to his ears and he indicated, with a jerky, mechanical motion, the waxed cotton strips he had stuffed into them beforehand.

Jeering laughter and bravado now seized the crowd, and Vlad could sense the turn. For the moment all the soldiers' weaponry and the monstrous winged dragon were all but forgotten. Then the wyvern lofted up from its perch with a bawling cry and flapped across to the bell tower, and Paille dove out of sight.

"What do we do, Hawk?" Foristek asked Vlad, shifting his scythe to the other shoulder.

Dobroczy regarded the huge man, saw the other farmers also awaiting his answer, and he realized in that moment that, despite his youth, his strength and aggressiveness had made him their leader.

He squeezed the long shaft of the pruning hook he carried. Gritted his teeth and called out to Ivar: "We don't know anything about this God-cursed crop plague. Why don't you leave us alone before you make one too many mistakes?"

Ivar swung his steed to face him, and the Landsknecht renegade nearest him walked his horse into the crowd to approach Vlad, his enormous broadsword resting on his shoulder as he watched the farmers part reluctantly before the horse's hooves.

Vlad gripped the pruning hook hard, and in that instant came the remembrance that he'd never killed a man before. And yet . . . he was certain that he could. Quite certain.

"All right, liver lips—come forward," Ivar said with an evil grin, waving suggestively. "Let's see how you sound from the stool—"

There came shouts from across the street. A pole-axebearing footman who had turned his back on the craftsmen took a shot to the back of the head that knocked off his lobster-tailed helmet. He fell to the ground, stunned.

Julian sent a mounted squad forward to drag out the attacker. The craftsmen formed a wall, tools held before them passively in an effort at blocking their passage. A pistol fired over their heads caused them to break in fear, but by now the attacker had melted into the crowd. The wyvern cried out and launched skyward, its battle shriek evoking peals of alarm from the crowd, erupting gooseflesh. It circled overhead, awaiting an isolated enemy it might strafe on Julian's command.

And in that mad instant, when the Landsknecht trooper turned away to eye the pursuit, Vlad Dobroczy lashed out with the pruning hook, jabbing the soldier hard in the skullcap and throwing him from the saddle.

But then he saw the look in Ivar's eyes, watched the high sweeping arc of the broadsword in the gloved fist, felt his heart racing, his breath catching, his feet turning to stone. *Oh no, they wouldn't kill me—they couldn't kill me—*

The sword slashed downward, but Peter Foristek's scythe caught the blow and turned it aside. The gray mare was struck by the recoil, and she lurched back on her hind legs. Vlad stumbled backward, and then there were rough hands on him, punching him in the back and head, twisting his arm. He could hear—feel—scuffling and fistfights breaking out all around him. And then he was dragged, kicked, pushed into the square. Slammed down at the base of the Ministry steps, he heard hoofbeats approach. He looked up apprehensively into the face of that sonofabitch Wilf Gundersen. Beside him rode his slant-eyed barbarian crony.

"So now what, Gundersen, you sore on a dog's ass?" Vlad heard himself cry out in the choking dust. "You and your friend riding with these bastards?"

But there was no one kicking him, or pushing him, or dragging him now.

Wilf and Gonji galloped through the tortuous walled alleys and back lanes toward Vedun's northern quarter, twisting and turning their mounts seemingly with every other stride. The ashlar and sandstone canyons, as familiar to Wilf as his own bedchamber, still yielded a new surprise at each dizzying corner, now, at the height of daily life. Children screamed and darted out of their way; startled dogs barked and yapped at their horses' hooves; men and women backed into doorways and cul-de-sacs, cursing in their wake, shaking fists. The alarm bell at the square began to sound.

Gonji yanked Tora hard left as they neared the market square. Wilf followed, guiding his steed surely and smoothly. But he saw the hanging laundry too late—

The samurai had ducked quickly enough to clear the clothesline, but Wilf had caught it full on the chest, snapping it, shock and discomfiture reddening his face as he slowed to tear away the nightshirts and undergarments that streamed from both him and his white stallion. He shook free the last of it, then snarled and launched after Gonji, catching up with him at the juncture with the Street of Hope.

Gonji slowed them to a trot as they neared the mad scene, urging Wilf with body language to assume a more dignified, less desperate posture. They clumped up to the Ministry as a band of footsoldiers struggled with a group of farmers. Wilf could make out the huge Foristek, brandishing his ever-present scythe defensively. Across the street mounted troops scuffled with another unruly crowd.

Shouts and screams, twisting bodies and lurching mounts in the eddying dust. Anatoly Gornick swung from a stool tied to the gibbet, Leo D'Amato's dead Dane hanging beside him. People leaned from windows for a better view.

Above their heads, the flapping, sailing monster bird, angling its red-eyed nightmare head for a strike.

Wilf sucked in a breath and slowed, allowing Gonji to pass him by half a length. He was suddenly aware of how small and vulnerable he was as his cold, sweaty palm gripped the broadsword's hilt. The soldiers in the square numbered about five and thirty. He had no idea what he would do next, what he was capable of doing. Gonji looked confident in his new armament, but Wilf saw the tremulous flicker in the samurai's dark eyes when he craned up at the wyvern.

And then he saw Dobroczy spilled onto the ground before him. His rival rose, railing at him with confusing fury. But the soldiers who had collared him now backed off uneasily, looking from Wilf to Gonji.

"What about Petrovna's woman?" someone was shouting from the midst of the tumult. "Who'll answer for her?"

Wilf eyed his fuming, hook-nosed rival narrowly. "What the hell are you babbling about, Hawk?"

"Whaddaya think I'm talking about?" Dobroczy growled, now realizing his mistake, the words spoken in frenzied anger. His nose and mouth were bleeding. He dusted himself off as he regained his feet. The knuckles of his right hand were raw and bloody; he drew them across his mouth in a dirty red swipe.

"What do you want with this man?" Wilf heard himself demanding.

None of the mercenaries spoke for a space. Two of

them held back the fallen Landsknecht, who brandished his broadsword dazedly, muttering imprecations at Vlad. A mercenary in brigandines clutched a sky-pointed pistol next to his ear threateningly. Most of them watched Gonji, who sat impassively astride Tora and said not a word. A cold harbinger of quick death. By now everyone had heard the breathless tales of the deadly spell those swords could weave; those strange gently curved blades whose hilts now jutted from his back like twin devil horns.

"He struck down a soldier," one of the men replied at length, indicating the angry Landsknecht.

Upon being addressed as an equal, one to be reckoned with, Wilf inhaled a prideful breath, his chest swelling, the fingers of his left hand massaging the sword hilt. But a sage voice within duly recognized that his new-found respectability was based on the company he kept.

"It seems to me he's been repaid," he spoke evenly.

Dobroczy cast anxious eyes about the grounds and, noting the decreased interest in him, began to ease back into the knot of cordoned farmers.

Wilf continued to sit aboard the white destrier, awaiting a reply, wishing for Gonji to do something to relieve him as the focus of the soldiers' attention. Suppose he was challenged now—then what? Still the wyvern wafted overhead, describing its terrifying circles, primed for the order by which it would rain down its foul brand of death.

Behind him, Gonji dismounted. Wilf looked back to see Captain Kel'Tekeli canter halfway across the street to them. He saw the mingled hatred and curiosity in Julian's eyes when his gaze met Gonji's. But the captain remained silent, watching as the samurai began climbing the Ministry steps to the open doorway that was now guarded by sentries bearing polearms.

There came a clattering of hoofbeats through the postern gate: Captain Sianno, heading up a double column of four and twenty Llorm dragoons.

Wilf joined Gonji on the Ministry steps, both turning to watch as Sianno and Julian engaged in a curt dialogue that could not be heard but was clearly less than friendly. The Llorm garrison commander gestured to two of his men, who dismounted and cut down Gornick from the cucking stool.

Gonji looked sidelong at Wilf, and the young smith knew that his own face must mirror Gonji's befuddlement over the occupation force's inconsistency and disorganization. Both good and bad, he had heard Gonji say.

Then they were mounting the Ministry steps.

"No entry without permission," grated a scowling German sentry.

Gonji stopped and stared icily. "I'm the Elder's bodyguard. I've come to check on his well-being."

"You heard him," the second sentry added.

Gonji took another step, and the guards crossed their pole-axes before him. The samurai took a deadly step backward, and Wilf held his breath, certain that both guards would be dead in a second. And then—?

"Master Flavio," Gonji called.

The murmur of voices within was choked off.

"Gonji?" came Flavio's reply.

"Are you well, Flavio-san? Have they harmed you in any way?"

"No-no, I'm quite all right, quite all right. Please—no trouble, I pray you."

"I'm coming in to see you for myself."

The sentries tensed. The man who had spoken first, a tall, beefy Aryan in corselet and comb-cap snarled and tilted his head sideways in threat. Gonji stood stock still a moment, looking from one to the other.

Then a clattering of hooves sounded below. The sentries relaxed to see the garrison commander assume responsibility.

"Let them pass," Captain Sianno said.

Wilf returned the stocky captain's thin smile, recalling the man's dignity and courtesy when he had come to search the smith shop, a more meaningful gesture now in view of the comradeship Wilf's father and Sianno once shared under Klann.

Gonji bowed to Sianno and entered the Ministry, Wilf following close behind, encouraged now by the comforting presence of Sianno. He emulated Gonji's swaggering mien.

In the Ministry were Flavio and Lorenz, plus several minor officials employed by the city government. A tall, gaunt Akryllonian national with dark hair and the lancing stare of a tax collector stood over Flavio, who was seated at his desk in the antechamber at the rear of the hall. The official, a counselor of Klann, swung around to regard them haughtily when they entered. Three mercenaries, clamping hands on sword hilts and pistols warily, closed in on them. Lorenz pushed himself up from the business counter.

"Wilfred?" Lorenz said, puzzled.

Wilf nodded at his brother.

"The business office is closed for the nonce—*gentils*," the counselor noted with undisguised contempt as he moved from the antechamber.

"Gonji—Wilfred—we're fine here," Flavio called over, rising. "Nothing to be alarmed about."

Gonji appraised the counselor's black-and-silver brocade doublet and feathered chapeau with disdain.

"So sorry—not to me, it isn't," he advised coldly.

"You're the fencing fellow from the banquet, eh?" the counselor remarked. "The acrobatic oriental."

Gonji ignored him. "What are they doing in here, Master Flavio?"

The three guards pressed closer as Gonji took two steps that brought him to the counter. They anxiously regarded the swords at Gonji's back and, Wilf noted with satisfaction, the young smith's broadsword.

"They're questioning us. And the farmers," Lorenz replied quietly. "Have you heard about the curious crop failure?"

"Something," Gonji said, looking past the Executor of the Exchequer to study the crestfallen Elder.

"And we have other difficulties," Flavio said.

Wilf turned at the new uproar in the streets. Two riders stormed up to the steps, citizens. One of them was Aldo Monetto, the loquacious biller, who was shouting something at the crowd.

"What do you mean, Flavio-san?" Gonji probed.

Lorenz answered for him. "A woman has been assaulted, in the early morning hours."

The wyvern shrilled low over the street without. Wilf gasped in spite of himself to see its baleful shade cast gloom over the menacing crowd. Screams and curses rolled through the doorway.

"Master Flavio! Master Flavio!" Monetto was pushing his way up the steps, held back by the sentries. "They're trying to arrest the prophetess!"

Wilf gulped and looked to Flavio, to his brother Lorenz. "The prophetess," he whispered. He saw Gonji spin on his heel and stiffen an instant, eyes flaring, control lost for the first time during the entire incident. And he wondered fleetingly why Tralayn should be of concern to Gonji.

The samurai stalked to the doorway. "Monetto! What did you say?" The biller struggled in the grasp of the sentries.

"Gonji! It's Tralayn—they're trying to take her—there's fighting at her house. Two men are dead already!"

"Who ordered her arrest?" Gonji demanded of the king's official.

"I did," he replied superciliously. "She's to be questioned like the farmers. In some ways the local witch woman is more suspect than they are." He pulled from a vest pocket a bulbous Nuremberg egg watch. "I'm wasting time here, I fear. I can finish with her at the castle. Remember, Flavio, no soldier of Klann, no Akryllonian national will ever know hunger because of the city's treachery. Not until every man, woman, and child of Vedun has starved to death first."

"As I have said," Flavio replied with evident strain, "the granaries and warehouses are full."

The official nodded brusquely and pushed past Gonji out onto the veranda, calling for Julian. The three guards trailed after him.

"Choléra," Gonji swore under his breath. "Wilfred-san—stay here with Flavio."

"Gonji, where are you—I want to go along." Wilf trembled, heart hammering, but he craved an outlet for his anxiety and frustration.

"Stay," Gonji commanded. Then his harshness became tempered with compassionate understanding. "You'll have your time in battle, sword-brother, make no mistake. But for now do this for me, *neh*? It's no mean charge I give you. If you fail to protect my employer, it is *I* who must forfeit my life."

Wilf swallowed and nodded, not fully convinced. They exchanged a bow, and Gonji clamped Wilf's right hand with his own—a rare gesture for him. Wilf followed him halfway down the steps to where the king's counselor spoke with the stern Captain Kel'Tekeli. He saw Gonji glare at the captain hotly before bounding aboard Tora to pound away from the square.

Seconds later Julian remounted and, calling over two other soldiers, clumped off with them in Gonji's wake. He felt a thrill of alarm, realizing Gonji's grave peril both before and behind. What would he do—what would the city do—if Gonji were to die now? He shook off the thought.

Without him they would do nothing. They would submit to the invaders' every whim.

Or would they?

"All right, Captain Sianno," the king's official ordered, "get the magician his . . . assistants."

The bells began to clang discordantly. The wyvern roosted atop the tower, shaking its head inside the belfry and battering them. The creature croaked out a jubilant cry that was chilling in its almost human anticipation. And even from this distance Wilf could see that its red eyes were no longer red.

Now they were diamond-black and shining with cruel promise.

Captain Sianno raised his arm in a reluctant direction to the troops. And madness reigned in the square.

Needled by the galvanic urgency of Tralayn's peril, Gonji pounded a zig-zag path through Vedun's carven alleys, retracing his recent route with abandon, if not with surety. He clung close to Tora's withers as they wove through the impromptu equestrian maze, the samurai trusting to his Spanish stallion's patient training as he shouted warnings ahead of him to playing children and curious adults.

Tora stumbled once on loose paving stones but righted himself adroitly just as Gonji heard the first pistol shots and the wyvern's strident war cry. He reined in sharply near the wagonage and patted the shuddering horse reassuringly. Looking back toward the square he saw the flying beast's vicious helldive, made out the jet of saliva it spewed earthward, heard the uproar beneath its strafing arc.

"Spirits of my fathers," he breathed, visions of the monastery outrage dancing in his head.

An unseen rider stormed through an adjacent street. "The dragon's attacking! Get to your homes!"

Gooseflesh broke out on Gonji's arms and neck. The scruples of *giri*—the sense of duty—beckoned him to return to the square. Flavio might be in danger, as well as young Wilfred. And he had an account to settle with the blasted horror that claimed Vedun's skies. But *ninjo*—the warrior's moral impulse, his natural conscience, whose frequent conflict with *giri* was a well-known source of woe to the samurai—assailed him with thoughts of the rightness of his quest, of the need to remain on his fated path in the solution of the Deathwind mystery. His karma was to seek the Deathwind; Tralayn might well hold the knowledge he needed.

Decide.

But he already had. Spurring Tora onward with a snarl, he galloped off toward the Gundersens' livery and smith shop, cursing his cheerless thoughts.

He spotted Garth at the corral and stamped up to him, dropping to a canter. Tora snorted and curvetted, now assimilating Gonji's tension and spoiling for action.

"Garth! Where is Tralayn's house?"

"Gonji!" the smith replied with a terrified grimace. "What of Wilfred and Lorenz?"

Gonji waved it aside impatiently. "At the Ministry—they're *all recht. Tralayn's*, Garth!"

"Straight down that lane, all the way to the walls," he called, pointing, as Gonji spurred off at a gallop. "It's the tumble-down place with sagging eaves—a bolt shot from the foundry—"

"Danke," Gonji yelled into the wind, leaning hard into the lane.

His heart pounded and sweat stung his eyes and healing wounds as he approached the broad southern lane that abutted the bailey wall. He swung Tora to the right, and immediately the mob scene at Tralayn's dwelling came into view. A small band of mounted mercenaries were held back from the house by twenty or thirty grim-faced citizens. Among the latter were Roric Amsgard, in bloodied apron, a meat cleaver at his side; and Karl Gerhard, his hunting bow nocked with a clothyard shaft.

Three men lay on the ground, at least one of them a Klann hireling. There was no sign of the prophetess.

Gonji reduced Tora's gait to a trot and set his face into a mask of self-assurance while his mind examined and discarded one course of action after another. He drew near the battle line, marked by the dead or injured, heads turning at his approach. Someone called out his name among the townsfolk. He restrained the impulse to draw the Sagami; no cause for that yet. The citizens seemed encouraged by his appearance. The small detachment of free companions shrank back a bit in implied warning, blades and pistols held at the ready.

The samurai rode up close, gingerly stepped Tora over the bodies of the dead—two citizens and a side-skewered soldier.

"What's going on here?" Gonji growled in Spanish, displaying the swaggering confidence of a personally involved high official.

"The prophetess—"

"These pox-ridden scum want to arrest her—"

"They shot Gyorgy and—"

Gonji waved them to silence. "Roric?" Gonji called to the provisioner, who moved forward to speak, but the mercenary leader spoke first:

"We have no quarrel with you, barbarian. We're here by order to escort the witch woman to the Ministry. And now we've got rebels to arrest as well!" He clopped ahead and pointed his saber at Roric, and the townsmen roared at him in defiance.

"You'll take no one, *scoundrel!*"

The mob pushed forward. Gerhard half drew his longbow and pointed his shaft at the leader.

"Stop this now—all of you!" Gonji commanded, calming the outburst. He picked over his thoughts, trying to choose the right words by which he might sort out the deadly situation. Still the prophetess had not appeared outside the house. But more citizens were gathering in the street, hefting staffs, clubs, and axes, threatening an escalation of violence. Now was not the time.

In the northern distance: the wyvern, shrilling and diving down at the square.

Choléra, it's all happening so fast, and so disorganized . . .

Then there was a clattering of hoofbeats along a nearby alley. Shouts of alarm, as people spilled to the sides of the lane before the charge of Julian and his cohorts. The captain brought them to a halt. To his rear rode the recent arrival whom Gonji had nicknamed "The Armorer": the sullen-eyed bandit aboard the armored black Turkish gelding who bore enough military hardware to open a battlefield stall. Blades at his waist and back, pistol half-hammered and aimed overhead, arquebus lashed to a weathered saddle, the mustached warrior sneered at Gonji under a sallet festooned with throwing daggers.

Four pistols now in evidence. Damn the devisers of these blasted firearms!

Julian walked his steed to the leader of the arresting

party and obtained the clipped and biased account of the resistance incident. And although his situation was precarious, Gonji knew that he must attempt to prevent the arrest of Tralayn by whatever means necessary.

"Well-met, good captain," Gonji said, smiling blandly when the mercenary had finished his account. "If you will pardon me, I believe you are just in time to—"

But Julian ignored him and clopped past to face the mob. "Who killed the free companion here? Step forward."

No one responded. The commander of free companions rose up tall in the stirrups and scanned them.

"You there!" he called to Gerhard. "What are you doing with a bow?"

He had spoken in Hungarian, and someone muttered a German translation.

"I've drawn my bow legally this day from your armory. For the hunt. The captain may check, if he wishes." The hunter and fletcher looked around him at his countrymen, and if he had been fearful before he was past fear now, Gonji noted. "But I'll use it here if our holy woman is threatened—" His final words were drowned out by the assents of the angry mob that shouldered together and raised their motley weapons in agreement.

Julian clenched his teeth and looked them over sullenly.

Gonji ambled over beside the captain, their eyes meeting levelly. Both their horses snorted in the prickling air. "The captain will do well to recall that this woman is sacred to them."

"*I* didn't generate the order," Julian spat defensively, and Gonji was emboldened to witness the captain's crumbling purposefulness.

"They'll not surrender her, I think, without much bloodshed. And the king would appear anxious to preserve the peace. Their dead currently outnumber yours," the samurai continued gently. "Perhaps . . ." He let the suggestion fill itself in.

Julian steeled himself against an angry tremor that afforded Gonji some small sadistic pleasure out of its rarity. He wheeled back to the arresting party.

"Pick up the dead man. Disperse them," he told the squad leader.

"And the witch?"

Julian eyed Gonji, his lip curling. "Leave her for now."

"But the adviser's order—?" The soldier's eyebrows arched in surprise.

"I'll take it on my responsibility," Julian snapped. "I'll answer to His Majesty. Get it done and report back to me."

And Julian rode off for the square with his party. Gonji watched him go, stifling his satisfaction, breathing a long sigh of relief. There were screams wafting up from the square. He cursed softly at their portent and shuffled Tora but decided to see Tralayn first.

When he dismounted, it was to much back-slapping and expressions of gratitude, which he growled at and waved off. But they saw through the facade, recognizing the shared sense of triumph and lavished their praise and thanks.

Gonji and Roric mounted the steps and knocked at Tralayn's door while several men turned to the grim task of removing the dead and apprising their families.

"This will get worse," Gonji said tellingly, indicating the two dead men. He studied Roric closely for a reaction.

The homely provisioner, an ex-cavalryman in

Austria, nodded gravely. "And we shall be ready," he replied.

Gonji caught the sincerity and determination in Roric's words, judged that they were backed by the same courage implicit in the saber scar that marred the man's face.

"This was a fine display of teeth and claws today. But your people will need a lot of bravery and solidarity to weather what may come. Not to mention training . . . planning . . . organization . . ." Gonji rubbed his stubbled jaw thoughtfully, then he hammered at Tralayn's door again. "How do you know she's in?"

Roric looked puzzled. "She entered just before this started. Told us not to worry about her."

Gonji scanned the milling, buzzing crowd again, saw the exhilaration in their quick gestures and sharp whispers that even their morbid task couldn't dampen. They bore away the bodies of the two dead citizens with grace and dignity. Julian entered his thinking again. It occurred to him that the captain always sent subordinates out to do the dirty work, ever careful to sidestep a fray. He had never seen Julian less than spotless except at the castle touch-duel, where he had evidently expected to win with ease and had displayed considerable loss of composure when victory had proven hard won. *I wonder how the dashing captain's courage holds up on the field? How does he comport himself under fire and sword? Common engagement too plebeian for him? Mmm. And Klann . . . Another mad outbreak of violence, apparently at his order. Seemed like a jolly enough sort who wouldn't be given to this kind of terrorism. Kami, but he's an unpredictable bastard. Can Garth's strange tale of enchanted linking be true? Does he obey the caprice of several minds? Choléra, the flying beast again . . . the square.*

207

His thoughts dissipated like smoke. Roric had pushed open Tralayn's creaking door: the house was empty. The butcher called her name. No response. They entered. Her parlor felt warmed as if by recent habitation but deadly still now. Dust and cobwebs whirled and floated in the newly stirred air.

"Your sanctimonious soothsayer has fled," Gonji said in Japanese.

"*Was*—what?"

"Gone, *neh?*"

And then they spotted the weapons: the monstrous battleaxe and broadsword suspended above the fireplace in symbolic reminder of the terrible annihilation curse that o'erhung Vedun. Their eyes locked in an instant of chilling awe, a shared sensation of momentary insignificance. And whether by their apocalyptic portent or their presence in the prophetess's home—neither man could have said—the weapons assumed an almost religious import.

Gonji moved forward gingerly and stood under them. He reached out and cupped the hilt of the sword, and with a great push he was able to raise the piece perhaps a span above its cast-iron mooring.

His name was William Eddings, and he had come to Vedun with his father, his brother John, and John's wife Sarah after his mother's death in England. They came seeking sanctuary from strife and religious intolerance, surcease of the rigors and heartaches of a peripatetic life that allowed no roots to be sunk; these were trying times for Catholics in England, and they were descended from a former Earl of Lancashire who had been an opponent of mad Henry.

Three days in Vedun had been enough to convince his kindly brother John that "this is our home—this is the place we've sought." Sarah and father Stuart were quick to assent, but William hadn't been sure. Indeed, still wasn't. The cosmopolitan populace was overtly friendly enough, but William, ever the cynic, ever mindful of the bleak turns of fortune that had dogged the Eddings name throughout history, was far less sanguine. He could not share brother John's sentiment that "mother might yet be alive had we come to Vedun long ago." His mother had been much like William; she too would have been suspicious of the multiplicity of languages that made daily commerce a chore. There were few who spoke French, and the English-speaking population was practically nil. They were outsiders, plain and simple, living on the fringe of the ethnic cliques.

The self-styled aristocrats who postured as the city leaders were no easier to chum up to. They would as lief hobnob with poor cobblers and sundriers like the Eddings family as they would mix with these bloody invaders. And there was talk now that they were soliciting recruits for a militia to oppose this savage army and its enchanted minions.

Indeed. That would bloody well be the day when William of Lancashire would send his high-born arse to this kind of fate on their account.

They were all there now. Representatives of the council leadership; the syndicalists from the trades, provisioners, and commerce, who really controlled Vedun. All standing hollow-eyed and slack-jawed, staring down, beyond horror now, at the revolting apparition in the streets before the chapel.

There were six dead, a dozen or so more, wounded. And this one. In which category did they place this one?

The soldiers had stormed into the crowd, singling out more hostages for the blasted "King Klown," or whatever he called himself. When the roughshod brigand had cornered the pack William was running with and his smoldering eyes had met William's own, the sundrier's knees had turned to butter. He had prayed earnestly that it would not be he who was chosen. So terrified had he been, that he feared he would wet his breeches. But it was not he; another had been shackled and dragged off, kicking and screaming—as William himself might have done; they'd all heard tales of what was becoming of those conscripted "servants."

Then it was over. The square looked like a crushed ant hill. Five dead by pistol and sword and trampling hoof, one more seared beyond recognition by the gruesome wyvern's terrible saliva, and *this* one . . . Befouled by its abominable excrement.

Dead? Alive? *What?*

Flavio was there, as was Michael Benedetto. And Wilfred and Lorenz Gundersen, the haughty Exchequer. And Phlegor, the loud-mouthed guildsman at whose urging the resistance had begun. Even he was beyond words now, all the fight wrung from him.

The man lay quivering, reeking of the filthy waste that slowly melted him away. His eyes rolled heavenward, all the pain emptied from them. What was he feeling? Thinking? He trembled so. Dr. Verrico bent over him and muttered to himself helplessly, poking with a tool at the awful ruin of what had been a man. He had ceased asking for help to move the victim. Not a man among them would aid him; all were paralyzed, staring with childish ambivalence, crossing themselves, lips curled behind rags held up to their faces to filter the ghastly odor.

William felt cold and numb and somehow inhuman and unclean to be in that place, empty now of monsters and soldiers, given over to the mourning and the dispirited, the dead and the maimed and the befouled. And he alone spoke the words any one of them might, if he were true:

"I'll never die like that. Not for anyone . . ."

Part II

The Sure, the Straight, the Brave

*There is nothing that a man need fear
Who carries at his side this splendid blade*
—motto engraved on Sagami

Chapter Twelve

"*Kiyai! Kiyai! Kiyai!*"

The double line of men swung their wooden blades. Over the crashing and splintering tumult they shouted their *kiyai*—the energizing cry of the warrior, though some cried out in pain, their partners having missed their marks, winces and sudden contortions all along the line betraying erring efforts.

Gonji and Roric watched one line closely; Garth and a Rorka Gray knight, the other. Again and again they clashed and clacked, lunged and parried, advanced and retreated, sweat, blood, and curses marking their progress in the echoing din. The leaders corrected errors, demonstrated proper techniques, then pushed them through the monotonous repetitions that rendered fencing techniques second nature. Those who displayed an aptitude for edged weapons, along with the previously experienced, were soon shunted off into more advanced training groups. Many of these men grinned and postured pridefully; their glee was short-lived. They presently realized that their reward translated into better odds at suffering bloody death. A creeping lassitude now could be seen to affect some of them. And yet another psychological demon had to be exorcised: Those who blustered with a dangerous overestimation of their nascent skills now trained side by side with those who grumbled that their hard work would surely bring them death.

But they worked on diligently, if not always in perfect accord, doubling their shifts so that they could work their normal jobs. Their leaders strove to cope with their fears and shortcomings, to understand each individual's needs and bring them into harmony with the needs of the group. There was no room for the weak link that might sunder their resolve and their ability to achieve their purpose.

In secret conclave Vedun's military council had been selected. It was composed of Baron Rorka, Michael Benedetto, Roric Amsgard, Garth Gundersen, and Gonji. The latter pair were held in disfavor. The revelation of Garth's former commission under Klann had shaken the popular smith's esteem, though it was obvious that the step down from his pedestal had been a minor one, and he was gradually restored to the people's good graces. Gonji, on the other hand, retained his enemies and antagonists: Phlegor and many of his craft guild followers, for instance, had refused to join in training under the samurai. And Gonji and Rorka found their personality differences irreconcilable, their disagreements over planning and policy many and deep.

The general plan was to prepare for an evacuation of non-combatants to the catacomb system, followed by a two-pronged assault against both the city occupation force and the castle, the latter facilitated by the tactically advantageous tunnel dug through to the castle dungeons themselves.

The catacomb system was amazing: the combination of natural cavern formation and persevering sapper toil by forgotten ancients. The main cavern, in which most training was pursued, was hundreds of yards across, flat at the center and cleared of boulders and rubble by Rorka's surviving knights. Jagged stalactites and stalagmites depended and jutted in places like craggy teeth. The rock walls were veined with mineral deposits that illuminated the cavern with a natural phosphorescence. The training ground could be reached from two points within the city and two without. The former two were Tralayn's fireplace and the sacristy behind the chapel's altar. Disguised levers in these two locations activated intricate series of pulleys, counterweights, and clockwork mechanisms that swung open mantel and closet, permitting entry into torchlit tunnels that descended in clammy, claustrophobic switchbacks to the caverns. The latter pair of entrances lay in the northern hills and at the base of the cliff beneath the city, in the southern valley.

Gonji and Rorka repeatedly argued over the intensity of the training. The baron favored a slow, steady process akin to the ascent of a squire to knighthood. Gonji, addressing the immediacy of their need, urged speed and vigor in bringing the militia along. His system was the one adopted for the nonce, the people being motivated by their frustration and terror over the occupation force's outrages. The leaders agreed that the fears of Mord's supernatural minions should be minimized, Gonji declaring that he would assume responsibility for the neutralization of Mord's monsters when the time came. The subject of the Klann multiple-personage legend was wisely not broached at all to the militia at large.

But when Gonji advanced the proposal that the castle assault team should have as an objective the firing of the treasure room, thus rendering the precious gold and silver unusable to Klann and unhinging his mercenaries' primary source of loyalty, Rorka vehemently disagreed. As he likewise did over Gonji's suggestion that the castle's gunpowder magazines should be detonated.

Worst of all, from Gonji's standpoint, the baron continued to hope in futility that his lost patrols or Holy Word Monastery would deliver them via allied or Church intervention.

Sooner or later, he knew, there would have to be an accounting of what Gonji himself had done to help shatter these groundless hopes.

By the third day of training, patterns were developing, a new order was becoming established. The logistics of the secret training, still vexingly laborious, were accepted with resignation. Supplies were brought to the caverns slowly and with nerve-wracking apprehension. Beverages, foodstuffs, and medical supplies were the easiest to move inasmuch as their discovery could be explained away. These were commonly brought via the catacomb entrances at Tralayn's home and the chapel. The latter proved the most useful, since citizens entering the chapel were never questioned about their purpose, and it was rare that a mercenary would slip in for a few moments of soul-searching or a Llorm regular would make a routine check. So the vital supplies were laid in with a minimum of risk, some being employed in the training, others stocked in the tunnels for use during the evacuation of non-combatants.

Gonji found the aforementioned tunnels—tens of them, snaking off from the great cavern in every direction—rather unsettling. Some simply dead-ended, evincing unfinished work. Others, bored pointlessly toward the bowels of the earth, appeared to have no end at all. Scouting parties sent to explore them would return hours later covered with grime, exhausted, and complaining of foul stenches that made deeper exploration unsavory. And more than one explorer would complain of an indefinable unease that gripped one the farther he ventured into their black depths.

The smuggling in of weapons was a stickier problem. Edged weapons—swords, knives, axes, and such—were legally and commonly carried; so their accumulation was a simple matter. The founders worked long and hard shifts, their forges ever fuming, in the production of blades. The well-carburized steel was kept for Vedun, while the brittler grades were used for Klann's ordered weapons.

Long-range weapons—bows and pistols—and polearms were a different story. Since the restriction on them, bows were in short supply, and for the first few days of training, there was not a gun to be had. Such long-range weapons would be crucial to their plans. Half the Rorka knights still possessed crossbows, but they were far outnumbered by the Llorm bowmen. Karl Gerhard, the dour hunter and fletcher, joined with Vedun's only two skilled bowyers in producing longbows of the English design and stockpiling cloth-yard war arrows with several different tips, in which craft Gerhard was a true master. But it was tedious work, and soon all three had smuggled down their tools and taken to spending all their hours in the catacombs. The bowyers presently abandoned their training altogether in favor of their vital trade, but Gerhard insisted on putting in twenty-hour days so that he might train the archers, over whom he was quickly placed in command.

Horses were needed in the cavern for cavalry practice. Much of the anticipated battle for possession of Vedun would necessarily be fought on horseback. And there was only one entrance that would admit the large animals—the concealed shaft in the southern valley, at the base of the cliff. When Gonji had first proposed their need for horses in the training, Baron Rorka had flatly rejected it, Michael and Roric supporting his contention that it was simply too risky an undertaking. But Garth had agreed with Gonji, and their arguments had ultimately won over the others. A corral was hastily erected, and horses were brought through the valley tunnel by ones and twos. Some by riders out for exercise who avoided the patroled southern trail and clumped down treacherous bramble-and-vine-covered slopes to the valley; others by small game hunters who dutifully returned their bows to the armory after their hunt—the Llorm armorer cared only about the weapons, and the mercenaries who guarded the gates kept no record of whether citizens passed through their bailiwick on foot or on horseback; and one night, under heavy cloud cover, an entire string of horses was daringly led the long way around the city—to the east and across the river—by the Provender's hostlers, Stefan Berenyi and Nikolai Nagy, in a carefully timed operation involving the opening of the sluice gates that cleaned the city's gutters and sewers, the torrential wash of riverwater covering their hoofbeats along the cliff base lest they be heard by sentries on the walls.

But the most difficult problem of logistics, one that would plague them for the duration of training, was the movement of the militiamen themselves. The entrances to the catacombs seemed terribly inadequate at first. Those entering through Tralayn's house — the fewest number were assigned here — did so with bated breath, for the free companions' garrison in the converted granary was close at hand. Likewise, the hill and valley tunnels' critical tactical positions caused them to be reserved only for those with legitimate reasons to be traversing the gates on a daily basis.

By far the greatest number of trainees were assigned the chapel entrance to the catacombs. Thus, new daily services were established at the chapel, presided over by Tralayn, and if the troops who constantly passed by the place of worship ever had taken stock, they would have been struck by the curious fact that all the women who entered the services at eight bells of evening and six of morning left an hour later with different husbands than those they had come with.

On the first day of training about two hundred citizens, mostly men, appeared in the cavern in a sporadic, chaotic flow and signed on with the militia. The first session was spent learning names; assigning translators for various unilingual groups (whose ethnocentricity would prove a nagging organizational problem); establishing rules of military courtesy and discipline (another hard-won battle, except among the former military men, who embraced it enthusiastically); assigning equipment and military specialties; completing the crude, cobbled-together training devices; performing agonizing conditioning exercises; and absorbing basic words of command, courtesy, and direction, some in Hungarian and German, but most, on Gonji's insistence, in Japanese.

The second day, due to aches and injuries, exhaustion and disillusionment, the trainees' number had diminished to approximately one hundred and fifty, counting the leaders and Rorka's knights. But by the third day, their number had again increased to two hundred, and a daily regimen was established. Now the lines of fencers clashed and cracked their wooden weapons together, more and more turning up at every session wearing gauntlets to guard against the earlier days' frequent hand injuries, while archers launched their volleys of whickering arrows under the head-shaking gazes of Gerhard and Gray bowmen, and squads of men groaned and complained as they stretched and scaled timbers and pulled themselves up ropes, only to descend again and be required to wrestle or run or respond to sham sneak attacks or try their skills at another new weapon, at last coming full circle to their weapon specialty for a more complex and wearying session.

Occasionally the valley entrance sentry would clang the alarm tocsin, relaying the message that a Klann patrol had been sighted along the southern road, and the training clamor would come to an abrupt halt as men grabbed for their weapons and hugged the musty ground in silence, each wondering whether the real moment of first engagement would so ice his spine and trigger the gooseflesh and cold sweat that now tingled him. But it passed. They returned to their rigors. But not without complaint and curses and stiff joints and teeth-gritting hatred for Klann and nervous stomachs that erupted in outbreaks of vomiting. And loathing and disgust for the training by some, who hawked and spat insolently to hear new orders being called out by Gonji, who had been ascribed the blame for the design of their toil.

Gonji knew their minds. He understood the stages through which their thinking must pass, enduring their silent hatred and behind-the-back sneers and insulting gestures. For he knew that he must abide it all with dignity, and as they distanced themselves from him so would they conversely bond themselves as a unit, dependent on one another, and fighting as one.

"It won't work," Rorka said flatly, hands clasped behind him. He watched wincingly as men engaging swiveling quintains failed to block or duck in time and were battered by the heavy beams. Beyond them, a motley cavalry unit charged, bellowing, at staked man-forms, slashed at them as their line thundered past. But some guided their steeds too wide for fear of colliding and swung at empty air; others reached too far and their momentum and the horses' motion tossed them from their saddles to crash to earth, dislocating shoulders and elbows and cracking skulls.

"*Dr. Verrico!*" sprang the outcries for the overworked surgeon.

"Your timetable is all wrong," Rorka elaborated. "Time is our ever-present enemy. Look at them."

Gonji mopped his glistening face and snapped his wet hand at his side. He set his face stoically, but his right hand squeezed the hilt of Spine-cleaver, as his spare *katana* had long ago been dubbed.

"So sorry, Rorka-san, but time is *everyone's* enemy, Klann included. The sooner we attack him, the fewer mercenaries he'll have in his hire. It's up to us to make proper plans for the uprising, to train them as best we can in as short a time as possible, and then use their training and their anger against the marauders while their blood runs hot."

"Oh, it will run, all right," Rorka said wryly, turning away. "It will run hot and red . . . *Festina lente*, Gonji—make haste slowly . . ."

Gonji's lip quivered. *Stupid lazy old bastard! Festina lente, my ass! What do you think this province will look like next spring? Picked clean like desert-bleached bones. And it's all your fault, you—ahh! Forget it. Control yourself. The baron is still rightful ruler of the province . . .*

Gonji's relationship with Rorka and his surviving two and twenty gray surcoated knights had been strained. They bore him great rancor over his quick accession to his lofty command position and responded grudgingly to his orders or suggestions. And he and Rorka shared a mutual dislike. But lately he had noticed that the inevitable bonding that cements men with a common purpose, especially a deadly one, had broken the glacial gulf between him and a few of the Grays.

If only Rorka would commit himself wholeheartedly, stop disagreeing with Gonji's every suggestion, quit appealing to the healing efficacy of dear, sweet time as if he expected divine intervention that would obviate all their efforts . . .

"Pay him no heed," Paille called over from the cavern niche where he worked.

Gonji ambled over to the alcove where the artist stooped under a ring of blinding torches, his eyes gradually adjusting themselves to the orange glare.

Paille wore a ragged bandanna in his hair. His paint-and sweat-stained tunic had the arms torn off unevenly at the shoulders. He reeked of clay and oil and cheap wine.

"His noble pantaloons are full from fear of losing his exalted position once the rebellion has placed Vedun in the hands of the people," Paille said without looking up.

"Perhaps," Gonji replied distractedly, watching Paille's talented hands ply their delicate work, "but I'm afraid we need him. And I think he fears his return to leadership as much as—what's that?"

"The mercenary garrison," Paille answered, moving the model into place, "near the soothsayer's house. See how easily they might be squeezed into the southwest corner of the city, cut off from their fellows?"

"Mmm." Gonji scanned the mock-up with fascination. Paille's in-progress miniature of the city and the castle was a source of endless interest and conversation. The alcove was often crowded with the curious, who couldn't pass by without peeking in to see how the diorama was shaping up. It was a marvel of clay and wood and stone, and Paille hadn't been able to resist supplying brilliant touches of detail, even to the point of adding tiny human figures. Here it was that the military council would plan tactics.

"And look here," Paille said, holding up the new pieces, "the calthrops and spiked barriers you requested. Don't look like much, do they?"

"Not in miniature," Gonji agreed, a frown furrowing his brow, "but in the field I've seen them take their toll of horses and men."

"Where do you want them placed?"

"In the walled-in lanes," Gonji said, pointing. "We lure pockets of soldiers into the alleys, then yank them or roll them into place. For a short time the alleys become effective killing grounds. Until the desperate find a way to scrabble over the bodies of the unfortunate." He smiled thinly, without humor. Angry shouts sprang up across the broad cavern, and he turned to go.

"Oh, Gonji—before you go, tell me what you think." Paille bounded over to a low bench whereon lay his tools and raw materials, plus paper, pen, and ink. He snatched up a stained and buckled sheaf of papers and thrust them at the samurai.

Gonji looked at the top sheet, which had written upon it in Paille's elaborate French script: *The Death-*

wind of Vedun Epic of Alain Paille.

"Go ahead, read something of it."

"It's French?" Gonji queried, making a sour face.

"Of course, *mon frere!*"

Gonji sniffed and turned to view the howling cavalrymen who pounded past in a mock skirmish.

"Later, *neh?*" he said, handing the manuscript back to the poet and resheathing Spine-cleaver. "I don't like the title, though. Where did you get it?"

"*You* suggested it! With your Deathwind quest and all. Only I've interpreted it to mean the destined Wind of Death that will sweep the world clean of the decadent aristocracy and the tyranny they promote. And it all begins in Vedun . . ." A faraway vision of social upheaval twinkled in the Frenchman's eye.

"*Iyé,*" Gonji said, shaking his head. "I don't like it. Why don't you call it . . . *Red Blade from the East?*"

Gonji strode off, a smile perking his lips, leaving Paille to stand, hand on hips, gazing after him.

"Well if *that* isn't the most pompous, conceited—!"

The training leaders worked long and arduous shifts, many overlapping their working hours for smooth transitions. Without the presence of Rorka and his Gray knights, it would have been impossible to pursue the simultaneous training in multiple warfare skills. But even these doughty souls were relieved, given the grueling double-shift training day of some twenty hours' duration, when they were able to turn up trainees sufficiently skilled and trustworthy to assume some of the tasks of leadership.

The knights were referred to as *rytier* (knight), *tanito* (teacher), or *katona* (soldier); Roric Amsgard and Karl Gerhard chose to be called *Lehrer* (teacher); and Garth, in his unassuming fashion, insisted on being referred to by name.

But no one was more feared or respected, if only with sulky or grudging acquiescence, than the leader who was referred to as *sensei*.

Gonji worked like a demon. His dynamic presence and surpassing skill with *bugei*—martial arts—caused him to swiftly become the final authority on all matters of training and tactics. He moved semi-permanently into the caverns, working straight through most shifts, avoiding the streets of the city unless accompanied, for he wished to stave off Julian's demands of fresh intelligence for his money. It was rare to find Gonji asleep or otherwise indisposed to the needs of the militia; few knew when or where he slept. And by the third or fourth day, the heavy regimen was taking its toll of him. His eyes were red and puffy, dark circles under them declaring the fatigue he refused to admit. And so it was that he studied the militia as carefully as did the other leaders, anxious to discover trustworthy subordinates who might relieve some of his burden. Not surprisingly, as a by-product, he learned a great deal about the men who would fight by his side, if the worst came.

Roric and Garth were Gonji's staunchest allies on the military council, his bulwark against Rorka and the brooding Michael when policy had to be decided. In addition, they delivered all he asked on the training ground. Roric, the ex-Austrian cavalryman, proved a solid, though unspectacular, exponent of *falchion* and polearm. The tall, uncomely butcher's steadiness and surety with weapons basics, coupled with an admirable calm and patience in directing his neophyte warriors, commanded him respect. He possessed a gift for dealing with hotheads and bridling outbreaks of temper. Of course, Gonji sometimes reflected in amusement, the jagged scar that cleft his jaw probably helped somewhat. Nor did the one or more vicious-looking, well-trained dogs that frequently accompanied him diminish his effectiveness.

Garth Gundersen was ever the gentle-strong enigma. The suspicions of his friendship with Klann had fled before the dazzle of his weapons skill: Double arms were his specialty: twin broadswords, sword-and-buckler, axe-and-shield, shield-and-halberd, axe-and-sword—Garth was a throwback to a nobler time, a time before gunpowder had popularized the easy, cowardly kill. Garth's skill with the francisca, a Frankish axe weighted for throwing, was remarkable; he could split a rail or shatter a melon at thirty yards. His province was power techniques with the heavier close-quarter weapons, and most of the city's bigger men could be found learning halberd, battle-axe, and two-handed broadsword from Garth. The smith was instrumental in helping Gonji teach craftsmen to use the tools of their trades as weapons. Under their tutelage Peter Foristek soon wielded the scythe and pruning hook in a manner that was something to behold. And one day, during *jujutsu*—empty-hand training—Garth and Gonji engaged in a wrestling bout that had the trainees talking and shaking their heads fondly for many shifts afterward. But for all the popular smith's assistance in preparing the militia, he still maintained that he could not raise a sword in battle again.

As for Wilfred, there was no question that the young smith ached for a chance to assault the castle. His jump on most of the others in fencing skill, plus his earnest desire to learn the ways of *kenjutsu* swordsmanship and the tenets of the *bushido* code, quickly established him as Gonji's second-in-command. Gonji declared on the first day of training that he had decided to award his spare *katana*, Spine-cleaver, to the trainee who best embraced the principles and practices of the *bugei* he would teach. From the start Wilf lustily entered the lists. The immediate upshot was that he was dubbed "the junior Japper" by his and Gonji's enemies and detractors. Stung by the insult, he nonetheless surged ahead with his training. But a certain distancing between Wilf and Gonji became apparent to those close to them. No longer did Wilf associate with the samurai in the fawning, tagalong way he had earlier. Used to being a leader and a loner, Wilf now manifested a more formal, equal-to-equal relationship with Gonji. He trained hard, displayed skill, anger, and tenacity in equal measures. And when the training was done, he worked dutifully in the smith shop, and longed for his Genya, and planned and prayed and wrought in his mind an endless gallery of savage scenarios he might have to survive in order to see her returned to him. Wilf's few close friends noticed his new moodiness and introversion. Some tried to pry him out of it, largely without success.

Jiri Szabo, for instance . . . Jiri was a young metal founder and probably Vedun's all-around finest athlete. A well built, though short, tawny-haired man with sincere blue eyes and a ready smile, Jiri would likely one day supplant Garth as the city's most popular fellow once the beloved smith had passed on. Earnest and guileless, ever more concerned with the feelings of an opponent he had beaten than with the thrill of his own triumph, eminently teachable and seemingly fearless, Jiri became the butt of Gonji's oft-repeated jest: "Szabo, what dirty things are you thinking about—*right now?!*" The samurai's sudden narrow-eyed focus on Szabo, coupled with the man's red-faced innocence, never failed to elicit hearty laughs. On foot, no one was faster. Only Aldo Monetto could keep up with him in climbing a rope or scaling a wall. He took to *kenjutsu* eagerly and learned well

Jiri's betrothed, a sweet lass named Greta who plied the weaving looms, often worked in the cavern in support of the training. The smiles and winks they sneaked at each other during breaks evoked much kidding, some of it plainly envious. Jiri had everything to live for. "It would be nice to keep the ones like him alive," Rorka observed once. Gonji had been irked by the baron's unnecessary caution, for he knew only too well that he was preparing Jiri for a very good chance at young death.

Lorenz Gundersen proved his father's match at springing unexpected facets to his background. Somewhere in the course of business ventures, the priggish Executor of the Exchequer had acquired passable adroitness as a rapier fencer. He moved surely and unflinchingly from wooden to steel blades, practicing vigorously, now and again even breaking a sweat. But he remained an opponent of Gonji's methods, particularly in regard to military discipline (degrading, in so motley an army) and security (insulting, implemented by an outsider), and when Gonji advised him that rapier alone, a weapon designed only for thrusting, would leave him ill equipped to deal with armored opponents, Lorenz countered cavalierly: "Finding the chinks—isn't that what it's all about?" Gonji shrugged and wished him happy chink-hunting.

Vlad Dobroczy showed considerable skill with the sword, was a fine horseman, and possessed a mean streak that would prove useful in combat. He had only one drawback—a hatred of Gonji, perhaps based in bigotry, perhaps on Gonji's friendship with his long-time rival Wilf. But it vented itself in insolence and discord, particularly when he was required to take orders from Wilf, and Gonji knew that he could tolerate such negative attitudes only so long.

Paolo Sauvini the wagoner exhibited another sort of

insolence. Sullen and withdrawn, a rather anti-social man who seemed widely disliked, Paolo had tried since Gonji's arrival to engage the samurai's attention through boorish staring matches. Now during the training of the militia his yearning for recognition had taken a new tack: anything for attention. Determined to excel with the sword, he hedged by pairing himself off with opponents he knew he could handle, sometimes coming on too aggressively in supposedly controlled practice bouts. He volunteered for everything; always was either the very first or the very last to respond to an order. After three days of censure by Gonji—the last time for bullying Klaus, the most easily victimized of the trainees—Paolo changed his concentration to the bow, where he performed quite well under Gerhard's direction. But Gonji frequently caught Paolo's hateful black eyes glowering from across the cavern, and he finally thought he understood why. As the top man, Gonji was the competition. The glory of soldiering success burned in those smoldering eyes of Paolo's, and until it became more important to him to *be* a soldier than to posture as one, he would be just another target for Klann's troops.

Karl Gerhard and Aldo Monetto were fine leaders and splendid exemplars of their specialties: Monetto with his biller's axe, conditioning techniques, and what Gonji called *karumi-jutsu*—techniques of agility in jumping, climbing, and dodging; and, especially, Gerhard with his magnificent longbow, which required four men to string. Under his guidance several fine archers were emerging. Each day the targets were moved back, yet roughly the same number of hits were recorded. And to watch Gerhard sight and quick-fire at the mobile target was a favorite sport in itself, always evoking whistles and cheers. Yet separating these two argumentative best-of-friends had done little to quell their wearisome bickering. Each day one would suggest a way to improve the other's teaching method, and the battle was joined. But their arguing was based on friendly competition, on the desire to intensify mutual respect and esteem.

What cemented the friendship of Berenyi and Nagy no one could say.

Stefan Berenyi and Nikolai Nagy were hostlers at the Provender. That was the extent of their similarity. Berenyi was the town comic, a man of twenty-two with long, flowing hair and twinkling hazel eyes whose lips were ever twitching at some anticipated jest, usually provided by him and often at Nagy's expense. Berenyi was the sort who always went for the cheap laugh, the low note of humor; the one irreverent voice in the otherwise polite crowd. A gifted mimic of voices and mannerisms, he kept his fellows in stitches, not always during the most appropriate moments. Yet he was the type one could not easily get angry with, and in any case there was no use in wasting one's anger—in seconds Berenyi could dispel the mood with still another asinine jest or foolish posture. Gonji decided that his brand of nonsense was badly needed. In Japan warriors masked their fears with faces of stone; in Europe they hid them behind laughter.

When Stefan unveiled his imitation of Gonji and was prodded into performing it for the samurai, Gonji was not sure whether to break his ribs or crack a smile. But the others were already chuckling at the samurai's barely stifled mirth, and Gonji joined in heartily. It was the first warm, boisterous laugh they ever shared as a group. Berenyi had helped form a valuable bond that day. And he possessed one other staple of the vulgar comic's repertoire: he could belch and fart at will. If Alain Paille was Vedun's intellectual jester, then Berenyi was its clown prince.

To everyone but Nagy.

Nick Nagy was twice Berenyi's age. Gray-haired and squinty-eyed, Nagy was a fist-shaking grouch who never failed to tell his tormenting partner where he could shove his latest jest—which he was quite probably the target of. Still strong, with thick, gnarled hands and wiry arms, Nagy trained harder than most of his young peers and refused to recount to anyone but his wife the toll these long agonizing days were exacting of him. Nagy's two children were grown, married, and departed from Vedun, and the Nagys were accustomed to having Stefan for dinner several nights a week. It was said that only Magda Nagy was exempt from Berenyi's jests, and in his less charitable moments Nick would call Stefan "the kid we had who died but then came back." Berenyi and Nagy could be vicious to each other, but as Paille observed, it was a "mutually salutary hatred."

Michael Benedetto presented Gonji a special problem. Ever Gonji's antagonist on the military council, ever the devil's advocate when the samurai would propose a new training technique or introduce a fresh tactic into their plans against Klann, Michael occupied the unenviable position of the least skilled of the leaders in use of arms. He further suffered embarrassment at being repeatedly remanded to *bokken* training from the more dangerous and demanding steel blades. The complete Renaissance man, Michael had been trained with the *schiavona*, the Venetian broadsword, during his education in Italy. He knew he was superior in skill to some of those Gonji had promoted ahead of him. And in his confusion, his rancor for the oriental increased.

But Gonji had good reason, for Michael was sword-shy. The council Elder's protegé showed fine coordination, speed, and balance; his thrusts and slashes were crisp and economical, his parries sure, his ripostes and combination attacks swift and clever. But he flinched under attack once restraints were removed and the bouts became freestyle. He did well enough against classically schooled fencing styles but tensed up and fell back, his form eroding, against a wild flailer—precisely what he'd be facing in many a mercenary. So Gonji was hard on him, sending him back again and again to wooden practice weapons, knowing full well the importance of keeping him alive, not only inasmuch as he was the city's pride and joy but also because of Gonji's own guilt. For he knew that Michael sensed the samurai's attraction to his wife. Sometimes Gonji would respectfully suggest that Michael switch his concentration to the bow, but the councilman would adamantly insist on staying with the sword, the elegant weapon of command. And always it seemed that when Gonji had occasion to embarrass Michael with a criticism, Lydia would be there, cleansing a wound or serving a beverage or repairing an item of equipment. She'd send Michael a nod and a gentle smile of encouragement, which he'd answer with a scowl.

Gonji was approaching his surfeit with this angry young Italian. In his bleaker moods he would resolve to let him have his head, to allow him to rush bullheadedly to his date with the executioner's blade.

To leave his fetching wife a widow.

And then there was Klaus.
"Owwww!"
Gerhard hefted the quiver of shafts and ambled over to the firing line, where a knot of archers, including Berenyi, stifled snickers at his approach. Klaus stood shaking his hand.
"Klaus, what's the problem?" Gerhard asked.

"Hurt my thumb on the string, Karl," the lumpish Klaus replied.

"Call me *'Lehrer.'* Here comes Gonji."

"Oh—I'm sorry, Ka—I mean *Lehrer*. I keep forgetting." Klaus was Berenyi's favorite *schlemihl*, the easy butt of his sometimes cruel jokes. A dimwitted fellow with unkempt wheat-shock hair and a pointless frazzle of near-invisible mustache, physical accomplishments always came hard for him. But he tried, and Providence had outfitted him with the patience of the social pariah. Ever sincere. Ever on the outside trying annoyingly hard to qualify as a peer. Ever the last in line.

Gonji strode over, a long, vicious-looking halberd leaning on his shoulder, to narrowly regard the bunch who now strung bows with businesslike chatter and very straight faces.

"Klaus, who told you to put the archer's ring on your bow hand?" Gerhard asked, knowing the answer. "It goes on the string hand, to protect your thumb."

"Stefan did," Klaus said vapidly, pointing to Berenyi.

Gerhard and Gonji looked at each other, then at Berenyi, who affected a defensive mask. "I'm sure I didn't," he replied. "Klaus, I told you it goes on *that* hand."

"Berenyi, go load quivers," Gerhard said flatly.

"Now, Klaus," Gonji said, directing with gestures, "let's try again. Nock your arrow—rotate over your head as you inhale and puuuuullll—now you're going to sight your target as you arc downw—"

Twaanngg.

"Look out!"

The cloth-yard shaft zanged into the cavern roof overhead, clacking sharply and lancing down toward the massed archers.

"Watch out!" someone yelled as they scrambled, laughing.

"Have a care!" Baron Rorka cried from halfway across the cavern. "Hit a stalactite just so and it will crush your skulls!"

They sorted themselves out, and Gonji and Gerhard separated Klaus from the rest.

"Really sorry, *sensei*, but I couldn't hold it—"

"Never mind that now," Gonji said. "Listen, Klaus, maybe there's another weapon for you. What sort of tools do you use in your trade? What do you do?"

"I make buckles," Klaus answered with simple pride.

"Buckles," Gonji echoed, crestfallen. He sighed.

"Can I try again?"

"Eh, Klaus," Gerhard cut in, "why don't you push the mobile target awhile—and keep your head down!"

"*Ja, Lehrer*, whatever you say." Klaus padded off dutifully. From behind he seemed shaped like the chapel bell.

Gonji looked at Gerhard, who stood shaking his head in perplexity.

(excerpt from the *Deathwind of Vedun* epic of Alain Paille:)

"*. . . there was good cheer and warmth of spirit in the catacombs where the Warriors of Vedun strengthened their wills and fired their thews in harmony and camaraderie, for it was by their unity of purpose that they would fulfill their age-old destiny to wrest the Soul of Mankind from the shackles of tyranny . . .*"

Wilf parried Vlad's *bokken* aside sharply, and the farmer closed with him, slamming into him, chest-to-chest. Grabbing one of his wrists, he forced Wilf's wooden sword high over his head. They grunted and cursed, teeth gritted in mutual contempt. Then suddenly Vlad elbowed Wilf hard in the face, snapping his head to the side.

Wilf growled and dropped his *bokken*. With a shrill *kiyai* he smashed a short, straight right into Vlad's jaw, then charged into him, bowling him over.

"Halt! Break it up!" Roric commanded, rushing over.

They were pulled apart, panting and glowering, a trickle of blood issuing from Wilf's nose.

"Let's save that for Klann, *all-recht?*" Roric advised, tapping them both with his heavy falchion. He extracted a curt nod from each of them and turned away. Before he had taken two steps Dobroczy launched himself at Wilf and the pair were on the ground again, pounding each other and swearing.

William Eddings braced himself. His turn would be next. Gonji reached the man next to him and glared at him with those oriental devil's eyes that bored into a man's soul. Eddings looked to his left. His brother John smiled and proffered a tiny head bob of encouragement, and in that instant the mad Jappo's shriek penetrated clear down to his bowels. There was a wicked smacking of wood, and Eddings felt his knees turn to jam as the man on the right parried with a two-handed overhead motion.

Eddings's heart thudded in his ears, and his breath whistled through his nostrils. The Japanese spoke to the man who had parried, whether words of criticism or praise, Eddings could not tell and didn't care. He would be next.

*Jesus-Mary-Joseph, all I ever bloody well wanted was peace of mind and a little private space to—*And then the Jappo was staring at *him*. He was vaguely aware of the interpreter who had eased up on the periphery of his vision.

"*Yoi-suru*—ready!"

Holy Mother of God . . .

"*Eeyiiiii!*"

Eddings's face contorted, and his *bokken* flashed upward.

"Unhh!" he cried—he had missed the parry. A sharp pain jolted his shoulder, but it subsided in seconds. The samurai's ferocious blow had somehow mystically ended in no more than a cautionary tap.

But Holy Mother Church, this bastard meant business . . .

Then the samurai was speaking to him in German, and when he had finished the interpreter took over.

"Eh . . . the *sensei* says that . . . so sorry, but you are quite dead. Don't freeze up. Relax. Empty your mind of conscious thought. You must not only make your parry, but you must be loose enough to complete the circle with a blow in reply. Practice . . ."

Eddings trembled all over. *Bloody madmen,* he thought. *All of them. Crazy if they think I'm ever really going to fight against* real *soldiers with* real *swords. Or that monster dragon that flew out of some bedlamite's delirium. That'll be the day when I'll dare that thing's flaming shit and spittle. Not me, not William of Lancashire* . . .

Dobroczy stamped forward, his broadsword held in two-handed middle guard. He described a figure-eight of steel that brought a confused, weak parry from Michael, whose form crumbled as his eyes began to follow the whirling swordpoint. Then Vlad feinted a lunge at his helmed head and followed with a short arcing slash to the left. Michael's *schiavona* twisted downward awkwardly as he went for the fake, his arm curling uselessly out of position in his desperate fear of being hit. And Vlad's swift circular slash to the right thudded against Michael's heavily padded jacket, knocking the wind out of him.

The protégé fell to one knee, holding his ribs, the *schiavona's* point digging into the rocky ground.

"*Sesshoku*—touch!" Gonji's command that ended the match echoed through the cavern.

Several men pressed forward to come to Michael's aid, but he threw down his helm and waved them off angrily.

Vlad walked up to him. "Sorry, Michael," he said softly. But the Elder's protégé said nothing.

"Miko-san," Vlad heard the Japanese say over his shoulder, "so sorry but your form still needs work. Back to the *bokken, dozo*. Dobroczy—to the quintains."

"*Da . . . sensei,*" Vlad replied, injecting all the venon he could muster into the infidel's title. Why in hell did he have it in for Michael? He wasn't as bad as some of the swordsmen who stayed with the steel weapons. Why did he have to keep on running him down like that?

And in front of his wife.

By the sixth day there were over three hundred trainees on the register. Council Elder Flavio and Milorad Vargo dropped in that day to appraise the training. They strolled about with folded arms, trying to look politely interested, but the strain on Flavio was showing in his stooped walk and the fresh pain lines that etched his brow and the corners of his eyes. He bore the onus of shattered ideals valiantly but not without effect.

The relationship of Flavio and Gonji had grown strained. They had already come to grips once over

Gonji's insistence on tight security, and Flavio vigorously opposed the brother-against-brother implication in Gonji's urging that needless fraternization with Klann's troops should be reported. Nor was he overly fond of the records of unusual or unnecessary traffic said to be kept by Old Gort the gatekeeper and others whom Gonji declined to name.

"Very sorry, my master, but this is preparation for war, if necessary, and I've seen too many campaigns left in heartbreaking ruin by treachery," Gonji told him.

"And if there is potential for such treachery in Vedun," Flavio replied defiantly, "then this is not the Vedun I founded and hence is not worth fighting for."

And Gonji had again found himself admiring the man's idealism greatly. But now there was another point of contention between them: Gonji's claim that the training ground had been compromised by a carnival atmosphere. Non-combatants were everywhere in evidence. The women who tended wounds and aided with equipment and refreshments were needed, but now there were many who came only to be entertained. The families of Rorka's men had moved underground, and sometimes children would be underfoot or blundering into dangerous places. Roric's dogs had seemingly invited their friends, and even some of the men who had eschewed joining the militia now shamelessly came to the catacombs to snicker and jeer. Most notable among these were Strom Gundersen and Boris Kamarovsky. Gonji's patience with these people was approaching its limit.

Changes were made. The dogs were banned, and the knights' families were moved back to the city, with daily visiting privileges. So far, so good. The first move Gonji made that raised any real opposition was the military training of the women.

"Hey, Nick!" Magda Nagy called as she emerged from the torchlit grotto into the cavern proper. "Better watch it next time you come home cock-eyed!"

She lunged forward aggressively with her poniard for emphasis, and those who understood Hungarian brayed and kidded Nagy mercilessly, Berenyi leading the jesters. Nick Nagy growled something at her that was drowned out by the laughter, his tangled and matted gray hair bristling like crabgrass as he tore off his burgonet helm.

By the second day of women's training, despite a torrent of protests on all sides, more than fifty women had begun to learn small-blade defensive skills against assault. While some broke into self-conscious giggling spates to be involved in so masculine an endeavor, and others frankly doubted that they could ever kill a human being, most women grimly agreed that should their children be threatened or their men fall, they would be grateful for the deadly knowledge. And so, with a prayer for merciful exemption and moral guidance—composed by Greta—beginning each session, they learned to employ and conceal dirk and misericorde, dagger and stiletto.

A tall, statuesque Germanic woman of Swedish extraction, named Hildegarde, came to Gonji one day and demanded that such women as desired be allowed to train with more offensive weapons. Many men scoffed, but Gonji recounted to them the tale of Itagaki, a legendary female samurai, whose skill with the halberd, which Gonji called the *naginata*, was unparalleled. In the climactic battle of her brilliant career she led a greatly outnumbered garrison against an army, dispatching scores of her enemies before succumbing.

So Hildegarde had her way, joining with Garth in learning the polearm. An extremely strong woman, and absolutely fearless, she displayed a gift for aggressiveness, and men soon treated her as an equal in the arts of war, overlooking the disarming fact that she was endowed with the sort of feminine ripeness that caused many of them to avert their eyes in intimidation and embarrassment. Gonji was fond of calling her "she of stout heart and mighty breast." And she in retort, referring to their shared Scandinavian heritage through Gonji's Norwegian mother, dubbed him "Gonji-Gunnar, the half-breed Viking."

Gonji was immensely fond of her and deeply proud and respectful of her skill at arms.

Some of the women took up the bow. Among them was Helena, who acquitted herself splendidly on the archery field. Her father, a Polish archer who had died in the field, had instructed her well, and her turn at the targets was a popular event in the catacombs. Whether out of pity for her affliction or genuine affection for her petite loveliness and spunk, the deaf-mute girl seemed to occupy a special place in the heart of Vedun. It was for this reason that Gonji regarded her archery involvement with relief. He was beginning to find her presence discomfiting.

Helena aroused in Gonji a complex blend of feelings he found as difficult to deal with as they were to define. His intense desire to be with a woman had to be restrained by his promise to Flavio that he would uphold the law of the land; the taking of pleasure-women was forbidden, and duty decreed that he acquiesce, though he at times doubted Flavio truly expected him to. Of late, however, he had been able to sublimate his passions in the rigors of the exhaustive training.

But whenever Helena's mother would allow her to descend into the cavern to aid in support of the militia, the girl would follow Gonji to attend on his needs.

Doe-eyed and artless, the coyness that typified romantic game-playing wholly alien to her, she would dote on him incessantly. At once attracted and repelled, Gonji felt oddly guilty, nervous and irritable, over the conflicting feelings she aroused. He didn't like the silly tittering of the other young women, the reproving glances some aimed at Helena. And most of all he resented the cold stares of certain of the men. He had no wish to violate their pet innocent and the rare flower they cherished so—the female equivalent, the thought occurred to him, of Michael Benedetto. *And I don't need anymore distrust of me among the militia . . . But I'm a man, and I have my needs, and so what am I to do about her? Choléra . . .*

She isn't even the woman I want.

Lydia Benedetto disdained the combat training as disgusting and unladylike. The province of men, and childish men at that. Men who hide their fear of lost control behind a threatening sword blade.

She eased up quietly behind Gonji where he sat and refilled his goblet with water. He half-turned but, upon seeing that it was she, averted his eyes at once. Too forcefully. There was no one else within earshot, and she recognized the sexual tension immediately. She needn't see his eyes to know that she was in his mind. Tipping up the leather budget too quickly, sloshing water on the ground, she spun to leave.

"You could use for your self-protection a little training," Gonji said in a rush, his Italian phrasing clumsy and forced. His voice quavered ever so slightly.

She thought a moment before replying. "I detest violence," she said finally in a voice barely above a whisper.

"It doesn't care much for you either, lady," he said harshly, rising at once to stalk away.

Well, she thought, whatever the hell did that mean?

Gonji stormed off, feeling awkward and stupid. He had felt the need to say something to her, to banish the tension between them, and as so often happened in such circumstances, what passed his lips had certainly not escaped from his brain. Damn her anyway, he thought. She looks bewitching even in that billowy tunic. What an asinine thing to—

Not far away, a small group of pikemen labored at performing a series of patterned movements against an imaginary opponent. Klaus chose that moment to stumble and sprawl on his face. There followed a few snickers among the trainees, but they were quickly belayed out of deference to Gonji's empathy with Klaus as a social outcast.

It was the silly, pointless, derisive sound behind him that needled Gonji's ill humor, caused his shoulders to bunch up, froze him in his tracks. He turned with terrible deliberation, like a death's-head in darkness.

Spine-cleaver whined out of its scabbard.

"Look at the monkey-man," Boris said from his seat next to Strom on the great boulder, "trying to move in on Michael's wife—uh-oh! *tsk-tsk*—he didn't like something she said. Must've turned him down."

"Shhh!" Strom cautioned. "Cut it out. He'll hear."

"Ahhhh, he doesn't understand Russian. Anyway, your father's here—oooh! Look at Klaus, the big jackass! Hee-heeee!"

Strom pulled out his reed pipe and trilled a merry little melody that underscored Klaus's oafishness and embarrassed effort at rising. He stopped abruptly and gaped to see Gonji draw the *katana,* to catch the irrational sparkle in the samurai's dark angular eyes.

A gurgle escaped Strom's constricted throat. He

heard Boris scream beside him. Gonji charged them at the run, arm extended rigidly behind him, that awful, gleaming blade pointing at the cavern ceiling. Together they scrambled down from the boulder and hurtled for the tunnel to the chapel.

"Strom Gundersen!" Gonji cried, surging after them.

There were shouts behind him, his name breaking from a dozen points in the training ground. He ran until he reached the egress, heard their yelps echoing in the dim lamplight of the upward-twisting tunnel. Then he turned back, the *katana* still gripped beside and behind him in a striking posture.

"Let him go," Gonji yelled in German at the crowd that pressed in, murmuring, "and let him and that rat-faced friend of his stay away from here until they're ready to come back as militiamen. *Look* at this place—do you people think this is a game? Your life or death is being planned here. Is that what you want—spectators watching you fall and bleed and die up there when the time comes? And then pipe funny little tunes for your departing soul? Then you don't need me."

Rationality returned to Gonji, and composure crept back into his features. He put up Spine-cleaver. Seeing his wrath abate, some of the leaders and his friends moved closer.

"Calm yourself, Gonji," Flavio urged.

"Diplomacy, my friend," Milorad added, "You needn't—"

"Calm myself," Gonji parroted. "That's usually not a problem. But look at this. It's a circus, and I have no desire to lead a troupe of performers. At least not before an audience until the performers are ready. I want all people who have no business here away from the training ground during practice sessions. We have everyone here except the hawkers and shopkeepers. Why not just move them all down here and abandon the city to Klann? There's scarcely a face I know in Vedun that isn't here already, except for Phlegor and his idiot followers. And what have *they* been up to the past week?"

"You have no cause to revile the city like that," Michael asserted.

"Haven't I—?"

"The people have done all you've demanded of them," Lorenz added, "and more, I dare say."

Garth stood behind him, silent, rather ruffled to have had a son threatened. He seemed uncertain of Gonji.

Gonji scowled. Then Tralayn glided through the parting crowd and stood before him, her lips pursed. She nodded. "Gonji is right to be angry. There must be no more nonsense, and we must redouble our efforts."

"Aye!" the voice of Paille cried from the crowd.

Wilf and Monetto and Jiri and some of Gonji's other supporters ringed him in and started to speak and to pledge their renewed efforts, but he pushed through them and stalked off toward the tunnel to the valley exit. They watched, whispering, as he marched past Lydia, who stood alone with raised eyebrows and downcast eyes; and then past Klaus, who scrambled up from his lonely seat on the ground to see Gonji approach and said, *"Es tut mir leid, Lehmer—I mean 'sensei.'* I'm sorry." But the samurai ignored him and strode into the tunnel. There was mild alarm among some that he might abandon them, but those who knew him better knew that he'd return. For he had left Tora behind, and lashed to his saddle, the Sagami.

Gonji needed to be alone for a space. He was tired. Tired of them, sick of their faces, their attitudes. He needed relief from the stifling atmosphere of the cavern. Needed to uncoil his knotted stomach. That had been very bad, losing composure like that. *The Western child part of me again, neh? Karma.*

He sat cross-legged in a quiet glade for a time and meditated, Spine-cleaver lying sheathed along his right side, arms on knees, hands hanging open limply, eyes focused on a point in the distance before him.

Back at the cavern the training resumed, sedate and serious. No one so much as cracked a smile for the remainder of the session, not even Berenyi. So ended the first week of the training.

And through it all the traitor had been there. Watching. Recording every detail . . .

Chapter Thirteen

Gonji stepped up the training's intensity and complexity.

More controlled fighting was done with steel weapons. Techniques became more specified and involved. Squads were selected. Actual battle plans were laid, objectives defined. Potential killing grounds were studied via Paille's detailed miniature of Vedun. Those less adroit with weapons were organized into harassing squads which would rush the deadly spiked-steel calthrops and barrier planks into place in alleys and courtyards. Then archers and polearmed footmen would descend on them like maddened hornets.

Dangerous skills were introduced: rider against footman; pikeman against rider . . . In the latter clash Hildegarde proved outstanding. Strong, intrepid, and with an aggressive abandon born of years of hearing exaggerated tales of the toughness of the male hide, she soon became a fearsome sight with a poleaxe to any rider bearing down on her. Garth was at last forced to caution her against ferocity when she had caused two severe gashes through leather jerkins and spilled a rider so hard that he had broken an arm.

And now the injuries, too, increased in proportion to the intensity of training. The elderly surgeon, Dr. Verrico, and his aides were kept busy, stitching and splinting.

"Butchers!" the doctor growled in Gonji's ear. "Every one of you—Klann and all his vermin included!" Verrico jabbed his needle a bit harder than necessary into Gonji's side for emphasis. The samurai's nearly healed duel wound had split in a fall from a broken scaffold.

"Easy there, old fool!" Gonji chided. "What kind of healer increases a victim's pain?" He gritted his teeth and pursed his lips, accepting it stoically.

Verrico grunted irascibly. "What kind of man sets himself up as a victim?"

"Would you have hurt Strom?" Garth whispered thinly, watching Gonji work.

Gonji paused and regarded him, smiling. *"Nein, mein Freund,"* he answered softly, "just frightened him a bit."

Garth nodded, satisfied. Under Dr. Verrico's direction the militia learned methods of aiding the wounded in the field. Gonji was in the process of splinting Garth's leg. Other wounds were described, the treatments broached.

Gonji caught the murmur of fear that rippled through the audience and began to extemporize in his inimitable fashion:

"The human body, you see, is like this piece of leather—" With his sword he poked at the cuirass of a man seated in the front row. Almost at once Gonji's German was rendered by translators into half a dozen languages. "—it has to be beaten and tanned, cured before it reaches its final toughness. That's how wounds are—that's the positive end they serve. When they're treated, when the skin grows back together, then it's stronger than it was before. The more healed wounds, the tougher the man . . ."

There were skeptical looks among the more educated, but mostly rapt attention. Gonji assumed an expression of smug conviction and mentally patted himself on the back for this fine bit of prevarication. Hell, it might even be true—that knife-long jagged scar along his shoulder blade, while itching like a column of chigger bites sometimes, certainly was twice as thick as the surrounding skin . . .

Then, while on the subject of wounds, Gonji launched into his recitation of where he had acquired his various body scars, omitting the shoulder scar with its poignant memories.

Dobroczy leaned over to Pete Foristek and whispered out of the corner of his mouth: "Listen to him. He thinks he's St. Paul the apostle . . ."

After the wound treatment business, a number of new pieces of armament began to turn up on the training ground: shields and bucklers, cuirasses and half-armors, legharnesses, pauldrons and vambraces, helms with buffes and low-cut visors. The militiamen of Vedun had decided to hedge their bets by providing every possible advantage against suffering the wounds they'd heard described.

The leaders encouraged them, instructing them in

the best cross between maneuverability and protection, given the nature of their enemy. And while Gonji used no shield himself, he showed how some, particularly the concave target-type shields, might even ward off pistol balls. The next day the already overwrought metal founders were inundated with orders for target shields, more than they could possibly deliver before the spring. But the overwhelming majority still wore only what oddments of armor they could cobble together, it being expensive and in short supply.

Even the children of Vedun did their part.

On nights when Gonji slept in the city, he would creep by darkness to the Gundersens' or Paille's, avoiding the room he had taken at Wojcik's Haven on the north side of town, then join with the workers going to their morning shifts and the militiamen heading for the training session. Linking up with Eduardo and the other children, the samurai would sometimes play with them, mug for them, perform martial arts *kata* to their yelping delight. Mercenaries from the garrison at the converted granary nearby would be drawn irresistibly, and trainees slipping into Tralayn's home to descend to the catacombs did so unheeded.

Gonji knew he was playing with fire. Julian would by now be desperate to have some further intelligence from him and was likely fuming over Gonji's dropping out of sight. Periodically soldiers would try to signal him that they wished to speak in private, and he enjoyed their exasperation when he would return their winks with bold gestures of greeting as he tumbled with the children. He knew he'd have to check in with Julian soon, but it would be on his terms.

During these play sessions Gonji grew increasingly fond of little Tiva. For her would be reserved the longest rides aboard the samurai's back and the gentlest tosses into the air. Her widowed father was an archer in the militia, a rather withdrawn, heavy-hearted man who had never overcome the death of his wife in birthing Tiva. Although the notion disturbed his sense of justice, Gonji resolved in the back of his mind to try to preserve the man's life. For Tiva's sake. The adorable urchin awakened in him previously untapped yearnings for fatherhood.

They were in Tralayn's house, and once again Gonji was transfixed by the sight of the great weapons slung over her mantel.

"Where did you get those?" he asked.

She clasped her hands in front of her and watched Gonji as she spoke, a hidden mirth flickering in her luminous green eyes. "They were found in the empty city when the pilgrims first settled here. For now they're only ornaments, awaiting . . . the warrior who can use them."

"They'll be waiting a while, I'd wager," he said, scratching his head. "I tried to lift one of them once."

Tralayn smiled in a way Gonji didn't like, as if she were appraising a child's fumbling ways.

"I've been out to see Simon Sardonis again," she said, Gonji's features perking with interest at the mention of the mystery man's name, "to try to enlist his aid for our purpose—"

"And?"

She shook her head. "Unfortunately he was gone."

"For good?" Gonji inquired.

"I don't think so," Tralayn replied, a far-off look in her eyes. "But it's possible that could be for the worse."

"Why don't you let me try to talk with him—warrior to warrior?"

"I've already told you, he won't see you. No one can pin him down without his wishing it."

"Really, Tralayn—" Gonji scoffed.

"Remember his fight with Ben-Draba, my friend. And didn't Klann's troops look like so many children when they tried to bring him down?"

"*Did* bring him down," Gonji corrected, a bit uncertainly.

"He *was* struck—but not downed, I assure you."

Gonji grew impatient with her doubletalk. "This is absurd, all this importance attached to a single man. And why won't so *valiant* a warrior join in your cause? He *is* in your debt in some way, *neh?* And he's obviously antagonistic to Klann anyway."

"Ah, but that would be telling too much, wouldn't it? Remember our bargain."

"And I've kept my half already," Gonji responded with annoyance.

"Patience," she said firmly. "There'll be more to tell soon."

Wilf clashed with Dobroczy, closed with him, slashing his *bokken* with the economical fury, the controlled passion Gonji belabored. But Hawk was a slippery bastard. His parries were quick and strong, and his classic European style would occasionally find him darting in to skewer Wilf. What mattered now was not Vlad but Vlad's blade and style; he must fight this man dispassionately—the passion was in the achieving of his purpose, not the feelings fostered for the enemy. And against a swordsman of similar style and skill, he soon realized, he would have to be quicker, more patient. He would have to favor *iai-jutsu*—defensive swordsmanship—over the more aggressive *kenjutsu*.

Then they slammed together suddenly, grunting

and cursing, and Dobroczy drove his knee up into Wilf's groin. Wilf shifted and caught the brunt of the blow on his thigh, but his breath hissed between his teeth, and he lost his head. He let go the *bokken* with one hand and swiped the wooden weapon upward, cracking the hilt against Vlad's jaw, knocking his sallet off.

Now Hawk lost his own temper, and Wilf froze in shock an instant to gauge the damage he'd done to his opponent—*oohs* and mumbling among the band that watched—Roric called out words of restraint—Vlad slammed his wooden sword down sharply, binding Wilf's awkwardly held *bokken* against the rocky cavern floor. Wilf's eyes bulged as Vlad brought his sword up—its arcing sweep would take his head off.

Clack!

Both men were disarmed with a single vertical slash of Gonji's *katana*.

"All right, tough men," Gonji declared in High German, "you have all this anger to spend, *neh?* Then spend it on a common enemy—hit *me*."

They stared at him, unmoving. He sheathed Spinecleaver and tossed it to Roric, who threw him a *bokken*. Sweat glistened on Gonji's shirtless upper body. He snapped off a vicious wrist-twisting blow that struck both men in their midsections, knocking the wind out of them even through their thickly padded jacks.

"Hit me! You want to play at childish fury, and I need the defensive training. Let's see how good you are. When you can strike me a blow, you're good enough to tilt with brigands. *Shiai!*" Gonji took a low-guard "invitation" stance, his sword pointed downward at his right side.

Wilf looked at Vlad. Their shared apprehension mingled in their eye contact, their mutual hatred abated. Vlad grinned at his rival and replaced his sallet, fastening the catch.

The watchers' excitement rumbled through the echoing cavern as they backed away to give them room. All other activities gradually ceased, an arena atmosphere prevailing.

Wilf charged, howling a *kiyai*, and slashed at Gonji's open belly.

The old Master Oguni exercise occurred to Gonji just about the time he saw the practice duel turn into a campfire brawl. It was time to add spice to the training, time to become for them the emotionless fighting machine they needed to test their new skills.

Wilf's telegraphed slash was batted aside, the circular, upward return driving Dobroczy's lunge up and over his head.

"Jaaa!—Hey-hey!—" came the cries from the audience as the pair resumed the attack with renewed vigor, but Gonji's seemingly effortless, lightning parries flicked their blows aside with a driving force that belied the magical grace of his small motions. Again and again they attacked and were rebuffed. They soon wore themselves out in their efforts. Their blows slowed. Gonji disarmed Vlad with a curling snap of his wrists like the sudden tautening of a rope, blocked Wilf's overhead slash with a breathtaking high parry, executed with his back to him, then with a blurring half-turn, still fighting almost totally with his back to his opponent, stabbed Wilf full in the chest with a short one-hand thrust under his armpit, his left hand pressed forward to lend reaction force to the blow.

A great cheer rocked the catacombs as the young smith stumbled backward, off balance. Dobroczy knelt on one knee nearby, shaking his head in frustration.

"All right," Gonji called out, waving down the cheering, "it looks as though these heroes need help! Who else would like to try to strike a samurai without fear of being unlimbed for it? A rare opportunity—come forward!"

Paolo Sauvini stepped forward with a *bokken*, working his jaw nervously. He removed his jack, eyes gleaming. And a moment later *three* men tried to deliver a blow to Gonji's unprotected torso and head. Without success.

"Hey, Hawk!" Berenyi called, leaping atop a boulder as they paused to catch their breath again. "Stab him with your nose!" A chorus of laughter at the hook-nosed farmer's expense, which he waved off exhaustedly. "Why don't *you* try it, Nagy, you old fart?" Stefan taunted his partner.

"Why don't you get off my back, you young stud!" Nick Nagy retorted from the crowd below.

Jiri Szabo joined the attack, and now there were three *kenjutsu* students arrayed against Gonji, but it was the single European-style fencer, Dobroczy, who landed the first blow, a glancing shot to Gonji's right shoulder after a deep lunge. Cheers rang out on the training ground. Vlad dropped to his knees out of weariness and gratitude, a crooked smile on his face.

Gonji sidled over to him and bowed. Dobroczy rose and returned it. "Everything OK now?" Gonji asked.

"Igen, jo," Dobroczy answered.

"I don't speak Hungarian."

The farmer's eyes became questioning slits, then softened. *"Ja—gut,"* he repeated in German. Gonji smiled and they exchanged bows again.

The exhibition resumed later, and Gonji proved to be, if anything, still more elusive. He broke his own *bokken* and Jiri's with vicious parries. But the militia had trained hard and well and were improving daily, and by the end of the exhausting match, both Wilf and Jiri had struck Gonji with clean slashes.

A festive mood took hold, and Gonji and the other leaders sensed that it was a good time for a break in the grueling training. The meal break was taken, and the usually disdained wine casks spilled their contents. Camaraderie and good cheer reigned. Even Rorka's Grays were warming to Gonji, if not the baron himself, as fully half of them came forward to share a laugh and a few words, either in a common language or a cobbled together *lingua franca*.

It was a warm, affectionate celebration, the first the militia ever shared. And even Gonji didn't shrink from the hearty back-slapping of well-wishers, as he usually was wont to do.

Klaus had studiously avoided the wine, as he always did, in his sincere effort at improving himself physically. It hadn't helped.

He clumped forward on a gray roncin, oversized burgonet jouncing comically on his head, and reached out with his broadsword to engage Lorenz, who stood his ground with a long, sharp *guisarme*.

"Just bat it aside, Klaus, that's all," Gonji muttered under his breath in Japanese as he watched.

Klaus swung his arm in a wide arc, Lorenz disengaged his polearm with a simple drop of the point, and the rider overreached, leaned too far, and spurred the roncin hard by accident.

"Look out!"

Horse and rider crashed to the ground in a jangling tumble. Klaus limped away, miraculously unhurt. The roncin had shattered a leg and had to be destroyed.

Gonji separated Klaus from the rest of the men. "Klaus, listen to me—have you any money?"

"A little," Klaus responded, face brightening.

"Why? Do you need some, *sensei?*"

"*Ja*, I—*nein, dummkopf!* Not for me, for *you!* I have a new idea."

"New idea?" Klaus looked perplexed already.

"Armor, Klaus. *Lots* of armor. I want you to see the harbisher and the foundry people. They'll tell you their orders for armor are backed up, between Klann's needs and the secret work they do for the city. But I'll speak with them, and they'll squeeze you in. Put all your money down on account, and don't worry about squaring up with them. That can wait. You just get yourself armor that covers you from head to toe, *verstehen Sie?*"

The samurai squared his shoulders and strode off but, remembering something, turned and called out, "And a bigger horse, Klaus! A big strong one, *neh?*"

And the slow-witted buckle-maker stood scratching his head, watching him march off.

Then a bad turn of affairs occurred: A tanner named Danko lost an eye in a staff-training accident. The hard-working Nick Nagy had delivered the blow during a rapid exchange, and he dropped his staff and roared for help as Danko hit the ground, writhing and screaming, holding the gouged eye tightly with both hands. A crowd of their peers gathered quickly to stare in horror, ashen-faced, as Dr. Verrico pushed through them. The younger members of the militia seemed especially struck, for although they had learned to live with daily pains and some serious accidents, this was the first permanently debilitating injury sustained during training. Their sense of imminent mortality was aroused.

Nagy surged around the crowd, jabbering nervously, crying out for forgiveness, trying to exonerate himself to any who would listen. Roric tried to calm him with gentle firmness, but he seemed inconsolable, and Gonji rushed forward, at once sensing the descent of an enervating new enemy—demoralization.

"Nagy! Nagy! Get hold of yourself!" Gonji snarled in a low, snapping tone. He pushed the babbling hostler away from the rest, guiding him into a recess along one cavern wall. "Stop it now—"

Nagy kept whining something repeatedly in Hungarian.

"—control yourself. Can't you see what you're going to do to them? You're older than these others, and you were a soldier once. You knew there was always this risk—and more! People may die in the coming conflict. They *will* die. But more will die without the training. Danko knew the chance he was taking. A slip the other way and it would have been *you*."

Danko's screams had dwindled to a soft moaning. Nagy relaxed, though he still stared over at where the man was being attended. At length he nodded that he was all right, but Gonji ordered him out of the catacombs for the rest of the session. Training resumed shortly, but with a notable lack of zest.

Danko took to wearing an eye patch and became a minor local hero, albeit one who provoked uneasiness whenever he would drop in on the training ground. He never again hefted a weapon. To the occupying troops he became nothing more than a curiosity, the occasional object of a cruel jest or insult. For none of them could interpret the black eye patch as the ominous mark it was on the horizon of their boorish aggressions.

(from the *Deathwind of Vedun* epic:)
"*. . . and the people of Vedun bore all injuries willingly and stoically, accepting all pain, embracing all hardship in the name of their noble purpose . . . and they laughed in the faces of their complacent*

oppressors, and went singing to their tasks, joined in heart and in spirit . . .

Clear, brilliant skies and the happy chirping of birds greeted them as the people who had just finished the night training session streamed from the chapel earnestly praying that their effort at washing from the trough in the catacombs had laved away the sweat and dirt and tiredness from their drawn faces. That their limps and aches would be sufficiently concealed behind their bright early-morning smiles and greetings and the Llorm dragoons they passed wouldn't be moved to curiosity. So to chase their winces and smother their aches, they sang on the way to their jobs. They sang folk songs and patriotic anthems, each ethnic group singing in its native language, competing with the others in volume and feeling in a great cacophony that was the war song of Vedun.

William Eddings walked alone from the chapel, his brother having stayed back to speak with the tanners. The tanners. Danko had lost an eye, and now listen to them all—singing! That was how the bloody fools would all go to the gallows one day. Singing. Slavs and Huns and Italians—peasants and barbarians all! He hated them, all of them. But most of all he hated the Jappo.

He marched grimly toward his tiny sundrier's shop, pulling his three-cornered hat low over his eyes so that the soldiers might not see their redness, then notice the weariness that weighted his arms and back and shoulders. His ribs ached with every step from the blow he'd suffered while fencing.

Damn fools. They'd even brainwashed his father and brother. He'd tried to talk with them about leaving this place, but neither his father, nor John, nor even John's gentle wife would hear of it. Wasn't this what they'd fled England to escape? Couldn't they simply flee again to some other, safer, saner place? But no, his father had said, they'd set themselves up here and would stay, come what may, even if it meant dying with these people.

He reached the shop and shuffled inside, breathing a sigh of relief that no soldier had stopped to question him. If they had, he was sure, he would have told them all, put an end to this madness. How many lives would be saved if the Jappo were strung up now, before he could do any more harm?

Throwing his hat into a corner, Eddings slammed over a table full of the gaudy trinkets and fake jewelry the mercenaries were so fond of bestowing on their strumpets. Table and contents crashed into a jangling, tinkling heap. He slammed the door and drew the shade. Then he dropped onto a stool with a heavy thud, rubbed at his pinched face, and all at once began to sob uncontrollably.

There was one birth and one natural death during the first week of training. Neither the christening nor the funeral was well attended.

Chapter Fourteen

The dancers whirled and gamboled and clapped their hands merrily in a great circle, the musicians driving them faster and faster until they had themselves reached a fever pitch, barely able to play in time. Flavio was pushed into the middle of the circle with Anna Vargo, whose arthritic joints caused her considerable suffering, but she made no complaint, so glad was she to see Flavio laugh and dance. A great cheer drowned out the strains of music as Flavio plunged into the dance with a spryness that belied his years.

Gonji cheered as loud as anyone, warmed by the company of so many new friends. He danced and clapped lustily, the social ritual appealing to his gregarious nature. The dance finished with a frenzied flourish, the dancers on their knees applauding themselves, exhausted but ready for more.

It was the annual feast of St. Stephen, a one-time king of Hungary, which coincided with the harvest. And despite the mysterious selective crop failure, the yield had been good, though there would be shortages. Bunting and banners proclaiming the event festooned the square. Gloaming shadows spread their cool tendrils over the city, and the moon, a bright ungular disc, rose early, racing after the first star of evening. Florid dresses swished by, their wearers chattering and laughing. Aromas of food and drink teased and beckoned, made one wish for the stomach capacity of a ruminant.

Gonji was in his glory, his kinship with these people growing. He stood mopping his brow in a group that included Jiri and Greta—who had dragged Gonji into the dance, Monetto and his wife, and several others, who were listening to Flavio relate how the tarantella was believed to cure the madness brought on by the bite of the wolf spider. Michael stood behind the Elder, smiling with arms folded, supporting the legend with stories of his own. The protegé appeared relaxed, darkly handsome in a corn-hued damask shirt and elegantly tailored breeches. His eyes had nearly returned to normal, but now in social garb it was more apparent than ever that his nose had sustained a permanent crook from the breaking.

Lydia stood with him, hand in hand, smiling the smile of a benign, all-knowing goddess; lovely in her swaying skirts, bonnet and bow; interjecting her quiet wit at just the right moments. Gonji stole glimpses of her in the course of long, casual pans of the festival crowd, determined not to stare. Their eyes never once met. She was the mistress of social grace, at once coolly discouraging prolonged male attention and reaping the homage of its ubiquitous presence. She knew well her attraction and had long since learned to deal with it to her favor. Her élan was annoying, and Gonji had always refused to compete on the terms such women set. But she was difficult to ignore, and he found himself fighting the well-known internal battle of the samurai, that of *giri*—duty vs. *ninjo*—natural impulse.

He suddenly felt awkward with this group, but Greta was a great help. Jiri sat while the bubbly girl took Gonji for her partner as the musicians broke into a rousing mazurka. Gonji and Greta became one of eight couples, and the samurai learned the step readily. When the dance was done they sat at a long table cluttered with food and drink, facing the marketplace on the Street of Hope.

The Festival of St. Stephen very nearly had been canceled by the city leaders for fear of trouble with the occupation force. But the traditional-minded and those who felt the tension-release was needed—Gonji among the latter—urged that it be held as usual. Captain Sianno had been alerted to the potential for mercenary bullying, and he had readily agreed to double-up the normal Llorm dragoon street patrols. Drunken, leering mercenaries had, in fact, been drawn irresistibly to the celebration, but they had been forewarned against aggression and remained on the perimeter of the square, leaning and sitting in surly bands who called out lewd comments and empty threats but proffered no physical menace.

Gonji saw a group of them exchange words with a few citizens—Phlegor and his craft guildsmen—across the square. A Llorm patrol clopped by and quickly put an end to it, dispersing the rowdy bunch.

He reached down to the bench for his swords. But they were not beside him. He remembered, smiling slightly, and then saw them. Wilfred had taken custody of the *daisho,* wrapping them in a silk cloth. They were being handed along the table from the end where Wilf sat sulking. Jiri held them out, bowing, but then he withdrew them from Gonji's grasp at the last instant.

"Wait," Jiri said, "let me place them." He walked around uncertainly to Gonji's left, started to lay them down, but stopped. *"Iyé,"* he said, remembering the significance of their position. Then he laid them on the bench at Gonji's right.

"Peace, *sensei,"* he said, grinning. They all laughed.

Gonji bowed. *"Hai, domo,* Jiri-san. No trouble tonight!"

A new dance began. Karl Gerhard took Sylva Monetto by the arm, leaving Aldo with the couple's three children.

"Hey!" Aldo shouted. "You dance with my wife you better behave yourself, *si?"* He closed one eye and fixed the other on Gerhard, shaking a fist.

Karl made a face and pawed the air in return threat.

"Somebody watch that sneaky Hun," Monetto declared as he took the children to the food stalls. Gonji chuckled with the others and tossed off the last of his wine. His head began to swim as he moved gently with the music. It was a grand time of sharing, and he felt warmed all over by the good cheer of friends, the smiles of pretty faces.

Nick and Magda Nagy dropped in at the table with Stefan Berenyi and the girl he escorted. Soon the two hostlers were carrying on a spirited argument regarding whether the corral at the Provender had been locked and who had been responsible for it. It culminated in the pair leaving their women and storming off to check, cursing and pointing accusing fingers at each other. The women sighed and spoke in Hungarian, exasperated.

Another woman came by with a small cask and refilled the empty goblets. Gonji accepted his refill with a grateful smile.

"When are you going to marry him already?" she said in German when she stood beside Gonji. She had spoken to Berenyi's girl, who tittered and whispered something in reply.

Marry. Gonji smiled hollowly and drummed his fingers on the table in time to the music. He began to feel bored, tense—something he couldn't quite define—as he sat surrounded by other men's women, wishing for some lively conversation.

Too bad Wilf had taken to brooding over Genya again. The young Gundersen sat swirling his wine at one end of the table, a pretty girl Gonji had seen somewhere before seated behind him, speaking to him over his shoulder. Wilf kept repeating the story of last year's Festival of St. Stephen, when he and Hawk Dobroczy had fought over Genya. The girl made sounds of sultry-sweet sympathy while she twined her hair seductively.

At the next table most of the men, including Flavio, Roric, Milorad, and Michael, rose to visit the stalls. The women remained. Gonji played a game of discipline: he resolved not to look over at Lydia even once during her husband's absence.

He looked across the grounds to where Phlegor and

his trade brothers had begun shouting drunken insults at passing soldiers. A strange reversal of the norm in Vedun. Those fools were going to create real trouble soon. Shaking his head and scowling, he panned around the grounds, stopped when his eyes fell on Helena.

The deaf-mute girl was staring back, her eyes widening in greeting when she saw him look. She was with her mother, who chatted with a group near the chapel. He felt a pang of desire to see her dusky beauty, deepened by the richly sensual hues of twilight. He waved to her and bowed, and she returned the wave discreetly. Then he felt abruptly foolish at the futility of the meaningless flirtation and broke the contact.

Jiri leaned across Greta and whispered to Gonji: "There's your friend."

Gonji looked to where Jiri pointed. Julian clopped past on a black roncin, whose color matched that of the captain's polished cuirass and ebony slouch hat. He cut an impressive figure, the midnight display counterpointed sharply by the gleam of his saber and the silver-handled pistol he now carried. Behind him rode the Armorer, his ubiquitous new companion, who still sported enough armament to sink a galleon. The way they arrogantly parted the crowd as they rode by made him mindful of the swaggering Navarez and Esteban.

He saw Julian glare when he had singled him out in the festival crowd, and in his ire and contempt for the man, now fueled by his amusement over Julian's frustration with Gonji's failure to report, the samurai brayed suddenly, "Hail, Captain!"

Those at the table became alert, following Gonji's wave.

Julian and his companion slowed, the Armorer

making as if he would steer his mount their way. But the captain dissuaded him with a head toss, and they went on their way.

Shithead, Gonji thought. Just keep looking back at me like that and riding east till you drop into the river. And take that armored porcupine with you . . .

A few fretful looks were tipped Gonji's way, but his friends soon resumed their merrymaking. Gonji knew he had been boorish, but his mood had taken an abrasive turn. All he could think was how Julian had tried to insult him, to pad his own reputation, at the castle banquet. Now that score was even.

Nagy and Berenyi's women excused themselves from the table. Gonji nodded to them, saw past them the smoky eyes of Paolo Sauvini, who sat alone on the fountain wall with his wife. Hell, even *that* sullen lout has a woman. Never thought *he'd* be married. She's not much, though, is she?

He rubbed his face vigorously, scratched under his topknot. Straighten up, Gonji-san. Pointless to try to share your karma, *neh?* Your bitterness is—

The rustle of skirts and rush of perfume had preceded her, but he was still not prepared for her abrupt appearance.

"May I?" Lydia asked, indicating the bench.

"*Hai,* of course," he replied, leaning forward and clutching the comforting solidity of his wine cup. *Choléra* . . . He took a sip. It went down hard.

"Enjoying yourself?" she asked, smiling gently. A smile that he would have described as . . . motherly. His insides churned.

"*Hai,* why not?" Go away, lady—*iyé,* stay!

She folded her hands in her lap, drew in her soft red lips, and stared at the ground a second. "Good," she said simply, a trace of uncommon nervousness in her voice. "You deserve it as much as anyone—*more.*"

What's on your mind, lady?

"*Domo, signora,* you flatter me too much. I do only my duty."

"Oh no—I—we—" she stammered, then looked at the flagstones again, arranging her skirts self-consciously. Gonji was beginning to enjoy her rare discomfiture, puzzled though he was.

"I think you've made a conquest."

Her simple statement struck like a hammer blow. His heart was pounding now, and his ears felt hot.

"*So desu?* Is that so? What do you mean?" The words had come out in a breathy whisper that he regretted.

"Helena—"

Oh.

"—she's . . . quite taken with you, Gonji. I—I only hope you understand, she's . . . she's just a child . . . you see, and—"

"And oriental brigands are well-known for their lusts," he growled low between gritted teeth, "for their intemperate—"

"I'm sorry," she breathed, rising and hurrying off.

By all the Seven Devils . . . Gonji felt like a spitted calf. He downed his wine in a single gulp. *Careful, Gonji-san.* Glancing around him, he saw that only Jiri and Greta had taken note of Lydia's hasty departure. They looked at each other curiously and soon also took their leave. Now only Wilf and the girl remained.

You can certainly clear away a crowd, samurai . . .

He lurched to his feet, having had enough of this night. He took up his swords, a bit unsteady. *Got to clear my head . . .*

"*Vive le samurai!*"

Paille trooped up behind him, a young woman in tow, and called for a wine cask. He clapped Gonji on the shoulder, already quite drunk.

"Sit, *mon frere!* I've been looking for you." Paille pushed the girl down onto the bench next to Gonji and spoke behind his hand. "Remember the nubile Torok daughters?" He winked with some effort and pointed down unsubtly. The girl looked up at Gonji and smirked coyly.

Of course, he thought, *the foster's daughter.* The girl with Wilf was her sister.

Paille annoyingly slapped him on the back again.

"My friend the poet *manque,*" Gonji slurred in the artist's beloved French. "And what can I do for you?"

"*Manque?*" Paille shouted. "Why—Your diction is terrible, *monsieur!* Use *langue d'oc* or *langue d'oil*—don't mix dialects! Where are those wine stewards?" He stumbled off in search of them, bumping into one and nearly knocking him down without noticing who it was, then kept going, grumbling all the while. The steward came and filled two goblets.

"What was that all about?" she asked, smiling. "You do speak German, don't you, Gonji?"

"*Ja*—nothing much. Your friend has quite a temper," he replied, sipping, his eyeballs beginning to sting.

"*Ja* . . . and the hands of an artist."

Gonji did a doubletake, wincing, then raising his eyebrows as he looked at her. He wasn't sure what she had meant, nor for that matter, whether it was even she who had said what he thought he had just heard.

She laughed. "You can call me Jana. My full name is a bore, my dear mother's idea."

Gonji smiled and nodded, his mood shifting again. She was very pretty, and the wine was very good.

"My sister's trying to pry Wilf away from Genya again." She shook her head knowingly. "It will never happen. Genya's a sorceress."

"I've seen that for myself. She's quite a woman," he added, grinning crookedly. Then he was presently appalled at his pride and familiarity in the silly statement. He was playing at Intimate Acquaintance with the Fashionable Youth—a game he hadn't played in years. He rubbed his face and blew out breath. Inhaled deeply.

Lorenz Gundersen came up to the other Torok girl and bowed elegantly. The musicians had begun a stately dance much favored in the French courts those days.

"I do believe I'm going to purloin your woman, brother Wilfred," Gonji heard him say.

The girl went along reluctantly, and Wilf grunted something at his brother, but Gonji had seen none of it. He was staring at Lydia again as she danced with Michael.

"Nein," Jana said curtly, sipping.

"Eh?"

"She's not for you. Not for anyone but her husband." She stared into her cup as she spoke.

"It shows?" Gonji asked rather painfully, knowing he'd drunk too much.

"Ja."

Paille clumped back to the table, carrying three goblets of wine. The two he set before Gonji and Jana had been splattered about so much that they were practically empty.

"Ah, finally found them," Paille declared.

Gonji rose to leave, sashing his swords, weaving just a bit. "I'll be turning in, I think."

"But you haven't finished your wine!"

Gonji looked down into the goblet the artist had brought. About a thumb's worth of wine remained. He drained it off.

"Merci," he said, "and *sayonara.*" He bowed to

them and stalked off, his mind a mulch of confused thoughts, anger and frustration stirring them to a boil. That was a bad sign after drinking, a clear one that he'd passed his reasonable limit. A samurai always knew his limit with drink, and that limit was always tightened when the mood it engendered was a dark one.

Too bad Paille had returned. He had begun to entertain an idea or two about the Torok girl. He snickered to himself mirthlessly as he untethered Tora in front of the Ministry and mounted, dimly aware that he was courting a confrontation with Julian's minions if he was caught riding alone.

Then two sharp claps attracted him to a shadowed doorway on the west side of the Ministry building. Helena stood there alone, her hands darting to her mouth to see how her bold gesture had startled him. Half in deep night shadow, the hood of her cloak billowing about her lustrous black hair, she looked ethereal, radiant, an apparition.

"What are you doing out here alone? Where's your mother?"

He had momentarily forgotten that she could not hear his words of concern. He smiled and motioned her to come closer. Her hands dropped from her face, revealing her own undisguised smile of affection. She seemed breathless as she approached Tora, her large eyes filled with longing, with a deep defenselessness that bared her soul.

Gonji's lower jaw worked nervously. Something wild and defiant stirred inside him. He tried to inquire after her mother, using halting signs that suggested her broad girth and matronly bosom. Helena laughed impishly once she understood and taught him her sign for "mother," indicating that Sophia had gone home to bed, where, apparently, Helena was also presumed to be. She appended a gesture that meant she was either in trouble or being very bad—perhaps both.

The samurai gazed about them, saw no one watching. The flambeaux across the street threw the festival activities into stark illumination, but this side was shrouded in gloom. He reached down a hand and drew her up onto the saddle before him. Their eyes met in a moment of deep longing, their breaths mingling, Gonji noting a trace of wine on hers. He wrapped his arms around her and took up the reins, spurring Tora into a walk. The charger snorted his disapproval of the increased burden but clopped off at the easy gait.

Gonji turned into a side lane that wended south toward the stables. The high rear walls of stone buildings dwarfed them on one side; a crumbling wall, raised in antiquity, on the other. Tora's hoofbeats resounded, halting in a confused clatter about halfway through the dark tunnel.

Gonji pulled her close to him, too hungrily at first, and in modesty she stiffened slightly and drew away. But his caress became more gentle, even as his insistence increased, and she yielded at last with a desire that matched his own. Her lips moistened, parted. They kissed desperately, yearningingly, drawing from each other, giving of themselves. Tora nickered and tossed his head at the heat of the unfamiliar emotion. There was warmth and sweetness in the dreamlike air they wrought of their commingled passion.

At length they broke the embrace, and Gonji signed his shame to have so disadvantaged her with a hand over his heart and his head bowed. But she perhaps perceived the gesture to mean something else, and with her fingertips she raised his chin. He saw the liquid gleam of acquiescence, innocent surrender in her eloquent eyes, and he squeezed her hand firmly and swallowed back the voices of wisdom and caution that rose to his throat.

They clopped out of the lane, rode past the stables and wagonage, continued westward to the gate. Llorm bowmen spotted them coming from the ramparts, slowed in their paces and regarded the samurai warily. Two mercenaries stationed at the gate snapped out of their boredom at their approach, seemed about to question them, but moved out of the way grudgingly to see Gonji's narrow-eyed challenge. When they had pased out of the city and onto the road upon which he had first entered Vedun, Gonji heard them sputtering. They hadn't even snickered suggestively to see him with the girl, and when the reason presently struck him, he laughed inwardly at their ironic confounding: They were perhaps under orders to convey to him Julian's displeasure, if they could catch him alone. And now, though his were the only ears that could have heard, Helena's presence had thwarted them.

Before they reached the first sentry outpost, Gonji turned them north, off the road and onto a trail into the foothills. Helena made no inquiry but only leaned back against him and sighed. They dismounted in the same glade where he and Wilf had practiced the sword many days ago. Then, light-headed and exhilarated by her presence, he set her down on the trunk of a downed tree and began to speak to her in Japanese, gesticulating broadly like a stage player to enhance his meaning. And he told her the story of a samurai's life, a life filled with pain and sorrow, but also with happiness and love of life in its strengths and frailties and impermanence.

It seemed that Gonji and Helena shared an enchanted nonverbal lingua franca, for the woman was amazingly attuned to the turnings of his tale, smiling at the indiscretions of a wayward young half-breed;

tensing over a warrior's moments of life-suspending peril; sensitively, empathically shedding large rolling tears when the nostalgic tang glistened in Gonji's own eyes.

And at the end, when the tale was done, whether by the mood, the wine, or Helena's own intoxicating presence, the samurai stood over her, drew her up and against him in a firm embrace. They kissed hard and longingly, reeling gently in their tracks so that they tipped almost off balance at the last and broke the embrace to stave a fall, laughing and clutching each other's arms, locking their fervent gazes as if they feared the enchantment would end should they look away.

Then they were reclining against the trunk, their passions inflamed anew, more urgent now as they mingled their touch with the luxuriant caress of the soft grass, the cloying scents of wildflowers and pine-tinged mountain breeze. They probed each other intimately, desperately, breaths quickening and hearts racing. Soon the moment of ultimate decision was reached. They broke the embrace by mutual consent, the stars above the glade twinkling their apprehension. Helena lay with a hand on Gonji's bare chest, her huge trusting eyes soft and moist, inviting.

She broke the eye contact and made a sign over her heart that could only mean a pledge of her love. Meeting his eyes again, she repeated the sign, more surely this time. And over the pang of guilt he felt, responding to his reckless desire, he deceived her, offering the same gesture in reply.

They lay back on Gonji's kimono, commingling their desires and their flesh, and for a time all else was subordinate to ecstasy.

Helena lay asleep in the crook of Gonji's left arm,

the sonority of her even breathing at his ear. A tingling mountain breeze soughed through the stillness of the glade. His other arm supporting his head, the samurai stared at the sky. He was mildly disquieted, now that the surfeit of their lovemaking had passed. The elements had withdrawn their translucent approval; the night was deep and hard-edged. Reality came to him, stern and implacable.

The aftermath was bittersweet. Gonji sadly realized that he didn't love this woman, regretted his lie to the contrary. There would be, he knew, a price to pay for his deceit. He couldn't fathom the guilt he felt. He resented it. There should have been no reason for it. They had simply satisfied a natural need, both of them. But it was never that simple among these Christian people. His spirit grew restive.

He was confused by his strange lot: having a woman he didn't want, wanting a woman he couldn't have . . . But one positive thought did occur—the spell of Reiko had been broken. Reiko. His first love, the woman he could never have, pledged to kill him despite their one-time mutual love. For the first time a woman he had been with hadn't assumed the dream-face of Reiko while in his embrace.

Helena's face shone with childlike innocence as she slept.

Plucked the little lotus . . .

He sighed restlessly. Something dug into his side. Feeling under him, he found the lump in the sewn-in kimono pocket. Curious, he fumbled out two objects: the crucifix of the late Hawkes, the mercenary who had befriended him while they rode with the 3rd Free Company; and the folded parchment containing the foul "faith chant" of Mord. Gooseflesh erupted on his arms when he beheld the paper—the crucifix had seared its shape cleanly through its folds.

Throwing both objects onto the ground, he lay Helena down gently and dressed. From Tora's saddle he obtained a blanket with which he covered the girl and flint and tinder he used to build a fire. When the blaze was strong he unfolded the hated parchment and lay it on the fire.

It refused to burn.

He poked it with a stick, turned it, plucked it out and replaced it— It seemed impervious to the cleansing flames.

Then on an impulse he dropped the crucifix of his dead friend onto the magically-endowed parchment. A loud *whuff!* and an orange burst of flame that nearly singed his hair—

Both objects instantly disintegrated into the kindling. And Gonji was left to ponder the eerie event's portent.

Chapter Fifteen

A traveling oblate arrived in Vedun the next day, and the city leaders prevailed upon him to stay for a time and minister to their spiritual needs in the absence of the visitants from Holy Word Monastery. By now the fate of the monks was suspected by all but the very young, and there was no more discussion of it among the grim populace. They took confession and communion gratefully at the chapel, Mass being celebrated there for the first time in a month, and those needing the last sacrament were attended by the itinerant priest.

When Gonji saw the sincerity of their faith and the

depth of their spiritual need, he recognized the centrality of worship as the rallying point for the vast majority of the militia. Thus, to reconcile their spirituality with the militant thinking they would need to oust the invaders from Vedun, and to indicate his respect for their mode of worship, he gave them the following prayer of his own composition:

> *"From all manner of wretched death and savage wound, Lord, protect me; but most of all suffer me not the death of a coward."*

They recited the prayer thereafter at the beginning and end of each training session, though there were those who cared little for its content and some who would not say it at all.

The leaders converged in the boulder-strewn tunnel area with the excited militiamen.

"Now what is so important—" Rorka began.

"Look!" several men cut in.

Jiri Szabo unfolded the bundled rag he carried. A new pistol lay within, polished and gleaming. Greta was with him. From a pouch lashed to her leg under her skirts she produced powder, pistol balls, and a spanner for the wheel-lock firearm.

"*Yoi!* Good!" Gonji said, hefting the gun.

"Where did you get it, Jiri?" Roric Amsgard asked.

"My father. He bought it last night from one of the traveling merchants, who smuggled it in concealed in his wagon."

"You'll need a lot more of these, I'm afraid," Gonji said.

"I thought you didn't approve of firearms," Michael observed.

"I don't care for them, it's true. They've unreliable

and ignoble, and one day fighting men of honor will abandon them for the elegance of sword and bow, the strong arm and stout heart."

Rorka snorted. "Are you really so naive, my friend?"

"*Iyé*, but I can dream, can't I?" He chuckled mirthlessly. "No, men with money who crave power will see that they're made better, and someday wars will be won by the rich. A sad fact of our time. I'm an idealist, you see, and the world has passed me by. A relic before my time—not so different from yourself, Herr Baron." He returned to the archery ground.

Rorka stroked his chin thoughtfully and pondered the samurai's words, admiring his aptness of observation.

In the next two days, three more pistols turned up in the catacombs.

By the middle of the second week, over three hundred men and forty women could be counted upon to attend any given day's training sessions. They were now past the attrition caused by frequent early injury, poor conditioning, fear, disillusionment, and disagreement over principle. Even Strom and Boris had by now returned to train, if half-heartedly, under Garth with the staff, though they steered clear of Gonji.

Now, too, the number of men swelled daily due to defections from Phlegor's guild, who had grown discouraged with their leader's shaky efforts at preparation with poor equipment and inadequate facilities; they had been training in small numbers in cellars and at a secret weapons cache in the hills. Phlegor was generously offered a command post on the military council, but still he refused, insisting that the action they trained for was too far in the future to do any good.

"He says he won't produce goods all winter for these

bastards while they pick the bones of Vedun clean," said the guild courier who took him the message.

Their fears intensified. What was the guild leader planning? Gonji found the situation vexing. The only sure answer was Phlegor's elimination, which he tried to make them understand via circumlocution: to broach the subject head-on was, he knew, dangerous to his tenuous position with some of the city leaders. The suggestion would be morally repugnant and unacceptable, and again Gonji would appear the barbarian savage in their eyes.

Thus was another dilemma added to Gonji's growing list.

Michael took a sharp crack to his morion helmet and went down on one knee. Paolo withdrew as several people rushed forward to check on the stunned young leader, who staved off their anxious ministrations.

Gonji scratched under his harness, but the nervous itch wouldn't abate. Michael had flinched again, reacting to a feint, thus opening the line of attack that might have crushed his skull. Lydia peered over at her downed husband from the grotto of the "Ladies Hospitaler," as the support group had dubbed itself, but she remained at her place, laving a gash on a Squire's thigh.

The samurai blew out a long breath. "Paille, what's that story of David, *King* David, from the Christian bible?"

Paille looked up from his diorama of Vedun, where he had been placing a figure of himself painting atop the Ministry building while a battle raged in the streets below.

"You mean David and Goliath? Are you planning to engage Tumo with a slingshot? I'm not sure God would so favor you, you heathen," the artist said jestingly.

"*Non*, I mean . . . about the woman," Gonji replied, his gaze distant, taking in something beyond the limits of the cavern.

Paille cast him a wily glance. "You mean Bathsheba, the one he married after first sending her husband out to be slain? That's one of the—What are you thinking, *monsieur le samurai?*"

"Nothing," Gonji responded, refocusing his eyes and moving off.

"Nothing good, I can tell you that," Paille shouted after him, a worried frown creasing his brow.

Patterns of armor and dress were taking shape in the training ground.

The men who chose to rally around Rorka and his knights emulated their dress, slowly accumulating, through purchase or improvisation, light field armor of steel, morion helmets, and shields or bucklers. The armor was worn only during full field exercises, and its emphasis was on protection. For normal daily training they wore tunics, jupons, or quilted gambesons, many of which sported Rorka's lion-and-cross coat-of-arms. These militiamen came to be called Squires.

Those who chose Gonji's *kendo*—the Japanese "way of the sword"—acquired still lighter armor of leather, scale, and thin steel plate, covering mainly the front of the body, and emphasizing maneuverability. They trained shirtless like the samurai, learned much of the Japanese language and manner, and took to wearing what Gonji called a *hachi-maki*—"headband of resolution". The leather sword harness for the back became a popular item of equipment as well, inasmuch as a great deal of mounted fighting was practiced and anticipated. These trainees came to call themselves *bushi*—"warriors," and there was keen competition between *bushi* and Squires.

Near the end of the second week, the militia held its long-awaited archery contest, the Gray knights showing their prowess with the crossbow at shorter distances, but the magnificent English longbow rising to the forefront as the targets receded from view.

Shot groups of three shafts at each distance were launched, the targets then moved back twenty yards. Eliminations were swift, and soon only Gonji and the splendid Karl Gerhard remained on the shooting line. They matched each other nearly shot-for-shot, miss-for-miss, the watching throng breathless. Gonji would score a perfect round, and Gerhard would follow in kind, his endearingly doleful countenance displaying no thrill of triumph beyond a curt nod with each hit. One man would miss a shot, the other would similarly fail. Then at 190 yards Gonji could manage only a rim hit, missing rather handily on both other shots. He unstrung his bow and bowed to Karl, but Gerhard declined the resignation and shot his round, missing narrowly on the first, hitting the second, and launching his worst shot of the day on the third, which skimmed the ground well short of the target.

"Are you toying with me, Sir Archer?" Gonji asked.

"Nein," Gerhard replied, "but we could do this all day, and I'm bored. Let's go for it all."

The militiamen stirred excitedly as the pair bowed and the target was moved back to the farthest wall, scarcely in view to some, the nearsighted among them waving their hands in surrender and walking away amid laughter and jests.

"Hey, old man," Berenyi yelled to Nagy, "why don't you go squint in front of the target so you can see?"

"Get off my back, you young stud, or you'll be wearing one of those arrows where it'll do you the most good."

Berenyi farted, and his companions roared and broke for cover.

"*Da*, you know where I'm talking about!" Nagy roared.

Wilf helped Gonji restring his bow.

"One shot per round, first hit wins," Gonji declared. Gerhard nodded and bade Gonji begin.

The samurai missed, planting his shaft high on the far cavern wall. Gerhard's shot wrung a hopeful groan from the audience—the spotters relayed that he had missed by a scant foot to the left. Gonji followed with a sleekly arcing, beautiful drop shot that hit a yard too high. An electric thrill ran through the audience as they groaned, shaking their heads. Gerhard's third volley caused the spotters to leap into the air, an action that transferred itself through the cavern in a gradual wave that lost its immediacy as it gained distance from the target. But the cheering was thunderous.

The target was rushed forward. Gerhard had missed the bull's-eye by a hand's width. They measured the distance the pair had been shooting: 340 yards.

(from the *Deathwind of Vedun* epic:)
"... *and the stalwarts did learn well under the Red Blade's direction, at the last striking targets with their unerring bows at distances in excess of six hundred forty yards ... and the Red Blade did dispense his sublime battlefield wisdom ...*"

"What about the monsters?" a voice whined from the seated tactics-briefing crowd.

"*You* what about the monsters!" Gonji yelled, spinning and pointing in the direction of the voice. "Don't let them catch you, and they won't hurt you!" A spate of nervous laughter.

"Seriously, *sensei*," Jiri Szabo spoke up, "do you have a plan for the wyvern and the giant, for anything else Mord might bring against us?"

"Of course," Gonji replied firmly, "I've told you as much. Next question!" He averted his eyes from Wilf, with whom he'd discussed the "plan," whose simple reality was all-too apparent to any who cared to reflect on it.

The skeptics who already had shook their heads sullenly.

"Remember that an enemy who regards you too casually probably has accomplices stropping their swords and leveling their guns just out of sight. Be wary . . ."

"Remember: They outnumber us, but we're better than they are. And we're fighting for your loved ones, your homes, your way of life. They don't rattle easily, but like you they freeze for an instant when something growls at them. So growl!" Gonji stalked before them, sword bared, as he lectured. "Eye contact!" he shouted. "Stare through them. Posture yourself like a champion, carry yourself like you've already beaten them. *Kiyai! Kiyai! Kiyai!*—*Howl* when you strike! They can be intimidated."

"What about their guns?"

"*Choléra*-pox on their guns!" Dead silence. "You have guns, and you'll have more. And you have the longbows—*and* the long swords, always better than guns, *neh?* They don't fizzle in the rain—and we'll probably begin our action in the rain—and they don't need to be spannered and loaded—"

"With all due respect, *sensei*," Vlad Dobroczy broke in, "suppose you charge a mercenary in the rain, and you howl and swagger and swing your sword truly, but his courage doesn't fail him and neither does his pistol? Then what?"

Gonji folded his hands behind his back. "Then you face the fact of death that is always with us, and you fall back on your final armament."

"What's that?"

"Your faith."

Grumbling and crestfallen looks. Rorka, standing at the back of the group, turned and walked off, shaking his head sadly.

They sat in Tralayn's parlor, sipping the jasmine tea Flavio had acquired from a traveling merchant, to Gonji's great delight.

"Tralayn," Gonji asked, suddenly serious, "what do you think happened to the crops?"

"Mord," she replied at once. "Mord destroyed them."

"*So desu ka?* To what purpose?"

"To incite a rebellion that would see the city crushed."

"Klann wouldn't want that," Garth declared.

"Perhaps not," she replied. Then she fixed her gaze on Gonji. "Gonji, I have a terrible suspicion, founded on an ill omen, that . . . something terrible has happened at the monastery. By your own admission you've been there since the invaders came. You must tell me now—what is the current circumstance of Holy Word?"

"You've been to the monastery?" Roric asked, surprised. He alone among them was not privy to the knowledge of Simon Sardonis or his connection with Father Dobret. "Why haven't you said anything? People have tried to get there to see what's become of the monks, but no one can get by the blockade of Borgo Pass, not without a fight."

Gonji's spirit sagged. The intelligence could be crushing to their morale and might shatter his fragile influence. But he decided to clear the air and told them what had become of Holy Word and the nearby peasant village, and of his part in the outrages.

"God in heaven," Flavio breathed. A funereal dismay seized them all.

"Zarnesti. The village must be Zarnesti," Michael said in a shaky voice, staring into his cup.

"*Ja*," Roric agreed.

"I'm sorry," Gonji said at length. "It was because of these things that I left Klann's free companions. I wish to make reparation at least in part by helping you free your city."

There were sympathetic nods and half-hearted mutters that he should not burden himself with guilt over what surely would have happened anyway. But Michael and Roric shortly took their leave of them, after agreeing reluctantly to Gonji's wish that he be allowed to tell Rorka himself in his own time.

"I suspected," Tralayn announced when they had gone.

"So there is no help forthcoming from the Church," Flavio added somberly, "unless Rorka's missing patrols are able to find it in Austria."

"*Iyé*. I'm afraid they never made it out of the province," Gonji advised. His companions crossed themselves.

"What was the message you had for Simon Sardonis?" Tralayn asked Gonji as the four sat sipping glumly.

"Just one of forbearance," he replied. "Dobret wanted him to go on alone, without seeking vengeance against Klann for what happened to him at the monastery."

"If you had told me when you arrived, I might have been able to persuade him to join with us in our efforts."

"If I had told you when I arrived, *I* wouldn't be part of those efforts. And you still owe me information about this . . . valiant loner Simon, *and* the Deathwind."

"Loner indeed," she said, smiling wryly.

"You still spread this business about the divine Deliverer among the militia. He's *gone*, Tralayn. The reluctant hero has fled Vedun in its time of need. I have my own idea about the identity of your Deliverer. And you yourself once wondered whether I wasn't the—"

"No, he's not gone. But we're not acting in concert either."

"What do you mean?"

"Two more mercenaries dead, on the road into the valley. I saw their bodies myself this morning. It was clearly his work . . . the work of the thing . . ." She drifted off dreamily. "Too late and for the wrong reason. For vengeance, instead of the restoration of Vedun . . ."

She bowed her head. "I shall not be with you much longer."

They looked to one another uneasily, troubled by the ominous portent of her words.

Stefan Berenyi came running out of the wide tunnel leading into the valley, arriving breathlessly at the center of the training ground. A harbisher and metal founder waited at the tunnel entrance for some signal from him. The three had been behaving curiously since the break between sessions began, carrying bundled goods from other tunnels across the cavern in mysterious fashion.

Now Berenyi formed his hands around his mouth and tooted a heraldic fanfare. He pointed to the broad valley tunnel—

Klaus clanked onto the ground aboard a massive armored destrier of eighteen hands, himself covered completely with old-style plate armor. He carried a huge shield and battleaxe, the buffe of his burgonet swinging open on its hinge to reveal his broad grin.

The catacombs rang with cheers and laughter.

The military council slumped around a table deep into the night. The late session had ended an hour earlier. The leaders were weary and irritable, and as always the sorest points of planning were dredged up at these times.

"So Phlegor continues to be a problem . . ." Garth mused.

"What do you suggest about him, Gonji?" Michael asked. "You have an answer for every other question of policy." There was neither sarcasm nor rancor in the statement, but rather an effort at levity.

Gonji shrugged. "I think my suggestion would be . . . unacceptable."

"Render him . . . *hors de combat*," Garth said, staring straight ahead, arms folded.

"Assassinate him?" Roric asked, shocked.

Michael shuddered. "But that's . . . murder."

"Not necessary to go that far," Garth corrected.

Tralayn rocked back on her stool. "If only we could destroy the evil wizard," she thought aloud.

"*Hai*, sounds easy, doesn't it?" Gonji said with a wry face. "Just mow down his monsters and—Anyway I'm not convinced Klann will do as he says, so sorry, friend smith. I don't think he's any more trustworthy than old goldface. And his hired killers will make Vedun a living hell."

"What about those monsters?" Rorka said. "Once and for all, what are we going to do? Gonji, what are these big plans you've saved for dealing with the wyvern and the giant and who knows what else—"

"What exactly do you suppose I've been planning? Isn't it obvious?" He waved his arm toward the weapons cache. "Longbow, spear, what pistols we have; polearms and swords against the giant, the flapping filth when he alights. The *hearts* of *men!* What other resource have we, in the absence of magick of our own? Faith and steel and righteousness—" The baron was rising petulantly, and Gonji raised his voice. "—and you've been no help at all, so sorry, with your defeatist attitude. You know they look to you for support of my every statement, and what do they see? An old man with head held low, slinking away . . ." He caught himself, regretting the words at first, but glad to have spoken his mind. The others were speechless.

"*Ja*, an old man," Rorka replied, reaching for his cloak, "but at least this old man will not have on his conscience the deaths of many young men who believed in the impossible. You've done a good job of molding their minds, preparing them for a death they can't even conceive. Your *bushi!*"

"So sorry, Herr Baron," Gonji responded, also on his feet now, "but you also did a good job of losing your castle in unheard-of brevity, and you all did a fine job of giving away your city. Now the only way to get it back is to fight, and some will die, and they must know that fact and accept it, or they cannot fight.

"And so sorry—" Gonji shouted, his rancor rising with every word, abandoning at last the self-control he lived by. "—but I think you should not leave until you've heard all there is to tell, while we're being honest with each other."

Rorka kept walking away across the cavern floor, and Gonji raised his voice still louder. It echoed through the cavern.

"The help you await will not be forthcoming! Do you understand?"

The baron stopped and turned slowly, like a man helplessly listening to his own death sentence. He shuffled back toward them, the lines around his eyes etched with dawning horror.

Roric stood and cleared his throat. "Gonji, maybe I'd better . . ." The provisioner took it upon himself to tell the story of Gonji's grim duties while a member of the 3rd Free Company of Klann. Gonji and Rorka glared at each other all the while across the wide table.

"Then it's finished," Rorka spoke with evident anguish when the tale was done.

"*Iyé*," Gonji disagreed, "now it has only begun. What I have done is my own evil karma. You bear the pain and I the guilt. We *both* have lost face, we share the shame. Now we must strive to erase it. We owe it to these people to help them cast out these brigands. It is our duty."

"*Duty*," Rorka spat. "Do you ever do anything on feeling?"

"More often than I care to admit," Gonji replied. "But the two are one and the same here. *Sayonara*."

The meeting was over, the two of them stalking off in opposite directions.

Wilf felt, more than saw, the flashing blur that was Gonji's *katana*, waiting, watching, holding back his *bokken* until his reflexes themselves dictated the proper moment to strike. He focused on Gonji's eyes, as he had been taught, knowing that they mirrored the opponent's soul. His motion had become more economical, swifter as a result, explosions of energy reserved for only the propitious moments in the fray. He knew Gonji reserved special attention for him, Michael and Jiri's blows causing him less trouble, probing more shallowly. But Wilf had to use their attacks to his advantage if he were ever to land a blow.

They turned and clashed repeatedly, the long minutes slipping away. Wilf emptied his mind of all intent, that his body might not betray him—*now!* Michael and Jiri attacked almost as one, Gonji's blinding parries fending them as Wilf lashed out and across, right-to-left. *Thwak!* Somehow, incredibly, Gonji had found his *bokken* and turned it in a twinkling, but Jiri struck downward immediately, the samurai's wicked high parry splitting his wooden sword as Wilf's wrists and forearms twisted with the well-oiled grace and speed of constant practice—

"*Sesshoku!*" Gonji cried.

"Halt!" Roric stormed at once, rushing forward.

Wilf's horizontal slash had again broken open Gonji's stitched ribs, blood seeping from the wound caused by Julian.

They bowed to each other as the trainees buzzed about the inspired bout. Despite his shock over having reopened Gonji's wound, Wilf felt a flush of warmth and pride. A great burden had been lifted from him. He no longer felt like a foolish child posturing himself after a role model. He was a warrior. *Bushi.* When he had landed the blow to Gonji in the earlier bout, the nagging suspicion that the samurai had allowed the trainees to hit him for the good of their morale taunted him. But this time he knew that it had been real.

And he knew that the others knew.

Now, soon, he would be ready to go after Genya . . .

"Come on, Klaus!—Do it!—You've got him!"

The clumsy buckle-maker, by now embraced by most of the militia as their favorite reclamation project, clanked forward aggressively, swinging his battleaxe in great circles over his head. Paolo Sauvini, waxing more wrathful by the minute, feinted and lured, stamped ahead with uncertain lunges of his broadsword, now using one hand, now the two-handed grip. He could make no opening, no headway against the sure, steady, uncomplicated advance of Klaus, who seemed to draw energy from the rousing cheers of support.

It was a dangerous exercise, endorsed by Gonji and Roric but opposed by Rorka and Garth. Klaus was clad—indeed, concealed—by his seventy pounds of armor, the buffe of his burgonet helm clamped shut. The head of his battle-axe was swathed in burlap to blunt the edge, a leather thong lashing the handle to Klaus's wrist to prevent him from dropping it. Paolo wore light half armor and a low-brimmed sallet. The object of the bout was to strike a punishing blow. Klaus had entered the contest willing but apprehensive, anxious to do his *sensei* proud. Paolo had been confident and arrogant.

Fifteen long minutes before . . .

"Swing, Klaus!" Gonji cried. "Leave no opening!"

The buckle-maker whirled the heavy axe, failing arm strength beginning to tell as the arc's radius shrank. Sauvini, drenched in sweat, his every clever trick repulsed, now turned to jeering and taunting. Klaus's groans of agony could be heard through the breath-holes of the buffe as his aching arms worked.

In the midst of a taunt Paolo sprang, timing the arc, everything he had left galvanizing his deep thrust. It struck Klaus's breastplate and glanced off with a steely whine—an instant before the axe-head crashed into the wagoner's shoulder, knocking him off his feet, his pauldron shattered.

Three-hundred fifty voices roared in approval.

"Decision!" Paolo screamed as he scrabbled to his

feet, clutching his throbbing shoulder. "My decision—I struck first!"

Gonji strode forward, the crowd noise diminishing in response to his hand signal.

"*Hai*, I see you've dented Klaus's armor," Gonji observed, rubbing his chin, "but I'm afraid *you've* lost an arm—the *victor!*"

As the cheering rang in the catacombs, Klaus fell to his knees, unable to rise. Several people helped him to his feet, raised his arm in victory. They opened his buffe to reveal a drenched red mask, grinning in happy anguish.

As for the look that washed over Paolo's face as he drew away, only the wagoner himself knew the source of the ugly spring that fed it.

But this moment belonged to Klaus, and while he was yet far from a seasoned warrior, Gonji beamed with pride over his achievement. The city's oaf had shown what might be done out of simplicity and sincerity, desire and practice.

Belief in the impossible.

Despite Gonji's having again fallen out of favor with Rorka and the Grays, things went fairly smoothly during training in the few days following the Festival of St. Stephen. It wasn't until the morning session of the third day thereafter that Helena again came to the catacombs, at which time matters took a definite turn for the worse.

She pattered in quickly from the chapel tunnel with scarcely a glance to Gonji and took up her place among the Ladies Hospitaler. Her eyes were red and swollen as she brushed away the tear stains. There were looks of concern and a few questioning signs to her that she ignored. Only Lydia and Greta thought to look toward Gonji for an explanation.

Wilf silently indicated Helena's sudden presence to Gonji, who cast her the merest glance from across the cavern, swallowing back the pang of guilt. He nodded sharply once, then continued with the training. He was teaching *karumi-jutsu*, the samurai's litheness technique for leaping and dodging, running along the top of the agility scaffold while militiamen speared and swung at him with staffs. Leaping and parrying with Spine-cleaver, his concentration was totally on his work, so that he didn't notice Helena's mother Sophia enter the cavern until her raging display had captivated everyone else's attention.

Sophia charged into the training ground, sputtering and swearing in Polish, shaking her fist at Helena once she had singled her out among the women. She pointed to the tunnel, still cursing, and when one of the other women had pointed out her mother's presence, a look of horrified embarrassment lit Helena's face and her tears began anew.

Gonji leapt down from the scaffold when the irate woman surged toward him. He felt hundreds of eyes boring into him. Perplexed and utterly shocked, he had no idea what to do as she approached. He could feel his embarrassment flaring through his neck and ears as his astonished friends backed away to give the wrathful woman space. She still shook her fist, livid with rage, railing at the samurai. Of the hot words she spewed he could make out only *"choléra"* and *"svina"*—pig.

He just stared, stoically absorbing the anger of the offended mother, for once impotent even with a sword in his grasp. For an instant he thought she would strike him, and he was prepared to accept it, knowing the justice of her fury, the shame the satiating of his passion had brought on both mother and daughter in the way of these people. But then two things happened: Sophia's ire was spent; and as she backed away, tight-lipped and shaking, Paille rushed up to her, tongue-lashing her in an absurdly idiotic manner:

"Get out of here, *fishwife!* How *dare* you so address the leader of the militia, the Liberator who will spare you from a fate worse than any you could imagine—!"

It was all foolish blather, Gonji knew, but he was grateful for it, for the filling of the breathless void in the cavern.

Helena ran into the tunnel, streaming tears. Her mother followed shortly after, militiamen parting to give her wide berth.

An ugly, leering moment. Feet scuffling softly. The muted tinkle of steel. Eyes casting about for private spaces. One woman's private concern had shattered the purpose of hundreds.

Gonji said nothing but marched off to a dark grotto where he sat cross-legged for a long time, alone. *Plucked the little lotus . . .*

Roric and Garth began shouting orders, resuming the training. But after a time some of Gonji's closest friends came to the grotto and wordlessly knelt or sat with him, a tight circle of men forming, their stomachs in nervous knots, as they were unsure of his mood and how his inner feelings might manifest themselves. He appeared to be meditating, staring at a space on the ground, his back against a mineral-veined rock wall. Those who joined him were shirtless like him, their heads bound with the *hachi-maki*. Wilf was among them, and Jiri Szabo, Aldo Monetto, and a few others. There were looks of surprise when, a while later, Michael Benedetto also entered the grotto to stand at the rim of the circle, looking on with an expression that beggared analysis.

Then, trancelike, Gonji began to speak, first in Japanese. Later, with a suddenness that startled and unnerved them, in High German. He spoke of his tortured soul, of the peculiar tragic karma attendant on the efforts at love in his life. He told them of his beloved Reiko, with whom he shared a compact of deepest love from adolescence. Of how his hated half-brother Tatsuya, second son of his father but firstborn of full Japanese blood, desired Reiko and lusted after Gonji's heritage. How his father was manipulated by Tatsuya's secret machinations to cement a clan rift by pledging Tatsuya as Reiko's betrothed, the union being completed despite all Gonji's desperate efforts. Reiko—the helpless pawn, pledged by *giri* to uphold her new, detested husband's honor by her samurai heritage. The secret tryst, the last kiss of ill-starred love, the entrapment and discovery by the triumphant Tatsuya.

The duel. Gonji's killing of his lifelong sibling rival. His resultant disaffection, the death of his brokenhearted mother, the vendetta sworn by Reiko's family. But worst of all . . . Reiko's duty-bound effort at killing him with her downed husband's sword, resulting in the ugly shoulder scar, the eternal reminder.

Then the words of a dying Shinto priest, his teacher-confidant, and the bizarre quest across mad Europe by the forlorn and dispossessed child of unsalutary birthing. The quest for the *shi-kaze*, the Deathwind.

And now Vedun . . .

After a long quiet space, his companions began to leave, one by one, until only Wilfred and Michael remained with Gonji. Then the samurai emerged from his somber meditation and rose.

"Come," he said, sighing. "There's much to be done."

They had ridden out of the catacombs under cover

of night and rain, the moon blindered by inky clouds, their horses' hooves muted with burlap. Fifty men on an exercise of stealth—discovery meaning unwanted engagement with Klann's troops; training in cavalry skirmish in the forested southern foothills; and finally, in the militia's grumbling estimation, a problem in misery and frustration.

They charged and clashed, far from the city and the reconnoitered Klann outposts, launched volleys of arrows through the cold and drizzle, slipped and flopped, slamming in the mud with spates of shouting and curses, the wincing jangle of armor and whinnying of steeds. Gonji, Roric, and three Gray knights led them through their paces again and again, dashing each renewed hope that the exercise was ended with fierce orders to engage still another imaginary battle line or monstrous foe.

Gonji knew that he was testing not only their battle skills but also their loyalty, and now was a good time to do so, with the memory of the recent shameful scene in the catacombs still fresh.

He watched with curiosity the whispers passing along the line, Berenyi and Wilf being the initiators, whenever a halt was called. Roric had no idea what was on their minds, nor did the Grays know what was transpiring.

When the final halt to the exercise was sounded, it was greeted not with the anticipated cheering and relief but with a confused shuffling and clumping of riders, Wilf and Berenyi calling out low commands, as the fifty formed a single long rank. The two leaders rode to the rear and center of the line that faced the five surprised instructors. Rorka's Grays looked at one another uneasily, but they all held their ground beside Gonji and Roric as the militia advanced by twos, pouring into a double column beginning at the middle of the line. When they were twenty yards distant the pair at the head of the column broke off in opposite directions, the lines following the leaders until the troop had formed a sort of flabby V, flanking the five instructors with the V's concavities. Wilf and Berenyi sloshed up from the point side-by-side, rain dripping from helms, armor, and mounts, bearing a banner between them. It was white, with the Rorka crest sewn into the left half, a representation of a *katana* on the right. Below the sword, a Latin inscription: *"There is nothing that a man need fear/Who carries at his side this splendid blade."*

Gonji smiled as he read it. It was the motto he had translated for them from the ideograms carved on the hilt of his Sagami.

Wilf and Stefan bowed and saluted. "First Rumanian Hussars reporting, *sensei,*" Berenyi said, suppressing his ever-present sly smile.

Roric and the Grays laughed, and their humor quickly infected the "Hussars." Gonji bobbed his head repeatedly, rainwater streaming off his sallet and down his back.

"All-recht, mein Hussars," the samurai declared, "let's return to the catacombs and celebrate the commissioning of this . . . new detachment."

There came muted shouts of enthusiasm, and they started back immediately, scouts being sent ahead to survey the road through the valley which they must cross again to reach the tunnel. One rider soon returned with the message that a patrol of four mercenaries traveled the road. The festive mood subsided, replaced by wariness. When they arrived at a rise overlooking the road, they assumed a corporate phantom-like presence, employing the darkness, the trees, the rain rustle as armor against prying eyes, hiding virtually in plain sight. The four mercenaries rode by within a dagger-throw, clearly feeling watched but too threatened to dare rousting out the watchers. Instead they spurred ahead, whispering and ceasing to peer about them into the looming forest.

Gonji watched his troop's confident smiles, felt their corporate thrill at the psychological victory, the vindication of a principle they had doubted. Had they failed in the joint effort, he, Roric, and the three Grays had been poised to launch themselves after the patrol and dispatch them as quickly and quietly as possible. But the militia had meshed as a unit; they'd been a single entity, a stealthy coiled serpent that had warded off an enemy via sheer projected menace, a metaphysical curiosity of aggression Gonji had never failed to marvel at in practice. For an instant the invading army had had the tables turned; their fears of the province had been stoked, and the lesson to the militia had been far more valuable than the violent deaths of an outnumbered enemy patrol.

Gonji swelled with pride. Vedun's militia were beginning to resemble soldiers.

At the cavern they broke out wine and ale. Roisterous cheer was the order of the day. Gonji keenly appreciated the camaraderie. He spoke to them of *giri* and *ninjo*, the battling forces of duty and inclination within the samurai, and of how for the first time in a long time these forces had found unity in the matter of freeing Vedun from the invaders' stranglehold. Despite all that was unsettled in his life, he felt relatively at peace and lacked only the fulfillment of his quest and his destiny in order to die happily and willingly.

Exhausted from the training, they ate and drank and sang lustily, pledged their fellowship and determination. Paille as usual threw himself into the toasting with gusto and soon was doing a reading, in his inimitable stentorian voice, from a novel excerpt sent to him by a friend in Spain. He was shouted down before long, Berenyi and his cohorts eventually binding and gagging the struggling artist, loosening his gag now and again so that he might sip from his goblet and blare an imprecation or two.

Wilf had purged his recent demon of self-doubt and emerged from Gonji's shadow self-confident and zestful as he formerly had been, more anxious than ever to invade Castle Lenska in rescue of his lady fair. He and Karl Gerhard presented Gonji with a gift from the militia: a magnificent three-man longbow and a quiver of thirteen-fist war arrows with armor-piercer heads.

Gonji was stunned by the gift. He thanked them with a rare warmth of emotion and replied by presenting Wilf with Spine-cleaver, the spare *katana* he had been using in training. There was no disputing Wilf's entitlement to the beautiful blade, for he had worked long and hard and improved by great strides in the art of the sword. Wilf sat down heavily in his place, goggle-eyed, cradling the sword, the only one of its ilk in Europe, save Gonji's legendary Sagami.

Not surprisingly, the tenor of the conversation turned to swordplay.

"Gonji," Jiri Szabo asked, "when it comes time for you to cross with that pompous ass Julian, you'll be able to beat him, won't you?"

Groans followed, the answer seemingly obvious to most of them, but Gonji's look quieted them.

"Pointless speculation," he declared, "something the warrior should avoid. Nothing works out as one expects. Concentrate too much on the stronger enemy, and you can be sure a lesser one will take your measure. It makes no sense, but that's the nature of things in warfare . . ."

"Still . . ." Jiri persisted, gazing up sheepishly, wishing some answer to his question.

Gonji chuckled gently. "He's mighty fast. Just about the fastest feathering touch with a saber I've ever seen."

"But you could beat him," Nick Nagy stated flatly.

"Not with a saber, no," Gonji disagreed, evoking gasps at the implication of Julian's brilliance.

"But with the Sagami, *neh?*" Wilf said, grinning.

"Mmmm. I don't know," Gonji responded, surprising even himself with his humble turn. Uncertain looks passed around the gathering. "His is a lighter blade, better balanced for quick, one-handed motion, more—"

"But you could beat him?" Jiri fairly pleaded.

He drew a deep breath, held it, expelled long and pensively, rather disappointed that they still needed assurances no man could give.

"Hai," he said at length, "but I'd have to beat him out of the scabbard."

Mutters of relief as they pondered Gonji's meaning.

"You boys yust get the baron's castle back for him," Hildegarde said, pointing with a staff for emphasis, her Nordic accent and cadence causing amused laughter. "Hildy will hold the city, no?"

"No doubt about that!"

A man named Tadeusz later voiced a fear that all the trainees yet bore:

"The sword practice is exhilarating, the sport of it all . . ." he began, forming words with his hands. "But to kill a *man* with a sword, feel his flesh part—I—"

Gonji's brow darkened. "Not *a* man—*many* men. The man among you who *cannot* kill—or can kill only *one* enemy and then lie back and stare at the corpse—that man is as good as dead."

"God," Tadeusz said weakly, head shaking. The

others stared at the ground, shuffling uncomfortably. Some rose to go, the celebration now tarnished by the intrusion of grim reality.

Gonji regarded their faces, ghostly in the torchlit cavern, wondering who among them might die in the days to come.

"If Flavio or Baron Rorka were here, they wouldn't like to hear me say this but . . . that's the way a warrior must think, my friends. Think on heaven—or hell—the final resting place. Sooner or later death comes. You believe in the afterlife. *Embrace* your belief. You have loved ones to fight for. If the fighting starts, it will have been forced on you." He rose and turned away from them, fists clenched. His voice grew small. "Blame Klann, if you need someone to blame . . . or blame me . . ."

He sashed the Sagami and strode off toward the tunnels.

Heat lightning cracked in the late morning sky as Gonji entered the abandoned dwelling in the city's southeast quadrant to confront Julian. Thunder boomed in the mountains.

"So the wayward one returneth," Julian taunted, looking like a cat who had cornered some helpless prey. But Gonji's confident pose would have ill befit a mouse as he bowed.

Julian ordered the mercenaries with him to leave them. "You know," he said when they were alone in the dusty, cobwebbed dwelling, "I've been thinking lately about wasted gold."

"You didn't waste your money. Here's what I've learned: It's the craft guild—they're the ones who've been planning an insurrection. They train in secret somewhere with their leader Phlegor. Have him watched and followed, and you'll keep them frustrated. They won't do a thing. Or you could have Phlegor arrested on some pretense. Suspicion, I suppose."

Julian's arch air dissipated. "Are you sure about this?"

"Of course. I take my job seriously. It just took time. That Phlegor's a distrusting lout."

"Who is this Phlegor? What does he look like? Where does he live and work?"

Gonji described the volatile guildsman, discomfort churning in his gut at having had to turn on citizens in order to contain and redirect the army's suspicions. But he had decided there was no other way.

"I wouldn't arrest him unless he gives you good reason, come to think of it," Gonji appended, egged on by his guilt. "He's a rather popular fellow . . ."

Julian studied Gonji's eyes, which were hard and flinty, revealing nothing of his designs.

"That's all I have for now. I'm still looking into this Deathwind business. It's very curious, and not a little frightening—"

"I believe there'll be a *few* arrests here shortly," Julian cut in, ignoring him. "More mercenaries on patrol have been slaughtered . . ."

Gonji nodded, affecting grave concern. Then he brightened, unable to resist the dig. "Oh, Captain—I hope you weren't offended when I greeted you in so surly a fashion at the festival. You should have seen the looks on the young folks' faces—it enhanced my cover, *neh?*"

Julian raised an eyebrow, his expression darkening when he recalled his similar words to Gonji once before. He eyed the samurai narrowly. "Where do you go for such long stretches? You seem to drop out of sight."

Gonji looked sheepish as he scratched self-consciously. "Well, you see . . . I've got a woman—*two*, actually, and, uh—"

"I *know* about the one. How much time can a deaf-mute occupy?" Julian said, his tone more insulting than the insensitive words themselves. "What about the other?"

Gonji's mind raced. *How did he know?* Oh, *hai*—the gatehouse guards on the festival night. But now what to—?

"That one had best remain my secret, so sorry. The wife of an official, you see . . . bad business if it were known. As a matter of fact," Gonji whispered, playing the conspiratorial clown, "I'm expected now. So, by your leave?" He bowed.

As he strode out the portal and into the humid mid-morning gloom, Julian called: "Free yourself from your women's embraces to do a little work for me now and again, won't you? And don't hoard those women—I have plenty of other men in need of their tender ministrations."

Gonji tensed to hear the man's conceit and callousness voiced, more poignantly now that the women he alluded to were objectified in Gonji's mind. But he strolled out into the gray light without response, to face the rogues' gallery clustered about Tora. He ambled through them calmly and stepped up into a stirrup. A hand grasped his shoulder, and he glared into the pale eyes of the now unhelmed Armorer.

"Do you know me?" the brigand growled. "They call me Salavar the Slayer."

"*Ah, so desu?* That's interesting. Never heard of you." He pushed up and out of the grasp, alighting in the saddle. Luba stood on the other side, glaring up at him, his bald dome glistening in the irritating swelter.

"You haven't, eh? Well, maybe you haven't traveled as widely as they say, Herr Red Blade from the frigging East—*ja*, I've heard of *you*—"

Gonji's eyebrows raised at the strange irony. The only man in the territory who had ever mentioned the samurai's widespread reputation . . .

"—and I've heard all they say you can do, with them swords and feet. I wonder if it's all true . . . and what else you can do." He had lumbered over to his own steed and spanked the deadly arquebus strapped to the armored destrier's saddle. A broadsword and short feathered lance bristled from the giant charger's other flank.

"Oh, not so much," Gonji replied. "Anyway, I've done with that sort of thing. Too dangerous, *neh?*"

Luba grabbed Tora's bridle as Gonji tried to spur off. The steed whinnied and lurched. "You making fun of Salaver, slant-eyes?"

Gonji caused Tora to rear so that Luba stumbled back before the threatening hooves. "Listen, baldy—"

"Luba," Julian shouted from where he leaned in the doorway. "You have your duties."

Gonji scowled at Julian, then at the slowly dispersing bunch. A rumble of thunder and a fierce bolt of lightning split in the valley. As an afterthought he swung Tora over to Salavar, who had begun tightening the myriad cinches on the bulky destrier's saddle and armor.

"Best watch yourself when the storm breaks," he said, pointing at the angry sky. "The fire god likes the taste of metal, *neh?*"

He cantered off, leaving Salavar nodding his head with silent resolve.

When he was out of earshot, Julian stepped into the midst of the tethered horses. "Umberto," he called.

A swarthy, bearded mercenary moved close, sword hilt and pistol grip protruding from behind his unfastened jack.

"Watch him, Umberto," the captain said, still eyeing the samurai's now vacant path, "watch him like he's your next meal."

Chapter Sixteen

The night, the storm, the jagged peaks of the Carpathians cupped the province in a malefic hand. Rain and wind lashed the battlements as the lone figure made the treacherous ascent up the pocked outer bailey wall of Castle Lenska.

Rampart sentries strolled their miserable watch swathed in hooded cloaks. When the chilling shadow slipped past them, each man in turn reacted with the familiar stomach-knotting and throat constriction with which one investigated an unwholesome presence in a darkened room. They hesitated, failing their charge in a way they would later deny, licking dry lips and grasping at the cold comfort of rain-slicked weapons.

Dogs barked in the wards, and once the cretin giant Tumo, aroused from the flapping canopy under which he slept, crawled out and sniffed at the air with his tiny nostrils. Gurgling a low growl, he returned to his slumber.

When the shadow had departed the ramparts, each guard gave silent thanks in his own way and reasoned that his atavistic terror had been nothing more than an effect of the ravaging elements.

"Oooh!" Genya cried, shocked by the thunderclap and flash of lightning. The tall windows of Klann's receiving chamber flared like iron-veined orbs.

The king laughed. "Such a spirited lass as you, who'd brave the descent of a sword—afraid of a little storm!"

She held a hand over her bosom daintily. "I've always feared storms, milord."

"Well you needn't fear them here. And do continue with your amusing tale of your beloved Wilfred's antics. Wilfred, the son of Garth Iorgens—now *there's* a man a king can count on! Alas! we can never ride together again . . . never again . . ."

Genya noticed the gloomy turn of the king's mood and at once resumed her happy tales of life as a youth in Vedun. It was important to promote his good cheer. Dreadfully important. Earlier in the evening the odious sorcerer had placed him in an ugly state. She had hung close to the king's private chambers, milking her tasks so that she might eavesdrop boldly on their heated discussion. More than once Mord had suggested that she be sent away, but Klann reassured him with the reminder that she spoke no Kunan.

But she did. She spent her days assiduously learning what she could of the difficult tongue, mainly from the chief steward. She gleaned great satisfaction from her ability to manipulate even that venomous old soul in the furthering of her purpose. And she knew enough now to learn from the conversation that Klann lived in fear of some predatory thing in the province that lusted after his blood. Mord seemed convinced that there was in fact such a creature hovering near but that it was something he *should* be able to enlist in their support. He seemed obsessed with the large key he carried at all times, which he insisted had something to do with the presence.

The idea of the spectral presence was new to Genya and terrifying in a way she couldn't describe. She had never known such fear in Vedun, and she couldn't understand Mord's assertion that it was in some way connected with the captive city.

And there were other things that gnawed at her. Things that troubled sleep: the scary murmurs among the servants, talk of mysterious crop failure in Vedun; of soldiers slaughtered by invisible things; of rebellious action by the citizens; and worst of all, the disappearances of the two servant girls who bore on their foreheads the red mark placed there by Mord, the mark they could not remove despite all tearful, frantic efforts.

"My men are killed in the forests at night," King Klann had told her when she brought him his mutton and wine. "Why do they do these things?"

But her winsome way had calmed him, and for once none of the ladies of the court had intruded. Soon she had allayed his suspicions of the people of Vedun with her stories of their happiness and brotherhood. She was feeling clever and sure of herself. Sure that she was on her way back to Vedun, whether by lubricious guile or outright deceit, the way paved by the controlled seductiveness that had never failed her. For if the king's paternal favor was withheld much longer, she would find another way to escape. Perhaps through the miller's gate, whose steward she had already dangerously approached about that very subject, though she was not desperate enough to pay the price he demanded . . .

"I'm tired now, and I have much to ponder," Klann told her at last. "Leave me now." He patted her face in the kindly manner he reserved for Genya alone, then turned his back on her and began to pace.

She left via the chamber's double doors, out the vestibule's heavier paneled door and past the sentries. The corridors were cold and dank, empty but for an occasional passing Llorm guard or scurrying dog or cat. The cresset lamps had burned low, some extinguished altogether. In the gleam of every licking flame she saw the burning eyes of Mord, remembered the way he had looked at her now and again, thought of the missing servant girls.

They say he does the unspeakable with 'em, Yola the chambermaid had said . . .

Genya pulled her collar close about her throat and hurried around the second turn on her course to the scullions' chambers. She stopped when she heard the muted clanking sound behind her. She couldn't tell how far behind or in what direction. Her hands were clamped over both her mouth and nose as she leaned against the chilly stone wall, listening. She tried not to breathe, fought off a spate of shivers.

Nothing. Silence. No . . . *breathlessness*. The sound that followed her stopped just after she had.

Emitting a single hot breath, she steeled herself, annoyed by her fear of the familiar fortress surroundings. She moved off again, hoping to pass someone, glad for the rustle of her skirts that filled the too-complete stillness of the corridor maze.

There—a soldier. Good . . .

She smiled more sweetly than usual when the Llorm dragoon passed and touched the brim of his helm. Grinned to herself and whispered a few scolding words over having behaved like a child, hearing the comforting bootslaps diminish behind her—

And vanish altogether with a single scrape, as if the soldier had been swept off his feet by something above him.

Genya gasped and trembled, pausing again to listen. Again the sounds abated just when she strained to hear. She lipped a fervent prayer and hurried on, her brows knitting as she clutched the front of her bodice, the fear within gripping her heart still tighter.

She turned right into the corridor that led past storage pantries to the servants' quarters. She gaped, open-mouthed: all the lamps had expired. But there was nowhere else to go. Now she heard the soft, loping footpads echoing in the halls . . . where? behind her? before? She couldn't tell.

Forward. She must run for the chambers—run! She hurtled onward into the darkness, her slapping footfalls and rustling skirts masking all other sound. The *thing* might be behind her, grasping, reaching out to touch her at any second. She had to look back—no! Mother of God, *no!*

Then she stumbled over a bucket in the darkness and sprawled on the floor. She barely felt the ache in her shin as she scrabbled into a seated position and . . . heard the laughter. She peered back flinchingly into the darkened corridor she had run through and saw the dim light from the intersecting hall. Then heard the comforting voices of soldiers.

"Uh—heeelp!" she cried out tentatively in a soft whining voice that made her feel foolish. She laughed when she saw them turn into the corridor and jog toward her, calling out. Two Llorm sentries, their sword hilts and burgonets glinting until they were enveloped by shadow.

By the huge hulking shadow that loomed over them and laid them both low. They fell to the stone floor almost as one.

The clatter of a helmet, bouncing against the wall. And the shadow approaching her, reaching out, piercing her soul with its inhuman eyes.

She tried to scream, but the sound caught in her throat. She lay across from the linen pantry. All she could think to do was run for the door, bolt herself within, and then scream and scream until she woke the dead, if need be. And if the pantry were locked—?

But it wasn't. It yielded at once to her frantic jiggling of the handle. She pushed inside and slammed the door, reached for the—*There was no bolt.* She dropped down like dead weight with her back to that slender portal and began to sob even as she pushed against it, digging her feet into the floor with the superhuman strength of the doomed.

"*Hsssst!*" the voice grated harshly under the crack. "Silence. Don't fear me, girl. I haven't come for you. Raise no alarm." It spoke in Hungarian. A voice she had never heard before but found strangely comforting.

She lay shaking in the pantry for what seemed a long time, but almost immediately the sense of oppression had lifted, for the presence was gone.

Mord stiffened in the dungeon chamber, as if a bolt had skewered him. He seized up the psychically endowed key, a look of triumph firing his crow-black eyes: "So you've come to me . . ."

He surged from the chamber, past the cells of puling, mindless half-human wretches, and up two flights of crumbling stairs, pushing through an iron-grated door that shrieked on arthritic hinges—

"Guards! Turn out the garrison! *We have an intruder!*"

The castle exploded with the tumult of shouted orders and stamping feet, jangling steel and the confused questions of the newly awakened.

"Look—this man is dead!"

Gasps and outcries. The corpse of a Llorm footman—the one who had passed Genya in her panicked flight.

"The king! See to the king's welfare!"

Soldiers and civilians alike poured through the corridors toward Klann's private chambers, lighting lamps and torches as they went. Others searched Castle Lenska from top to bottom, through every corridor and drum tower, through kitchens and larders and every cellar and dungeon and rat-infested subterranean cell save those only Mord knew of.

Outside, the dreaded wyvern roused itself from sleep and shrilled at the storm as it banked around the castle spires and walls, gradually widening its radius of search. Two hundred mercenaries camped in the outer ward and beyond the moat on the piney slopes grumbled and cursed as they, too, joined the search in the heavy downpour.

"What the hell we lookin' for?"

"This is crazy!"

Tumo bellowed and kept pointing into the forest to the west. Retrieving his great spiked truncheon from under the canopy, he leaned it on an elephantine shoulder and pointed again, canine sounds and braying groans emanating from between his flaccid lips. He looked up to his master Mord, who stood atop the ramparts, gazing with a strange fixation into the forest. Beside him there was a frenzy of activity, one soldier babbling about the apparition he had seen but couldn't stop, his dead partner being examined by an anxious group. A dagger still jutted from the dead man's breast.

"No, Tumo," Mord ground in his murky voice. "Not now." The sorcerer seemed deeply puzzled. He hefted the key in a gloved hand.

At the king's chambers: madness. The two sentries who guarded their king had been stabbed to death. No one had seen the assailant. King Klann leaned against the wall, unable to arrest the trembling that had begun when he had come out to see why his guards failed to respond to a command.

"I saw him . . ." Klann kept saying, distant and

unsettling to those who listened. "I *think* I saw him. He's—he's showing me that he can destroy me whenever he wishes. He might have done so, if—if—"

"Calm youself, milord," Lady Thorvald pleaded. "Let me help you into—"

He pushed her hand away roughly. "What must I do to have security here?" he shouted in a cracked voice. "Sleep with a regiment at my bedside?!"

He still displayed the effects of his horripilation; his face was pallid, his hair bristling.

"Another dead sentry on the south middle curtain, but *this* man says he struck the intruder, sire!" came an officer's voice.

The babbling Llorm guard was pushed forward, his drenched face an almost comic fright mask. He was helmless and quaking.

"Well—*speak*."

"I—I—I struck him, sire, slashed him as he went by . . . He—he—Kirka, he stabbed Kirka, and then I sliced open his arm but . . . but then he was *gone*."

"You missed him, then, idiot."

"No, sire, I did hit him. See here—his *blood*."

Half-clad soldiers and civilians in nightshirts pressed forward to see the valiant sentry's bloody sword, sighing and muttering in impressed tones.

"I don't want his blood, I want his *corpse*," Klann railed.

"Here, let me have that." Mord pushed through the crowd and took the weapon. "Draw another from the armorer."

"You—Mord," Klann cried in an accusing voice, pointing. "Where were you during all this? You're supposed to be one step ahead of such unnatural attacks against me."

"It was I who raised the alarm, milord, having sensed the presence—"

"A fat lot of good it did." Klann still shook.

"On the contrary, I succeeded in contacting the thing." Gasps from the onlookers. "I was right in thinking it ought to be something which might aid us. I called to it, and it tried to come, but . . . somehow it was restrained. I don't understand all about this being yet—"

"Well, *do* something! Subjugate it, drive it away, destroy it, but *do your job!* We'll not be threatened by the supernatural while you dare to call yourself a sorcerer in our employ." Klann's pallor had by now been replaced by a lurid flush. Mord bowed to him and departed with the sword.

"Gorkin," Klann said to his castellan, "get me a scribe."

"Milord?"

"A scribe and a courier. I must see these people, go to them. First thing in the morning I want the message sent to Vedun. This has got to stop. We can't live with this oppression, and they know—oh, yes, Gorkin, they know what it's about."

A peal of thunder rumbled in the mountains like the drums of an advancing army, and Klann grabbed his head as the angry counsel of the Brethren rose until it filled his ears and clouded his vision. Lady Thorvald and General Gorkin and two or three retainers caught him as he swooned, guided him back into his chambers.

"Garth . . ." he muttered in his delirium. "We must speak with Garth . . ."

Under the lambent glow of the lapping torch, Mord examined the sentry's sword with eager eyes. The blood that dozens of people had marveled at moments before . . . was gone. And suddenly the simple weapon felt unsalutary, radiating a threat the likes of which he hadn't known in centuries.

Chapter Seventeen

The training had been long and hard during the night, the militia grim. There were several incidents of lost temper and a general lack of harmony. Gonji knew the reason.

Radetzky the foster had been caught trying to smuggle a pistol to the militia. Rushing through the streets toward the chapel with his concealed prize, he had had a chance encounter with a band of sharp-eyed mercenaries, who had been tipped off either by the over-cautious way he walked that morning or his instant flush of guilt upon being espied. No one was sure, and it didn't matter. Radetzky had been beaten near the rostrum, kicked and battered until his teeth lay loose all around him and he coughed up blood from a mouth that no longer resembled a mouth. And at the last they had loaded the gun and taunted him with its deadly promise. Then, just before Captain Sianno had arrived with intentions of stopping their brutality, one of them had blown a large hole through Radetzky's forehead.

He had told them nothing.

Treated as Vedun's first military casualty, the foster was buried in the catacombs in a somber ceremony.

The new social order was becoming intolerable: The city seemed in a state of undeclared martial law since the Radetzky incident. Citizens were questioned and searched without cause at the whim of the occupation force, which led to a general escalation of aggression. Resistance met with brute force, which soon evolved into popular sport, whenever the mercenary troops could get away with it. And sport quickly led to other passionate pursuits: it was no longer safe for women to travel the streets unescorted. This despite the fact that as mercenary recruits straggled into the city to enlist with Klann, so also did women of easy virtue arrive in increasing numbers, word having traveled fast of money to be made in Vedun.

Flavio's dream was turning into a snake pit under his tortured gaze. And the militia, raised for the purpose of crushing the invaders who had descended like a horde of locusts, was anxious to flex its muscles. Whatever Klann's true intentions for the province, his noble Llorm regulars were now far outnumbered by the mercenary companies and had surrendered control of the city to them.

Only three people still exerted an arresting influence over the mercenaries with respect to their bullying and brutalizing of Vedun: Captain Sianno, commander of the crack Llorm garrison, who could not be everywhere at once, although he was committed to preserving the peace as King Klann would have it. Julian, who could be cruel and sadistic when given even slight reason, but whose lust after the vacant Field Commander post prompted him also to court the king's good graces by keeping Vedun in one piece. And Gonji, whose status was slipping fast as the free companions swelled their numbers and grew bolder.

"Come on," Gonji said as they slipped out of Tralayn's house and into a relatively quiet dawn, "let's take a ride and then gather the council. I've something I want to discuss with the rest of you."

Wilf and Garth agreed, though the smith was expected at the metal foundry and his son had work backed up at the forge. The storm had spent itself, the clouds having blown far to the east, molten now in the rising sun. Already many mercenaries were out patrolling the streets.

"It's not going to get any easier to sneak down to the catacombs," Gonji observed. The night's trainees had been cut by half their usual number, attributable to fears over the heightened vigilance of the invaders. "How many would you say they number by now, Garth?"

The burly blacksmith shook his head, frowning quizzically. "Hard to say."

"Judging by what I've heard and seen," Gonji advanced, "I'd say . . . six hundred, maybe. And they'll continue to grow."

Wilf whistled tonelessly. "Well when do we sweep them out of the way so that I can tackle Castle Lenska?"

Gonji chuckled, and Garth clucked his tongue. "That's never going to be necessary, Wilfred, whatever your glorious dreams," the smith told his son. "Sooner or later *she* will find a way back to Vedun. She always gets what she wants, doesn't she?"

"Why do you hate her so?" Wilf asked.

"We've been over this a thousand times. She's not the girl for you. You can do better, believe me, if you'll only—"

As the Gundersens pursued their domestic debate, Gonji observed the day's burgeoning activities, the furtive movements of the militiamen heading for the day-session training. The harvest was in, a good one despite the mysterious blight, and produce wagons laden to bursting joined with others filled with sundry goods ordered for the castle.

They breakfasted at Wojcik's Haven, where Lorenz joined them and passed along the encouraging news that there would be few shortages. Both the king and the city would survive the coming winter. Lorenz looked refreshed, having skipped the night's training so that he might deal with the day's anticipated heavy business at the Ministry.

When they were mounting up to leave, Eduardo and Tiva's little band of urchins accosted them.

"Hey, samurai!" Eduardo called, rushing up to bow impressively. The others scurried over, and Gonji reached down to scoop Tiva into his arms.

"*Ohayo*, little ones. Been keeping out of mischief?"

"Never mind that," Eduardo said. "I know something you'd like to know."

"*Ah, so desu ka?* What's that?"

"So sorry. Need money first," Eduardo replied, fluttering his fingers, palm up.

Gonji's brow furrowed in mock animosity. "Ohhh. Gentlemen, I believe I'm being taken. But all right." The children grinned and jostled each other when Gonji set Tiva down to reach inside his kimono and extract a gold coin. They gasped in awe when they realized its value. "Uh-uh—" He withdrew the coin from the grasping Eduardo. "First tell me this valuable information."

"A man followed you all day yesterday."

"Eh? Is he around now?"

"*Si*, at the hostelry across the street. Don't look now, wait till we go! He has a black beard and a pot helmet. He carries a sword and pistol. He watched your horses all the while you ate. Is it worth your money?"

"Oh, very so. *Hai, domo arigato, kiku-san.*" He flipped the coin to Eduardo, and the children pranced off with their new-found wealth. "And take care of Tiva, scamp!"

Gonji looked at Garth and Wilf. "Is he there?"

"*Ja*," Garth answered wearily.

"Matter of days now for me," Gonji said. "Maybe hours . . . Let's get the military council together for my proposal."

They headed for the Ministry. On the way they were attracted by a noisy argument in an alley off the Street of Hope. They steered toward the ring of shouting men to see whether any Vedunians were involved. Gonji cast Wilf a look that urged readiness when the sound of clashing steel emerged from the alley. Pulling up behind the bunched mercenaries, they saw at once that no innocents were threatened. Instead, two free companions had drawn arms over some disagreement. They had been gambling with dice. Gonji recognized one of them as Stanek, who bore under his lip the ugly scar of Julian's slitting saber.

Their swords whined and clanged, sparks flying as they dueled lustily but with unrefined technique. Every earsplitting clash would evoke a wince and a withdrawal from both men. Saber against *schiavona*. An interesting fight until—a freakish turn that drained them of hostility, then redirected it: Stanek's vicious slash caught his opponent's Italian-style blade on the flat of its forte, breaking it cleanly in half.

"Hey! I just bought this god-cursed sword. What the hell kinda trash are they sellin' as armament here?"

The others pressed in, grumbling. Gonji, Garth, and Wilf wheeled their steeds and slowly clopped away from the alley.

"Good workmanship," Gonji said archly.

"*Ja*, we've done our work *too* well, I fear," Garth added.

"Tell the swordsmiths at the foundry to raise a stink if they're questioned. Make it sound like a rare accident, impurities in the steel. And tell Lorenz to be properly indignant if the soldier demands credit."

"That shouldn't be too hard for my highbrow brother," Wilf advanced caustically.

"This just deepens my resolve about what must be done." Gonji spurred Tora into a determined canter.

A while later the three of them sat around the table in Flavio's parlor along with the Elder, Roric Amsgard, and Michael Benedetto. Gonji made his proposal:

"Zarnesti. We're going to free Zarnesti."

"*Cui bono?* To whose benefit?" Flavio protested.

Garth agreed. "Much too reckless an enterprise."

"Nothing we could do could be considered reckless any longer," Gonji said, "and as for who would benefit—Zarnesti, of course, for starters. I was there. I know what the situation is. It would help erase my guilt over what I did there in the name of misbegotten duty. And most importantly the militia needs to be blooded—so sorry, but a small foray is necessary to test their mettle and to fire their confidence. Garth, how would you rate the militia's chances against the occupation force?"

The smith spread his hands on the table, seemed to slump under a ponderous weight. "Not good, I'm afraid. There *are* promising individuals . . . some of the unit drills are looking up, but . . ."

"You don't know," Gonji concluded, "and neither do I. Or you, Roric, and that's as good a reason as any to find out."

"Sounds dangerous," Michael said. He was in the grip of some inner struggle. "Inflammatory, I mean, to Klann. What might he do in retaliation?"

Gonji snorted. "What hasn't he allowed already in your city? Who'll be beaten to death next? Whose woman will be assaulted, eh? We must prepare for the worst. No help will be forthcoming from the baron's allies, we all know that. The baron himself appears only halfheartedly committed to the entire enterprise. That's bad. And things are getting tighter for me, also. My time here is running out. I've already had to take steps to buy more time. Julian demanded additional intelligence. All I could come up with was to caution him to watch Phlegor and his men—"

They looked surprised and not a little hostile.

Even Wilf's eyebrows raised at the disclosure. "That wasn't very charitable," he said.

"*Hai,*" Gonji sighed, "that's why I had to do it myself. None of you would have. So sorry, but Phlegor is planning something, judging by what we've heard, *neh?* The wrong action at the wrong time . . ." He shook his head somberly. "And it got Julian off my back briefly. But he doesn't trust me. He's having me watched now—"

"I still feel a bit sorry for Phlegor," Roric broke in with his gentle-strong voice. "Shouldn't he be warned?"

"Do that and I'd wager he panics and tries something crazy. *Iyé.* If he plans action independently of the council, then I'm afraid you must begin to think of him as militarily expendable." He paused and lowered his eyes, a grim set to his lips. When no one spoke, he went on. "The poor weapons they forge for Klann have already come to light, also. Only a matter of time before they begin testing the pieces they buy from Vedun. Things are mounting against us. And so I propose a foray into Zarnesti. It may be the remotest outpost, so the chances of repercussion are slim. There would be no reason to suspect Vedun. Twenty-five or thirty volunteers from the militia should be all we'd need . . . That's all I have to say on it for now. Shall we vote?"

There was silence for a space, then a few throat clearings.

"I'm inclined to agree with Gonji," Roric advanced.

"That's two 'ayes'," Wilf observed enthusiastically.

"*Ja,* and one against," Garth followed at once. "There's no need for this sort of thing until we've had a chance to clear the air with Klann."

"I agree that that effort should be made, *mein Freund*," Gonji noted, "although I can't share your optimism about the result. Why haven't you made the attempt already? I should think you'd be the one person from Vedun that Klann would see."

Garth looked stung. "I shall do so," he responded defensively.

"Well, you all know what my vote would be if it counted anymore," Flavio said with uncommon ire. They all dropped their gazes in shared embarrassment over the Elder's loss of influence in the current state of affairs. Flavio called in a servant, whom he sent to the cavern to obtain Baron Rorka's vote on the matter after a careful briefing. Another servant entered with wine and cheese, and they whittled away the anxious time, debating the proposal.

Just when they began to wonder about the servant's prolonged absence, the secretary from the Ministry arrived, breathless, in the foyer.

"Master Flavio, Master Flavio—the king—King Klann comes here! *Michael*—the king is coming!"

"*What?*"

They rushed over to hear the news.

"Here—calm yourself, Vito," Flavio urged. "What are you saying?"

"The king is coming to Vedun," the messenger said, pop-eyed. "A courier came, brought a message. Milorad has it at the Ministry. Klann wants a conclave with all the city leaders, perhaps over a return banquet—"

"All right, all right, slow down. When is he coming—today? Tomorrow?"

"Day after tomorrow. Milorad and Lorenz and the others have begun preparations already. We *need* you, good sirs, please come." Vito rushed back out and sprinted back to the Ministry.

"Well, that changes everything, doesn't it?" Flavio said with smug relief.

"Perhaps," Michael added uncertainly.

"It does indeed," Garth agreed flatly.

"Nein," Gonji said, giving them pause. "It makes things even better for us."

"We could kill Klann while he's here," Wilf said with shining eyes.

"Nein! I forbid such talk!" Garth bellowed, pointing a thick arm at his son. "Wilfred, you're out of place here. Leave us." Wilf glared at him but made no move to go.

"I should say that's out of the question," Flavio added. "Wilfred, I'm surprised at you."

"Be at ease," Gonji told them. "That's not what I meant. It isn't necessary, and in any case the militia isn't ready for so ambitious an undertaking yet. By all means, make your appeals for peace and sanity to Klann. Flavio's dream deserves every chance to survive. But I think he's coming here to threaten, to make a big show of royal indifference over your efforts at salvaging the harvest. And he'll surely be under heavy guard. Patrols in the province will be thinned. That makes the foray to Zarnesti easier on us, if we do it while he's in Vedun, and all the city leaders will be here. There'll be less reason to suspect local involvement in such a far-off place." His vision grew distant. "The one big problem is that the Elder's bodyguard won't be present . . . That can't be helped. I'll have to risk it, create a cover story. The rest of you can just feign ignorance of my whereabouts."

"Why can't you wait until after Klann comes?" Garth asked, looking pained.

"Because, my friend, if what he has to say doesn't appease you, he'll *surely* suspect the city for any subsequent action, however far away."

"I remind you that the vote isn't in yet," Flavio said. They returned to their wine, sipping quietly and exchanging lifeless small talk.

The servant returned from the catacombs, looking sheepish. Baron Rorka had rejected the proposal. Shredded it, to be more exact. "You'd have thought it was *my* idea," the servant declared.

"Well, that's that, then, eh, Michael? . . . Michael?" Flavio's relief abruptly turned to anxiety. Michael stared across the table from behind clenched hands.

"Gonji . . ." the protegé began thoughtfully, "I'll vote in favor of the foray on one condition: that I can go along."

Flavio gasped. Garth stared, open-mouthed. Roric drew back in surprise. Wilf's rapid breath whistled through his nostrils.

"The leaders will be expected here, Michael," Gonji reminded.

"Those are my terms."

Gonji glanced around the room. "Then I suppose I must agree to them," Gonji's pulse raced, his thoughts a-boil. *What's he trying to prove? I've enough to worry about without . . .*

Michael nodded. "Three-to-two in favor of the foray."

"Michael," Flavio said, frowning, "what's become of you, the boy I once knew? The education, the careful nurture of a promising young statesman? I thought you'd arrested this . . . unspiritual passion for vengeance."

"People change," Michael responded. But he averted his eyes from his father's lifelong friend.

"*Sì*, but it is always hoped that change comes for the better . . ."

"You'd better see about the planning," Garth told Flavio, "for the meeting with the king. We'll wring good from this, I assure you, my friend. This opportunity will not be wasted." The massive smith leaned forward determinedly on his meaty fists.

"You go in my stead, Garth," Flavio replied, slowly ambling from the parlor. "I'm afraid I have no heart for these deceitful preparations. I'd just like to be alone for now. Make yourselves comfortable in my home, gentils."

When he passed Gonji the samurai stood and bowed deeply. "I am truly sorry, Master." But Flavio ignored him and left the room. Gonji ground his teeth over the Elder's dismay, his own insides in turmoil.

Lydia selected from among her gowns in the bedchamber's closet, winnowing out those she deemed unsuitable for the banquet, laying out the three finalists on the bed. "Dignity and grace. I need the best combination . . ."

The argument was over, and as usual even in apparent defeat she had won. Her arrogant dismissal of the matter annoyed Michael. He couldn't drop it.

"So I'm going on the sally, and that's that," he said with the forcefulness of the victor, feeling none of it.

"Stupid," she said daintily without looking up from her selecting. "What are you trying to prove? Your mother disowned you because you'd rather lead an insular colony of peasants than assume a more promising career, and now you want to die as a savage."

"These are violent times, Lydia. Why is it all right for other men to change with the social order but not me? And don't think I haven't seen you admiring other men's prowess in the cavern. It's a different matter, though, when I show my skill with the sword, isn't it?"

She began disrobing.

"Whatever are you talking about? Whomever you've seen watching with fluttering heart, it hasn't been me. Do you think I should wear the chemisette, or would the ladies of court be scandalized if I—"

"I don't give a damn about the gowns! I won't be there anyway." He slumped into a chair, brooding.

She peered over him. "Talk sense. You're no killer, you're a statesman. The future belongs to men who can use their intellect, not just their vulgar muscle. There's a time and place for fighting, and the kind of men to do it, but . . ." In her poise and self-possession she had always failed to understand one thing about herself: the power she seemed to have that made men posture as what they were not, act insincerely, and play coy games. Even her husband.

She thought about it. *Si*, now was the time.

"Men are such fools," she said amusedly. "Look at me."

He glanced over disdainfully. She stood naked in the flattering soft lamplight. He looked away, smirking.

"What do you think you're going to do—seduce me out of my resolve?"

"That would be unfair. And I think unnecessary. *Look* at me."

There was a girlish humor in the quality of her voice that made him regard her questioningly. He felt an immediate pang of desire. She had struck a sultry profile. His eyes coursed over her exquisite hair, her proudly jutting breasts, limned in the alluring flicker of the oil lamp.

"You're getting fat," he teased.

"*Si*—very."

He looked closer. "Oh—*Sancta Maria!*—Lydia—you—*when?*" He rushed over and embraced her.

She laughed softly. "In the spring."

He drew back and held her at arm's length, the

present taunting him. "That's a long way off, isn't it?"

Her face took on a hard edge. "You're going to be a father . . . if you live."

A sudden trembling seized him, made speech difficult. "Lydia, I'm committed, and that's that." He turned away.

"Listen to me, Michael. We must not do this terrible thing. Life must go on as it has. It *will*, if we allow it. If you go out and die on this crazy adventurer's sally, I—I can't swear to you that I'll honor your memory to our child." She made a tiny sobbing sound. "God forgive me, but you bring out the viper in me sometimes." She wrapped herself in a robe and stalked out of the bedchamber.

Michael grasped the bedpost, his mind sifting through his anguished thoughts. It suddenly occurred to him how reason weighed against Gonji's foray, and how many reasons there were for him not to go along.

"*. . . a weak conjurer of smoky serpents when I found you . . .*"

Quite so, Mord thought, smiling to himself as he sat with arms folded in his subterranean sanctum far below the castle halls and ramparts. Yes, that's what you were led to believe: an inept magician with erratic sorcerous potential. Someone who might be of limited use to you in your undying quest after the Akryllon that loathes you. Is that what you think, *Your Majesty?* Good. Your own folly aids the Grand Scheme. And now . . . time for a new turn, which you yourself have facilitated, O Five-in-One Most Sublime! I was unsure what to do. My mana grows weak; I cannot drain your people *too* quickly lest I cast suspicion on myself; and you grant me these sacrificial provincials only with reluctance, and in insufficient numbers. Soon . . . in a matter of days . . . the full moon—the faith chant at its most efficacious—a new imputation of power. And until then *you* have made it easy. Your foolishness could not have been better channeled. After the city conclave I'll be rid of both a weak, fearful king *and* the place I loathe.

He thought of his parents, cult worshipers of the serpent demon. Could they have ever guessed how great his stature would one day be among the Dark Master's acolytes? And of the long-dead priests of ancient Vedun—long dead whilst *he* stalked the earth, immortal!—who had marked him as a monster to the world of men.

And lastly he thought terrible thoughts of his plan for the new colony of cross-worshiping pilgrims who would suffer countless agonies for every crime the priests had perpetrated upon him.

Chapter Eighteen

Gonji awoke, startled, to find Tralayn seated beside his cot, smiling wanly.

He remembered: Several trainees had napped there prior to the morning's training session, an important one, where plans for the next day's foray into Zarnesti would be hatched. Now all the men were gone save he.

Nine bells rang in the distance.

"Spirits of the dead—nine bells!" He swung his legs off the cot. A headache made him wince slightly. "I often wondered what it would look like to wake up and see your face. Now I know—*why didn't you wake me with the others?*" he finished in a rush.

"You have time. You have other matters to attend to

this morning," she replied enigmatically.

The samurai, still bound by webs of sleep that parted only with effort, pondered her words dully.

"I've waited to break my fast till you awoke. Will you join me?"

"Mmmm," he grunted noncommittally. She took it as an assent, brought him bread, fruit, and fresh milk. He rubbed his eyes and stretched for a bit, then washed himself and sat to eat.

"Your place is like a brothel these days," Gonji observed, an irreverent eye twinkle punctuating his words in just the right place.

Tralayn grinned, an infrequent gesture, judging by the freshness of the crinkles around her eyes. She was pretty, Gonji decided, in her way. Her age couldn't even be guessed at.

"You know you keep trying to irk me," she said. "You're the only one in this city—aside from the soldiers, of course—who dares to do that. Do I frighten you?" Her eyes flashed like a stormy emerald sea.

"Don't be ridiculous," Gonji replied in a low voice, viewing her askance. "More milk, *dozo.*"

She poured. "Do you know why I like you? You remind me of the child I never had, whom I would imagine would comport himself just the way you do around me. A child is always the last to treat his parent with respect. I think," she continued, leaning her chin on her clamped hands, "that unde.neath your *hubris* you're really just a lonely person, desperate to be loved and accepted, perhaps a bit—"

Gonji slammed his goblet down and scratched his beard stubble. "I think that will do, eh? It's a little too early in the day to be picked apart by a soothsayer. What is this business you have for me today?"

She leaned back and spread her fingers on the table.

"Today you learn what you've asked. All that I can tell you. I fulfill my end of our bargain."

Gonji strove to contain his excitement. "Ahh, *yoi!* It's about time, *neh?* But . . . why so suddenly?"

"Because yesterday, when I received word of Klann's coming to Vedun, it became clear to me that my death has been arranged."

Gonji asked her no more until they had descended into the catacombs, where Gonji found Tora saddled, as well as a bay colt for the prophetess.

"Where are we going?" he asked.

"I'm taking you to meet with Simon Sardonis. We're going to confront him, *if* he will see us, for whatever that may be worth to you."

Gonji's pulse raced. He looked himself over carefully. He had on his stained tunic. That would have to do. His kimono, which he favored for social encounters, was at the Gundersens', and his light armor he fancied too bullish. Again he was overwhelmed by the sensation of destiny in unfolding revelation.

They rode out into the southern valley and carefully crossed the heavily patrolled road. When they were deep enough into the forest trails to resume normal speech, Tralayn began the chilling tale of the being known as Simon Sardonis, who might—or might not, Tralayn observed—be the legendary Deathwind whom Gonji sought.

While Simon's mother carried him, her husband was murdered and she abducted by a Satan-worshiping cult leader, a demonic agent who called himself Grimmolech. In a foul ritual the young woman was raped by the evil priest, effecting in her womb a *secondary* conception, an energumen, a bestial body and soul which would coexist with that of Simon. Rescued by priests led by Father Dobret and sheltered in a convent throughout her tormented pregnancy, the woman died giving birth during a full moon to a raging wolf-child—a *werewolf*—whose only apparent connection with humankind was its bipedal structure. But for the intervention of Dobret, the monks would have destroyed the unholy thing on first sight.

But in the morning, after Dobret had kept a prayerful vigil over the snarling whelp, it was transformed before his eyes—in a pitiable, painful wracking of its form—into a fair-haired child, strong and healthy, its only unnatural mark being a pure white cross that blazoned unmistakably in his left palm. This Dobret took as a sign of divine favor on the unfortunate innocent. The young priest named him Simon Sardonis—his human father's given name coupled with a perverse surname that occurred to Dobret in a moment of anger that the Lord would permit so accursed a birth. He took the orphan in as a ward of the Church and raised him as a Christian.

Simon quickly evinced uncanny physical and intellectual prowess and a ready spirituality, but for the one night each month—the night of the full moon—when the energumen would again hold sway, its own wolfish appearance bursting through the human flesh in an agonizing transformation which, as described by Simon himself in relation to a strange primitive memory of his mother's birth agonies, was akin to giving birth over the entire course of his body.

It was found that if the werewolf could be kept from killing and partaking of the flesh and blood of any warm-blooded creature on this night, he would be free of the savage spirit's corporal takeover until the next full moon. But if he killed, the transformation would occur each night for the entire month, with the important exception that *he*, Simon, would be in command of the taunting energumen's awesome physical presence. Yet this was something he loathed, for its achievement meant that he had killed. Restrained by specially fashioned shackles during the full moon, he came to call this the Night of Chains.

When, on his twenty-first birthday, he was told the full tale of his shocking origin, Simon became embittered that God would so curse him. He left the monastery, obsessed with the vengeful notion of tracking down and destroying Grimmolech. Dobret journeyed with him, his sole confidant in the world of men, all the while endeavoring to steer Simon from this angry vendetta and into thoughts of the great purpose God must have meant for his incredible powers.

Dobret viewed him as an angry spirit who should be directed against the evil things of the night, the Wrath of God. But Simon could see himself only as an accursed soul, shunned by the world of men and animals alike, who could sense in him an inhuman strangeness even when he was in human guise. Throughout their itinerant years together Simon and Dobret had even found it difficult to find monasteries that would shelter them.

About a year ago their journey had brought them to Tralayn at Vedun. And although the monks at Holy Word refused to shelter Simon, regarding him as possessed by the demon that cohabited his body with his own soul, the outcast did find sympathetic acceptance by Flavio, Garth, Michael, and Michael's younger brother, Mark, with whom he formed as close a friendship as any he had ever known. Dobret convinced Simon that a spiritual respite would do them both good, a sabbatical during which Simon would study with Tralayn, searching the Scriptures and other ancient writings to try to shed light on his purpose.

Residing alone in a cave at the base of the wooded mountain slopes, shackled each full moon with heavy chains wrought by Garth and released the following morning by the key carried to him by Mark, Simon had lived the last year on the fringe of the unsuspecting city of Vedun. But he had grown restless and frustrated with his fruitless study, and had been on the verge of leaving with Dobret to continue his quest after the priest's next monthly visit to Vedun. By now, however, he had doubtless gone for himself to Holy Word to discover the outrage that had been done, and it seemed clear from the reports of slaughtered Klann patrols that his vengefulness had been rekindled.

Gonji began to laugh, an embittered, humorless sound. "You're quite mad, woman, do you know that?" There was anger in his tone, and pain. He seemed bemused, victimized by the turnings of the cosmos.

She cast him a look filled with pity. "That's . . . what Simon himself has also told me," she replied tellingly. "I'm sorry . . . but it's all quite true . . ."

Gonji spat. "Madwomen, fanatical priests—first Garth's crazy story about Klann, and now . . ." He waved a hand aimlessly. "You people of Vedun are nothing but wild story-tellers." But then acceptance dawned, belief born of his own experiences with things supernatural, and he waxed bitter over the irony of his own quest. "Have I really come so far, wasted the years of my youth, in search of . . . a *monster?*"

"Do not judge him so harshly. He is the most tortured of men." She closed her eyes and sighed expansively. "I rail at him when he reminds me of that, but I'm afraid it's only too true."

"Everyone has his pain," Gonji said trenchantly. "That is karma. We must all bear it, each in his own way. Why should he think himself special?"

"His suffering is unique. He is a faithful follower of

the Lord who is denied the exercising of his faith. The energumen clings to his soul like a leprous thing, taunts him incessantly within, channels its evil impulses into his every human weakness. He has killed many times under its influence, and the evil is not his alone; yet he bears the guilt as if it were. He can never be a man at peace with himself or his world."

"You keep defending him—why?" Gonji snapped. "You all sheltered him, coddled him, suffered these—anti-social ways of his, and now he goes off on his own and places Klann's sword at your throats. But you feel sorry for him. *Why?*"

"I pity him. We all do. And his potential as a soldier against supernatural evil is tremendous."

Gonji snorted, struggling with his wrath, his loathing of the karma that had fallen to him. He found it difficult to think straight. "Do you think he's the Deathwind?" he asked, a curious edge to his voice.

"I'm not sure. The alternative name of Grejkill springs from a Nordic legend of a man-beast believed in by certain northern folk. It tells of an icy devil-wind that accompanied the Grejkill's birth. Dobret has said that when Simon was born in Burgundy a great wind almost tore the monastery from its stone foundation. Yet the Lord sent a great calm after the wind, and his mother died peacefully during—"

"*Iyé*, Tralayn, I think you're wrong about him," Gonji cut in, abandoning his stoicism for a rare instance of self-pity. "I think that *I* am the Deathwind. My quest has been circular, as is all the cycle of life. I've been the fool. Seeking myself all the while, chasing after my own unreachable tail. Why haven't I seen this before: Death-laden winds have certainly dogged my footsteps throughout this Europe of yours . . ." His words drifted off, and for a time they didn't speak, Tralayn granting him space for his sullen ruminations.

They turned onto a trail Gonji recognized as one they'd used during the night of cavalry skirmish training.

"We practiced here the other night. In the rain."

"*Ja*, you were very near to his cave," she said. "He probably watched the entire exercise."

"I hope he enjoyed the spectacle."

Tralayn only smiled. From his effort at wry humor she deduced that he was coming to terms with his frustration and disappointment.

Tramping through fresh-scented pine forests, their horses' hooves squelching in mud puddles and bogs formed by the recent rains, they neared the northern slopes of the Carpathians' southern curve.

"Is he the beast these nights, then?" Gonji inquired, his face once again an impassive mask.

"*Nein*," the woman replied. "When Mark was captured he was bringing the key to *release* him." She saw his expression of surprise. "*Ja*, he's unusually gifted, even without the savage strength of the wolf-thing. His power is greater than any man's. That is why he has wreaked havoc with Klann's patrols, struck fear in their hearts. He can meld into shadows in the night. The elements, within a certain limited distance, seem to obey him, or at least to reflect his moods. Something even he cannot adequately explain. And his recuperative faculties are remarkable. Yet . . . I think he wishes at times that they were not. I'm afraid Simon longs for the peace of death." She drew a deep breath. "I believe that, more than victory over these brigands, he wishes to go to the grave, taking along as many of them as he can . . ." She peered sidelong at the samurai. "Can you understand my meaning?"

Gonji looked from the prophetess to the trail ahead, his vision parting the way, at last forming a bridge between his own soul's disquiet and that of the mysterious cave-dweller.

"*Hai.* I've known the feeling."

They arrived at a glade overgrown with thick grasses and tangled weed. Facing them was a steep rocky slope matted with scrub and bramble. Their horses nickered but displayed no alarm. They dismounted.

"He may be here," she whispered, listening to the unnatural stillness. Not a bird twittered in the enveloping treetops, nor did any land creature scurry in the underbrush.

"Or it may just be that we've scared the animals into cover ourselves. Where's this cave?" He seated his swords properly, tightening his *obi*. Then he raked the twigs and pine needles from his hair and adjusted his topknot. Dusting himself off, he caught up with Tralayn, who was already padding through the soft grasses.

To Gonji it appeared they must certainly be heading for a climb; there was nothing before them but a wall of rock thatched with vine and bramble. But then they reached the facing of the rocks, and Tralayn swept aside a fall of vines to reveal the hidden cave entrance. Gonji stopped and peered into the forbidding blackness. An inner cry of caution placed him on alert: Was this some sort of trap? *No, don't be so suspicious.* Telling a story such as she just told was no way of lulling a victim into complacency.

Producing flint and tinder from her cloak, Tralayn struck fire to a torch in the entrance tunnel.

"Simon," she called, "forgive me. You've made it necessary for us to break our solemn oath."

A chill surged through the samurai to hear the words. Choléra, they treated him like a godling. But the fight . . . Remember how he so easily dealt with Ben-Draba. And those eyes—those inhuman silvery eyes. . .

"Come," Tralayn said, motioning him into the cave.

Gonji followed her, breath held in check, hand on the hilt of the Sagami. They both exhaled as one. The cave was empty. Only the severe appointments of Simon's habitation flared into view under the flambeau's harsh light: a low oaken table and chair, two oil lamps, several books and scrolls and some scattered writing materials, an opened bedroll, some bundled clothing, a water bucket, and some foodstuffs.

Tralayn picked up a well-worn prayer manual. An almost mystical atmosphere prevailed in the cave, and Gonji avoided touching any of the man's personal effects for no particular reason than the strangeness of it all.

"No, he hasn't gone," Tralayn said. "He stays, for his own selfish purpose, for vengeance."

"Sometimes that's as meaningful a duty as any."

"No. Not for one raised by the teachings of the Christ."

"Mmm. All right for an infidel samurai, though, *neh?*" he found himself probing only to hear her answer. But it was a discomfiting one.

"You have other reasons, and you know it. Your quest . . . you have friends now . . . and Helena—you care for her, don't you?"

He swallowed. *Discretion.*

"*Hai. . .*"

Part III

"Le Roi Est Mort!"

Chapter Nineteen

There were no training sessions on the day of the foray into Zarnesti. The council decided it would be best for the populace to be in the city for that day's banquet meeting with Klann. A dawn assembly of the militia was held in the main cavern, at which the final selection of volunteers for the raid would be made. But although the attack plan had been embraced lustily and the training for it enthusiastic, the morning's formation of the volunteer band was curiously tentative.

Everyone seemed to stand around and wait to see who would go first.

Gonji and Roric stood before them, along with Wilf, already posturing like a leader, Spine-cleaver proudly angled from the sash he now wore. About two hundred men shuffled uneasily in the ranks, nervous snickers and jests issuing from them as, for the first time, their confidence in new fighting abilities was put to the test. Several former military men were turned back for a time, first priority being given to those with no soldiering experience.

Baron Rorka stood nearby with some of his Grays, eyeing the proceedings imperiously, smugly amused at the initial difficulty they were finding in culling the thirty men Gonji sought. Michael was with him. Flavio's protegé had shown up with a curiously different deportment this morning. He had declined to go on the foray, to Gonji's relief, admitting that he would indeed be expected at the meeting with the king. Yet he refused to change his vote, having cast the deciding one, and he seemed at ease for the first time Gonji could remember.

"All right, so who's going?" Gonji called in German, the other leaders translating his words as he strode before them with hands clasped behind him.

Paolo Sauvini was the first to step forward. He spoke not a word, just looked at Gonji squarely, his hand on his sword hilt. Gonji studied him a second, then nodded and indicated that he should stand with the leaders.

"Oh, what the hell . . . you guys are going to need *somebody* to lighten it up." Relaxing laughter accompanied Stefan Berenyi's strut forward and the deep bow that so precisely imitated Gonji's own.

Gonji smiled wryly. "Well, we have a man who can fix wheels and one to laugh at him! Keep coming."

Jiri Szabo came next, looking wide-eyed and expectant. Ready but nervous. Gonji welcomed him. A few more men followed in a slow trickle. It was obvious that few wished to risk death so far from the city.

"What about me, *sensei*?" Klaus asked.

"Not this time, Klaus," he responded gently. "Soon, *neh*?"

Wilf approached Vlad Dobroczy and spoke to him quietly. The farmer stood at the front of the ranks, arms crossed, but made no effort to join the band.

"What about you, Hawk?" Wilf asked. "You're always spoiling for a fight."

"Oh, sure," the farmer replied, sneering, "works out just right, doesn't it? He takes out the best fighting men, comes back alone, says they were hit before they knew what was happening—No, thanks. I'll sit this one out and see what comes of it."

Wilf glared at him. "You haven't been listening. He's not asking for the best, just the ones who need it most."

Vlad stiffened as if he would jump at the smith, but then eased up, a look of surprise on his face to see Pete Foristek stride past, the huge farmer joining the raiding party.

"Welcome, big man," Gonji said, grinning. Pete shook his hand firmly and took his place beside the others.

When they were about twenty, Nick Nagy came forward. "I fought with Magyar cavalry in my younger days, but you better let me come along or that young smart ass Berenyi will never let me hear the end of it." Gonji laughed and assented.

Berenyi broke wind. "Well, chalk this one up as a defeat." They began to argue, and the tension eased out of the assembly. A few more men came forward.

"I'm going, eh?" Karl Gerhard asked, leaning on his deadly four-man bow.

"*Hai*, we'll need your shooting eye to help overcome the pistols. We're not taking any."

"Well then you'll have to take me along, too," Monetto advised, shaking his head, "for the same reason Nick's going—unless you plan to lose Gerhard and Berenyi somewhere in the mountains!"

"All right," Gonji declared, "get to your mounts and saddle them."

Thirty-one volunteers ambled off across the cavern with mixed pride and apprehension.

"Why so many for only—what?—fifteen bandits, maybe?" someone called up from the assemblage.

Gonji rubbed his neck. "We're going after victory,

not valor. Battle plans aren't formed on the basis of fairness to the enemy. You produce a couple of giants, and I'll cut the raiding party in half!" There was much good-natured laughter.

When the raiders had been armed, mounted, and briefed, goodbyes and well-wishes were passed around. Many loved ones mingled with the mounted party to lend them encouragement and pledge their prayers. Brief group prayer was offered, including the one Gonji had composed for them.

Hildegarde came up beside Tora and slapped Gonji on the thigh. "You know Hildy would go along, Gonji-Gunnar," she said in her thick Nordic accent, "but I don't waste my time on these little skirmishes!" They shared a hearty laugh.

Wilf rode up alongside him and guided his horse through a prancing complete turn. Gonji had made him change steeds, declaring his favorite white roncin a too easily spotted target. The new horse was a jet-black gelding. Gonji nodded.

"Bona fortuna," Flavio offered, standing before them with Garth. "And ride with God."

Gonji bowed to him. Wilf and Garth exchanged strained farewells as the people were guided back to the tunnels for the cautious return to the surface.

"And the best to all of you," Gonji called, "on your efforts at establishing peace with Klann. My wish is for you to pick up the pieces of your dream, Master Flavio."

The samurai had Roric form them into a double rank. He walked Tora back and forth in front of them, looking them over carefully, seeing the tension that manifested itself in twitching and itches, sweating palms and faces, skittish mounts. Most of them wore armor and helmets of one sort or another. A wide assortment of weapons was on view. Gonji wore his cuirass, pauldrons, and vambraces, but no helm, only his *hachimaki*.

"When the sluice gates open and we hear the water rush down the cliff, then we go. Mute everything that makes noise as best you can." They were again using the opening of the waste-clearing sluice gates to cover their noise from the city wall sentries high above their heads.

A Rorka knight named Anton, a middle-aged man with a balding pate, clopped over to Gonji, clad for battle in half-armor and his gray surcoat with the baron's crest.

"I go along," he said gruffly. "I have kin in Zarnesti—*had*, the last I heard."

Gonji met his smoldering eyes, nodded. "You do so under my command, then, and you respond to my orders." Anton shrugged sullenly but cast Gonji a salute and joined one end of the front rank.

The wash of water came to them from outside, the fetid waste gully splashing nearby with the day's offal.

"Let's go—quietly."

They were off, under the concealment of heavy foliage. Scouts were sent ahead to watch for patrols along the southern road. A small party of mercenaries approached from the south not long after they had begun their ride. The raiders split and broke into the forests on either side, waiting breathlessly until they had passed.

"The relieved sentries, probably," Gonji said when they had reassembled. "From Borgo Pass. They've just been granted a stay of execution."

Some of the men gulped and wrestled with private fears to hear the words. A few were beginning to have second thoughts, if their lack of color was any indication. But they rode on.

They reached Borgo Pass in the early afternoon,

stopping within sight of it to share a meal in silence. Even Berenyi's light-hearted gesturing and mugging seemed forced and evoked only the merest polite smiles. Gonji sat apart from them in the lotus position, arms folded, watching their anxiety without expression.

Tethering their horses in the swampy valley, they came near to the pass on foot. From their concealment on the eastern side they could make out the enormous rock formation that resembled a leaning crow. Three mercenaries in jacks—open in the midday heat—lounged on a rise tucked between boulders, a cooking fire serving up heat waves in their midst. Their armament could only be guessed at over the distance. One bow could be seen protruding from a saddle, unstrung.

Gonji pondered a while, crouching at the rim of the tangle of brush. Gerhard scrambled up beside him.

"We could drop them with shafts from here, no?" the long-faced archer posited.

Gonji grunted. "No good. If they have pistols, they could squeeze off a warning shot that might be heard for leagues. Anyway I want to involve a novice, if possible." He watched as one of the brigands removed his jack to slump down shirtless against the boulder facing with his meal. "Come on."

They scurried back to the others. "Someone get me a horse—not Tora!" Gonji commanded. A man hustled off to comply. "I want one volunteer to work with me on eliminating those guards. Someone to—" Paolo Sauvini rose and stepped up to him. He looked him up and down, then past him to the others. "—someone who can climb well and doesn't fear a drop from that boulder. You're going to land on top of one of them while I engage—"

"I'm your man, *sensei*," the swaggering wagoner interrupted. His forte was the bow. He had never shown any special agility.

"I think not," Gonji countered in a low voice. "Anyone?"

Paolo swallowed hard, not liking the taste of rejection. He rubbed his nose rapidly and shuffled off, apart from the others.

"Jiri?" Gonji questioned hopefully. A sheepish grin broke on the young athlete's handsome face. He shook his head with a tiny fluttering motion that denoted embarrassed unwillingness.

"Not just yet," he replied, gulping and looking down with a nervous rolling of his shoulders.

Gonji fingered an ear pensively, frowning. Monetto bounded up. "Better let it be me."

Gonji eyed him sidelong. "Ever kill before?" he inquired softly in Italian.

"Did you have to ask me that?" He winced.

The horse Gonji had called for was brought to him, a roan mare. "I may have to use your beauty here for cover," he told the man. "So sorry, but Tora is too valuable to me. Don't worry, though, my plan is to avoid it."

Gonji removed his swords from their back harness and seated them in his *obi*, which was still cinched about his middle. They moved ahead stealthily as a group to watch the operation from concealed vantage. Monetto circled behind the rocks and scaled the boulder behind the encampment. When he was above the brigands he waved a signal. The sun strobed the raiders' faces through the brush, causing them to squint from its glare in the peaks as Gonji led the mare back through the trees a few hundred yards, finally emerging onto the road and leading her by the bridle toward the outposted sentries.

"Come on, damned horse!" Gonji was calling petulantly to her as he dragged her along, leaning forward, panting and wheezing. "Come on!" He jogged with her now, twisting and turning back to shake his fist at her muzzle, then pausing either to rub his buttock or relieve the friction of a heat rash.

When he was about even with the concealed raiders, the mercenaries heard him, two of them moving out to investigate.

"Sonofa—!" Gonji gasped, waving to them and half-smiling as he fought for breath, clutching at his throat, his chest heaving.

The lead mercenary drew a pistol and spannered it tight, checked its charge and load. Replaced it in his belt. The watching raiders held their breaths. The seated man had set his plate down but remained in place, watching his fellows' backs, still out of sight of Gonji. He leaned over and hefted another pistol, readied it, then stuck it behind him.

"They'll blow him a new asshole," Anton whispered harshly.

"Hsssst!" Roric ordered, the knight scowling.

Gonji waved affably, still panting in feigned exhaustion, and drew near to them.

"Julian—I—he—" he rasped, holding his chest. "—damned horse—Julian—"

"What do you want, slopehead?" the pistol-wielder demanded. His partner gripped his sheathed broadsword suspiciously.

"Ohhhh!" Gonji dusted himself off, two yards away, his breath still choppy as he bent over. "I'm—supposed to—"

"I said *whaddaya want?*"

"To relieve you," he said, looking up. The bandit cocked an eyebrow and leveled his pistol.

The raiding party gasped as one and lurched forward.

In the instant Gonji swept the Sagami out of its scabbard, Monetto dropped down on the seated mercenary. With a slash right off the draw, Gonji sliced his opponent's arm off at the elbow, blood spouting from the wound, the pistol and severed arm still in the air while the returning glint of steel tore open the swordsman's belly before his blade was half drawn. They lay on the ground writhing in agony, Gonji's finishing strokes silencing them. He turned at once and peered at Monetto, who rose shakily from the slumped sentry at the boulder. There was blood on the biller's shirt. Not his.

"Aldo—you all right?"

Monetto waved weakly and bobbed his head. The rest of the band charged forward excitedly, Roric sending several of them after the horses. Gonji saw the horror etched into their faces at the sight of the carnage.

"There can be no witnesses, *nicht wahr?*" Several heads assented silently.

Monetto shambled up to them unsteadily, eyes still gleaming from the adrenalin rush, blood throbbing at his temples. He blew a whistling breath and smiled crookedly at Gerhard. "That's one for me, *neh?*"

"A fine attitude for a Christian, blustering like that before the Lord," Gerhard said, scowling.

"These are *evil* men!"

"How can *you* judge them?"

"Stephen Sie!" Gonji commanded. "Let's move. Get the horses, and let's ride like demons. There should be only one more outpost to take."

Roric and Anton took up the pistols of the dead men, and the rest of their weapons were loaded, their horses taken in tow.

"Shouldn't we bury them?" Jiri asked.

Gonji looked over their anxious faces. *"Hai.* We'll

keep it civilized, then, for as long as we can. But quickly. No time to dig—in the rocks, over there."

They found a cleft beneath the beak of the great crow formation of Borgo Pass. There they consigned the corpses of the sentries to the earth's keeping, piling rocks atop them to confound the scavenger beasts. With muttered prayers and signs of the cross they edged away from the common grave and remounted, pounding away along the mountain trail on a westward course.

Gritting his teeth against the jouncing ride, Wilf wondered to himself whether it ever went away. The tightness in the stomach, the constriction in the throat; the parched mouth and sweating palms and prickling spine . . . The symptoms which added up to fear of battle, of dying by searing wound of pistol ball or sword. He wondered what it had felt like to be one of those unfortunates Gonji had dispatched so swiftly, so coldly. Gonji hadn't looked at him accusingly when he had failed to volunteer to join him against the sentries, but he thought he could detect a certain disappointment.

Got to get over this, Wilf, he told himself. *It's a long way to Castle Lenska . . . and Genya . . .*

The old man had been driving his rickety dray on his annual visit to Vedun, there to sell the modest surplus yielded by his small plot of land. With the money he might lay in his winter supplies. Not that he cared much anymore. Nothing was the same since his wife had died.

It was the Turks. Her fears of the blasted Turks and of the bandits who ravaged the countryside had finally sent her to the grave. Ever since, the old man had felt his zest for life ebbing from him, and with it had gone certain other things. He couldn't remember what, but they had been important once . . . he thought. *Boh*—God, but he could scarcely remember even his beloved wife anymore.

When he saw the devils attack the small campsite, he guided the swaybacked draft horse off the road. There he cowered in fear until they had gone. Bandits, that was sure. They'd taken everything. He hated bandits. He'd seen their leader—a Mongol, and he hated Mongols. He'd have to tell the authorities, that was what he'd have to do. But who? Who was it that ran this territory? Some . . .

Baron. A baron, that was it. Baron—Ruka, or Hrurka. Something. The one who lived in the castle not far from Vedun.

He'd go there. Go and tell the baron about the Mongol with the hair tied like a tulip bulb on his head. The one who had killed the men camped at Borgo Pass.

"My turn?" Paolo asked sarcastically.

The samurai eyed him up and down. "Go," he said simply. "And no needless heroics. Just get it done quietly."

The wagoner made no answer but grinned foxlike and ambled off with a cocky strut. He disappeared up the slopes, as the others waited, a half kilometer from one of the two passes that led into the mountain valley wherein lay Zarnesti. Nestled with their steeds in the lee of a cliff off the mountain trail, they waited for a time that seemed too long to some, while others prayed that it might continue forever, if that would keep them from what was to follow.

"Monetto, you're Italian, too," Gonji said, squatting down next to the biller, "what's the matter with this Sauvini? What are his aims in all this?"

"Glory," Aldo answered.

"To be a big man in the city," Nagy added in German, "like this smirking brat here." He indicated Berenyi.

Berenyi sneered. "Drop dead, old man, and I'll pile stones on you like we did to those brigands. Don't listen to him, Gonji. Sauvini's just a . . . man nobody likes. Always braying that he's going to be important someday. Thinks all the women love him, too, when really they love this old fart here." He jabbed a thumb at Nagy.

"You mean he's not the quiet kind, the way he poses in training?" Gonji asked, mildly surprised.

A few knowing laughs.

"That's just when you're around," someone spoke farther down the line.

Jiri Szabo piped in: "Usually he asks too many questions. Always nosy: 'What are you doing? What's going on? Tell me what happened.' "

"*Ah, so desu ka?* Like Klaus, eh?" Gonji said, chuckling affably. His congeniality spread quickly to the others, who were anxious to stave off their apprehensions. Quick translations were followed by nervous laughter. "Klaus is a fine, honest fellow, though, *neh?* A lovable lummox."

"At least him you can put off, if you show he's annoying you," Monetto said.

"*Ja,*" Gerhard agreed, "Paolo always wants to fight."

"I feel sorry for his wife, though," Roric said sadly. "Good woman. Made the mistake of falling in love with what Sauvini is instead of what he wants to be. She's too good for any man to think his dreams are too high and mighty to include her."

Then—the sibilant whistle of an arrow—*thuck!* It planted itself in the road. To a man they hushed and stared at the shaft. Something was affixed to it. A shred of cloth.

Gonji clopped out onto the road and peered up. Sauvini stood there grinning with self-satisfaction. The samurai looked down at the arrow, dismounted and pulled it free: Tied to it was a piece of bloody bandanna, a souvenir of Paolo's sally. He shook his head.

Seconds later they were on the road again at a gallop. They passed the post of the now dead sentry, and the cliff cave where Gonji had shivered on the night he had nearly been killed by the 3rd Free Company. When was it? Ah . . . the full moon, the last full moon. *The Night of Chains* . . .

They found the delve through which Captain Navarez had taken Klann's mercenary company, negotiated the rugged climb, their mounts whinnying in protest. And soon they were descending the treacherous shale-and-bramble slope into the misty mountain valley. Gonji cautioned them to guide carefully, recalling a nasty horse fall he had seen there. Evening shadows lay across the valley when they dismounted and made their plan. Six men were chosen to hold down the village perimeter with bows, polearms, and a pistol lest any mercenaries escape.

They crouched on the south of Zarnesti, just across the meadow. Gonji's pulse pounded when he recalled the rainy sprint he had made there in darkness on a night so buried by recent memory; and his eyes narrowed to think of the swarthy Navarez and his toady companion Esteban, and of insults he suffered; Riemann, who'd tried to shoot him.

And Jocko. That crazy old bastard Jocko. He'd best tell them what to expect . . .

Captain Francisco Navarez slumped in a chair in the

former magistrate's two-room fieldstone dwelling. His feet were propped on the pine table, his dark face skewed by the drunken torpor that sagged his whole being. He felt sluggish and useless, jaded by the carnal excesses of—what? three weeks? a moon?—in this backwater hole. He looked around at the woman, crumpled into a heap on the blanket-strewn floor. Snoring. The bruised eye angled up on the side of her face he could see. *Whore* . . . He was tired of this, tired of easily taken women and dispirited men who knelt on command or fought their neighbors at gunpoint to save their worthless skins. Tired of wine and slovenly women and horseshit and cold quiet nights under silver mountain moonlight.

Tonight the moon danced behind scudding clouds, and a whistling wind snaked out of the mountains. Good. He'd go out in a few moments and clear his head. Then . . . then? Then maybe they'd leave this place. *Si*, why not? King Klann had abandoned them here. No relief, no word . . . *Dios*, maybe Klann and the whole army were in—

The screams and shouts dispersed his confused thoughts but at first didn't cause him to move. Probably just the company trying to chase their boredom again. Then more screaming—he thought he heard his name called. He sat upright and listened.

It was the gunshots that finally sent him lurching for the door, reaching for the pistol and shot on the table.

Peter Foristek was the first to strike.

"Let me take that one, *sensei*," the big farmer had asked of Gonji while they hunkered in a ditch as darkness fell. They saw the brigand have his way with a young girl in the tall waving grass behind a barn.

"Call me Gonji," the samurai had responded. "You're not on the training ground now." Pete had interpreted the grin as an assent to his request.

It was a timed operation. They all counted as they darted into position around the village, readying themselves for the strike. The single bandits and pairs first. Watch for pistols most of all. Try not to let any be fired. *What else?* Oh, the old man, Pete recalled. That's right. And leave the Spaniard with the big black mustache for Gonji . . .

Then his count was finished, and his crawl had brought Pete to the corner of the barn. The wind moaned in the mountains. Laughter and shouting in the street, and the screams of men in pain: villagers made to fight each other for the mercenaries' entertainment.

Then the girl's small whimper. And Pete peered around the corner, squeezing the shaft of his great halberd, and he saw. Revulsion roiled around his stomach. The girl couldn't have been more than thirteen. She wasn't even struggling, the brutalization of these people having had time to take its toll. She only emitted tiny whimpering sounds as the bandit lay atop her, thrusting and grunting, his breeches down around his ankles. And all Pete could think was how much the girl reminded him of his sister, whom the occupation troops had once tried to assault . . .

Tuh! the small puff of breath escaped his hot throat despite his effort to contain it, but the bandit never heard it in his ecstatic throes. Pete stood over him, easing the razor-sharp halberd point against his ribs.

"Yeeooowl!" the bandit cried, rolling off the girl and grabbing at his side. Then he stared at the angry giant above him in disbelief. He panted, grimacing in shock and confusion.

Then he reached for his pistol, but Pete anticipated the move, the quick lash of the halberd tearing the pistol loose and splitting his hand open. He didn't scream but rather lurched to his feet and stared in horror, a rhythmic gagging sound coming as he held the injured hand.

Pete growled and threw down the halberd, clutched the man's throat with both hands, and lifted him off his feet. He slammed him hard against the barn and squeezed with those hands that could uproot saplings. The bandit flailed and tried to kick with his bound up legs. Foristek raised his knee and pinned him against the rough wood. The bandit turned red, then purple, his bloodied hand smearing Pete's face and cuirass. The farmer gritted his teeth and squeezed harder, grunting. Something snapped, and a gout of blood blubbered out from between the man's lips when Pete relaxed his death grip. The bandit's eyes bulged and his head fell like a sack onto his chest. His bowels loosed in death.

And the girl started tossing and screaming on the ground, the horror of it all penetrating her, welling up buried emotion. Pete called for her to hush, fearing that she'd compromise the raid. But already the sound of conflict in the street had begun. And the gunfire.

Jiri scuttled between the huts, lithe and circumspect. One hand touched the hilt of the sword strapped to his back. He knew he'd have to be careful, would have to choose his opponent and the tilting ground. Conditions would have to be right, or he feared he couldn't see it through. Terror rippled through him like an undulating serpent, threatened to paralyze his will and, worse, his thews.

Suffer me not the death of a coward . . .

Just remember what Gonji taught, relax, empty your mind—

He heard the surly laughter and shouting from the street. *Da,* you'll be laughing when we . . . Before the huts he could see water troughs and part of a canopied well, loose objects fluttering by in the wind. It seemed safe. He peered around the corner.

The mercenary nearly bumped into him, snarling in surprise. *Omigod.* Jiri's first impulse was to run when he saw the man claw at his belt, but there was no pistol, only a saber and dirk. Jiri leaped out from the cover of the huts and drew steel, came to two-handed middle guard, eyes popping.

"So you wanna fight, eh, kid?" the mercenary said in German. "Hey, Eugie, look at this!" But the partner the man had left several huts down the street was already dead, two militiamen standing over him with bloody swords.

They engaged, the mercenary probing, testing with his saber. Jiri parried his every attack crisply, but his *iai-jutsu* technique lacked completeness: he wasn't finishing the circle, riposting after his parries. He fought totally in defense, backing, retreating, too timid to take the offense and dare the man's blade.

Then he noticed the figure creeping up behind his ever more confident opponent. Jiri maintained his concentration on the man's eyes, all the while sure that he would be dead in seconds if it were another free companion who approached.

But it wasn't. It was Paolo Sauvini. The wagoner moved forward with catlike strides, the whites of his eyes shining in the darkness, both hands clutching his sword in a horizontal thrusting posture taught by the samurai.

There was a sickening sound of rending flesh and innards as Paolo's running, driving lunge shot his blade completely through the man's torso. And what came out of his belly with the point of the blade caused Jiri to grimace.

He turned away, gagging, as the brigand's soul-chilling scream shattered the night.

The village of Zarnesti exploded into violence.

Some of the brigands, assessing the raiders' number and seeing their hopeless plight, scrambled to the stables for their steeds.

Many of the foray party gave chase, most trying to run them down before they could take to horse, some hoping the others would get to them first.

Screams and curses sounded in the village, doors slamming.

The trooper named Riemann rolled off the cot in the hut he had taken for his own and fumbled on his trousers. The woman made small puling sounds, and her child began to cry fretfully.

"Shut that child up before I do it myself," he grated. She couldn't understand, only knew from his tone that her child was menaced and that if she couldn't calm her the monster would kill her just as he had killed the woman's husband.

Muttering curses, leaving his jerkin behind, he loaded and spannered his wheel lock, then grabbed his sword belt and rapier and moved out into the night. Adjusting his eyes to the darkness, trying to make sense of the carnage and hurtling shapes and pounding hooves.

"Care to try another shot, Riemann?" came a voice in the shadows, and he spun down onto one knee and pointed the pistol at . . . what? *Where had he heard that chilling voice before?*

A dagger chunked into the earth several feet away to his right. He rose and leveled his pistol in that direction. Too late, he heard the soft padding behind him. Whirled. Saw the glint of moonlight flash his death sentence—

The Japanese . . . that terrible sword raised high

over his head—He never even had time to aim the pistol, the shot tolling his death knell squeezed off at the earth.

Gonji drew one quick breath and kept moving. He slammed the door shut on the screaming woman and child and launched off into the main lane.

People were running in all directions in bewilderment now; doors and window shutters burst open and were clamped shut. The sharp reports of pistols along a side lane—

He saw some of the raiders dashing about in terrified confusion, feigning toughness by growling and waving their blades and polearms but seeking no action. He called out a few brusque orders, sending them toward the activity at the stables.

Then he saw Esteban. Navarez's toothy sycophant rushed through the street at the head of three others, one bearing a flaming torch. Esteban's good eye was cocked toward the far end of the main street. He held a pistol at the ready, another one angled up behind him in one of his followers' fists. Gonji slipped into a doorway and waited until they had passed. He sprang after them.

"*Komban wa*—good evening! Pox-ridden scum!" Gonji cried at their backs. The four spun and fixed their gazes on him, wide-eyed with dawning terror.

"*You—barbaro!*" Esteban gasped. "Franco-o-ooo!"

And then Gonji hurtled into their midst, his *katana* singing, tearing through flesh and bone. One pistol-wielder shot his crony in the back in his frenzied effort to get at Gonji. Esteban himself never had the chance to recover from the shock of the apparition. He lay dead atop his still undischarged wheel lock.

Gonji saw the horsemen lurching out of the stables, some of the militia engaging them. He knew the danger should any of them escape. But Gerhard and

Roric and Anton were there, and he turned instead toward the magistrate's dwelling, where he knew Navarez had taken up residence.

There, peering dimly out into the street, a pistol hammered and leveled at his waist, stood the hated captain who had brutalized Gonji's duty.

Anton surged into the stables after the fleeing bandits, who rolled and scrabbled aboard neighing, bolting mounts, some unsaddled. Two horsemen lurched past him, knocking him aside. He slipped and fell in the hay. But a third bandit had been thrown from his steed. Anton peered up, leveled his pistol, cocked it. Sighted his downed adversary in the shadows. Too late—he caught the glint of the other's pistol barrel in a stray beam of moonlight.

Both guns cracked and belched smoke at once. Anton cried out with the searing pain that jolted his leg, spun down onto the damp, pungent stable floor. But he heard the other's groan, looked up tentatively through the cloud of smoke. In his gasping agony he felt a flood of relief: his pistol ball had split the brigand's skull.

He collapsed, succumbing to shock and pain.

Outside, a sword-swinging mercenary on horseback engaged the wily Roric, whose pike pointed steadily at the chest of the oncoming rider. The swordsman howled his berserker's cry and lashed down and out. But Roric sidestepped the slash and lunged—

There was a horrendous scream and chunkering of honed steel against plate and bone that caused heads to turn nearby. The free companion's momentum skewered him on the pike, tearing him out of the saddle. The horse galloped off, riderless, as Roric felt the great weight on the end his polearm that wrenched his grasp downward. The weapon's head had nearly gone completely through the rib cage.

Monetto bounded up, open-mouthed. "You—you—" He couldn't catch his breath.

"Look out!" Roric yelled.

Two more horsemen were upon them, splitting up to skirt the carnage. One whirled a cutlass, but the other was aiming his pistol for a passing shot.

There was nowhere to hide.

Wilf heard the cries behind him as he clashed with his opponent between the huts. Spine-cleaver flashed and whined, backing the Austrian highwayman, who waxed increasingly desperate, though he sneered and taunted Wilf. The young smith held his concentration.

Clang-clang-süzzzzz!—a rapid exchange of attacks and ripostes and Wilf's leap over a low slash designed to hamstring him. The *karumi-jutsu* training had made the timing feel natural and easy. His confidence grew.

He backed his man down the lane, steel, teeth, and eyes gleaming in the darkness. Wilf felt his stomach knotting. *(have to finish it)* They passed from murk through shards of yellow light from an unshuttered window that illuminated their sweating faces and back into deep shadow again. *(for the city, for Genya)*

He missed a parry and the saber whanged off his sallet, knocking it awry. He flung the helm off as the brigand took a step back and, encouraged, lunged into a straight attack. Spine-cleaver deflected the blade, slid along, shot forward in a two-handed lunge—

A wet gurgle and a spout of dark blood.

Wilf withdrew his point from the man's throat like a shot, as if having been caught doing something he shouldn't. The soldier fell heavily in the lane.

"Get down, Wilf!"

The cry had come from behind; the pistolier stood

in his path, not ten paces distant. Wilf dropped like a wet sponge. Heard the report of the pistol and the sizzle of something overhead. A falling body—the bandit's.

He looked up, then behind him. Karl Gerhard stood there, nodding curtly, his now emptied bow lowered to his side. Wilf blew out a hot breath.

"You *all-recht?*"

"*Ja, danke,*" Wilf replied.

"*Kommen Sie,* then—the stables."

Gerhard sprinted off, reaching back into his quiver for another cloth-yard shaft. Wilf rose, recovering his sallet, and stared at the bandit he had dispatched. Walked around him twice in disbelief.

"*Choléra.*"

Nick Nagy charged the pistol-wielding horseman from the blind side, slashing his exposed ribs. The horse's flank brushed him, and Nagy stumbled backward, cursing. The wounded bandit fell in a jangling heap at his side. Nick had lost his blade, reached for it as the groaning mercenary tried to rise, pressing in his rent side. But Paolo Sauvini rushed him and finished the job with a savage blow across his neck and shoulders.

Nick pulled away as the brigand crashed to earth almost on top of him. Roric and Monetto surged over to them, as Paolo leapt back, crouching, chest heaving, looking for more enemies to engage.

"Holy shit! Stop him, somebody!" a voice cried.

They all looked down the street: The other horseman had evaded Roric and Monetto as they dove for cover from the pistol. He was headed for the gate far down the main village road. If he were to escape, get to Klann with word of this . . .

Roric seized the downed man's pistol, took careful

aim, and fired—missing. "Perimeter guards will have to stop him," the butcher said, all of them looking after the fleeing bandit anxiously.

But then through the shrieking and pounding of feet there came a sizzling hiss. An arrow skewered the fleeing free companion full in the back. They looked across the street. There stood the saturnine Gerhard, his great longbow still vibrating from the magnificent shot that had spilled the man over his horse's withers. The animal continued to gallop out the gate, but now it bore only a dangling corpse.

A dozen men cheered as Karl simply nodded with finality as he did on the archery field. Then Roric muted their celebration.

"All right, all right, calm down. We've yet to—"

It seemed over for the most part. Two things beckoned their attention: the shouts for help from behind the stables and the crowd that gathered before the magistrate's house. They split up to check them out.

Gonji charged Navarez, the Sagami trailing behind him, pointed rigidly upward in his right hand. He dared the captain's cocked pistol, racing at him with flaring nostrils, zig-zagging with the litheness of a leopard.

"*Barbaro?*" Navarez whispered dimly, squinting against the harsh light that flared from wind-whipped torches. "*Barbaro!*" he shouted at last, recognition gripping him with the certainty of oriental justice.

He waved the pistol and fired, missing badly.

"*Barbaro*—Gon-shee—I—" he stammered, fending off the charge with raised hands.

Then Gonji was on top of him. The *katana* arced sleekly, struck the captain's head from his shoulders. The tarantula-mustached head thudded on the steps, jaws still working mutely.

One of the militiamen ran up behind Gonji, saw the gushing neck, the rolling head. He fell on his knees and began to vomit. Others gathered. The villagers began to leave their homes and congregate at the magistrate's, their deliverance becoming understood.

Paolo came up beside Gonji, triumph in his bearing. Seeing the horror on some of their faces, he intoned, "Well, that's the way it looks, boys." Then, turning to Gonji: "What's our next move, Gonji? What's the plan? Vedun next, eh?"

Gonji made no answer. Suddenly he was Gonji's equal, full of tactical questions, his sullen introversion gone. *Proven yourself, have you?*

"Let's restore order," Gonji called out over his head. "See to our men. I want a head count. Check the perimeter. Someone start a body count of the—"

The shouting from the stables cut him off. "*Kami!*—I—"

Gonji bolted to the stables, the curious and concerned following him. He arrived there to find four of his men holding the crusty old cook and hostler Jocko at bay. Sort of . . .

"Pilgrim!" Jocko shouted to see Gonji. "Sonofabitch! Ya told me you'd be back like a conqueror, and goddamn if ya didn't do it! Hee-heeeee!" He rushed forward, past the now relieved band at whom he'd been waving his rusty cutlass, "Kingslayer," and embraced Gonji like a son.

"What a grand day it is! How 'bout some wine fer you an' yer pals? Say, y'know," he said in a low voice, "I don't like ta say nothin', but ya better get yerself some good boys. Why, if an old codger like me can hold off four of 'em, well—"

They were speaking in Italian, some of the men at a total loss to know what was going on.

"I told them not to hurt you, you old relic. But go

ahead, break open the wine casks. Later we'll reminisce. My friends, this is Giacomo Battaglia—"

"Just Jocko," the old man growled.

"—who saved my life from these brigands a while back."

Angelo, Jocko's mule, began braying and kicking in the smith shop.

"Awww, shut up, Ange! I'm comin', I'm comin', dammit!"

"All right, *bushi*," Gonji said, "let's see what we've done."

They moved off to sort out the village, voices in translation relating tales of the fray. It had been a new experience for most of them.

Anton's leg was patched. He wouldn't be fighting on foot for quite a while. And Stefan Berenyi had come forward clutching a bloody rag, pale as the harvest moon. When the rag was unwrapped, it was found that he'd lost a finger. "Oh, is that all it is?" he joked to stave off the fainting spell. They quickly got him drunk so that the old woman who served as village physician could cauterize the wound. All the while Berenyi sat in a cold sweat, shivering, telling jokes that Nagy for once suffered in silence.

But that was the extent of the militia's casualties—not a single death, and most of them seemed encouraged, if a little unnerved to have seen Gonji's savagery in battle for the first time. And the samurai, for his part, understood that some of them failed altogether to take part in the exercise, these having at least gained something from the grim sight of it all, he thought.

"I didn't do very well today," Jiri said to him when no one else was around to hear.

"Forget it, Jiri, that's the way it is sometimes."

"Don't give up on me, eh? I feel more comfortable

about it now. All I need is some extra work in *kenjutsu*—"

"Jiri, this isn't a competition to please me. This is war. Do what you must to feel good about yourself." And with that Gonji left him to ponder what he had said.

Later Gonji stood alongside Wilf, watching as the bodies of the last fifteen members of Klann's 3rd Royalist Free Company were loaded onto wagons for burial. The samurai cleansed his *katana* blade with a silk bandanna taken from the dead Esteban. He saw Wilf staring at the man he had killed. "Are you *all-recht*, Wilf?" he asked gently.

"I think," Wilf breathed.

The wrapped corpse of Navarez was the last to be brought, Paolo carrying his head, which no one else would touch. The manner of the captain's death still evoked terror and revulsion among some of them, Gonji knew, and he decided to probe them about it.

"This man did me grave insult and offense. He tried to kill me—"

One of the grimacing militiamen spoke his mind in a way that brought the band to tense silence:

"Who are you? *What* are you? Are you a god or a spirit or a demon, that you can fight like that? You—you—"

"I'm both very good, and very lucky," Gonji replied evenly, "but still a man. When my time comes I'll fall like any other. Maybe I'll fall a little more gracefully . . ."

His arch tone on the last word brought a few chuckles, but his detractor continued, impassioned now:

"You make light of it! I'm talking about the way you kill. You kill men like—like—like you're gleaning in a field. Like they—"

"I'm sorry that you don't approve, friend. Battle is like that. I didn't make the rules. I just survive, that's all. Just because men die when I slash them doesn't mean I don't believe in human dignity. I'm sorry that I'm so good. I'm what my father expected me to be. Can you say the same? What were you hoping, that I'd die back there? That one of those bandits would be better? Your hope was misplaced. Better start hoping that none you meet on the field are better than you—"

"It isn't going to matter, because I'm not going to be on any battlefield." With that he turned and walked away, and another followed him. They left the village and returned to their horses.

"Shouldn't we stop them?" Paolo asked.

"*Iyé*—it's their right. Maybe they'll turn out to be smarter anyway."

A new magistrate was appointed in Zarnesti. Gonji recognized him as a burly villager whose life the samurai had spared when he had helped the mercenaries take the village. The man thanked Gonji through an interpreter, relating that he had felt he was a good man when he had seen how the bunch had tried to kill him on that miserable night. The militia left him many edged weapons and half the bandit pistols with which to help defend his village in the future.

Gonji went alone to the widow of the smith he had killed to try to convey his deep sorrow, but she would not receive him; nor would she even hear him out through an interceding villager, saying only that she wished he were as dead as her husband and would pray that he would soon end up that way.

Gonji was profoundly pained by this, his heart heavy with guilt. But there was nothing he could do. Karma.

When the militia mounted to leave Zarnesti, deep in the night, Gonji said his farewells to old Jocko, having tipped a few cups to their mutual good fortune. "And what will you do now, old sourface?" Gonji asked.

"Well . . . seein's how ya made me unemployed . . ." He shook his head.

"You won't go up and tell Klann what we've done?"

Jocko's grating laughter blared forth. "That'd be pretty stupid—I saved yer cursed life fer ya! No, I think it's kinda funny, one li'l bugger like you givin' Klann's whole army an' monsters and God knows what-all else fits! Only you be careful now. These're small fry ya done in here. No, I kinda think I'll stay around here a bit. Ya killed their only hostler, ya dumb ass! But that's work fer me. And then, I dunno . . . I got this notion I ain't too long fer this world, and I got a grandson I ain't never seen. Maybe I'll spend some o' that time with him. Who knows?"

"Well take care, my friend, and may the spirits of your ancestors guide you to a place of gentle respite when your time comes."

"Well now I don't know about that, sonny, but you just watch yer arse. Y'hear, pilgrim?"

"*Sayonara,* old man."

They rode out of Zarnesti exhausted, wounded, but in high spirits. Anton clopped up beside Gonji when they slowed. He didn't look well.

"My cousin is all right. Thought you'd want to know."

Gonji glanced at the balding knight. "I'm pleased."

For a time they rode on in silence, something on Anton's mind besides his pain. Finally he phrased it: "They lost something back there, your *bushi,* no?"

"Eh? What's that?"

"Their innocence. They won't be the same now that they've spilled blood. The war has begun."

Gonji nodded, but it was not of the militia that he was thinking.

If he killed, the transformation would occur each night . . .

Chapter Twenty

They rode into Vedun early in the evening, King Klann under heavy Llorm guard but apparently in good spirits. The main hall had been decorated to celebrate the event, and the citizens had even fashioned a modest effort at pomp and ceremony, a band on the rostrum striking up a military tune as Klann rode by. People cordoned along the sides of the streamered Street of Hope watched with decorum in their best attire. Some even threw blossoms in the column's path, a symbol of hoped-for peace.

We'll see, Captain Sianno thought. He sat aboard his destrier in dignitary array but with weapons at the ready. He mopped his brow discreetly and licked his beaded lip as they pulled up before the city meeting hall, liking this not at all. The king was being very foolish, and what could be accomplished? The farther he stayed from these people, the better off he was.

The troop dismounted, and Sianno ordered the bearers to set down the palanquin so that Mord could disembark. Damned sorcerer postured as if *he* were king. If Klann weren't counting on Mord's aid during the spring voyage after Akryllon, the aides might be able to talk him into dispensing with the conjurer. There was something terribly wrong about him, the way he divined things in advance.

Sianno stayed at Klann's side during the entrance and seating ritual. The banquet aromas hung appetizingly about the hall. The Llorm quietly but efficiently inspected the environment for evidences of deceit, any possible threats to Klann's well-being. A network of Llorm dragoons and footmen patrolled the area without, surrounding the hall. No one—nothing —could get in or out.

The greetings were long and tedious. Sianno scanned all in attendance closely for concealed weapons, any kind of trick, the slightest twitch that might reveal anxiety over a hidden threat to the king.

Flavio; Milorad; the protegé, Michael; their holy woman, Tralayn, looking subdued for once; Garth Iorgens and his son the Exchequer—a wearying parade of local dignitaries. And only Garth had aroused a flicker of real interest in the king.

"A splendid display of goods for the castle," Klann was saying to the crowd. "You've done well indeed. This crop failure, whatever caused it, has been overcome by your diligent efforts and, I'm sure, some belt tightening." Strained laughter. "It's all well appreciated, I assure you."

The leaders seemed anxious to have the festivities done with so that they might speak. Klann, in turn, seemed eager to talk with Garth, frequently casting him nervous glances. Whatever he had to say to him must be important for him to risk coming among these devious people. Could he be planning to offer him a commission again?

No. Never. Their alliance was precluded forever.

Gaily clad women who had prepared the food now fussed about the king, trotting out their concoctions for the head table at which sat Klann, his retainers, and the local leaders. Bright-faced, freshly scrubbed children from the city were employed in the tasting ritual that assured no threat of poisoning to the king. During this time Sianno excused himself and moved to Garth's end of the table, where he engaged the ex-Field Commander in a muted chat.

"Iorgens, for past favors, I'll advance you this: His Majesty comes principally to see you. I think he'll want to ask you what's afoot in Vedun. Will you answer him true?"

Iorgens looked mildly miffed, Sianno thought, as he responded: "What's afoot is that people are dying inside to know what's become of their loved ones. Those taken without provocation and held as hostages. What's happening to these people, Sianno?"

The captain was stung. He suspected, as did all at the castle, that they were being foully used somehow by the accursed sorcerer. Yet it was for some purpose that was to benefit the king, and with his sanction. And they had their allegiance to Klann—all there was to live for to a people without a land to call their own.

"They're needed," he answered sternly, "for the king's service. That's all a conquered people need know. The king's will is law, and his followers will die to uphold it. You used to believe that, Garth. Once *you* were willing to die for Klann's will, isn't that so?"

"That was a long time ago . . . another king . . . another me." Garth turned away, the strain of time and other burdens—things Sianno cared not to probe into—knitting his brow.

The captain returned to his place.

". . . my mother made it herself!" a freckle-faced red-headed boy was telling the king as he took his seat.

Yes, that's wonderful, child, Sianno was thinking, *but let's get on with it, shall we?*

Even the sorcerer seemed on edge as he surveyed the hall. As usual there was no place setting before him. What did he eat?

Sianno banished the thought.

Then the food was dished out from the children's serving trays, "none of them having fallen dead in the generous time allotted," as Klann's chief steward was given to say in his sardonic manner. Klann sampled a little of everything, commenting to each child and frequently to the preparer of the dish as well. Klann's rare displays of magnanimity to a conquered people were always the most wearisome days of duty, Sianno decided. And tonight he was playing the benevolent monarch to the hilt. I wonder what—

The piercing scream from the kitchens off the hall proper caught everyone off guard, so lulled were they by the mood. The Llorm guards fisted their weapons as all lurched from their seats.

"The king!" Sianno cried. "Surround the king!"

The bastards were using some diversion to—

Two bodies came flailing, entwined, out of the kitchen, the faces of the nearest guards contorting as they watched what couldn't be seen clearly from the bunched throng that now ringed-in Klann. The king pushed at his retainers to see what the trouble was, insisting that he was quite safe.

It was the red-headed boy. His mother struggled to hold him still, sobbing and muttering incoherently in a Slavic tongue. The child spun madly in her arms, gagging, making a terrible dry retching sound. She shrieked for a surgeon, calling out the name "Verrico! Verrico!" repeatedly.

Then the boy slammed into a table facing them, and they saw . . . His face was bright purple, his tongue dark and protruding. His belly looked distended. No breath passed his lips. Yet it seemed as if he were grinning evilly somehow, even in his death throes. He lurched over the table and landed on the floor, stunned people scrambling out of his way. His mother pushed the table out of the way to get at him, but his body already sagged in death, his last breath escaping hissingly.

Soldiers filled the room as the dawning horror struck

Klann's retainers. They backed away like helpless children, casting about for some idea of what to do, as the king clutched at his belly, looking down at it with awful understanding, then gazing about him, his face a twisted mask of pain and pleading. He gurgled once and lurched about in a sudden seizure, smacking the nearest retainer in the face. Then he fell behind the table as the Llorm rushed forward to bear him away, some calling for the city physician, while Mord spouted orders.

"Forget their doctor! They're the ones who did this. Back away—give your king room to breathe," the sorcerer shouted. "Prepare to leave this place. Mount the guard! Place this city under martial law!"

Then Mord ordered them all to back away from the place where the stricken king lay, including Sianno, and bent low to attend him.

"Does he . . . does he die, Mord?" Sianno rasped.

"He dies," Mord's bass voice sounded like the closing of a crypt. "But he shall live again." He straightened and began walking about the downed Klann in rapt fascination. "Get them all out of here—all of them!"

The wailing and confused citizens were pushed out by Llorm pikemen, the kitchens cleared of all help. Sianno caught Garth's eye for just an instant before he was ushered off. The captain's hard glare brought no guilt in response from the city's chief blacksmith. Sianno called out his orders. Then only he and a few advisers remained in the breath-stopped hall with Mord and the body of the late king.

Sianno saw Mord's diamond-black eyes widen. He took two steps forward when he heard the first deep rush of inhaled breath.

"Stand back, Sianno!" But the captain crept closer, feeling the chilling crop of gooseflesh as the hand appeared over the edge of the table and the new figure rose shakily from the corpse of the king. Sianno held his breath in check.

Yes, yes, it was a man. A new king for Akryllon. Or would be. He wasn't finished yet. He seemed vague in outline, his features still settling. Sianno hadn't seen the last Rising. It was truly as awesome as they said . . .

"Ohhhh . . ." The new Klann drew long, deep breaths, appreciating the invigorating rush of life for the first time. "Mo—Mord—I—We . . . are *four*."

"Don't waste your new-found breath, my liege. There will be much to do soon." The sorcerer bent and wrapped the residue of the transmogrification.

Klann felt his new face. "Ahhh, this life is as wonderful as the Brethren spoke, but . . . I'm still changing, still resolving, Mord—quickly! Get me a cloak to hide my face! None may see me until *I* do! Yes-yes . . . yes, my Brethren, it *is* as glorious as they say. Soon . . . soon you must all be free . . ." Klann drifted off into the near-catatonic trancelike state of communion with the Brethren that his followers knew so well.

Mord had a cloak brought to him. He wrapped the king in it. "The wretched curs," Mord snarled. "*They* did this to you. I warned you of this. They'll see the quest after Akryllon dashed—!"

"Enough," Klann commanded. "To the castle. Hurry."

Outside in the now lamplit streets, a terrified throng was pushed back by scores of Llorm dragoons. Both garrisons had been turned out, hundreds of soldiers now milling about in disarray, awaiting orders that would seal Vedun's doom. The mercenaries, long since chafing for action, rubbed itching palms in their bloodlust, having no idea what was happening. Tales spread quickly that the king had been assassinated, but the old-timers allayed any fears of lost wages,

Julian and Ivar keeping them steadfast in their duty.

All watched the mysterious proceedings before the hall as fearful speculations passed in half a dozen languages. The king was dead, some said. People crossed themselves and offered tearful prayers against repercussion. Mord rushed the cloaked figure out of the hall, several guards ringing them in until they gained the palanquin. He moved the concealed figure inside, then ordered the city's finest barouche delivered at once for his own use. The palanquin bearing Klann was sent off with the entire Llorm escort, while Mord remained to wait for the coach.

The sorcerer threatened them with all the terrors of hell, advising them to count as precious the hours of life left to them.

"You think Klann is dead?" he roared as he stepped up to the hastily procured coach. "Klann is the Invincible—*long live Klann!*" And with that the barouche clattered off under mercenary guard led by Julian, leaving a strangled city in its wake . . .

Captain Sianno stayed back in command of the city garrisons. Mounted now, he stopped in front of the blank-faced Garth. "There'll be hell to pay. Feel you *nothing?*" But Garth made no reply.

Tralayn and Flavio looked at each other long and tellingly in the lambent torchlight, speaking not a word. Michael stood before the fountain with Lydia, stewing over a course of action in his capacity as a military councilor, ultimately deciding that nothing could be done to take advantage of this disorientation of Klann's forces. They'd have to wait to see what the army did first. But—what in God's name would they *do?* Lydia could only press against him fearfully, offering no counsel, her blue eyes wide with the innocent terror of life imperiled.

Garth watched the course of the palanquin long

after it had departed, understanding, wondering, fearing the changes to come. The changes that always came. And Lorenz stood at his side, following his troubled gaze.

Paille watched it all from the chapel belfry, eyes alight with fires of predestined certainty, the flames of epochal social change.

"Le roi est mort . . ." he spoke to the indifferent night.

Strom Gundersen sat among the rolling hills that marked his flock's favorite pastureland, unmoved by the strife and trauma of political and social upheaval. He watched the ride of the long Llorm column that bore the palanquin back to the castle, torches streaking the night in their wake. He idly played his reed pipe as they passed, legs crossed, one foot kicking in time to his tune. When they were gone from his view, he put up his pipe and gestured to the figure huddled in the brush that it was all right to come out.

Chapter Twenty-one

The *bushi* arrived back at the catacombs like seasoned conquerors, quickly forgetting their puzzlement over having had to slip in singly with some apprehension when the sluice gates failed to open at their appointed time.

Even Baron Rorka received the briefing of Gonji and Roric Amsgard with a quickened pulse and eyes that mirrored renewed hope. While the raiders tipped flagons to their success and engaged in back-slapping retellings of the foray, Gonji received the baron's sincere handshake and congratulations.

"*Prosit!—Na zdravie!—*"

"Where's Verrico?" Gonji asked. "Anton's burning up with fever. Berenyi's wound probably needs to be looked at too."

"He never came. None of the leaders did." Rorka remarked gravely, pulling Gonji aside.

"No one?" the samurai pressed.

"Not even Tralayn. We know nothing of the meeting with Klann. I fear there must be trouble."

"Mmmm." Gonji waxed reflective, his brow furrowed with concern and indecision as he rubbed the exhaustion from his numb face. "We'd better get up there and see what's happening. You prepare for the morning training shift. These men will take the day off to recover; they've earned it. I'll be back later with the news from the city leaders. First we'll assess what Klann had to say, then plan our immediate future." Baron Rorka nodded his agreement, and Gonji moved back to the vibrant celebration. Berenyi, still rather ashen, was explaining for the third time how he lost his finger.

"Some of you men bring a litter for Anton. He and Stefan will see Dr. Verrico when we get to the surface."

"*Da*, Gonji-Gunnar," one of the men answered good-naturedly as a few of them moved off in response.

"Never mind that," Gonji replied with mock indignance. "Don't get so familiar until you can fight like Hildegarde."

Anton was placed on the litter, and the band of about twenty-five passed through the massive iron-bound portal to the small cavern, used now for stores, that branched into the tunnels to the surface. Their ascent was laborious in their weakened state, but the mood was light despite their anxieties over the city. Talk of their victory and of the food and drink to come kept their spirits bright.

At length they arrived at the rear of Tralayn's broad fireplace, and Gonji whanged a rock off the iron frame to signal that someone wished to pass through. They waited impatiently for a response, as security measures dictated. The passage behind the fireplace was tiny, cradled between two shallow chambers of the house, and it dropped off almost immediately to a steep stairwell carven from rock. On this most of the men were clustered, staring up into the grimy lamplight. The air in the passage rapidly became difficult to breathe, for so many.

"She must not be in—let's go through—"

"*Nein!*" Gonji shot, startling them all. "Someone almost always guards this entrance now, whether she's around or not. Something's amiss." He thought a moment, raised the rock to strike again.

Then the pulleys and counterweights began to perform their smoothly oiled functions, and they all inhaled sharply, Gonji reaching for the Sagami at his side.

Tralayn's ghostly face appeared in the crack as she halted the fireplace's travel. Air gushed in all around her, carrying the antique scents of her parlor.

"No, stay right there," she commanded as they began to push forward, their relief suddenly dashed.

"What's happening, Tralayn?" Roric Amsgard asked.

"The worst—Klann has been murdered in Vedun."

"Klann—*killed?*—how?—what happened?—"

"Hush! This house is being watched by soldiers. Soon they'll come for me. You cannot leave by this way. I'm not sure you can leave the catacombs at all."

"How, Tralayn?" Gonji asked. "What happened? Did he—?—"

"I'm not sure, but it seems so," she replied to Gonji's veiled reference to the rising of a new phoenix-Klann from the body of a dead one. "Mord would allow no one to see what transpired immediately after his death. Then he emerged with a cloaked figure that may have been the new Klann. He was poisoned while he ate—and the boy from the city who tasted for him—"

"Oh, God," someone said, all heads bowing with the grave revelation.

"—we're under martial law now. I can't say what will happen. The people are confused and terrified—"

"What is this business of a 'new' Klann?" Monetto asked.

"Best tell them," Tralayn advised.

Gonji and Wilf related Garth's tale from the Akryllonian parchment. "No one is sure whether it's true," Gonji concluded. "It was thought best to keep the tale under wraps. Now, though . . . that decision may weigh against us, if the people's confusion causes them to balk at action. But we still don't know whether it's true."

"I must say that I'm inclined to believe it now. At least we must act as if it were true. That's what the Llorm are saying. Mord has manipulated well. Satan's minions do not lack for cunning. To Klann he has created the appearance of a city cold and cruel enough to mask regicide behind the sacrifice of their own children. And he's made the populace fear him still more in thinking he has the power of life and death, that he alone raised Klann from the grave."

"*Mord* murdered him?" Gonji asked, his face twisting.

"Of course—who else?"

"But *why*, Tralayn? How can that possibly serve his purpose of eliminating the city—"

The *bushi* stood by, whispering translations for

those who needed them, murmuring in shock at these portentous concepts.

"—killing the supreme military leader?" Gonji shook his head in disbelief.

"Who knows the workings of the diabolical mind?"

"He can't get away with it . . . can he?" Wilf offered hopefully at Gonji's side.

"Perhaps not," Tralayn agreed, considering. "Perhaps this time he's taken on too much. But it matters nothing if you cannot get the city to oppose him. And *now* is the time, Gonji—now it must be done! The troops—even the Llorm—seem in disarray. The mercenaries grumble amongst themselves in fear of lost wages. The army's morale is at low ebb. You must meet with the council. Plans must be made swiftly, the evacuation to the catacombs begun even as the battle rages. And Gonji—" She paused breathily. "—you *must* confront the Deliverer of whom we've spoken. Tell him he must help us at all costs. Tell him it was my dying wish—"

"Forget your unwilling hero!" Gonji railed. "*I* am your Deliverer, *neh?* Who has sacrificed the most with the least to gain in this bloody venture?" Then he composed himself. "What do you mean your . . . 'dying wish'?"

"I shall not be with you again," she said evenly. "The evil sorcerer will have his way with me. Just one more confrontation. Perhaps I can make Klann see the truth, if things be as Garth says. Mord will see this city destroyed. He bears it a grudge fortified by centuries of hatred. Scrolls found hidden in the chapel tell of great evil forces which twice before besieged Christian communities in Vedun. And the last time, centuries ago, a demonic sorcerer was disfigured by militant priests, branded so that men would recognize him wherever he roamed. But in their zeal they fought evil with evil and were ultimately destroyed by malevolent forces. They are gone, but the *branded* one lives on, wearing a mask to conceal his disfigurement. It is *Mord*, and he will not rest while stone lays upon stone in Vedun."

"*Jesu* . . ." someone breathed. The foul air was making their breaths come in gasps.

"Go now, and do what you must," Tralayn said. "Be firm in faith and courage, and strong of arm."

Anton moaned somewhere below.

"We can't all go the long way around," Gonji declared. "We've injured men who need attention." He scratched, nerves and anger erupting all over his body. "*All-recht*—two-thirds of you go back through the tunnels to the cavern and brief the baron. Tell him I'll be back later to work with him on the plan, once I've spoken with the others. Spread the word that we're on evacuation alert, but everyone must go to their jobs until they've heard official word of . . . anything else. If nothing's happened, meet me back at the cavern tonight. The rest of you come with me—those who kept any weapons, come along this way. Bring Anton up."

Enervating fear gripped them, and no one moved.

"Let's go," Roric commanded. "We haven't time for weak spines now. You're past all that."

They were galvanized. Anton was passed up with some difficulty.

"I've told you, you can't come through this way," Tralayn admonished. "The house is being—"

"Then you're going to have to leave," Gonji said quietly. "So sorry, milady, but if you leave, they will follow. Then we may be able to sneak away singly or in pairs. You'll be in violation of curfew . . ." His words trailed off.

She thought a moment, then bowed her head.

When they were in her parlor—nine men, counting the injured knight—the fireplace was resealed. With a final farewell, Tralayn was gone into the night, headed for the chapel, where she knew Flavio would be.

They watched her furtively from the windows. Sure enough, a small mounted party followed her, keeping her just in sight down the lanes. One mercenary strolled over and began to mount the steps to the house. Gonji cautioned them to silence. The soldier stopped halfway up and sat, drew out a pipe and lit it.

Seconds later Gonji peered out from behind the rear corner of the house, glancing around the area circumspectly. He timed the pace of the Llorm crossbowmen on the ramparts, then went back inside.

"Let's go," he ordered. "Make it to the alleys and you're safe for a space. Remember, it's after curfew. If you're stopped you'd either better have a damned good story or you'll have to try to take them. Get Anton and Stefan to Verrico. Keep your ears open for word from the council. If you've heard none, then meet me at the cavern tonight."

They slipped out the window, making Anton as comfortable as possible. A loose tile on the sill, dislodged by Foristek, shattered on the stone pavement. They froze, eyes prying at their sockets, heard the rasp of steel from the steps. If the guard cried out . . .

The mercenary reached the corner of the house, blade raised high overhead. "All right—" he growled low.

Then Gonji's clamping hand clutched his throat, tearing a small keening whine of air from the vacuum of his gaping mouth. The guard flew over Gonji's hip, landing hard with a clatter of armor and the bounding sound of the loosed sword. In seconds he was dead. Gonji dragged his body into the deep shadow of the house.

Two horses trotted up along the street from the direction of the granary that now billeted free companions. Gruff voices argued in the stillness.

"Go!" Gonji whispered. They all darted away into the darkness, two of them bearing the moaning Anton between them. But Wilf edged up behind Gonji.

They both readied for a spring, hands on sword hilts. The clacking hooves stamped by, sparking off the paving stones twenty feet from the concealed pair. A pistol-grip glinted in a broad belt. The mercenaries talked on, disputing hotly in a language Gonji didn't know. Then they were gone toward the east.

Gonji tapped the smith, and they pulled the dead mercenary into the back lane, looking about frantically for a place to hide him. They abandoned the effort when the crossbow quarrel shattered against a hut, just above Wilf's head. An eagle-eyed rampart sentry had spotted the dim figures far below and was now pointing them out to his partner.

"Dear God in heaven," Wilf gurgled.

"Run!" Gonji spat.

And they were off in a low crouch as if all the Seven Devils cackled behind.

"Genya—Genya, I must speak with you."

"Hush, now, Richard," she replied, "something's afoot." All the servantry had been roused by the fearful tumult that swept the castle. Richard had come up behind Genya in the vaulted chamber in the central keep, now alive with a flurry of activity.

"Genya—Lottie's gone," the baker persisted, his voice pained.

"What? Gone . . . where?" She gave him her full attention now.

"I—I don't know. She's disappeared. I haven't seen her in two days now. Early yesterday morning one of the scullions saw her in a corridor of the southeast drum tower and—"

"The one where the sorcerer stays?" Genya queried, grimacing.

"*Da*—and that's the last anyone saw of her. Genya, you've got to help me look for her. I'm *scared*."

"All right all right, relax. We'll search as we can."

"I've already searched the larders and pantries and stables—the gardens she sometimes tends—and I've worked my way over to the armorer's tower and the prison tower, but—I—I—"

"Why haven't you tried Mord's tower, where she was seen?" Genya asked in a strained voice.

"You know I haven't any reason to be about there. I was hoping . . ."

"That *I'd* try there, is that it?"

"*Da*," he gasped, excited, "could you?"

She'd thought as much. Richard wasn't noted for his valor. She clutched at the neck of her robe, pulling it close, recalling the foul magician's hungry looks.

"Well, I . . . I suppose."

"Oh, Genya, you're marvelous!"

Da, thanks a heap, she thought as he leaned over to kiss her cheek, but then she stopped him with a hand on his chest. She moved forward a step, staring like the others at the strange figure that strode into the chamber, parting the milling servantry before him.

The castellan, General Gorkin, roused his wife from sleep. "Stir yourself, good lady, and attend on us—hurry!"

She rubbed at her heavy-lidded eyes. "Are you out of your mind? What hour is this?"

"Never mind, just get up—there's been a new Rising." His words were weighted with near religious awe.

"Wha-a-a-t?" She was fully awake. "The king is *dead?*"

"Yes—poisoned in Vedun. We've a new monarch to . . . break in. Perhaps we can start on the good side of this one, eh?"

"*I* shall have no trouble there," she declared haughtily. "*You're* the buffoon who can never read his moods. Ah, I shall immediately prevail upon Thorvald to use her 'charms' to seduce him to let us stay in this place forever—that's a laugh."

"Mind your tongue," Gorkin said, combing out his hair and beard in the mirror. "Have you no sensitivity? The scion of the Akryllonian throne has again given a life in the pursuit of his people's home."

"Oh, screw your Akryllon. Who can love a home they've never seen?"

"Have a care, lady," he warned, "the servants are everywhere. I've got to go turn out the royal grooms."

"Royal grooms," she sneered. "Has anyone told Thorvald yet? Bel! She'll have an orgasm just thinking about her new possibilities!"

"Hush! Get yourself ready."

"Oh, shut up and do what you have to do, Sten. I'll be along with all my courtly grace . . ."

Klann stared into each mirror in turn in the counseling chamber, which his dead Brother had reappointed as a throne room. He touched every part of him that reflected back, gazing with the innocent bewilderment of the newly unblinded. His hair was black as jet, here and there touched by strands of gray that he found not unappealing. It was long and wild and tangled, streaming down his back in a lifetime's growth. His wavy beard similarly coursed down to his waist. His eyes were a deep, piercing brown, narrow and close-set. His face was sharply chiseled, with an aquiline nose and pointed chin. His body was taller, more slender than that of his predecessor, erect and dignified, his posture planklike. The long, curled fingernails on both hands, by now half broken off in his passion to touch the stuff of physical life, lent him an eerie oriental bearing.

"All new," he spoke, the dozens of people crowded into the throne room following his every movement, hanging on every utterance. "Everything new . . . all apprehended only . . . second-hand before. Ohhh . . . I'm going to like this life."

To those who listened, the assertion sounded foreboding.

"You can't know—none of you can know—what it's like to *feel* your kin *die,* crying out in their anguish, seizing upon your life essence for—" But abruptly the spell was gone. Then: "Bring me food—I'm ravenous! A sampling of everything the kitchens can deliver on short notice. The king demands it!" Servants scrambled to do his bidding, running into each other in their haste. Klann laughed to see the result of his every spoken whim. The room was cleared of all but his advisers.

The grooms came forward then to attend on him. These personal servants of the king were Akryllonian nationals who had been schooled from birth in the ritual grooming of a newly risen King Klann. The generation before them had no opportunity to use the traditionally passed ritual. In times past many generations had gone by without a Death and Rising of Klann. These grooms would long retell the proud tale of how they had trimmed the beard and hair of the newly risen king, how they had manicured him, bathed and dressed him in his finest raiment, setting, at last, the Diadem of the House of Bel upon his brow.

The food was served, and he wolfed it down with no

care for table manners, so eager was he to experience as quickly as possible the fullness of life. The Chief Botiler brought him a variety of wines to sample, discreetly limiting his consumption so that he might not disgrace himself on this first intemperate night.

Advisers, astrologers, and military people arrived; the ladies of court put in their most attractive appearances, vying with one another for the grandest entrances so that they might curry the Newly-Risen's favor. But no one caused more of a furor with her appearance than the seductively clad Lady Thorvald, who glided along the chamber wall to stand at one end of the table set before the dais, leaning against a marble column with heaving bosom and expectation in her heavily painted eyes. Her nightdress had been chosen well to reveal her ample charms and still potent allure.

When he had finished his repast, Klann pushed the table away from him—too hard. It tilted over and crashed to the floor, servants hurrying to clean the mess even before the yelps of shock had died out. The newly emerged personage of Klann the Invincible felt the muscles in his arms.

"Yes . . . I'm the Strong One. The one you've all awaited these many long years and despairing generations. The one who will at last bring you to your home . . . to Akryllon. There will be changes, make no mistake. I'm not like my soft Brother who feared shadows in the halls and brooked the slaughter of his men by conquered peoples. They will know *fear*. They will know *obedience*. We—will—not—be—defied!"

Klann was seized by the trembling and glazey stare that his most intimate confidants recognized as the trancelike state in which the Brethren communicated their counsel. But he began to growl in a most unseemly way for a monarch, causing the more timid among them to back away. This the aged scribes, the keepers of Akryllon's history, identified as the primitive wrath of the Tainted One, less diluted now by the rational caution of the remaining Brethren. A female voice passed Klann's lips once, saying something in the Kunan tongue that was too garbled to understand. The court whispered in rapt fascination. But soon the rigidity of the seizure relaxed, and Klann's eyes returned to the throne room.

It was at that point that the golden-masked sorcerer knifed into the room, courtiers scurrying to clear him a path. He bowed to the newly risen Klann.

"I await your word, my liege. What punishment shall we visit upon the brazen city that has caused you such suffering?"

Klann eyed him suspiciously a moment, then his gaze softened. "For the nonce, a tightening of the fist will suffice, I think. Perhaps a change in local government . . ."

Mord's fathomless eyes reflected a certain disappointment. "It was that devious sorceress who likely did this to you—"

"Yes," Klann interrupted. "Have her arrested. I should like to hear these superstitions she spreads from her own lips before I seal them. *And* her defense of what you accuse."

There was instant muttering at this bold command, experience reminding the more sage among them of the danger of such a radical measure.

"Sire," one of the advisers spoke up, "isn't that rather extreme before the facts be known—?"

"*Extreme?*" Klann exploded, charging at the man. "What is extreme? Did not your king *die* in their city? Have they not opposed our every wish? I have a plan for these militant people, and it begins—what is *this*? What have you brought me here?"

A Llorm corporal-of-guards came forward, knelt,

and indicated the toothless old man he had brought. "Milord, this old fool has, I think, intelligence of an urgent nature."

The old man shambled forward and squinted at Klann, who made a face back at him that caused the court to chuckle. "Come-come-come, what is this all about?"

"Are you . . . Baron Rumka?" the trembling man inquired uncertainly, squeezing his cap between sere brown hands.

There was instant laughter mixed with gasps at the senile faux pas when the words were translated into Kunan. The Llorm guard cuffed the old man on the side of the head. "I've already told you whom you're addressing, you idiot! Just tell what you told me."

"This had best be worth our while," Klann warned.

With the Llorm's prompting the man related the tale of the ambush he'd seen, perpetrated by the militia. Klann's ears reddened as he listened. The room buzzed with translations.

"Bandits!" he cried at last. "Bandits—do you hear that, you military experts? Why aren't they working for *us*? Has the whole province gone mad? What kind of bandits, old fool? Turks?"

"Oh, no, sire," the old codger whined, "just . . . bandits." He grinned and cocked his head, a vapid cast to his ancient eyes.

"Where is that outpost?" Klann asked of his advisers.

"I think the leader was Mongol . . . *da*, that's it," the man babbled on, only now no one was listening as the king spoke with his military leaders. The corporal-of-guards began to push him back toward the archway and double door.

"It must be at the Borgo Pass, sire."

"Yes, that's it. Is it strategically useful to us—?"

"*Da*, a Mongol—" the old man continued as the Llorm strove to calm him.

"Quiet now, you silly old bastard, His Majesty's speaking."

Klann walked with hands behind his back. "You'd best fortify it again with better men. And check *all* the outposts in the marches. Raise the wage for outpost duty to attract better men. We can afford the additional numbers by now, surely—"

"A Mongol with—with—with his hair tied up on his head like a tulip bulb—" The Llorm had his arm twisted and was carrying him off.

"*Wait!*"

Klann had heard. And understood.

He had the farmer brought back in to repeat what he had just said. An interpreter rendered it all into Kunan at the king's behest. Whispers and gasps. Klann was staring at Julian, smiling evilly.

The captain of mercenaries had blanched. He swallowed hard, trembling.

"Soooo, Kel'Tekeli," Klann said as he approached him slowly. "The man with hair tied like a tulip bulb on top of his head. Your spy, eh? Yes, my fine captain paid good gold to the leader of these rogues who've been marauding in the roads and marches! Just like your father, aren't you? Leave it to a Kel'Tekeli to sell out reason and logic to anyone who'll promise him power! Uh, you needn't purchase any more intelligence from your faithful employee Gonji. I think you've gotten your gold's worth." He glared hard at Julian, who looked as though he had swallowed a rat. "*Get that damnable oriental.* And hang the old man, the *august* Council Elder. His *bodyguard* indeed," Klann sneered.

"Have I said anything to anger the baron?" the old man queried in a small, weak voice, having understood nothing that had been said.

"Silence, you fool!"

"No let him speak," Klann told them. "He's the only one providing answers around here, and you idiots haven't the sense to listen to him. Men like this old peasant are running you all in circles—feed him, give him wine. See, Julian, what information I've gleaned without having parted with a single piece of gold!"

Julian had known no greater embarrassment in all his days of sterling service to his liege lord. He left the castle that night with blood in his eyes, and the face of Gonji in his head, on which his imagination visited agonies as formless as they were unspeakable.

Mord stood alone with Klann in the king's private chambers, the auburn-haired wench having been banished once the king had taken his pleasure with her. The sorcerer studied the king's seizure with profound interest, saw in his eyes, heard in his outcries things both promising and unsettling to him.

Her counsel—that of the lioness to come—was troublesome to the dark enchanter's plans. But the bawling cries of the mindless one could well be an indication of potential assistance to the Grand Scheme from the unlikeliest place of all: within the persons Klann themselves . . .

Later they spoke.

"Now that my weaker Brother is out of the way, I think we're of one mind as to how to handle these rebellious folk, Mord."

"Oh, indeed we are, sire."

"Mord, I want results—soon—on the charm of division you seek. The Brethren must be separated. I want to know the feeling of precious aloneness. I want only my own counsel in my head . . ."

Oh, yes, hopeless fool, the Brethren shall emerge in full. One way or another. Beneath his gold mask

Mord's lipless mouth smiled its terrible smile.

In the cellar where they had practiced their battle skills for days, Phlegor and his faithful craft guild followers met in secret conclave.

"Klann is dead," the feisty guildsman told them. "Of that we're sure. Now is the time to strike."

First one man assented, then another, and soon the cellar burned with determination and blood-rage.

Chapter Twenty-two

Lydia's cook started at the rapid pounding on the rear door. Her hands went to her throat as she leaned against the pot-bellied stove, burning her behind and emitting a sharp, strangled cry.

"What's the matter?" Lydia asked, entering the kitchen, her face drawn by sleeplessness but now animated with concern.

The sharp rap came again at the lower door panel, and the cook could only stare. Lydia moved to the door stiffly and peered out the shutter. There were several horses tethered in the courtyard but no one in sight; the gate was shut. She opened the door a crack and gasped as two bodies tumbled in — Wilf and Gonji, sword scabbards scraping on the floor. Hoofbeats resounded down the back lane.

"Close it, please," Gonji ordered.

She complied. Then the night's horrors came back to her in a rush. "Omigod — have you heard what's happened? Michael!" she shouted, rousing her husband, who lay napping with his head on his arms in the dining room.

A babble of sleepy voices as they all moved into the parlor.

"We've heard," Wilf replied curtly.

"Michael," Gonji engaged the protegé, "quickly, tell me the current military status—and, good lady, so sorry," he added to Lydia, "but we've not eaten since yesterday. If you could—"

"*Sí*, of course," She called out a string of directions to the terrified cook. As Michael explained the martial law situation with much face-rubbing and anxious posturing, food was brought to them. Several people slumped in the parlor, dispirited, men and women alike, a few from the tragic banquet, and a couple of militiamen who were friends of Michael. There was no milk to be had this morning, so they drank ale and wine.

Gonji listened while he filled his belly, thinking, calculating. A knock at the front door caused them all to scramble, but Gonji commanded them to relax and keep their places. He and Wilf concealed their *katanas* behind the sofa. Then the samurai waved for Michael to open the door. The first soft hues of dawn flooded the aperture, the chirrups of birds combining with them to bathe the figure that stood there in a heavenly aura.

Paille burst into the foyer.

"What's the word, Michael?—Gonji! I thought you might be here. I've spoken with some of the foray party. They tell me you met with splendid success. *Vive la liberté!*"

"Calm yourself, Paille. The streets are filled with soldiers," Michael cautioned.

"*Oui*, frightened ones," the artist-poet declared, sitting and helping himself to the wine. "Do you know what the invaders are say—"

"*Hai*. And our sally into Zarnesti *was* successful, as

you've heard," Gonji said. "Everyone back alive. But no time for that now. Michael, tell me, what have you and Garth decided? How are the people talking?"

"How do you expect them to be talking? Their resolve has been shaken by this madness. No one even knows what's going on yet. *I* don't even know, except that—"

"You mean you and Garth haven't thought how vulnerable the occupation force is, with this talk of Klann dying?"

"Vulnerable?" Michael laughed shakily. "That's ridiculous. You can't be seriously considering attacking them *now*."

Gonji set down his goblet. Hard. "Of course, now. They must be—"

"Listen to what you're saying," Lydia broke in, aghast. "It's perfect *madness*."

"It's madness, all right," Paille interjected. "Do you want to know what your fine leaders have been saying, Gonji? Garth is spreading a tale about Klann being literally *immortal*. He says he died last night, just as the magician said, but then he rose again as a new person—they're talking about him as if he were the *Christ*, for Christ's sake!"

Gonji winced and rubbed his temples against the thrumming that had begun.

"There, you see," Michael accused, "that's *your* doing, Gonji. That's the result of your decision not to tell the people Garth's story of Klann's enchanted origin."

"Wait a minute," Gonji growled, "why is it my fault alone? We agreed, so sorry, that it was best withheld. Who could've known it would come to this? Anyway, can any of us truly say that that's what has happened, even on the good smith's word?"

"Mother of God," one of Michael's friends

whispered in awe, "the king is immortal?" He crossed himself. "Why weren't we told what evil sorcery we—"

"Then the legends we heard are *true*—?"

"Stop that talk," Paille snapped.

"No one knows for certain *what* our enemies are pulling," Gonji reminded, pouring more wine. "Michael, we must make a plan for—"

"Stop creating enemies," Lydia ordered. "You make enemies by wishing to find them everywhere."

Wilf snorted, spilling his wine. "No, they're not our enemies. They killed Radetzky and all the others because they like us."

"Forget it, Wilf," Gonji said low.

"Wilfred Gundersen, if I didn't respect your good father so," the councilman's wife said, "I'd make you leave for speaking to me like that."

"No one leaves here," Paille countered. "This is the military council now, and martial law is hereby declared." He tipped his flagon at Lydia.

"Paille, for you I have no respect—you can leave now!"

Michael stepped forward, lips pursed. "Lydia, enough. Please stay out of this."

"I can't believe Garth is spreading this discouraging legend," Gonji said, perplexed.

"He decided it best that everyone know . . . *now*, before Mord comes up with anything worse. He tried to make it look as though *he* raised Klann from the dead."

"What do they have on their devious minds?" Gonji wondered aloud. "It's all rubbish! Did anyone— anyone whose word we can trust—witness this transformation? *See* the new Klann?"

They looked from one to the other. Shook their heads uncertainly.

"Then it was all faked to produce exactly the effect

we're seeing, making the people wilt out of a false sense of guilt and responsibility. What a fine act," he drawled, gazing around the room sullenly, offering his goblet, reddened eyes glowing, "and all of you fell for it."

"Correct," Paille agreed. "I've seen the soldiers—they're scared. They haven't been let in on the game yet either. But the *townies* are *cringing*—it's a contest of cowardice, with defeat as the prize for those who can cower the longest! Now is the time to *fight*, while they fear the city's quiet toughness."

"Hear-hear," Wilf offered.

Michael's brow furrowed as he considered what was being proposed. *Such a decision . . .*

"Shouldn't . . ." Michael began tentatively, "shouldn't the *whole* council be in on so important a decision?"

"*Hai*—"

"Michael, you can't be serious," Lydia breathed.

"Lydia—*please*."

"I agree," Gonji said, "but it wouldn't be taking on too much responsibility for you and me to at least alert the militia of the possibility of conflict. And the difficulty of the evacuation—*that* would no doubt have to be done under fire. That can't be helped. Be we must do something *soon*, before they beef up the garrison again. They made a big mistake, riding out of here with so many men, if what you've observed was accurate. Almost . . ." Gonji grew pensive, fighting back the sting of exhaustion, the heaviness of the wine, "almost as if they *wanted* the city to do something. But *why?*"

"I can't believe you're all considering this," Lydia said, seating herself, trancelike.

"Nor I," someone added.

"*Nein*," another agreed.

"Ahhh—cowards!" Paille slurred, his breath an alcoholic breeze from a night of tippling. He slugged at his wine, refilled the cup with a mock-chivalrous bow to Lydia.

"What are you thinking?" Michael asked Gonji, anxious to know what troubled the samurai.

Gonji mopped the moisture from his lips. He formed the words as he spoke. "If they—if they wanted to crush the city, then they needn't resort to tricks to foment rebellion . . . so Klann couldn't be in on the trick . . . so he *was* poisoned, and either they're hiding that fact—there was no corpse? Nothing they carried out of the hall?"

"No—*nem*—*nein*—"

"All right, all right, then . . . then he was poisoned and it failed, and they decided to make him look immortal, for the morale factor . . . or they rushed him to the castle *before* he died, and there'll be hell to pay when the furor is over, one way or the other . . . Or—or he died . . . and Garth was right." He looked up, eyes twitching, mind racing. "But if he was killed, then there was a killer. Tralayn said it was Mord—"

"Mord? But why?"

Gonji raised his hand. "I don't know. I don't see how it could serve any purpose, unless Tralayn was right about his wanting to see Vedun in ashes. *And* Garth would have to be right. He couldn't destroy Vedun without an army. No king, no army. Unless he thought they'd rally around him. But I doubt if the Llorm would. They seem loyal only to Klann. And could Mord hate Vedun so much that he'd take that kind of chance?" He shook his head violently and asked for water to lave his face. "Ah, swine-karma! I wish we could all sleep before we had to make a final decision . . ."

"*Ja*," Wilf agreed, "I can't say I feel much like doing

anything right now. Everything sags . . ."

"Michael . . . could Tralayn have killed Klann?" Gonji asked suddenly.

"That seems possible," Lydia opined. "She's been in favor of violent overthrow since the occupation."

"But would she kill a child of our own?" her husband probed. He shook his head negatively, refusing to accept it.

"*Iyé*," Gonji agreed, "I don't think that sounds like her either."

"Well, what are we going to do, gentils?" Paille asked, weaving before them.

"Michael?" Gonji asked. "It's your city."

Michael slumped into a chair. His voice was meek, resigned. "I don't think we can do anything until we see the next move generated by the Castle."

"That's it, then," Gonji said, his mouth twisted. "We drop it. More wine, *dozo.*" Paille obliged him. Lydia looked at them with distaste.

Gonji's bewilderment over the mystery of the king's assassination dovetailed with his disappointment over the city's attitudes to cause him to eschew sleep for a sullen drinking bout. Paille and Wilf joined in lustily, though the young smith succumbed to slumber before long, and even Michael embraced the bleariness of drink over more lucid pondering of his city's dreadful future, of the terrible circumstances into which his child might be born. And before long thoughts of the coming child caused him to withdraw from the drinking. Soon Flavio's protegé fell into quiet brooding.

Paille and Gonji exchanged banter, ever less sensible with the passing of the hours. The samurai recounted the details of the Zarnesti raid.

Lydia paced from room to room, wringing her hands nervously and scowling at them when she passed, occasionally peering out the shutters into the harsh blue light of day. The sky was cloudless, the city uncommonly quiet. Many had gone to their jobs in a hopeful effort at normality, but there was little commerce. The Benedettos' other guests excused themselves one by one, having become stir crazy, and braved the city's streets. Soldiers clopped by in increasing numbers, and by three bells of afternoon, Lydia decided that her house was being watched, as was Flavio's nearer the square.

Gonji waxed maudlin, surly, and vulgar in alternating mood shifts that worried her. No one had ever seen him so totally devoid of his much vaunted self-control.

"Cowards," Paille brayed at the windows.

"*Hai*. And it was my bad karma to fall in with them," Gonji said gloomily. "Their own God must laugh at their childishness. Twice cursed past and thrice in the future—that is you, Gonji-san . . . the lark recalls my duty . . . the tainted one—what's that?" Gonji wondered dully. "Paille, who wrote of 'the tainted one'?"

"I don't know, *monsieur* . . . not I."

Lydia peeked through the crack in the shutters again. No question—they were watching the house. At least four of them. Fully armed. The looks they leveled at the house were stone cold sober.

"Looks quiet," the free companion in the slouch and leather jerkin told his companion.

The fat man riding beside him snorted. "Yeah, they're scared shitless. I don't blame them. Who could live in this place? What about this stuff the captains are saying—" They guided their steeds down a walled lane. "—you think everything's right up at the castle? This army comes up with some wild stories. But I guess they know what they're sayin' when—"

The marauding band charged them out of nowhere,

slamming them off their whinnying mounts with staffs and pikes. The bandit in the slouch was dead before he hit the ground. The fat man's shrill cries were silenced with a single blow of a woodsman's axe. Their armament was stripped, their horses commandeered in seconds.

Phlegor bounded astride one of the horses, his face glowing with the flush of success over the bold daylight attack.

"All right—" he said, breathless, "—onward. Split up and take these lanes. Pistoliers and bowmen hold them. You run into big trouble, you lead them back to one of our snares. Got it?" They assented readily. "Let's go."

About forty craft guildsmen under Phlegor divided into small squads and began their hit-and-run attacks against straggling mercenaries. Emboldened by their early success, they swiftly spread their skirmishes from the center of the city toward the fringes, avoiding only the square and the areas where the troops were garrisoned, on the extreme east and west ends.

Soon they were joined by a dozen militiamen under Paolo Sauvini, he being the only one among them who had taken part in the Zarnesti raid. Paolo had gone home and related his tale of personal valor to his indulgent wife, then had ignored her urging that he lay low at home, heading instead out into the streets to see what effect the alleged murder of Klann was having. Linking up with curious, if badly shaken, *bushi* and Squires, inspiring them with his report of the foray, he encountered Phlegor and a band of about ten near the provisioning district. The craftsmen had ambushed three Austrian highwaymen, dispatching them shortly and savagely.

Phlegor tossed Paolo a pistol. "How about it, Sauvini? You ready to free your city?"

Paolo hefted the piece. "What about the militia leaders? Gonji and the others?"

The guild leader cast a thumb over his shoulder. "Your monkey man's down in the southern quarter. I saw him there myself. He's left *us* the tough job up here. You game?"

Paolo nodded resolutely. "All right—rebellion, then," he said to his companions. "*Kill* the invaders."

They mounted and surged into the twisting, narrow lanes, bloodlust in their eyes. Soon the revolt was joined for fair.

Phlegor's killing grounds were hastily established but effective in the early going. Pockets of mercenaries were lured into alleys and culvert lanes to be tripped up with ropes or blocked by debris, arrows and bolts raining down on them in their frenzy. Their armament was swiftly appropriated and used against other bands.

Word of the revolt spread through the city, people closing their shops and sealing their homes against the upheaval. Confusion reigned. Some of the militia began to wander out to investigate, unsure of whether to become involved. An alert plan for such a rebellion had been established, and no relay teams had spread the word that this was a sanctioned action by the council; yet the fighting was fierce and spreading in both outreach and intensity.

Soon there was open fighting in the main streets. Screams could be heard from all points of the city.

The turning came quickly. It began with the mercenary messenger who alerted Captain Sianno at the Llorm garrison. The captain turned out the skilled troops and sealed off the city gates against all traffic. The Llorm dragoons' disciplined search methods, coupled with their hard-hitting tactics and superior firepower, soon turned the tide against the insurgents. The craftsmen's inadequate weapons and numbers and the shallowness of their planning began to tell.

Sianno deployed his dragoons in long lines of skirmishers in the broad avenues, infantry troops climbing walls and roofs to establish high-ground dominance. The renegade element from the German Landsknechts, adroit with the polearm, plus bowmen and pistoliers, established solid defensive positions. Now mounted mercenaries were directed into a containing posture, sweeping across the city from east to west, surely and methodically, enveloping the rebels, containing them toward the center of the city again. Volleys of bowshot and pistol fire rooted the ambushers out of their killing grounds, some wisely seeking cover where it was to be found in houses, shops, and available niches; others scrambling out into the streets to be slaughtered by Sianno's positioned troops.

The rout was on.

Lorenz pulled up to the stables just as Julian led his band of mercenaries away. The captain scanned him closely, recognizing Garth's eldest son and, seeing no weapons, gestured to him with a head toss.

"Get in your home and stay there," the captain commanded. Lorenz tipped his hat with foppish grace and dismounted, entering the shop through the canopied portal as the troop thundered away to the east.

The parlor was empty, and his father was not in any of the chambers. He was drawn to the soft scuffling sounds in the cellar. Descending warily into the damp enclosure, Lorenz saw his father seated on the trunk in the dim gray light. He was gripping the haft of his old broadsword with one thick hand, and other feeling along the cutting edge. A strange expression was set on the smith's face, stony and grim.

"What did they want?"

Garth didn't look up from the sword. "Gonji," he said simply.

Lorenz's eyes shrank to slits. "To arrest him?"

"*Ja.*"

"What's on your mind, father? Will you, too, join in this madness?"

"Kings can change whole lives, their own and others'," Garth answered evasively. "Why can't common people change their minds?"

"Can Christians change their minds where violence is concerned?"

"I don't know. I don't think our beliefs apply here. Anyway, I wasn't speaking of my faith . . ."

Lorenz watched him for a time. "All right," he said finally, running up the steps to return moments later, strapping on his rapier. "Then maybe the time has come—let's go out with the rest." And then Lorenz was gone, leaving Garth to shift through his clashing thoughts, to examine his feelings.

His sons were out in the violent streets. Wilfred was no doubt somewhere with Gonji, who was to be arrested. Garth held the sword before his eyes and stared at its dull sheen, his face twisting with the coiling of his innards. Then he flung it against the wall and slumped forward, burying his head in his hands.

The criers had begun to call out the mandate in the streets: All citizens were ordered indoors until the rebellion was quelled.

Vlad Dobroczy was among the first to hear the order.

He knelt in a woodshop near the chapel, his sword resting against his knee, squinting through a chink in the shutter. He heard the chilling cry of the wyvern as it skirred past overhead, then strained to see the source of the growling, as of some monstrous dog, that accompanied the tattering hoofbeats that sped through the postern gate.

A long double column of mercenaries pounded through, escorting the barouche in which Mord had ridden out of the city the night before.

And following the coach, bearing on its shoulder the most terrifying weapon Dobroczy had ever seen—a huge spiked tree trunk, came the cretin giant Tumo.

Paolo rode at the head of twelve men, mixed militia and Phlegor-trained craftsmen, who galloped frenetically back and forth through the southern sector, seeking escape from the seine of troops that gradually hemmed them in. They would pound toward the west, only to clatter to a halt at the massing of bowmen who readied their volley farther on. Swerving hard, faces betraying their terror of inevitable entrapment, they'd race madly to the east again, their way blocked just as menacingly by mounted pistoliers.

"This way!" Paolo shouted at last in desperation, nodding to a long, sinuous walled alley, whose farther end could not be seen. "Down the lane and *disperse*—get under cover."

"Where?"

"Anywhere—it's every man for himself now," Paolo yelled, belting his discharged pistol.

They clumped into the lane, snaking through its turns, past barrels and reeking chamber pots, tools and hanging laundry. A horse stumbled in a gutter, slamming its rider against the sharp rock wall, leaving him stunned, his arm and face badly abraded. The horses shrilled and jostled as the other riders guided around him in a shuffling knot. They pushed off again, seeking shelter. Ever nearer to Provender Lane, the avenue they would soon intersect which ended at the Inn, they knew their dire peril when they heard the clatter of hooves and shouts of command in an adjacent alley.

They lost the race.

Out of a branching alley just ahead, a band of mercenaries emerged, blocking their path, jamming their steeds flank-to-flank, swords and lances upraised in gauntleted fists. The Flemish brigands carried shields, which they linked in a warding wall. Their smiles were portentous, promising something somehow worse than a skirmish.

The rebels yanked to a halt, appraising the enemy, and Paolo was about to wave them through the blockade when the formidable Salavar the Slayer turned into the alley before his men. He sat aboard the great destrier, scowling at the rebels through the viewslit of his sallet, a shimmering apparition of death in the sultry heat waves, bedecked in his array of weapons.

"Better get out of here," Paolo whispered. "Better not get involved with—"

Behind them, riding up slowly and with a terrifying calm in his eyes, was Julian.

"Welcome to the hunt, gentlemen . . ."

Paolo had seen none of it, his own engagement a nightmare blur. He was the first to take a sword cut from the toying, arrogant captain, who snaked in with his blade, wounding them at will. And then Paolo was leaping painfully up the rear steps of a dwelling, clutching at the door lintel, groaning with the agony in his ribs, his feet scraping the rough stones. He heard the shouts, the report of pistols. The sizzling of balls and shafts rending the air all about him.

All he could do was run and run and cry out in his terror, at last collapsing in an exhausted heap on a rooftop. He had no idea where he was, and he didn't care.

The metal founder lay beneath the straddling Julian, bleeding from numerous wounds all over his body. The saber point pressed against his throat.

"All right, craftsman," Julian said coyly. "You want to live? Tell me where the oriental is. Where is Gonji?"

"I—I don't know. I haven't seen him. I swear to God, you must believe me. They made me do this—they—"

"Come now. You're not protecting him, are you? He told me who you were. He fingered the craftsmen as the rebels. He sold you out to me for *gold.*"

The founder swallowed. "The Gundersens'. He stays at the Gundersens'."

"Mmm, I'm afraid you're behind the times. That's old news. Ah, well—I presume you have nothing left to barter," the captain said archly, shrugging.

He jabbed the saber point through the man's throat.

The marketplace had become an arena of ghastly sport.

Bands of rebels routed out of the lanes were chased into the main avenues, where they found the fresh mercenary companies waiting. But the adventurers held back curiously, giving them pause. With dawning desperation they realized that they had been led into a killing ground. But they were not prepared for the full reality of it. When a squad of about twenty craftsmen had gathered, mounted and on foot, before the market stalls, the slavering cretin giant lumbered out from between two shops. His awesome spiked club leaned on one flabby shoulder, a dozen feet above the ground.

Now they understood. And broke in panic in all directions.

The soldiers watching roared their anticipation as the giant bounded forward to swing his fearsome weapon. Men were crushed to pulp under the monstrous blows of the club, horses shrieking in terror and throwing riders, who were repulsed by sadistic troops in their efforts at gaining freedom.

Tumo blared at the rebels in his excitement, which had begun to stir as soon as the soldiers had dressed him in his great plate armor. His kettle-sized helm bore a pair of animal horns that enhanced his atavistic presence.

Sweeping one horse and rider into the air on the skewering spikes, Tumo ran down another screaming man and squeezed him until blood issued from his mouth and ears, then flung him down and stamped him in a manner that caused even the mercenaries to flinch.

Men who tried to fight their way through the cordoning troops were dropped by arrow and pistol fire. And the wyvern swooped overhead, strafing individual runners, *skreeing* in triumph whenever its searing saliva and jetting corrosive waste would ravage a man or steed.

And when no rebels remained alive in the center of the city, the mercenary companies dispersing to engage remaining pockets of resistance, Mord directed the giant against people watching from windows. Shutters and doors were bashed in, and the bawling creature's massive arms thrust inside dwellings and shops to crush and gouge even the unmilitant, the innocent.

Then, to the surprise of the now thinned troops in the corpse-strewn market square, a band of militia and non-militants alike, led by Aldo Monetto, streamed out of the granite building that housed the weaving looms. They began to shout at the giant, some firing arrows and stolen pistols, others hurling rocks or hefting tools. One shaft struck the giant in the bulging fat of a thigh, causing him to yowl and charge toward the offender.

Monetto watched in helpless horror, knowing his axe would be useless against the monster. Squads of mercenaries began to return to the marketplace in response to the din. And the wyvern slashed down suddenly to strafe the breaking mob. Aldo thought he saw Roric, but then the figure disappeared. He had no idea what the council had decided to do. Few militiamen seemed to be taking part in the melee; yet the rebellion had begun. Where was Gonji? He had to find him. Without Gonji they couldn't succeed in this mad display of undirected anger.

Captain Sianno returned to the market stalls, sought out the leering sorcerer standing atop the barouche.

"Mord, that's enough," the captain shouted.

"They need a good lesson," the enchanter replied.

"Enough, I say! Their spirit is broken. They've suffered enough. This isn't warfare. This is vile sport. Even animals wouldn't sink to such brutality. Call off your beasts!"

Mord regarded him sullenly. He bowed, stiffly and not without a trace of mockery.

Calling out to Tumo to desist, making a sign in the air that caused the flying dragon to veer out toward the river with a final raucous cry, he climbed down from the coach. Sianno pulled on the reins and guided his horse away. He regarded the slaughter with a heavy heart and a military mind that knew the point of no return had been surpassed.

The sorcerer watched him plod away. So close . . . so near to achieving his purpose had he been. Still there was a chance—the sounds of isolated conflict could be heard throughout the city. No. No, it would soon be brought under control, and the damnable captain had ended his effort at incitement before they could be driven mad enough. Mutual slaughter had to be inspired. Crush Vedun; break Klann.

Tumo loped up to the coach on his knuckles, crying like a timid child over his superficial wounds.

"There-there, my big fellow, don't whine. Pull it out—pull the arrow out of your leg. Do it now, you sniveling coward, or it will hurt worse later!"

Tumo grasped the hunting shaft by its stole and gave it a tug. The barbed head tore his flesh as it was withdrawn, and the giant wailed in agony and began to sob, slumping to the ground with a jangling din like the collapse of a hardware hawker's wagon.

Flavio and Tralayn turned with the rest of the supplicants in the chapel when the doors flew open and the Llorm squad marched in. There were a few strained screams. Some people sobbed openly in fear of death. Women pulled their children close. Several people rose and formed a determined knot around the Elder and the prophetess, but Tralayn ordered them away.

They looked deeply into each other's eyes and exchanged a nod of resolution and mutual commitment to go peacefully with and arresting party.

Tralayn took the Elder's hand and squeezed it in warmth and affection.

Julian's lieutenant, Ivar, headed up a party of mercenaries searching for Tralayn. They tried her house first, bursting through the door with drawn swords, their fears of her witch's notoriety making them not a little anxious. Some of them grumbled. Accosting a witch was extremely hazardous duty that ought to earn them a bonus.

Their fears were soon allayed: the house was empty.

But then they caught sight of the awesome weapons slung over the mantel. They looked from one to the other, speechless, the huge pieces arousing primal fears none of them would care to voice later. As their leader, Ivar knew it was his duty to quell such nonsense as he now saw in their eyes. He puffed up his chest and strode to the fireplace.

"Make a good set of weapons for Tumo, eh? Just about his size—"

The brackets gave way at just that instant, and the huge pieces fell to the floor with a thunderous echo. The stillness in the parlor was almost a palpable thing.

"I'll . . . come back for 'em later, eh?" They were already backing out, even as the tremulous words quivered Ivar's lips.

Chapter Twenty-three

The sounds of the revolt poured into Vedun's skies. The din of battle reached Michael's house on the Via Fidei, the main avenue near the center of the city which, though surrounded by frenzied activity on all sides, was as yet fairly quiet, the eye of calm at the center of the clash.

Inside the Benedettos': terror and confusion among the gathering refugees; concern for what was happening both without and within. For Gonji and Paille were by now irretrievably drunk. Gonji had fallen to vulgar introspection, snarling at those who would try to disturb his maudlin self-pity. Paille crashed about the house, blaring heraldic outcries. Wilf slumped on a settee, one leg hanging over its back. He seemed ill, his face twisted; he alternated between short fitful naps and glassy-eyed staring matches with Spinecleaver, which lay across him.

Lydia wrung her hands as she peered through an upstairs shutter, Michael at her side, his face a mask of fear and indecision. She whimpered softly, an angry tear rolling down her face as they watched the search party enter Flavio's manse farther down the Via Fidei.

"This is what your military preparedness has brought upon us," she accused, sniffing and brushing away the tear.

Michael made no answer, just kept staring as the searching mercenaries left Flavio's and clattered off with a howl toward the sounds of fighting at the market area.

They hurried down the stairs at the sound of beating on the rear door behind the kitchen. Michael set his sword in a nearby pantry and inched open the door—several militiamen stood without.

Monetto led them in, followed by Roric Amsgard, Jiri Szabo, and three others.

"Where's Gonji?" Monetto cried in a rush. "The rebellion's on. Who gave an order?"

"Not I," Michael declared.

"Nor any of us," Roric agreed. "This is Phlegor's doing, I'll wager. We've got to decide what to do now. Most of the militia await an order, and I doubt Rorka's heard yet, unless someone who was in the chapel when—"

"Roric—look!" Galioto the dairy farmer cried, standing in the archway to the parlor, staring in disbelief. Galioto was an intense and serious Sicilian who constantly complained of tension headaches from the way the world had of confounding his idea of how it ought to work. He it was who was the first to see Gonji in his deplorable state. Galioto grabbed his head and began shaking it hopelessly. "Oh, no, Gonji . . ."

The others surged into the parlor.

"Found your leader, have you?" Lydia said at their backs.

Monetto rushed up to the now seated samurai. "*Gonji*—it's begun, Gonji. We need you at the square—everywhere. They're fighting, Gonji, fighting and dying with no plan, no organization . . ." He pulled Gonji upright, grasping his soaked tunic.

The samurai glared at him with watery red eyes. "What are you doing here?" Gonji slurred, grabbing his wrist. "Why aren't you training?"

"To the caverns!" Paille yelled.

"Hush yourself in my house, you drunken fool," Lydia ordered, surging forward and pointing. Paille glowered at her.

The wyvern shrilled in the city's skies. Somewhere: the bawling idiot roar of the cretin giant.

"Listen, Gonji," Roric urged, "the *beasts* are here. Mord's familiars. They're destroying people in the streets. We've got to do something." Whispers and the shuffling of the terrified through the house.

"Calm yourselves," Michael directed. "Nothing can be accomplished by panic."

Wilf pulled himself up and listened, casting about for something that apparently wasn't there. The *katana* fell off his lap. He looked as if he'd vomit.

"The foul dragon," Gonji breathed reverentially. Then he growled and surged to his feet. "Come, *bushi*—the time to fight is now!" He staggered forward two paces and stumbled, falling heavily. They looked from one to the other in desperation as they picked him up from the floor.

"Oh, Gonji—" Galioto whined, still holding his head.

Paille leaped atop the Benedettos' dining table. "To

horse! Assemble the Hussars! Let freedom win the day! Someone bring me quill and scroll!"

"Get off there, you idiot," Lydia shouted.

"Gonji, come on, we've got to get you—"

The samurai pushed them away violently, swung a backfist at Jiri, who ducked and tripped backward over a stool.

"Get hold of yourself, for God's sake!" Roric stormed at him. "Get me an emetic," he shouted at the trembling cook, who padded off in response.

Roric grabbed Gonji from behind in a bear hug, calling out for help. The samurai growled and broke the hold with a snap of arms and hips that knocked Roric back, his wind *whoofing* out of him. Monetto seized Gonji's arm and hung on for dear life as the samurai began to claw for the Sagami. Jiri latched onto his other arm. Gonji tried to kick, but his sense of balance had long since fled.

"What are we going to do now?" Galioto cried, sagging into a chair, where he hunched forward.

Three of them now had a grip on Gonji and began to half-walk, half-drag him around the shambles of Michael's parlor. The wyvern skirred over the house with a sucking rush of wind. A woman's voice puled in prayer in another room. Paille stomped atop the table, marching back and forth, singing a French battle hymn, a taper held before him in lieu of a sword.

The cook's emetic concoction arrived from the kitchen.

"Paille, get down from there before I knock you down," Michael shouted, advancing.

"Benedetto's joined the enemy!" The artist leaped down from the table and staggered behind the sofa, extending the candle in defiance. "I shan't be taken without a fight!"

Roric poured the emetic down Gonji's throat while

the others held him. Gonji choked on it, gasping. Wilf was standing behind them now, his face askew. He stared dimly, trying to make sense of his surroundings. "Genya," he whispered thickly. "Got to save Genya . . ."

"You're not going anywhere," Monetto ordered. "Someone grab Wilfred." Two men took him by the arms and spoke gently to him, and he sat back down without a fight.

Gonji gagged at last on the emetic, having drained it off. They started to walk him around the room again, his arms around Jiri's and Monetto's necks. Lydia stood in a doorway, gazing on the scene in disgust. Her house stank like the Provender on harvest home.

"Give me my sword, you cowards," the samurai blustered, sagging between the two *bushi*. Monetto and Jiri strained under his weight, his feet dragging.

There came a pounding at the rear door again.

"Merciful heavens!" the cook cried.

Lydia's face contorted. "This is *madness*. Michael—this is your house—*do something!*"

Michael turned around once, twice, tipped between helping them sober Gonji and responding to the knocking, which came again, this time more insistently. He moved to a wall cabinet, thrust it open and pushed aside a clutter of linens and tableware. Opening a secret panel in its rear, he withdrew a pistol. Lydia espied the weapon with shock, its presence unknown to her.

Michael cocked the pistol and strode through the kitchen, followed by Roric and Lydia. "Open that, please," he said.

Lydia crossed herself as the butcher complied. The door swung open, and there stood Karl Gerhard, his English longbow at his side.

Michael breathed a sigh and lowered the gun.

"Michael—Roric—" the dour archer said in surprise. "The people are in revolt—there's no one to lead them—"

"Has the militia turned out?" Michael said.

"Most of them are waiting for official word, I think. The craftsmen started it and . . . and now it seems there's no turning back." Gerhard moved into their midst, the door closed behind them. He continued in a grim whisper. "The beasts are here, gentlefolk. They're killing people at the square. We've *got* to do something."

Cries came from the parlor. "A chamber pot—quickly!"

The cook came charging through, retrieving the pot from the garderobe and rushing back with it—too late. The sounds of Gonji's heaving came to them. Lydia walked back into the kitchen slowly, eyes closed, jaw trembling.

"Gonji's in there," Michael said.

"What?"

"Indisposed, I'm afraid."

Gerhard grabbed Michael's arm. "He's to be arrested. Soldiers are searching for him under Julian. They'll *kill* you if he's found hiding here."

"Mother of God," Galioto prayed, listening from the doorway.

"We've got to get him out of here," Gerhard said. "Michael, you and Roric must get to the market stalls and give them some kind of leadership. They're dying out there like—like animals." Karl pushed through to the parlor, saw the grotesque spectacle there. *"Himmel,"* he muttered.

Michael and Roric looked at each other, and the protegé slowly stuffed the pistol into his belt. They nodded their resolve and lashed on sword belts and baldrics.

"Michael!" Lydia shouted, horrified. "Michael, don't go—*please*."

"It's our duty," he replied. "We must. I'll . . . try to put an end to it." Lydia stared through the space he vacated as Michael and Roric went to the cellar and returned with helms and half-armors, buckling them on. A moment later they were gone into the night aboard two steeds from the courtyard.

Gerhard and Monetto gazed in mutual astonishment at the base display the amazing oriental warrior had made of himself. He lay face down, snoring sonorously, the smeared effects of his retching all around him. Both knew, even from what little they had absorbed of the tenets of *bushido*, that there would be a terrible price to pay for his loss of self-control this night. If he survived . . .

"We've got to clean him up, Aldo, get him away from this. He's—"

"Soldiers are coming!" a man cried from a window. "They're searching house to house."

Gerhard stiffened. "I saw them earlier—didn't think they'd reach this street so fast."

"What'll we do?" Monetto asked, panting in his fear. "We can't let them take him like this."

"I know—I know—Lydia, is there any place we can hide him?"

"Nowhere," she replied. "You've got to get out of here—all of you. Go out and help Michael."

Monetto looked around: the others would be of no help. Paille had slumped against the wall behind the sofa, his head lolling on his chest. Wilf was deeply asleep.

"The cellar," the biller said in sudden inspiration. "Let's see what they've got in the cellar."

They raced down the stairs and rooted about.

"There's nowhere to hide him down here," Gerhard complained.

"I'm not looking to hide him, idiot. We need something to carry him off in." He ran his hand over the top of a bulky old armoire.

Gerhard shook his head. "That's too damn heavy. We couldn't even carry that thing through the streets *empty*."

"How about this?" Monetto fished up a pile of Lydia's old clothes from a wooden crate. "We could dress him up in—" He saw Karl's look of ridicule and dropped the garments.

Then they spotted the brine barrel. It had been used for pickling, and its stench, when the lid was removed, welled up at them, overpowering.

"Whoo!" Gerhard breathed. "Forget it."

"No-no, this is just what we need. Help me get it up the stairs."

With a skeptical frown the hunter complied. They poured the reeking liquid out onto the cellar floor and carried the barrel up without much trouble. Under Lyda's perplexed stare they carried Gonji into the kitchen, washed him off, and wrestled him into the barrel, folded into a fetal position. His swords were dropped in with him.

"Hurry—they're coming here next!"

Gerhard pounded the lid into place. Gonji groaned inside. Then there was a pounding at the rear door again. Karl swiftly nocked an arrow and pulled back on the bow. The first man through was marked for death. But when Monetto threw open the door and raised his axe, it was at a flinching citizen.

"Are you *crazy*, Monetto? Signora Benedetto—Michael's been hurt!"

"Wha-a-a-t?" Lydia cried, rushing up to them. "Oh, dear God—where? how?"

"An arrow, I think—he's at Signor Vargo's."

"Go, Lydia," Monetto urged, pushing her to the

door. "That's where we'll meet you—at Milorad's."

Michael's wife rushed out with the messengers, but they all jostled to a sudden halt: two mercenaries rode through the opened gate and into the courtyard, blades drawn.

"Where you people going?" a gruff voice called out.

"My husband—" Lydia shrieked at him. "He's been hurt."

But before the words were finished the first shaft sizzled the air from the cracked open shutters and a mercenary was torn backward off his saddle. The second soldier lurched his whinnying steed and swung toward the gate. Gerhard leapt to the portico, nocking and launching in one motion—the second man spilled over onto the horse's neck as it bolted out into the street.

"Drag that body into the lane," Karl whispered harshly. Two men complied, another catching Lydia in her swoon, hurrying her toward the gate.

"Go on, get moving!" Galioto ordered from the parlor arch. "I'll try to put them off when they come." He shook his aching head, wincing.

Gerhard and Monetto hefted their burden, grunting. They lugged the barrel to the gate. The others had already run halfway up the street, past the advance of the search parties, which could be heard shouting on the Via Fidei. Twice they had to set Gonji down and duck into cover; once for a clattering Llorm troop, a second time for a band of galloping rebels, a mercenary squad in hot pursuit. Both times the barrel came perilously close to being a surprise stumbling block.

At last they reached the rear yard of the house across from Milorad's. But they still had to cross over the now deadly Street of Faith. A short sprint—without the barrel and its precious cargo.

They knelt in the shadows between the houses, panting for breath.

"We may have to just . . . just leave him here somewhere," Gerhard observed despairingly, "come back for him later."

"Don't be stupid," Monetto countered. "What if he comes to and climbs out at the wrong time?"

"He has the Sagami, *dummkopf!*"

"Against all these soldiers? Come on, Karl, we're not *that* tired."

"We still can't run across, and we'll *have* to run. Besides, what about my bow? They're sure to spot that."

A Llorm party pounded past, crossbows clacking at distant rebels.

"Hope they made it *all-recht*," Karl breathed, thinking of Lydia's bunch. A sudden notion: "I know what let's do—let's roll him across."

Monetto's face contorted and his stomach churned just to think of Gonji's situation. "You're crazy."

"*Nein*, it's the only way. A good push—a *really* good push. It wouldn't do to have him stop in the street. And then we follow fast. How about it?"

"Stupid," Monetto assessed the idea. But in the end he had to agree it was the only way.

Gonji moaned pathetically inside the barrel. "Sleep, *sensei*. It'll be all right," Monetto said, slapping the lid.

They waited until the most propitious moment. Then, running behind the rolling barrel and injecting all their remaining energy into the push, they sent Gonji bouncing and scraping across the tumult on the Via Fidei. Holding their breaths and grimacing with every bounce, they watched it rumble over the cobblestones, hit the sewage gutter at the center of the street and lurch over with increased momentum, then begin the roll up the slight grade to the far side of the street. With failing speed it struck the tiny curb and jumped up onto the fieldstone walk, where it settled. More soldiers thundered past. They waited anxiously a long time, or so it seemed. But at last they were able to sprint across the avenue safely.

Picking up the barrel once more they struggled to the rear courtyard, where they were met by a grim party of citizens who lent them assistance.

Phlegor was dragged to the square, bound and bleeding.

"Keep fighting, Vedun!" the guild leader cried. "Fight the invaders until not one of them is left alive! Their king is dead!" A Llorm footman slapped him sharply across the face. He was brought to the ominous black barouche in which Mord sat with arms folded. Even in his fury and resignation to death, Phlegor paled to see the giant seated in the fountain laving his wounds, its long red tongue running over blubbery lips as a low rumbling growl evinced its pain. Mercenaries bandaged Tumo's wounds as he glared at Phlegor.

"So, you think King Klann is dead, do you?" Mord said. "Since you don't believe in the Invincible, you shall have to see him for yourself. First you may enjoy the fate of your brave followers." The sorcerer pointed to where soldiers dealt with the arrested rebels all over the square. Some had been hanged and shot; others beaten; still more huddled together to await the punishment for their crimes. So far, seventy citizens were known to be dead, along with twenty-six troops from the occupation force. No one could even guess how many more were injured.

"Bring him when you're finished with him," Mord told Julian, "along with the witch." He indicated Tralayn, who stood nearby in shackles, head held up proudly, her flashing jade eyes fixed on Mord accusingly. Julian nodded, and Mord rode off in the coach under mercenary escort, his monstrous familiars following. Tumo carried his pot helmet in one hand, the now splintered truncheon in the other. He lurched behind the barouche, apelike, while the wyvern flapped down from the north, aiming a last keening cry at Vedun.

"Where is Gonji?" Julian asked Phlegor, walking around him arrogantly, saber in hand.

"I don't know, and I don't care," Phlegor grated.

"You ought to care—he sold you out." Julian leered at him, bringing his face close to the guildsman's. "He's the one who told me you were the leader of this . . . abortive action."

Phlegor hawked and spat, catching himself short of directing the shot at Julian. "Don't speak to me of that yellow monkey-man. All he ever did was talk. He's probably running halfway to Vienna by now with the city's money."

Julian thought about the man's words. He felt sure Gonji was still in the city somewhere but was fairly convinced that he wasn't thought of fondly in Vedun any longer. *No backbone for a real fight* . . . Thirty against three was his kind of odds. Julian's first assessment of the barbarian had been correct: he was merely a self-serving rogue who made a living playing both sides against each other.

Phlegor and Tralayn were led away to the castle. Julian passed along his order that Gonji be found and brought to him alive: "Shoot him, if need be. But bring him to me with life left in him. *I* want the privilege of bleeding him dry."

And as Phlegor disappeared through the postern gatehouse, Boris Kamarovsky moved out into the open, unbothered by the soldiers—for it was he who had revealed where they would find the guild leader hiding.

One less troublemaker, he thought. *And next the filthy barbarian* . . . A smug smile curled his lips.

"Hang him," Julian ordered calmly. "On the cross he loves so much."

And so the great cross at the square in the shadow of the chapel's comforting spire became a gibbet on which Council Elder Flavio last beheld his beloved Vedun, now the shattered relic of the dreams and work of a lifetime. He gave no complaint but only offered up a last prayer for peace and placed his neck in the noose almost with relief to be departing so troubled a world.

The shouting, rock-throwing mob's action was brief. Little harm resulted, as Captain Sianno and the Llorm dragoon company that took charge exercised great effort to contain them with a minimum of violence. At the last the captain looked on the body of the kindly Elder and realized with a great ache in his heart that the final bastion of peaceful coexistence had been breached.

Chapter Twenty-four

When life has taken a lamentable turn and the dawning promise of a new day's rising shifts to imminent threat, one's entire being rushes to his defense. Thus it was that, deep in the night, Gonji's sleep parted in successive curtains, each revealing a vague new shape of guilt and despair and dread . . .

. . . it seems quiet now . . .

The headache manifested itself, so that he clamped his eyes shut tighter, grimacing at the pounding in the back of his head and neck. Certain foul odors began to penetrate the screen of sleep . . .

". . . *no, milady, he won't lose the leg* . . ."

Who won't lose the leg? What leg are we taking about? *Kami*, what the devil happened to me today . . . yesterday?

"Look—he's coming around."

Shuffling.

"Gonji—" Wilf's voice.

With a groan the samurai rolled into an upright position on the cot, hands on knees, wincing back the pain. He breathed deeply and stretched, then blinked awake.

"What's going on?" he asked, looking around the small damp room, framing the several people there in turn. "Where the hell are we?"

"Milorad's cellar," Wilf answered. "We had to hide you here."

"You're to be arrested," Gerhard clarified.

Gonji stood up, bemused by it all. "What? Wait a—" Then he saw Michael lying on the cot across the cellar, his leg thickly bandaged. Lydia sat beside him, weeping softly. He seemed in pain. Dr. Verrico rose from his side, casting a critical eye Gonji's way.

"That's all I can do for now," the surgeon said. "He won't be walking with that cocky Italian strut for some time, I dare say—if at all." He peered at Gonji. "Now I must go. I've already neglected many others who need me more." The doctor collected his things and climbed the stairs wearily.

"What's going on, Garth?" Gonji asked, picking up and sashing his swords.

"Gonji . . ." the burly smith began in his childlike

voice, "there's been a revolt. A terrible mistake—"

"A *revolt?* On whose order? Why wasn't I alerted?" But the taunting voice in the back of his mind, coupled with the sudden downcast looks all around, answered his last question with shame-filled certainty.

"What matter who began it?" Garth replied. "It's over. Crushed. Mord came with his beasts—"

"Here in the city?" Gonji grated, scowling.

"*Ja.* I'm afraid there were . . . many casualties. Hundreds, maybe. No one is sure yet."

"Tell him the worst, Garth," Lydia said with hostile trembling, her eyes on her feverish husband as she mopped his brow.

"Tralayn's been arrested . . . taken to the castle. And Phlegor." But even these words sounded evasive.

"He started it, they say," Wilf added.

Gonji's eyes narrowed, seeing nothing in the room. "And the *bushi?*"

"Forget your *bushi,*" Lydia spat. "They're probably all slaughtered by—"

Roric cut her off. "I was there, Gonji. I don't think many became involved. Mostly craftsmen—it was all over . . . so fast . . ."

"Spirits of my fathers," Gonji breathed, the terrible apprehension of having done something dreadful coming to fruition, "all while I lay in a stupor—"

"To hell with your self-pity," Lydia shouted. "Tell him the *worst*, Garth. Tell him how well he discharged his famous *duty.*" She crumpled into sobbing despair, her face buried in Michael's chest.

Gonji felt sick again. "Garth—? What is she saying?"

They looked at one another, all fearing to speak.

Wilf inhaled a deep breath. "Flavio's been *hanged,* Gonji. At the square, on the big crucifix." His eyes bulged as he watched the *sensei* swoon.

Gonji's mouth gaped as he fell slowly back onto the

cot, head hammering. His face twisted, his inscrutable dark eyes mirroring a terror none of them had ever seen before. Running a hand through his hair, the samurai began to pant for breath. *"Iyé,"* he said, shaking his head, "it cannot be . . ."

For a time no one spoke. Then Lydia raised herself from the cotside. Michael's breathing was labored.

"I'm going upstairs," she announced. "Does anyone want anything?" No response. "I'll bring water and a little food . . ." She paused halfway up the stairs. "All the male swaggering and fight talk of the past month have come to this—death and horror."

A dreadful silence fell for a space after she ascended into the house, and then Gonji looked up. There was a calm on his countenance now that seemed somehow more ominous than the frown he wore in battle.

"Wilfred-san, get me writing materials."

Wilf complied at once, the others espying him curiously.

"What are you . . . going to do?" Gerhard asked from the corner where he sat, curled up and despondent. But Gonji said nothing in reply, watching Lydia descend with a tray.

The samurai washed himself in a basin and dried with solemnity, taking the paper and quill from Wilf with a bow and giving him his soiled tunic. Cleaned and shirtless, he began to inscribe Japanese ideograms on the paper. They all watched him with silent expectation, even Lydia. Michael, too, was conscious now, absorbing the apprehension in the gloomy cellar.

At length he finished.

"Wilfred-san, see that Paille gets this, *dozo.*"

"What is it?"

"My death poem. He will understand. I wish it inscribed on my grave, and I'm to be buried with the Sagami."

Shock gripped them. Gerhard rose slowly from the floor.

"Are you going out there?" Lydia asked, not without concern. "Giving yourself up?"

He smiled without humor. *"Iyé*, that is not my way." Then he drew a mat to the center of the floor and laid the Sagami on it, scabbarded. He sat in the lotus position, the *ko-dachi*, his short sword, carefully set on the mat before him.

"Oh, my God," Garth whispered.

Lydia looked from one to the other of them, but none would meet her gaze. "What's he going to do?" she spoke with widening eyes. "Merciful Mother, what does this mean?"

Gonji at length pulled himself into a kneeling position. "Wilfred-san, I will need your assistance."

Wilf gulped and looked at his father.

"Wilfred, I forbid it," the smith cried.

"Oh, dear God—*no!*" Lydia screamed. "Are you *mad?*"

Ignoring her outcry, Gonji spoke in a ritual tone: "For failing in my duty to my Master and the city, for numerous failures in upholding the code of *bushido*, by which I live, I offer my life in *seppuku*—"

"Are you crazy?" Lydia persisted. "You—you—*here*, in Milorad's house? This is barbaric savagery!"

"Here it must be," Gonji replied calmly. "If I could perform it at the square beneath my Master's body, I would. But I would never get that far. Please do not deny me this final dignity in my wayward life. Wilfred?" he appealed to the hesitant smith. "Are you my best friend?"

"J-ja," Wilf responded shakily, moving forward.

"I will not let you do this," Garth growled, imposing himself between them.

"Then you must assist me," Gonji said to Wilf.

"Should I cry out, or fail to complete the cut, then you must strike my head off immediately. *Do you understand?*"

"*Jesu Christi,*" someone prayed.

"Gonji, you can't ask this of any of us," Roric advanced.

The samurai withdrew the *seppuku* sword from its sheath and gripped it in both hands, the point angled at his lower abdomen for the plunge and the subsequent cut, upward and across, which would spill his bowels in the time-honored manner of the ritual suicide.

"No!" Lydia shrieked, her cry drawing Anna Vargo halfway down the stairs. Milorad's wife began to shake at the vision in her cellar, her face set in abject horror.

"Stand behind me, Wilfred-san," Gonji ordered.

Garth grabbed his son, holding him back. They began to struggle. "Gonji, I'll never permit this!" Garth roared as they wrestled. The smith flipped his son to the floor. Wilf struck his head on the edge of the cot and, enraged, slammed a fist against the side of his father's head. Garth drew away from him at once, and Wilf, seeing what he had done, sucked in a breath, slumping back against the cot.

Garth lifted himself from the floor, glaring at his apprentice son. For the first time in his life, Wilf saw loathing in his father's expression. It frightened him in a way he had never felt before. He lay back, unmoving.

"*Es tut mir leid,* Papa," Wilf offered in quaking apology.

"Shut up, you young fool," Garth replied spitefully. "How did it feel to strike your father?" He turned his angry gaze on Gonji. "Why don't you just leave us? It's finished, all this madness about peace-loving people fighting to the death over—over arrogant principle. I once fought because I believed it would lead to dreams fulfilled, and it ruined my life. Now I've given myself over to helping train fodder for militant men again, and what has it brought me? My son raises his hand against me—my other two sons I haven't seen all night. They're probably *dead*. And how many other fathers are grieving for lost sons this day?

"You've never truly understood us. Just tried to make the city over into your strange vision of what it should be. You can't change the world to make it your . . . lost Land of the Gods. Why don't you go back to it . . . instead . . ." He turned away, seeming to regret the words, rubbing his face in a nervous effort at calming himself.

Lydia moved past him. "Perhaps it's best," she said gently, "that you leave us now. It . . . isn't necessary to do away with yourself to show us how you feel. We appreciate it. You needn't feel guilty—" She stopped when she saw the disgust that caused Gonji's lips to quiver. He rose with clenched teeth.

"You understand how I feel?" he said with barely controlled rage. "You know *nothing* of how I feel. None of you. You won't even allow me the dignity of finishing my miserable life in the way I've been taught from birth. Have I ever reviled your ways? your beliefs? Yet you deny me the peace I seek. You demand that I continue living with this intolerable shame—"

But he broke off, sensing the futility and unfairness of trying to make them understand. A fleeting thought came, something spoken by the mad artist-poet. Something about the mitigating of cultural responsibility when one moved amidst a strange population. He seized upon it, dearly hoping that his ancestors would allow for such adaptive compromise . . .

Externally, Gonji was soon composed. But now, in the face of denied honor, what was he to do? There was only one thing: He must leave, as he had been asked. Only Wilf would meet his glance among those in the cellar, and the young smith's actions betrayed his emotional trauma, his grave misgivings over what had just happened and, perhaps worse, over what was about to happen. For Gonji's manner was now subtly different. For the first time in nearly a month, he walked among them as a stranger.

Gonji bowed solemnly to the group. Garth muttered a half-heard apology, then grasped him by the shoulders as if he would embrace him, but Gonji's icy exterior put him off. Garth stepped back and bowed uneasily. From the cot Michael offered a weak salute. Gonji shambled up the stairs, all of them following save for Lydia, who remained with her wounded husband.

Paille had been sleeping in a chair by the front door. The commotion caused him to start, wild-eyed. He raised his dagger in bleary threat. "*Qui va lá?* Who goes there?" he burst at them but then settled back at once, groaning with his hangover.

"A fine sentinel," Gerhard grumbled at him.

Anna fluttered about them, relieved, preparing a light meal that Gonji accepted gratefully. He fended off their endeavors at conversation with monosyllabic replies. Milorad was absent, having gone out to aid with the sorting of the wounded and the dead, the assessment of the night's carnage. About the time the meal was done, Helena arrived with a bundle under her arm: Gonji's kimono and the Italian riding boots he had bought, retrieved from the Gundersens'. Her tears began to flow to see Gonji glum and taciturn, still bedraggled from his ordeal.

"She was here almost all night," Anna whispered to Gonji. "Helena—such a chance, you took . . ." She ignored the girl's inability to hear, as she always did, guiding her to a seat at the table and taking the bundle from her. Gonji nodded to her, his steely gaze mellowing ever so slightly.

"You're not really going," Wilf said, desperately hoping for reassurance.

"I must," Gonji replied. "What time is it?"

"Four bells of morning was the last I heard, I think," Roric responded.

"I'll want to see the body of my Master before I go down and turn the shambles of the militia over to Rorka."

"You can't go out there," Garth said in mild caution, "the chapel area is like a beehive."

"I must. If they're picking up the dead, then there will be many citizens about, too. I'll mingle with them, if only briefly . . ."

Gonji cleansed himself again and donned his kimono, sashing his *daisho* ominously.

"You're going out there to die, aren't you?" Wilf said, an edge of hostility in his voice. "You're going to take as many them with you as you can and then you're going to die with a big show of courage—a fat lot of good *that's* going to do anyone! The soldiers will shoot you to pieces and then spit on your corpse, and what will you have left behind?"

"Calm yourself, Wilfred," Garth cautioned.

"*Nein*, I won't calm myself—you promised you'd help me rescue Genya," Wilf accused Gonji. "What will happen to that promise?"

Gonji paused and thought for an instant but avoided Wilf's eyes and moved to the window to scan the streets.

"If you go out there, I'm going too," Wilf announced.

"You'll stay here," Garth ordered.

"*Nein*, I'll do as I please," Wilf responded, turning

on him. "Don't say anything—just listen to me. I will never live down having struck you, Papa. It was unforgivable. But I'm still a man. I have a mind of my own, and I believe we're *not* through. Have we trained so long, suffered through so much, to give it all up because Gonji's pride has been hurt?" He saw the samurai stiffen as he stood behind him, but he continued: "*Ja*, that's why you're leaving as much as anything else. You know they don't want you to leave, whatever they say. My father spoke in anger and exhaustion and fear. Nobody knows what in hell to do about all this, but your leaving isn't going to stop it. The prophetess was right. Mord isn't going to stop killing until we're all dead, and some of us won't stop fighting until we've won or died trying. *I* won't stop—even if no one will help me—" He burst into tears of rage. "I'm going to get inside the castle," he raved, *"with you or without you."* He slammed off into another room, leaving deadly silence in his wake.

By now Paille was awake and, having taken in what was occurring by random snatches, he came to understand the tragic circumstances of Vedun and the fact that Gonji was going to leave them. He registered his protest with a rambling tirade that was largely ignored.

Gonji moved to Helena, who still sat weeping softly. She shook her head when he approached, indicating that he should not leave. She signed to him that she still loved him. He took her hands in his and set them on the table, nodded tenderly that he understood, but he closed his eyes with an eloquent finality that caused her tears to stream anew.

Lydia mounted the steps. Gonji aimed a telling look at her, one that was fraught with the strange ambivalence she had aroused in him during his stay. The knock at the front door broke the spell.

"Monetto," Garth said, opening it. The bearded biller entered, out of breath.

"Greetings, gentils," he said. "Gonji—good to see you up and about. Listen, everyone, they're cleaning up the city. The body count of citizens seems something upwards of fifty—very few militiamen, I gather. But it's awful—*God*, it's awful what they've done. I saw some of the Zarnesti party, and some others who want to know what to do. A lot of them are sneaking down to the catacombs, I think. What now?"

Gonji remained speechless.

"That's where I'll head, too, once I've checked on my family's well-being," Roric announced.

Gonji finally spoke. "Signora Vargo, let me borrow your husband's capote, *dozo*, to cover myself as best I can." She bobbed her head and brought him the hooded cloak. "The boots I'll leave for whoever wants them. Can't imagine why I ever bought them," he continued distractedly.

"I'm going along with you," Wilf said, returning to the room, the firmness in his voice smothering his father's disagreement. Garth turned away from him.

"*Sayonara,*" Gonji said to all, a note of reluctance detectable in his tone. "Do what you must." He and Wilf slipped out into the pre-dawn gloom, a shroud of fog helping to mask their surreptitious movement. Moments later, Gerhard and Monetto left in a different direction, followed shortly by Roric.

"Well," Paille began, watching through the shutters as Gonji and Wilf disappeared through the narrow rear lane, "there goes the best fighting man among us."

"And the finest leader."

They all turned at the sound of Michael's voice. The protegé leaned against the cellar jamb, supporting his weight with both arms. "But still a man, who needed understanding like any other man . . ."

They darted through the darkened lanes, using the shadows and the fog, weaving their way to the square not far off.

"You can't go," Wilf kept whispering, his voice ever on the edge of tears. "I didn't think you'd ever let those cowards influence you."

"Quiet, Wilf."

"What about those who trained hard to become *bushi*? We still need training. If we can't overthrow them now, then why not next week, next year—*sometime*?"

"Stop it before someone hears you, dammit!"

Wilf snuffled in a breath. "I'll not surrender this sword. You'll have to *kill* me to get it back."

"Oh, shut up already—Spine-cleaver is yours to keep forever. You know that."

Wilf grabbed his shoulder as they hunkered down in a cul-de-sac, waiting for a mounted party to pass. "How was I supposed to be sure? Can I believe any of your promises? You also promised to show me how to get into that castle and free Genya."

Gonji threw off his hand and glared back into his eyes, but Wilf didn't flinch. Gonji turned away, struggling internally. "Come on, they've passed."

From between two market stalls they viewed the terrible result of the night's slaughter at the square. Bodies of the dead were heaped near the chapel for identification by survivors. Soldiers' corpses were loaded onto drays. The square crawled with troops. There was no getting to the chapel entrance to the catacombs for them, but Gonji's mind was not on that problem now. His grim stare was fixed on the lightly dangling body of Master Flavio, swinging with the air currents from the ironic gibbet of the great crucifix between the fountain and rostrum.

Gonji nodded. "May Iasu take him to the reward he lived for—let's go."

"Where?"

"Tralayn's."

Chapter Twenty-five

Mord had worked feverishly through the night since his return from the too easily thwarted rebellion in the city. He had failed there, thanks largely to the traitor's inability to get to him sooner. That owed much to the blasted oriental's security measures; there'd be much to pay him back for once his usefulness was done. But there was nothing for it now but to forge ahead with an alternative plan. Specifics would be pursued later. For now . . . the groundwork.

He hastily prepared his subject for the dramatic presentation he would make to Klann. The king had to be appeased in his renewed demands. And the thing he would show, Mord thought, should prove quite convincing. After all, what did any of these common mortals understand of magick gramarye?

Next—a fresh imputation of mana for his further work. Soon, the invocation at full moon, and such extreme measures of acquiring dark power would be unnecessary. And *this* full moon would be special, he felt sure. It would mark the achievement of his and the League's Grand Scheme, with the sorcerer annexing to himself both the manpower and the wealth left from the holocaust. But for now . . .

He lured five Akryllonian children into the tower,

using as an enticement the strange malleable man-forms, the "dolls," they all loved to handle, the ones that moved when the children ordered them to. Next he told them a story—and how they all were rapt by Mord's way with tale-spinning! They would sit hand-in-hand in a circle while he wove his mastery about them, all the while draining them of their life essence, drawing from them the mana he would need to work his sorcery. Soon they all were asleep, exhausted. Their parents would blame the late hours they had kept, or their miserable peripatetic life, or changes in diet, or the spirits that roamed the territory, called down upon them in curses by the despised people of Vedun. They would blame anything, in short, except the dreaded sorcerer, who was, of course, working on their behalf. And the children wouldn't tell them where they'd been; they were all forbidden to bother the magician in his tower.

Mord had them carried to an unused chamber by mercenaries who drew pay both from the king and from him, though Klann knew nothing of their latter employment. Then, with some remonstrance from Mord at their childish cowardice, they brought the wrapped subject that would be shown to Klann.

Now remained the most difficult task of all: dealing with the holy woman, who had been granted a hearing rather than the summary execution Mord had hoped for.

"See how the sorcerer bleeds your people!" Tralayn cried, raising her shackled arms to swing them over the audience in the main hall. "He has poisoned you, and now he is killing your people!"

"Yes, keep talking, by all means," Mord blared from the gallery, where he stood flanked by mercenaries, "this is all quite fascinating to the king and his subjects alike, witch woman. You guards with her, keep her arms down, that she may wave no vile enchantment over anyone in this hall. We've seen quite enough of her power lately."

Murmurs in the crowd. They had momentarily forgotten her notoriety, so shocked were they by her accusations against Mord, her denunciations of their king.

"Indeed, tell us more," Klann commanded, glancing toward Mord suspiciously.

"I have no more to say to you," she replied, her impassioned obloquy at an end, "save to say that you've been the fool, Klann. You've opened yourself to use by the Evil One, chosen evil as a shortcut to power that is denied you. And your folly will see your life dashed." People began to shout her down, cursing in the Kunan tongue and crying out for her blood to hear their king so reviled. "The Lord God will send to Vedun his Deliverer," she continued, shouting now over the din, "he who will turn your blood to ice for his very sight!"

A Llorm pikeman leapt forward and thrust his lance through her heart, and there came a blinding flash of light in the hall that tore screams from their throats as they buried their faces in their hands. But when they timorously uncovered their eyes, everything had returned to normal.

Tralayn lay across the table, her face set in the peace of death.

The king and his retainers craned their necks from their side of the gallery. "What *was* that, Mord?" Klann asked.

Mord stood unmoving, hands pressed against his chest. A moment earlier he had felt there a burning pain and known the fear of kindled righteousness. The same fear he had felt fleetingly a month before, when Austrian troops had surged after them under the cross of Christ, the massed power of their faith arrayed against him, confounding his waning sorcery through the might of arms of those who truly believed . . .

"Her—her final weak attempt on your life, sire. I—I dispersed it, fortunately, at the last instant. Forgive me for not foreseeing it sooner. It's the flagging of certain of my powers, you . . ."

"It's your *duty* to foresee such things, magician," Klann roared. "I'll not be threatened within my own castle again, or *your* head will roll in payment!"

"Quite so, sire," Mord replied, bowing obsequiously. "You men," he called down to the hall floor, "burn that witch's body and all her effects. And tomorrow, burn her house in the city as well."

"Julian," Klann shouted down, "come forward." The captain marched out to the fore of the massed troops.

"Sire?"

"What about that oriental rogue? Has he been arrested?"

Julian paled. "No, sire, I'm afraid not. He—"

"Slipped you again, has he?" the king taunted.

"No, milord," Julian said defensively. "This revolt kept us busy throughout the day, and he seemed to have no part in it."

"Is that so?" Klann said skeptically.

"True, my liege. He was nowhere to be found, and the rebels are saying he's *not* their leader, that he's fled. But I have the troops alerted. If he's about, he'll be apprehended. Have no fear. I shall deal with him."

"See that you do—now what is it *you* want, courier?"

Mord listened in amusement while the Llorm messenger related the lost contact with patrols sent to check on outposts in the territory. Probably more of the oriental's doing; or the newly freed and more vigilant peasant village. Or perhaps it was the work of the enigmatic presence. The Deathwind . . . But then Klann was speaking his name.

"Uh—sire?"

"The charm of division—what new developments?" Klann pointed an accusing finger. "You swore there'd be results to show soon."

Mord bowed and snapped his fingers. Three of the mercenaries with him licked their dry lips and shuffled off to the chamber at the sorcerer's left. They came out moments later with the slender wrapped figure that undulated in their tentative grasp. An unearthly moaning sound emanated from under the wrap. The crowd in the hall whispered and pointed.

Mord undid the fastenings and unwound the shroud—

"Behold!"

Screams and epithets howled from those gathered below. Women covered their eyes and turned away into comforting arms. It was a ghastly sight: A fragment of what had once been a human being, split vertically through its middle such that no scar could be seen, the flesh covering the head-to-groin severance appearing like melted tallow. It was naked. A one-armed, one-legged, half-headed monstrosity that had to be supported by the quaking mercenaries, whose breaths hitched at having to touch it.

The creature babbled hideously out of the bit of mouth left to it.

"The latest experiment, sire," Mord announced proudly. "A living, breathing division."

The crowd's shock passed. Now many of them became coarsely amused at the apparition, their esteem for the sorcerer's abilities also increasing.

"Just mind that *I* don't end up like that," Klann bellowed.

"Oh, of course not, milord. This was but one puny

man, while you are *many* men. Soon I shall be ready to work the charm to the end you seek."

"Well, get that . . . *monster* out of here," Klann ordered. "Have it sent to the city as a further warning of what to expect should they attack us again."

The crowd began to disperse, shaking their heads in wonder over what they had just witnessed, glad for the power of Mord that protected them from the enchantments of their enemies.

"A drink?" Klann offered archly. Then he smiled. "No, of course not. You don't drink anything *we* would find palatable, do you?"

Mord's lipless mouth smiled under his ornate mask. "Your wit becomes a scion of Akryllon, sire."

"Indeed? What do you *really* know of what it is to be the scion of Akryllon's throne?"

Mord tensed imperceptibly, uncertain of this wry turning of the king's humor. "Milord?"

"You know . . . if I could believe for a second that the witch woman's accusations were true—"

Emitting a great, patient sigh, Mord clasped his hands loosely before him. "So, milord, she has done her work well, caused just the sort of rift between us that she would have hoped. Somewhere her shade grins over what she's wrought . . . I make no response to her accusations, if that's what you seek. Your very entertainment of the plausibility beggars any response. What do I say to such mad—"

"Say nothing," Klann said curtly. A strange mirth danced in his eyes. "Suffice it to say that what happened did indeed happen." His voice dwindled to a whisper. "But that you will prevent its ever happening in such a way again. Have I made myself clear?" The magician nodded slowly. "And you will separate the personages so that there will never again be . . . such a Death and Rising."

Mord's mind raced with unruly thoughts. Was Klann telling him he suspected that Mord had, in fact, murdered him? Was this personage sanctioning it by virtue of his delight in being freed? The sorcerer's unholy soul cackled. *Things are indeed looking up.*

"Your wish, milord, is ever my duty."

Knowing that Mord was occupied with the hearing of the prophetess and sensing that it might be her only opportunity, Genya slinked into the ground floor corridors of the sorcerer's drum tower, bent on fulfilling her promise to Richard.

She had to find Lottie, and the three of them must flee this awful place.

It was all wrong. Something inside her despaired for Lottie, told her that her friend was dead . . . or worse. But she had promised, and she was motivated by her own determination to discover what had become of her longtime companion.

So far, so good. She had made the circuit of the ground floor, checked the empty chambers that weren't locked, and found nothing. No sentries were on duty, most of the garrison also at the hearing, so she hadn't found it necessary to employ her questionable cover story; but Mord's confidence was disarming. And as she ascended the first cold staircase that rose to the darker, mustier second level, she was seized by the certainty of one thing: If Lottie could not be found in the tower, she would never, *never* descend into the subterranean levels, from whose nightmare pit crawled those dim moans of inhuman things in torment . . .

Second level. A full, cautious circuit—this tower might well be abandoned. Or she was being played for a fool. The notion angered her, summoned an indignant courage that caused her to press onward. And upward.

Halfway around the third level's girdling main corridor, the obvious—so readily arrested under stress—occurred to her. Why not simply call out Lottie's name? Why *shouldn't* she be looking for her missing friend out of honest concern? Even the fulsome enchanter would have to—

The scuttling sounds in the chamber on her left stopped her wispy breathing like a swallowed plug. It was very dark, she suddenly realized. Only starlight strained to illuminate the passageway through the grated windows. *Why didn't I bring along a lamp? I can't even light a tor—*

The soft scuttling sounds again. Just beyond the rusting chamber door. Her eyes studied every inch of the forbidding portal. The sounds *might* be the struggling of someone bound and gagged on the floor. Might be . . .

Her hand stretched out to touch the verdigris-stained knob, closed on it. She withdrew it when she heard the muffled voices through the thick ashlar walls. *In this chamber?* No. No, they were coming from the next room.

Madonna, do I move on or turn back or—*sssst!*

Footsteps ascending the winding stairway. Low voices. The clump of boots and the jangling of—*Merciful Father!* The jangling of keys—the ring of keys Mord always carried when in the tower!

Genya's face twisted like that of a child in pain, but she made no outcry. Instead she did the only thing she could: She tried the knob, and it yielded. But the footsteps were approaching rapidly—*Mord* . . . Mord's voice speaking in those sepulchral tones amid other men's voices, and by now she could see the orange glare of their torches rising to the third level, and they were coming, they were coming, and there was nothing to do but—

Creak . . .

435

Genya pushed in the door as gently as she could, but still it made its small telltale noise on rusty hinges, and all she could think to do was send up to heaven the most fervent prayer of her young life. Then she was lapped up by darkness, her back to the door, eyes shut tightly, lips drawn inside her mouth, where they continued their trembling.

And the scuttling sounds were near her feet now.

Rats.

"Stay there," Mord's voice boomed in echo, "and allow no one to pass."

She bit her lip. Her whole body went numb to hear his striding past her place of concealment, and she prayed that he possessed no sense that might divine her presence here in the foul-smelling darkness.

She shuddered in the rank chamber, hearing Mord enter through the door wherein she had heard the voices. And now despite her circumstances, her undying curiosity was stoked. Who was in there? Dim light shone here and there through cracks in the ancient mortar that separated the chambers. She heard a woman's voice—and a man's—and Mord's deep basso profundo twice as loud as either. Something was familiar about the woman's voice, but Mord kept drowning her out just when Genya would begin to identify the lilt. It was all infuriatingly muted. Perhaps if she could get closer—

The cracks flared alight, a lamp having been lit on the chamber wall. Up near the low ceiling: a sizeable chink through which yellow light gleamed unfiltered. If she could get to it, it might be—

". . . better, isn't it?"

Genya gasped. It was the man's voice. Near the wall. He must have lit the lamp, and now *his* tone had a remarkably familiar quality. Her head itched, nerve ends prickling. She had to know.

Slowly, inching along with a balance and control that would have done any *bushi* proud, Genya moved across the cluttered room. Her hands reached out sensitively, feeling her path . . . a set of stocks or a pillory from the days of the rampaging bandits; along one wall, a huge arm of a catapult or mangonel, disassembled, rusting . . .

The wall. And the familiarity of the woman's voice again.

The chink was a foot above her head. She reached a hand up and felt the warmer air that soughed through it. *The man—a dreadful inkling. No, forget that, it couldn't be . . .*

She reached down along the wall. There must be something there to climb onto. She felt along the clammy stone, down. A rat ran over her foot at the base of the wall, and she lurched back, bumping the mangonel arm and clamping her hand over the hiss of her sharp inhale. She froze, listening. An agonizing minute. The conversation continued unabated.

Reaching down again, Genya found something cold and crusted, an iron object that seemed solid and almost flat. It wouldn't yield when she tried to shake it.

Her heart pounded as she mounted with a deliberation that made her muscles ache. Her fingers found purchase in the chipped mortar and stone, and she brought her eye to the chink and peered through. For an instant the lamplight was blinding, but almost before her eye had adjusted, her mind began to accept the testimony her ear had presented.

Trembling like a winter-born foal, she heard little of what they were saying, so bewildered, so frightened was she by the figures she saw gathered.

The man, the woman, Mord. The woman—the man—what was their connection? Why did they conspire with the evil sorcerer? Then she began to make sense of it, to realize what the connection must be. And their identities, in the context of what was being said, so horrified her that she lost her concentration momentarily. One hand slipped its purchase, and in her anxiety to maintain her hold she grabbed at a section of mildew-rotted mortar that crumbled at her touch and spilled onto the floor.

Beneath her feet: the scrambling of furry bodies. And in the adjacent chamber, all three heads turned to regard the wall.

Mord's laughter boomed. "Edgy, aren't we? *Rats*, you see."

The woman sighed in relief. "Of course I'm edgy. Meeting with you like this—working behind the king's back—Why must you continue to work in secret? Why not let Klann in on what we know? Haven't you done away with those in the city whom you hated so?"

"All quite cleverly manipulated, if I do say so myself," the man added, idly twirling his sword in its scabbard.

"No, I'm *not* yet finished with them," Mord replied. "And it remains to my advantage to have you operating on my behalf. I still wish to court the king's favor, you see, by imparting to him bits of intelligence that no one else might, from time to time."

The traitor from Vedun chuckled in a way that caused Mord to hiss softly. "I should think your magicks would be sufficient to turn up such intelligence, eh?"

Mord suffered the insult silently. This fool would pay. "Mmm, perhaps. But there is much that you do not understand about sorcery. Be mindful only that we are all in this together now, each for the thing he—and she—wants. But now—where were we? Ah, yes . . . the catacombs. What an advantage they shall be. Rorka and his men should be alone there now?"

"For the nonce, I think," the traitor replied.

Mord nodded. "Good. The sooner he's dealt with, the better."

"Why?" the man asked.

Mord paused before answering. They were beginning to ask too many questions. "Because I hate him, also. More than the others, in some ways. He might well raise considerable trouble against us—allies and such."

"I don't think that's possible anymore," the traitor said.

"If that's what you think, then perhaps you haven't done your work well enough," Mord said haughtily. They were both staring at him speculatively. "In any case Klann expects that Rorka's dead already, true?" They looked at each other. The woman nodded slowly, uncertainly, but the man tossed his head back and giggled, a rapid sound that was quickly strangled off.

"Power games," the man said, "how endlessly fascinating they are."

Mord eyed him closely. He was going quite *mad*, and that could be dangerous.

"What about this Gonji?" Mord inquired. "Is he gone as they're saying?"

"Of course not," the traitor replied.

"Then why didn't he lead them in full revolt so that Klann's forces could crush all the rebels?"

"They had no plan. It all began because of the guildsmen."

So, Mord thought, *then my timing was wrong. But the proper turn of the ratchet at just the right moment...*

Mord folded his arms. "Do these upstarts truly think the taking of a peasant village proves them worthy opponents of both Klann's army and my power?"

The traitor shrugged. "It seems so."

Splendid, Mord decided. That oriental rascal —double-agenting! He had to admire the fool's cleverness and hubris. But he feared that this latest abortive effort may have crushed the city's fighting spirit, making the mutual destruction more difficult in view of the king's pigheadedness about keeping the city in his peaceful thrall. An interesting problem: How to eliminate the Rorka threat while at the same time inspiring the militia to rebel again in such a way that Klann will be swept into internecine conflict. Moving too obviously could cast dangerous suspicion upon him, perhaps compromising the Grand Scheme. *But what risk isn't worth taking after murdering Klann himself?*

"The Deathwind legend—what does it mean? What do they say of it now?" Mord snapped. "And who is this Deliverer supposed to be?"

The traitor leaned back. "It's . . . just a legend they're using to strike fear in the superstitious soldiery."

"Oh, there's more to it than that, you can be assured. Much more." Mord paused, worrying in his mind at the thing that troubled him most. He would have to move swiftly, his intuition told him. "The witch woman knew. Too bad she's gone. Ah—she would never have talked. But it's more than a legend, this . . . confusing thing that's torn by the clash of cosmic forces."

He snapped out of his reverie when he saw the pair staring at him. And then he had it.

"It just occurred to me," Mord said in an amused tone, "how I'll deal with the elusive baron. Specters of things past nestle in the ground beneath our feet, did you know that? One never knows . . . I shall take my leave of you now."

"And I shall follow soon after," the traitor added. "I'll be missed before long."

Mord bowed to them and moved quickly through the corridors, his guards trailing behind. He descended to the dungeon level, where he laughingly retrieved the homunculi the children were so fond of handling. A short while later, while Mord recited the words of an arcane spell of sympathetic magic, he wrapped all but one of the figures in articles stripped from the bodies of slain knights after the castle siege. The last was rolled in a garment taken from Rorka's bedchamber. He began to chant, the figures slowly, eerily moving, writhing to its rhythm. Then, obtaining a shapeless handful of the same malleable substance that formed the figures, he began to knead and work and roll it in his hands, drawing it out, sculpting it.

Soon the sinuous thing took definite form. Movement. Life, of an imitative sort. He set it on the stone slab amidst the man-forms, where it performed its hideous work.

An hour later, the complex, wearying rite completed, Mord hurried to the dungeon subcellar the traitor had described. A torch's illumination revealed the discolored outline of the concealed door of stone, moisture having seeped through the slender crack. Mord found the disguised lever with little difficulty, depressed it. The stone and metal mechanism scraped and groaned from years of settling, but the aperture gaped open, causing the sorcerer to toss his head back, a gravelly laugh filling the cellar.

Seconds later he was off into the tunnel, heading for the training cavern to witness what he had done.

Several levels above, Genya rushed from the tower, only minutes behind Mord's conspirators. She was badly shaken, her entire world disintegrating. What in hell was happening here? What would be the fate of Vedun, given the monstrous things she'd heard and seen? She could no longer trust even those she might have counted on.

It was late in the night, yet the castle was still crawling with activity. She was unimpeded as she moved hurriedly through the wards and halls, snatching the sack from the scullions' chambers, putting off the chambermaids' curiosity with evasive words, not even tarrying long enough to hear them speak of the ill omen that attended the horrible death of the prophetess.

Alone, she sped through the central keep, through the inner curtain's tunnel which led to the miller's gate, situated between the castle's westerly towers. The impregnable gate, rarely used, was cut into the west outer bailey wall and led into a fortified casemate, a defensive outwork set on a causeway over the moat. Beyond it camped a company of mercenaries. But she had been promised safe passage through them, if . . .

This was the last resort she had dreaded, she reflected as she donned the man's breeches, tunic, jerkin, and slouch hat in a dim and cluttered corridor. The unthinkable last resort. She had been planning to find another way out with Richard and Lottie when the time was right. But that was not possible now. Now she had to get out alone, quickly, though she knew she couldn't pay Tomas's price. Tomas—the leering Keeper of the miller's gate. How repulsive he was. She had heard all the disturbing stories about him, but they had to be put behind her now in her urgency. She would have to count on her persuasive charms to bluff her way out.

She stashed her clothes in a bin and waited for a band of soldiers to pass. Then, inhaling to steel herself for the confrontation with Tomas, she sprinted to the guardhouse before the miller's gate. Knocked—two long, two short—as she'd been instructed.

"Enter."

The iron door rasped open under her push, and she slid inside to see Tomas's unseemly smile. He reclined in a curve-backed chair near the gate, his feet propped on a dusty flour barrel. He slapped at flies lazily with a short riding lash as he watched her enter. He was alone.

Peering at the face under the low-brimmed slouch, he grinned, mildly surprised. "Well, Genya—never thought I'd see *you* here. The miller's gate is quite an attraction these days, is it?" He swung his feet down and ambled up to her casually, the lash draped over his shoulder.

"Tomas, we've been friends for a long time—"

"*Friends?*" he said airily.

She swallowed. "A-all right—acquaintances, co-servitors—call it what you will. But we're fellow citizens of the province and—"

He flipped the slouch off her head with the lash, her dark curls rushing down over her shoulders like seafoam against a moonlit shoal.

He snickered as he sidled around her. "Still protrusive and callipygian, even in a man's clothes. Do you know what that means?" She stiffened with the impact as he slapped her bottom with the lash. But she remained in place, raising no protest.

"Tomas, I need to get out of here. *Now*, tonight. I'm going mad in this place. I *must* get home for just a few hours. I've got to see my parents, be sure for myself that they're well after all this—"

"More likely to curl up with your friend, uh—Wilbert? Wilhelm?"

"Wilfred," she said sternly, "and I *swear* to you that's not what I have in mind. You know I've got to be back here by tomorrow noon, else the king will be sending troops after me. I'm his personal servant, you know."

Tomas grinned cruelly. "So I've heard. Been ministering to His Majesty's needs, have you? Tell me . . . what's it like to . . . cavort with kings."

He probed at her breasts with the handle of the lash. Loathing welled up to her throat. She wanted to spit into his face, to jab out an eye, but she instead forced a shaky smile and stood fast under his fondling.

"Listen, Tomas, I can't pay you the price you ask tonight. I simply *must* get home to see my parents, to breathe the air outside these walls before I go *mad*." She reached up to caress his face. "But tomorrow—"

He grabbed her hand and squeezed it. "I must get out tonight, but *tomorrow* I'll pay," he mimicked through clenched teeth, frightening her. "If I had one taler for every time I've heard that, then *I* would be king and Klann would be down here collecting favors." But then he let go of her hand suddenly and waxed serious.

"Wait here," he said simply, departing through the door she had entered.

Frost needled her insides to hear the turning of the key in the lock. *Oh no . . . he's going to report my attempted bribe. I'll deny it, I'll—*No, she was at their mercy. What to do, what to say? She felt defenseless. Terror broiled now at the pit of her stomach, the turmoil making her nauseous.

Minutes later Tomas returned, but not with soldiers. With him was the brutish Steward of the Larders, the one they called Chooch. She tried hard to ignore his presence, to address only the smug Tomas, for she remembered well how Chooch once had been flogged and made to do public penance for trying to force his embraces on a milkmaid.

She felt the clutch of panic. She had to get out of there.

"All right, Tomas," she said with affected aloofness,

"you won't let me go tonight, then neither will I pay your price tonight. Perhaps another night you'll . . . see it my way."

With a casual flutter of her eyelids she turned to the door, but Chooch imposed his hulking form between her and the portal, slamming it. Her eyes widened, her self-confidence shattered.

Tomas chuckled behind her, circled around and locked the door with a screeching twist of metal against metal.

"You have it all wrong, my dear. *I* don't want you. *Chooch* is the gateway to your freedom. I shall simply resume my perch and monitor the proceedings—no sense wasting time on second thoughts while we're all together like this. Proceed," he finished with amused detachment, sitting and flicking out at the heat-maddened flies in the stuffy chamber.

The huge man stalked her slowly, grinning, and whether by the thickness of the walls or the familiarity of the sound, Genya's screams aroused no interest outside the gatehouse.

Later—a timeless, woeful outrage later—she lay on the powdered floor, her face streaked by tears which would no longer flow. The vile gatekeeper stood over her, his beastly companion having drawn away from her, exhausted.

"Well done," Tomas said archly, clapping. "Was it truly so bad?"

She curled like an animal at bay against the lash's feathering course along her nakedness.

"Like everything else," he taunted, "freedom has its price. But wouldn't Wilbert be pleased to know how badly you wish to see him?"

"Bastards," she whispered with undisguised revulsion, her tears flowing briefly again. But now they were tears of rage, and for the first time in her life she knew what hatred felt like.

Tomas kicked her clothes over to her. "Get those on and go. You begin to bore us."

She rose at once and dressed, averting her eyes from them. A cold, ugly feeling radiating a dead emotionlessness inside that vaguely bothered her. Just get out of here and be done with it, that was all she could think now.

"Which one of you . . . sees me through the free companions?" she asked in a cracked voice, replacing the slouch hat. The dead cold feeling had reached her glazed stare.

Tomas feigned surprise. "Oh—whatever is wrong with me, Chooch? I forgot to tell the lady. You see, the demand for freedom is so high that our risk has increased lately. We've had to raise our price. *Three* nights now . . . you see." He flicked his lash at the flies that clustered on the walls. "The door is unlocked. Good morrow."

She gulped back the sickening taste of bile in her throat and shuffled back through the grating iron portal, numbly drifting along the tunnel and turning into the corridor where she had left her own clothes. When she had slumped to the floor next to the bin, her tears came again in the cheerless shadows, this time accompanied by wracking sobs.

Once two soldiers were attracted by her weeping, but she sent them off, bewildered at her insensate harangue. But it had seemed to do her good. No longer did she think only hateful, vengeful thoughts; the futility of killing the perverted swine and then herself came to her with dismal clarity. What was done was done. And her thoughts of murdering Klann and/or Mord melted under the white heat of returning reason: Klann would only rise from the dead again, and the evil magician might divine her purpose before she could see it through. No, however dreadful the plight of the city, she doubted whether she could be of help now.

But no man would ever do such an awful thing to her again. Of that she was starkly sure. She would get a dagger. And she would use it . . .

O Madonna, I've been an awful woman, just awful, she prayed. So sure of myself. So quick to use my charms. My *charms* . . . And then she prayed for Wilf, prayed in intercession, that he might be spared the horrors that would surely come.

Chapter Twenty-six

It was well past a hazy gray dawn when Wilf and Gonji's furtive efforts at last brought them to Tralayn's house. Their proximity to the mercenary garrison had kept their progress slow, but they gained the slain woman's dwelling without incident and entered via the window by which they had last left it.

Passing through the fireplace, they made the descent into the catacombs hastily, Wilf having fallen silent, brooding over Gonji's refusal to honor his promise. Soon they caught sight of the glowing torches in the nexus cavern between the tunnels and the training ground. Many anxious voices could be heard as they approached, and when Gonji appeared at the tunnel adit, several of them greeted him excitedly.

The samurai experienced a mixed warmth and guilt to see how many of the *bushi* had faithfully crammed into the small cavern to await him. Something over fifty men pressed forward amid the babble of voices.

Most of the foray party were there—Gerhard, Monetto, Nagy, Foristek; Jiri Szabo, looking breathless and apprehensive; Paille had also come, sober now and full of nervous energy. By the sheepish looks of some, Gonji deduced that the story of his shameful breach of duty had already been spread, and in his introspective search for the right words to convey his apologies to the faithful militiamen, he failed to notice what was different about the vestibule chamber, the source of their disquiet.

He bowed to all of them. "Listen to me, all of you—"

"Never mind that now," Paille rasped harshly from across the vaulted chamber, "there's something dreadfully wrong here—*look.*" He indicated the iron-bound door, all the others clamming up. The portal was closed. It never had been before.

"Locked," the artist whispered loudly. "Barred from *within.*"

Gonji rushed up to the door as the others crowded in. The small storage and receiving chamber was jammed now, more men straggling in. A baking swelter of massed body heat. Gonji hushed them and strained to listen at the cracks, twisting his nose at the foul stench that seeped in.

"*Q'est-ce que c'est?* What is it?" Paille wondered.

"*Shhh!*" Gonji commanded, listening. The sounds of whinnying and clumping—the horses were loose from the corral. But no human sounds emanated from the cavern. Gonji tried the door, one hand on the Sagami, but it wouldn't budge. A sensation of primitive fear coursed through them all.

The samurai cast about, his mind a-whirl. "What weapons have we?"

"Few," Monetto replied.

"There are tools here," Peter Foristek called out.

Gonji considered it a moment, then nodded. *"Allrecht,"* he spoke in German, "let's open it . . . and see . . ."

Foristek led a small band with prybars in working free the embedded hinges on their side, then gouging the stone door jamb so that they could get a bite on the door. As Monetto had said, there were few weapons; most were in the grotto used as an armory. Some had their swords, and a few staffs were in evidence in glistening fists, but there were only three pistols, and only Gerhard had dared smuggle down a longbow.

As the work progressed, their tension spread contagiously, men crumbling into fearful sobbing that they would try to smother by beating tools or swords against the rock walls.

"Courage," Gonji urged in a gentle voice as he walked slowly around the cavern, hand on the Sagami's hilt. "Time for prayer now, or meditation . . ." He palmed aside the sweat beading his brow, soaking his light beard. Water skins were passed around by those who had brought them. Those containing wine were drained off the quickest.

"There might be . . . just about anything on the other side of that," a man observed in a tremulous voice.

"We're sure not going to surprise anybody," Szabo said in a weak effort at humor.

"Might be . . . a whole army on the other side," the other man continued.

"And if there is," Gonji said, "then you can be sure there'll be one on the other end of the tunnels as well. So there's no point in fretting. Karma."

A few men, some of the married ones in particular, began to worry about the safety of their families in view of what Gonji was suggesting. If the catacombs' secret had been compromised—Some of them broke under the stress, bolting back into the tunnels to ascend to the city. Wilf and a few companions moved to stop them.

"*Nein*," Gonji called, holding up a hand. "Let them go."

A bolt shrieked free of a timber on the other side of the door—only one coupling left fixing the door to the bar. The work party eyed Gonji.

"Get ready," he ordered quietly. He and Wilf drew their *katanas* and raised them in a striking stance, other men moving behind them on either side of the door, swords at the ready. Gerhard and the pistoliers stood facing the arch, longbow and guns loaded for a volley at whatever came through. A table was turned on its side and set before them as a crude shield.

Gonji bobbed his head. "Finish it," he whispered.

Pete and the others gave their prybars a mighty wrench on the side with the remaining coupling. The iron door wavered and fell inward.

There were sharp cries of horror when they saw the thing on the other side, and one pistol-wielder fired into it in panic. It jolted with the impact and then fell in toward them, draping over the horizontal door bar that remained anchored in solid rock.

"Oh, *Jesu!*—Holy Mother of God!—Damn you, Sklarz!—"

"*It's the baron!*"

It had taken seconds to identify him in the state he was in. Sklarz, the man who had fired the shot, clamped his hand over his mouth and dropped the weapon.

"You stupid bastard!"

"Shut up, all of you," Gonji growled. "The shot didn't kill him. *Look* at him."

They eased him gingerly from the bar and onto the floor.

"Look at his back . . ."

His corpse was swollen, his skin a mottled blue-black, as if his whole body were one huge bruise. They laid him face down and examined the deep gashes on his back, the rent flesh around them.

"Don't touch that," Paille warned. Something bluish seeped from the wounds along with the now dried gouts of blood, and around them the swelling was most pronounced. His back had the contour of an anthill.

"Gott in Himmel—what is it?"

"Some kind of . . . venom, I should think," the artist mused.

A few more men abandoned the terrifying scene for the tunnels.

"All-recht," Gonji said, standing. "Pull him inside, and don't touch the wound. Anyone else who can't enter with us, leave now."

"We're going in?" Vlad Dobroczy asked, moving close to the samurai. "But that could be suicide. Who knows what's—"

"Everything we've trained for is in there," Gonji said. "Our main armament cache. There may even be survivors who need help. All the finest horses—If no one else goes, *I* want to know what's happened here."

"Well . . ." Gerhard said, moving up to the arch. He kissed his longbow and seated his quiver of arrows comfortably on his back. "We're wasting time, *nicht wahr?*"

"Just let me get to a halberd," Foristek ground out through clenched teeth, staring at the baron's corpse.

Something came to their ears, echoing dimly in the cavern: a hissing, and then a grinding of rock. Then it was consumed by the tight, rough breathing of the *bushi*.

Gonji slid the bar out of their way and stepped into the cavern.

As they moved in, the horror was compounded in their unblinking eyes. More dead men, similarly bloated and discolored. Three knights—two militiamen—weapons scattered about their bodies: they had covered the baron's flight. Or had it been flight that had motivated him?

"Why didn't the baron get away, having made it this far?" Wilf whispered behind Gonji. "Why did he—?"

"I . . . don't think he was able, Wilf. I think your baron died a hero. With his last effort he tried to protect us from . . . whatever it was that did this."

They moved into the main cavern, where the unsaddled steeds raced about in a frenzy. A wild herd. Gonji glanced about for Tora, but the stallion was nowhere in sight. The training ground was a shambles in spots, the corral having been caved in on two sides. Two dead horses lay atop the wreckage.

"Get to the weapons," Gonji called low, and a large party broke off and scrambled for the armament grotto.

"Gonji—*look*," Monetto said in anguish. He was pointing at the area of shelters used for sleeping and privacy by Rorka's Grays. They were smashed to bits, bodies strewn amidst the debris, bloated and gouged like the others, many of them naked, having been overtaken in sleep.

Gonji rubbed the back of his neck in wonder at the portent of the carnage. What could have done such a—? Then he descried the drag marks in the dust, the long trails that all led to . . . the shallow flat outgrowth of rock on which many training lectures had been held, near the center of the cavern. And about the same time, as the others took note, gasping, they began to hear the slithering sounds in the ground beneath their feet.

"Stay clear of the rocks and tunnels," Gonji commanded. They all froze, looking about cautiously, wide-eyed. The men who had gone after weapons slowed, listening, hushing one another as the sound moved toward the pounding of their massed feet—

A resounding cracking of earth and stone. And the horror erupted in their midst, spewing rocks and shale and screaming men in every direction as it burst up from the bowels of the earth, mewling with a shrill echo like a thousand cats in a cathedral. Beyond its sound it bore no resemblance to anything natural.

In seconds the monstrous creature had snared a shrieking man and dragged him back under the earth, slithering down into the depths. The stunned survivors of the eruption crawled away, some moaning in pain with injuries sustained in their fall.

"*Choléra*—what in all the hells *is* that?" Gonji breathed. Then, shouting: "Get to the damned weapons! Fan out. Head for the sides of the cavern. Hurry—we need bows and guns—"

"It's a serpent," someone behind said in awe.

"*Nyet*, it had *claws.*"

"We've got to get to the tunnels, Gonji," Wilf cried. "We can't fight that thing."

"Get hold of yourself," the samurai shouted.

"There's no one left alive here to rescue!" a man screamed. "Let's get out before we're next!"

A rumbling eruption came again from the direction of the tunnel that exited into the hills. Then the subterranean scraping came again under the cavern floor. Swift and ominous. The creature slithered under their feet impossibly fast.

"Then let's get out of here now," Gonji agreed, swallowing back the lump in his throat. "You men with the armament—grab what you can and get back to—"

"Gonji!" Paille was yelling, sprinting out of the southern valley tunnel, three men trailing behind him. "Gonji, that thing's burrowed up into the tunnels, blocked them off with tons of earth! We can't get out this way!"

"Back to the city tunnels," Gerhard yelled, waving them all toward the way they had come. But the explosion of rock before the door through which they'd pried their way in stopped them in their tracks. The beast emerged, triumphantly clacking its clawed tentacles, and its segmented, wormlike body—thirty feet of flexing and extending rings—bowed and stretched eerily in place, churning up rocks behind it so that the portal to the city tunnels was effectively blocked in seconds.

It reared up on its tail and wove its beaked, eyeless head, birdlike, as if listening. The men in the cavern all stood and stared in abject terror, their claustrophobic shock paralyzing them. Every man now understood what was happening. The training cavern had become a larder, a livestock pantry for the worm-thing's casual feeding.

Its pair of grasping appendages sprouted from its body for about a third of its length. These were similarly segmented and ended in the vicious talons that now rubbed its beak, as if cleansing lazily while it sat, coiled with detached unconcern.

"Stand still, everyone," Gonji shouted. His voice echoed, and the monster's head twisted again. It tensed and extended the awful tentacles, sliding forward slightly. "Move only on my commands." It slid forward half a length, its motion, when above ground, like that of an inchworm.

"Karl," Gonji whispered. "Try one."

Gerhard drew back on his mighty bow, launched—the shaft embedded in its soft gray underside with an almost pulpy sound. The beast emitted a high-pitched whine like a startled bird and raked the air before gliding forward. A knot of men panicked and bolted at the center of the training ground, and the monster undulated after them.

"Stop, you fools—it can't see you," Gonji cried. "It has to feel your footfalls."

The worm was terrifyingly fast for its size. One man stumbled, and the creature was led unerringly to the sound of his falling body. It descended on him as he screamed insanely, seizing him with the talons, immobilizing him with the venom from the spurs that protruded from the base of the talons, like extruded stings. Then it gouged his belly open with its hooked beak, and the ghastly sucking sounds began.

Suddenly the cavern was alive with panic-stricken militiamen, who scrambled for cover anywhere it might be found. The worm fed casually on the freshly killed prey.

"Come on, you men," Gonji yelled to the staring bowmen and pistoliers, and they rushed forward. "Follow me," he said to the bunch within earshot.

"Where?"

"To get weapons and mounts." He began to run.

"But that thing will follow our footsteps!" Wilf shouted after, trotting with eyes fixed on the worm.

"Just follow!"

Several men ran with him in answer, Gerhard launching a parting shot that pierced its hide, disturbing its feeding. It lashed about blindly a second, then followed after the running footfalls, even as Wilf had feared.

"Fire!" Gonji ordered, and a fusillade of gunfire and bowshot exploded and whistled into the monster's soft flesh. It rocked with the impact, a banshee wail spewing from its maw. There were shouts of released tension when its mesmerizing hold was broken, but now the pistolmen had to retreat to reload, and the beast bore down on the shouting band of archers, who fell into disarray and broke into flight rather than resuming their attack.

The maddened creature coiled and sprang off after Gonji's sprinting party again, slithering into a course that would intersect theirs before they could cross the cavern. But Gonji yelled for men to bring mounts and weapons, then led his band into the training facilities that sprouted in the middle of the cavern. They reached the quintains and jousting posts just as the worm reared for a strike and darted through.

Gonji slashed right and left with his *katana* as he ran through the practice field, setting the man-forms spinning and squeaking, the others following his lead. The worm hesitated in its confusion over the cacophony. Then it sprang downward, catching a quintain and tearing it to shreds. It moved forward into the practice devices and was slowed, becoming entangled in the wood and burlap and rope of the twisting training aids.

By now Dobroczy and Nagy arrived aboard two reined but barebacked horses, another pair in tow. Gonji and Gerhard bolted under the *karumi-jutsu* scaffold and leapt astride the skittish mounts. Gonji grabbing a bow and quiver tossed to him by a man on foot. Monetto ascended the scaffold with a lance and awaited the creature's approach.

The archers reformed and sent another volley into the worm's slimy rings. It clawed at the irritants ineffectually. The pistoliers charged forward again and blasted a torrent of lead balls through it broadside, so that it spun unnaturally, screaming and crashing down onto the quintains.

Gonji and Gerhard galloped in circles about it,

firing war arrows into it. The creature bled darkly now from a hundred wounds.

"Pour it on!" Gonji roared, riding ever nearer the beast in his battle-frenzy.

Now pikemen appeared on the grounds, spears tearing into the bewildered worm-thing as it snaked its rending talons about in futility, the sounds of its tormentors coming from all directions at once. Defensive posturing was something new to the predator from far below the earth's crust, its natural prey placid and inoffensive.

Sklarz and Foristek began to work in on foot with halberds, slicing through the gelatinous rings with razored steel. But they moved too close—Sklarz became ensnared on a tattered quintain, and the monster heard his scream beneath it. Half Sklarz's head was torn off by the twisting slash of the beaked head. Foristek went mad at the sight, screaming his friend's name and burying his halberd a foot deep, penetrating to the worm's vital organs. It lurched high into the air over their heads, men scrambling to avoid its descent. Elongating into a blood-freezing strike like the spurting of a severed artery, it launched itself full length in the direction the wound had come from, landing atop the big farmer and knocking him senseless. Then it lifted him into the air with some difficulty in its mortal agonies, shredding him before the anguished gazes of his sword-brothers.

"*Sado-war-a-aaaa!*" Gonji's war cry rent the cavern, echoing as he leaped off the horse and bounded atop the monster's back, screaming with berserker frenzy. He had both blades out now, slashing repeatedly at the worm's back and neck. It lurched, but he stabbed both blades into its soft flesh and held on as it dropped Pete's lifeless corpse in its maddened efforts to dislodge him. Its catlike mewling shrilled as it rolled and at last threw Gonji off, nearby steeds neighing and tossing their riders in fear of its violent movement.

Then it loomed above Gonji, leaking its vital fluids, unsure of his position as he froze beneath it, only the Sagami in his grasp now, the *seppuku* sword lost in its flesh. It leaned near the agility scaffold, and Monetto's lance gored its ear slit, its most sensitive organ. It slashed sidewise, but the lithe biller had already dived off the scaffold.

Its other tentacle raked under its belly, and the keen flash of the Sagami's arc sliced off its taloned end, fluid spouting at once.

"Mind his venom!" someone cried, but Gonji had dashed off with the momentum of his swordcut.

When he looked up it was to see a fresh blast of pistol fire from close range send ragged chunks of gray-green flesh tearing toward the cavern ceiling. Then the monster worm emitted a final piercing whine and fell like a downed tree, skewered on a splintered jousting post.

They pulled themselves up slowly. Horsemen dismounted. It was a long time before they would stop circling the thing, staring at their hard-won prize. Longer still before their last war whoops had died and they had stopped embracing and pounding one another's backs in the pressure-release of victory.

But at that point some of them could only collapse in tearful exhaustion. And the bodies of the dead lay all about them, reminding them of the price they had had to pay.

Gonji withdrew the *seppuku* sword from the dead thing, cleansed his blades, his eyes still red and glazed over. He looked at the cloth-yard arrow that had driven through its lower jaw and continued on straight up through the upper, splitting the base of its beak. He couldn't recall having seen the shot.

Gerhard and Wilf came up beside him. "My parting shot," Karl related, "just before it almost fell on me. Not bad, eh?" Gerhard grinned shakily, his chest heaving. It was the first time Gonji had ever heard him express pride in a bowshot. "Do you know what this means?" the archer said, his tone suddenly changing.

Gonji began to shake his head, his mind a maelstrom of his own thoughts, motives, suspicions.

"That the prophetess was right about Mord wanting to see us all in our graves," Nick Nagy snarled, removing his soaked tunic and scowling.

"Worse," Gerhard corrected. "It means that there's a traitor among us."

They were stunned by the assertion. Gonji's eyes narrowed, focusing on something that twisted his lips.

"*Why*, Karl?" Monetto asked.

Gerhard shrugged. "The catacombs, eh? I don't believe he stumbled on them, whatever his powers. And that . . . *thing* didn't blunder up here. Even Tralayn never spoke of any such creature ever showing up before." He unstrung his bow with assistance from the others.

They mulled it over, each man offering his opinion, while Gonji continued to stare off toward the castle tunnel.

"That's just my hunch," Gerhard concluded at last to those who disagreed.

"Sit down, all of you," Gonji said gravely. "Let's rest and . . . reason this out." They complied, food and beverages being passed around from their stores, accepted wearily.

"It can't be," Wilf said, wagging his head as he sipped his wine. "Klann would've sent a whole army through here to wipe us out, *neh?*"

"Unless your father is right," Gonji countered, "*and* Tralayn is right. Suppose Klann is being straightforward with us as your father insists, but that Mord is working at cross-purposes to him, as we all heard Tralayn say a thousand times. So Mord employs a *traitor*—" He spat the word, revulsion for its connotation bringing a bitter taste to his tongue. "—as Karl suggests. Someone hateful enough—*insane* enough—to brook murder and savagery and the decimation of his neighbors—"

"Or *her* neighbors," Paille reminded.

Heads were shaking.

"Who has opposed all our efforts?" Gonji asked. "Vehemently opposed them from the start?"

"*Himmel*—that covers a lot of non-combatants, for starters," Gerhard advanced.

"Maybe it's just the opposite," Nagy observed, scratching his head. "Maybe it's somebody who's been too militant. That's what Mord would want, isn't it? Somebody to start trouble so that he could crush us?"

They all looked to him, grim and thoughtful.

"Phlegor?"

"He was arrested."

"That could have been a ruse."

"What for? What else could he do now that he's gone, expected not to return?"

"Wait," Gonji commanded, giving them pause. "I remember now—Jocko, good old Jocko, telling me something about this army of Klann's having too many bosses. He would say that orders would come from Klann, then separate orders would come from Mord, always for the mercenaries. It was in response to such orders that we committed the outrage at the monastery . . . *Great Kami*—Mord's purpose may even be inimical to that of Klann *himself!*"

"What are you talking about?"

Gonji stood, eyebrows knitting. "Add it up, gentlemen: what Jocko told me—the mystery crop spoilage—the poisoning of Klann--this-this—filthy worm from the depths . . . And there's another thing. I recall Tralayn speaking of *mana*, the force drawn from the living so that the sorcerer can work his devices. Tralayn said there was always a price to pay for black sorcery. These mercenaries who ride with Klann—I can tell you that they seem more devoid of humanity than any bandits I've ever known. Could Mord be draining them through this 'faith chant' they offer for him? And the children of the Akryllonians—I've never seen such pathetic looking—*damn you, Mord!*"

He ran toward the castle tunnel, the others jumping to their feet and following, apprehensive.

"If the militia training plans are known, then certainly there are more effective ways to quell us," Gonji spoke, inflamed by the revelation of it all. "He wanted *Rorka* destroyed because he fears Rorka's *Church* connections. That's why they were in flight, the *3rd Free Company*—" He drew a ragged, wrathful breath. "—when I encountered them."

Gonji's eyes bulged with fury now. His friends had never seen him so hostile, not even in the Zarnesti fray.

"He wants the city destroyed, and he has his spies report our every move," the samurai continued, simmering now. "He must know everything about us—as if that will do him any good . . ." His voice had shrunk to a boiling whisper.

"You're staying," Wilf said behind him, eyes shining with renewed hope.

Gonji turned to him, trembling with pre-volcanic emotion, at the moment unconcerned with his unseemly Western display.

"*Hai*, Wilfred-san," he whispered, clasping the young smith's hand, "there is evil to uproot in this good place. And a castle to be taken."

Wilf's jaw set with determination as they stared into each other's eyes. Then the entire band looked into the castle tunnel.

"Fire that tunnel," Gonji ordered. "Collapse it. It can only be harmful to us now. All our planning has been compromised by a traitor—may the Great Kami allow me to live to face him."

"Her," Karl reminded again.

"Him or her, the time will come," Gonji said with finality. "I don't like having been a plaything. I don't like being regarded as a fool whose efforts are futile. And you *bushi* will prove Mord wrong. He thinks we're playing at being knights, that Rorka was his only worry. We may yet provide him with a surprise or two." He waxed reflective as they moved back to the center of the cavern to view the creature's carcass again.

"He went down kind of easy, when you think about it," Wilf thought aloud. "I mean, in spite of—"

"Hai," Gonji agreed, "that's what I thought, too. He wasn't meant to crush the militia, just to inspire us to rebel in full force."

The tunnel to the surface had been cleared, and the runner sent to check on Vedun confirmed that nothing unusual had occurred during the day. Their agreement over the truth of their situation was enhanced.

It was about that time that Paille came dashing madly from the alcove that housed his diorama. He was hurling imprecations at the downed worm-thing, his dagger held on high. When he reached the carcass, he began to slash at its tentacles.

In the alcove they found the reason for the artist's sudden choleric outburst: his painstakingly constructed miniature of the city had been crushed. Shaking their heads in collective frustration, they were about to depart when Monetto tapped Gonji on the shoulder.

The tiny figures of crushed militiamen had begun to writhe hypnotically of their own accord, as if in the throes of death.

"Burn it," Gonji directed, his voice now devoid of emotion, his control reestablished.

Tora could not be found, many horses still scattered throughout the tunnels; so Gonji had another steed, a gray roncin, saddled and readied for him. He left orders for them to report back to the city and begin the careful removal of weapons, armor, and other useful equipment to the surface.

"Tell your father what's happened, Wilf," Gonji said. "Tell him that if anyone can stop Mord now without bloodshed, it will have to be him. He may be the only person who can gain Klann's confidence. Move the horses back slowly—find Tora for me, and take care of him, *dozo*—"

Wilf nodded indulgently, but interrupted him. "Where are you going?"

Gonji seated his swords in his *obi* and pondered his words before replying. He smiled thinly. "Let's just say I'm off to meet with a legend." He chuckled at Wilf's puzzled frown and clapped him on the shoulder. "If I succeed, you'll know soon enough. If not—it isn't going to matter."

They were drawn to a group huddled around the dead worm.

"Send that vile thing up in flames already, will—?"

Gerhard held up an armor-piercer arrow, its tip strangely discolored. "Look at that stuff, eh? The worm's venom—it impregnates anything it touches. Do you think—?"

"Is that my quiver?" Gonji asked.

"*Ja*," Gerhard smiled. "Might be worth a try, *neh?*" Gonji cast him a sly glance.

"Finish the job. I've got to move."

Soon Gonji was aboard the roncin, swords sashed at his waist, his three-man longbow lashed to the saddle, the quiver tied behind him.

He turned the steed at the tunnel, the last rays of evening fading in the entrance.

"Sayonara," he shouted, bowing sharply and spurring the horse out into the valley.

They watched him go, their fears and hopes mingling wordlessly. Then they shuffled heavily back into the cavern to begin the difficult work ahead. Each man wrapped into his own thoughts, the prayers of the group an open book to all.